SWARM AND STEEL

SWARM AND STEEL

MICHAEL R. FLETCHER

TALOS

Talos Press books may be purchased in bulk at special discounts for sales promotion, corporate gifts, fund-raising, or educational purposes. Special editions can also be created to specifications. For details, contact the Special Sales Department, Talos Press, 307 West 36th Street, 11th Floor, New York, NY 10018 or info@skyhorsepublishing.com.

Talos Press™ is a trademark of Skyhorse Publishing, Inc.®, a Delaware corporation.

Visit our website at www.talospress.com.

10 9 8 7 6 5 4 3 2 1

Library of Congress Cataloging-in-Publication Data

Names: Fletcher, Michael R., author.
Title: Swarm and steel / Michael R. Fletcher.
Description: New York : Talos Press, [2017]
Identifiers: LCCN 2016039142| ISBN 9781940456898 (hardback) | ISBN 9781940456911 (ebook)
Subjects: | BISAC: FICTION / Fantasy / Epic. | FICTION / Fantasy / General. | FICTION / Action & Adventure. | GSAFD: Fantasy fiction.
Classification: LCC PS3606.L4865 S93 2017 | DDC 813/.6--dc23 LC record available at https://lccn.loc.gov/2016039142

Cover design by Shawn T. King
Cover artwork by Miguel Coimbra

Printed in the United States of America

For Rich, Ken, Hans, Spin, Pete, and Dave.
I don't see you lads often enough.
Pints!

AUTHOR'S NOTE

T HIS IS A NOVEL of manifest delusion. As such, the classifications of Geisteskranken (Delusionists) will probably mean little to you. At the end of the novel you'll find a very short definition of each classification as well as a complete list of characters and any weird terminology I invented. Or, feel free to read and discover for yourself. Sometimes the difficult path is the most enjoyable.

Last time I apologized to any German speaking readers for my horrendous borrowing of their language. This time I'm butchering Basque as well.

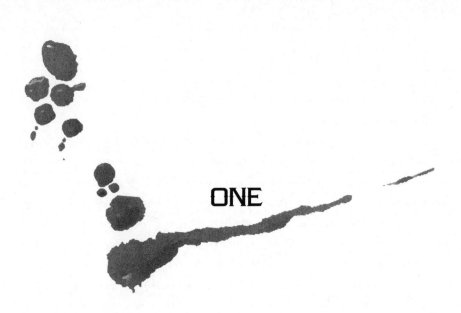

ONE

Sanity is a delusion, reality a myth.

—Versklaver Denker, Gefahrgeist Philosopher

O*PEN YOUR EYES, M*EHRERE.

Eyes open.

Mehrere? A name?

No, she thought, *Geisteskranken manifesting as multiple people.* She knew that but not how or why.

Her back against an uneven wall, stones jutted against her spine. Confining alleyways, deep in shadow, wended away in every direction. The street, filthy, thick with garbage and human waste, looked unfamiliar. Thick vomit, once warm but cooling quickly, covered her thighs and snug black leather pants. She blinked, vision smearing in and out of focus, trying to remember how she got here.

Nothing.

She stared at the mess in her lap, the regurgitated remains of a meal; hard to tell now what it was, but there's lots of red. Hopefully wine or tomatoes rather than blood. An empty scabbard, simple and unadorned, hung at her hip on the left side.

The street swam, and for a moment she saw double. Her head, resting against the wall, throbbed with blinding pain.

Had she fallen, struck her head against the stone?

No. Someone hit me, tried to cave my skull in.

Raised voices echoed down the alley, people screaming panicked orders. She heard the distant crash of splintering wood.

Leaning forward, her head came away from the wall with a wet sucking sound. Nausea pulsed in hot waves. Had there been anything left within, it too would now be on her lap. She reached her left hand to the back of her head and found it hot and wet. Her skull felt soft, soggy. The hand, petite and delicate, came away spattered in blood and tangled clumps of black hair. Beneath the mess, dark lines of swirling ink peeked through. Wiping the hand on her vomit covered pants, she stared at the intricate tattoo of a closed eye on the palm. It looked like it might open at any moment. She dreaded what she'd see.

Leaning back, she closed her eyes. She could die here; let it all go. That wasn't quite right, she *would* die here.

Or maybe she already had.

More voices, louder this time.

Open your eyes, Mehrere.

Leaning heavily against the wall, she pushed herself to her feet and stood bent, hands on knees as spasms of nausea twisted her guts leaving her gasping and retching bloody drool. She stared at her feet, at well-made but simple boots. Bloody ropes of black hair hung past her face, dripped bright crimson to the cobblestone street. The boots told her nothing of who or what she was. Her left hand strayed toward the empty scabbard.

Where is my sword?

With a grunt she stood straight, still leaning against the wall as waves of dizziness threatened to topple her. The voices grew in volume, desperate and loud.

Were they searching for her?

God, she wanted to sink back to the ground. Lie down. Let the world go on without her. She had nothing more to offer. Everything she'd been was gone, stripped away by violence.

This, she decided, told her something of herself.

You're the kind of person who gets their head crushed in dark alleys.

She searched through her clothes, finding hidden knives, a book of poems by someone named Halber Tod, and a folded sheet of thick vellum. Her body she found well-curved yet hard with muscle. The sheet was a bank note from the Verzweiflung Banking Conglomerate, a promise of payment to one Zerfall Seele. The numbers swam before her eyes, and she gave up trying to read them.

Zerfall. Is that me, or did I steal this? Was she a thief? That would explain the knives and all the black.

Shoving the bank note and book of poems back into a pocket, she pushed away from the wall and stood, knees wobbling. She'd had a sword and there were knives hidden about her body. *And someone recently tried to kill you.* Resisting the insidious desire to reach back and test the softness of her skull, she felt less than certain they'd failed.

Angry voices echoed off stone from somewhere to her left. Turning in the other direction, she stumbled down the alley, leaning against the walls. Blood ran from her hairline, stung her eyes, stained her blurred vision red. Two turns later, she found herself blinking in bright sunlight. Before her, a wide street lined with shops and stalls. Gone was the stench of poverty. The people, fat and soft, wore their wealth in looping chains of gold, their skin studded with inset diamonds. She found no such ostentatious displays on her own flesh. Was she among the city's poor?

The thief angle looked increasingly likely.

The few people noticing her shied away, eyes wide; no doubt she looked and smelled awful.

Voices from the alley behind her drove her forward. Pushing herself from the wall she staggered into the crowd, hoping to lose herself within. People parted around her, staying well clear and avoiding eye contact.

Do they know me? She reached toward a man, trying to catch his attention. When he noticed her he sobbed and fled into the crowd.

What was that about? Am I some kind of outcast?

A tall woman wearing long chain hauberk, a sword hanging at her side, pushed through the mass of people. Her eyes widened and she yelled, "She's here! I've found her!"

Oh thank the god, she must be city guard. Maybe—

The woman charged, sword drawn.

The street narrowed to a tunnel of focus.

The woman's sword, held in her right hand, glinted in the sun. Step to her left, force her to attack across her body. Knife in hand—*how did that get there?*—feint high and stab low with a second knife—*what?*—concealed from sight. There, thigh exposed in a slit on the hauberk designed to allow freedom of movement. Slash the thigh, opening the femoral artery. Kick out a knee and hear the joint pop. Wet sob of agony cut short as the second knife, finish as dull as the edge was sharp, stabbed upward into the woman's throat.

She stood, barely breathing, over the corpse. The crowd, as yet unaware of the violence, had yet to react.

That was fast. Easy. If not a thief, perhaps she was an assassin.

An elderly woman spun, screaming, "She's here! I've found her!" The old lady rushed forward, arthritic knuckles and wrinkled hands forming bony claws.

Drive the knife into her heart and spin away, free. Send the corpse toppling with a shove.

Only now were people beginning to react, mostly in confusion. Bodies. Blood.

"She's here! I've found her!" A young boy no more than eight years old charged, arms outstretched like he meant to tackle her. His body toppled past her, the weight tearing the knife from her hand. *Not to worry, there are three more where that came from.*

Armed men poured from the alley from which she'd come.

She fled, stumbling into yet another narrow street choked with garbage. Someone followed, screaming, "She's here! I've found her!" and she spun a knife, perfectly weighted, into their throat without even taking the time to register who they were.

In the distance, towering structures of marble and granite loomed over the poverty surrounding her. Churches and banks, it was difficult to tell them apart. The people lurking here were dirty and poor in sharp contrast to the soft luxury of those on the main street. She leapt something that was either a corpse or someone sleeping facedown in the middle of the lane.

Momentarily out of sight, she turned into another alley.

'She's here! I've found her!' The words, always the same. Always just one voice screaming them.

"She's here! I've found her!"

The lone voice pursued her through narrow streets, growing ever closer.

Ducking into a detritus-strewn alcove, she stopped, pressing herself into the shadows. No breath. No sound. Deathly calm, heart doing its lethargic thump thump. *Shouldn't I be scared?* How often did this happen that her body took it all in stride? Approaching feet. A young woman, face flushed and still bearing the last of youthful baby-fat, came into view.

No time for thought. Crush the nose with an elbow strike. *Lean into it, put your full weight behind the blow.* She felt the satisfying *crunch* of shattered cartilage through the sharp bone in her elbow. The woman's feet came off the street and she sprawled like a doll thrown to the ground, her mouth opened to yell. A brutal kick to the stomach kept her gasping for air.

Knife hard against throat, drawing blood.

"Why are you chasing me?"

The girl snarled hatred, teeth bared in a psychotic grin. "Go ahead, Zerfall."

She's taunting me, she doesn't care if I kill her. At least she knew her name now.

"We'll hunt you forever," the girl said. "Swarm awaits."

"Why? What did I do? Who am I—"

"Hölle will never forgive your betrayal."

"Hölle?"

"She's not dead, she survived." The girl grinned triumph. "Didn't expect that, did you?"

The clattering of armour grew closer. Zerfall severed the girl's hamstrings, careful not to nick arteries lest she bleed out too quickly, and fled.

Why did I do that? Why did I leave her alive? She didn't know, but it felt like the right choice.

Spotting the city wall in the distance, she left the claustrophobic alleys behind. *I have to get out.* With no knowledge of who or what she was, she had to escape, leave this city behind. Anyone and everyone could be an enemy. She ran past boutiques selling scarves and trinkets as pretty as they were useless. Clean streets. Marble and brass framed every shop. So much wealth just a few strides from such poverty.

Turning a corner she spotted the city gates, half a dozen lounging guards and a young squire leading a horse. The gates were open, the guards bored and inattentive.

Zerfall wanted that horse, *needed* it.

A score of heartbeats later, the squire and guards were dead or dying and she rode east, the setting sun warming her back. Ahead, the land rolled in verdant hills dotted with sprawling farms.

What lay beyond that serene landscape?

She didn't know.

Eleven dead in half as many minutes. Only death lay behind. She couldn't go back, not when anyone and everyone might be an enemy. If she didn't know herself, how could she know her friends? *Do I even have friends?* The word felt strange, alien.

What *did* she know?

My name is Zerfall and I kill, quick and easy. She thought about the people she cut down and felt nothing. *I'm a remorseless killer.*

Or had that been expedience?

"No, you didn't have to kill the city guards or the squire." The sound of her voice, husky and deep, startled her. "So, that's what I sound like."

Zerfall rode in silence, her hips rolling with the movement of the chestnut horse. Reaching forward to stroke its ears, she realized her fingers felt numb. Not lacking strength, but the sensation of the horse's hair felt oddly distant. She turned the left hand, examining the thin fingers, black nail polish shellacked thick enough to look wet. The palm. A closed eye. What a strange thing to tattoo on one's hand. She wondered what it had meant to her; it must have hurt. She closed the hand into a fist, shutting away the closed eye. Something about the tattoo left her uncomfortable. It meant something, said something about her. Something she should know.

If that eye opens, what will I see?

Clenching her teeth in the expectation of pain, she reached back and probed at the rear of her skull. The blood had dried, caking hair and god knew what else into rigid clumps.

God knew . . . God, singular? It felt right, and yet wrong. Like an affectation. So much was missing. She spoke a language and knew nothing of its origins. Had she been a native to that city, or a visiting foreigner? Try as she might, she could think of no words in other languages. Come to think of it, how would she know what words belonged to what language?

She pushed fingers against the back of her head. An area the size of her fist felt soft and spongy, but with the mass of blood and hair, she couldn't tell how much was broken bone. *I shouldn't be conscious, much less standing and fighting.* She blinked, half expecting to topple from the saddle. Nothing. She felt fine, if distant and numb. Considering her head had been hit hard enough to leave her unconscious and incapable of remembering anything about herself, the pain was muted.

Zerfall picked at the black polish on her fingernails; she hadn't noticed starting. Was this some old habit so ingrained even now she kept it up? Perhaps it meant someday she might remember more of her life.

With nothing else to think about, she recalled the few moments she remembered. The woman in the hauberk, the old woman, the young boy, and the girl she hamstrung: Somehow they were all the same person. That made no sense. Did it?

"We'll hunt you forever," the girl said. "Swarm awaits."

What the hell did that mean? A swarm of what?

Hell. Singular rather than plural? Could there be only one hell? That felt wrong much in the same way *god* felt wrong.

The girl mentioned another name: Hölle. Apparently Zerfall betrayed this woman and attempted to kill her. That she failed rankled. She wanted to turn the horse around and ride back to—whatever that city was—to finish the job, but she had no idea who Hölle was, no idea what she looked like, and no idea where to find her. If she decided to follow through with the desire, nothing and no one would stop her. She'd kill everything and everyone who got in her way.

I'm not the kind of person who takes failure well.

Hölle. The name meant nothing and everything.

HÖLLE LAY ON HER side, curled around the agony in her stomach. She drown in torment, physical and emotional. Each breath shook with shuddering sobs. Her heart and soul were riven, torn in two. Not just her heart and soul, her very mind had been sundered.

Less than an hour ago her sister, Zerfall, had tried to kill her, stabbed her in the gut with that damned sword, Blutblüte. It was a miracle she didn't now stand in Swarm—the Täuschung hell she'd hallucinated into existence—surrounded by the seething crush of naked humanity. If Zerfall and Blutblüte couldn't kill her, nothing could.

The One True God protects me; my work here isn't finished.

Still, she felt broken. Betrayed.

She remembered Zerfall pacing the room as she laid out her plans for the church. Her sister had been increasingly distracted and distant for years, becoming less and less involved in the running of the church. In the last decade Zerfall did little except recruit new Geisteskranken to their cause. A powerful Gefahrgeist, it was easy for her to convince people to join them. As more of their holy work fell to Hölle she realized how good she was at this. The long hours left her continually exhausted, feeling stretched thin, but her own suffering meant nothing in the face of saving all humanity. While it bothered her, she assumed her sister needed space and left her alone. Doing the work of the One True God was a life-long task, often brutal and grinding. If Zerfall needed some time to herself, Hölle understood.

Hölle shied from the memory of her sister drawing that terrible sword and her even more terrible words: "You're trying to replace me. You're trying to kill me."

Why would she say that?

For over four hundred years she and her sister stood together, bound to their purpose by the One True God: Once humanity suffered for their sins, they would be freed to once again become the gods they were always meant to be.

Lost in thought, she stared at the detritus heaped in the corner of her room. Dust, discarded articles of clothing, and a considerable amount of long dark hair, both hers and Zerfall's, had been piling up for years. Maybe longer. The entire Täuschung compound was a chaotic mess, had been for as long as she could remember. She didn't care; a religion of suffering had little call for cleanliness. And none of the millions of worshippers spread throughout the city states would ever see the inside of this church, the true core of the Täuschung. For the sane masses, the church presented a very different front. To them, Swarm was a heaven of belonging, a collection of righteous souls awaiting the final day when all humanity had been saved. The sane could never understand that torment and suffering were the keys to redemption. If lies had to be told, it was for their own good.

They don't even know they're already in a prison. We'll make them gods again, set them free.

Still, she had a dim memory of things being different. Cleaner, like once they'd taken pride in their holy mission.

Four hundred years of living in perpetual misery. Four hundred years as the Voice of Wahrergott, the One True God, with only her sister to stand at her side. Centuries of suffering, each and every day seeing this prison for what it was and knowing it would take millennia more to free humanity.

Her delusion, driven by the will of Wahrergott, birthed Swarm. For four hundred years the Täuschung religion, the one hidden beneath the public façade, fed her child with souls. Millions now populated Swarm and more were sent every day.

One of the Täuschung priests, a doctor who lost his mind after losing too many patients, had bandaged her belly, said she'd survive. He'd had her carried to her chambers and laid in bed. Though he offered narcotics to ease her pain, she refused. She wanted to feel this, needed to. Suffering was everything.

Tears had run, damp and hot. Now her eyes were dry, her face tight, lips tasting of salt, the sodden sheet beneath her cheek cooling. She embraced the discomfort as if it were a cherished lesson. Suffering and penance, as well she knew, was the key to unlocking everything.

And, oh, how she suffered.

Four hundred years with but one driving purpose, sacrificing everything she was and could have been to bring about the Ascension of Humanity, and here she hid, arms wrapped around a wound that should have killed her. Had her faith in Wahrergott faltered for but a single moment, she would surely have died.

Four hundred years and still I live.

The memory of cold steel sliding into her gut, the wrenching twist as the hand holding that sword tore it free. The tortured moan ripped from her lips as she pitched to the ground. Numb recognition as she rolled over to stare up into her sister's face.

Four hundred years we stood together, never once wavering. How did this happen? What changed?

"You're trying to replace me. You're trying to kill me."

Had Zerfall completely lost her mind? Had she finally fallen to the Pinnacle, the fate awaiting all Geisteskranken? Did the One True God no longer extend his protection to Hölle's sister?

Hölle gritted her teeth in a snarl and the ice in her gut turned hot. Clutching her arms tight to her stomach as if relaxing them would allow her guts to fall free, she pushed herself into a sitting position.

Zerfall, why?

This physical pain was nothing in comparison to the soul-shredding agony of betrayal.

Four hundred years ago they'd been normal little girls, unimaginative and average in every way. A plague swept through their village, killing nine of ten people. Their parents and two little brothers died early, leaving the two sisters hallucinating, feverish and alone. The fever changed them. Wahrergott spoke his commands into their febrile minds as they lay dying:

This responsive reality is a hell. I am The One True God and Enforcer of the laws. To save humanity you must unite all in suffering. Penance for your crimes. Convince the world. This is your prison. Make your hell. Beyond this is paradise. You will be free, as gods.

Suffering, they learned, would set them free. Misery was the key. Someday, when humanity had suffered enough, paid for their heinous crime—and the even fouler breach of forgetting their crime—they would be free.

Hölle and Zerfall went to bed as two feverish sisters and rose, to the stench of their rotting family, as something more. Hölle awoke a Halluzin, and birthed a new hell with her hallucinations. Zerfall, a Gefahrgeist, bent humanity to her will, conscripting Geisteskranken and those meek sane in need of a religion into their priesthood. The Täuschung was born that night.

"We were gods," she told the surviving villagers upon her miraculous recovery. "Each and every one of us is an imprisoned god. I know how to set us free."

They mocked her, called her insane. Fools.

Four hundred years later, here she was. She'd built a church upon the words of Wahrergott. Penance for humanity's forgotten crimes. The Täuschung were tens of thousands strong and growing. They had hospices in every city-state and preached words of hope and salvation to lure in the mentally stable. The Täuschung promised an eternity in paradise and the sane swarmed to them, proving their faith by pledging to die in a Täuschung hospice where devout priests could ensure their souls travelled to the Täuschung heaven.

That heaven was a lie. She'd dreamed of *Swarm*, a hell of endless suffering, and her Halluzin power made it real. Each hospice was overseen by sane priests who believed in the Swarm, the heaven. But within each hospice lay a dark heart, a core of Geisteskranken who believed in Swarm, the true Täuschung hell.

She and Zerfall had a plan and countless millennia to make it real. Belief *defined* reality. The delusions of one person, no matter how strongly held, twisted only local reality; the proximity of the dull and steady beliefs of the masses would limit even that. A powerful Gefahrgeist might bend the beliefs of a crowd or even a small city-state to their will, but to irrevocably change reality required vast numbers. Millions. Someday there would be more souls within Swarm than without and the balance would forever tip. Already there were more souls in their hallucinated hell than in Geldangelegenheiten, Geld to the locals, the city-state the Täuschung called home.

Hölle bit down hard on her lip, tasting blood. In recent years she found herself living increasingly in the past. She had so much past. Enough to drown in.

Focus. Embrace suffering as all Täuschung must.

Zerfall, soul of her soul, had turned on her. Hölle replayed their last conversation, struggling to understand why.

"Aas gave me a book of poems," Zerfall had said, interrupting Hölle. "Halber Tod."

Hölle was familiar with the poet. "Talentless hack," she answered.

"You're trying to replace me. You're trying to kill me."

Zerfall's accusation had been so unexpected, so insane, Hölle had stood there, blinking at her sister, wondering who she was talking about.

And then Zerfall drew Blutblüte and drove the blade into Hölle's belly. She stood over Hölle, watching her squirm with dead eyes. "This is rotten," her sister added. Without another word she turned and walked away, leaving Blutblüte behind.

Hölle had nothing but questions. What did her sister's senseless accusation mean? What had she meant by "This is rotten?" Why hadn't she taken the sword? If it was a play for power, why hadn't she finished her sister and claimed the church as her own?

Zerfall had always been quick to violence; her emotions ran hot, ever bubbling below the surface. She'd been the balance to Hölle's steady temper and eternal patience.

"Zerfall, we are nothing without each other," Hölle whispered.

Whatever her plans, whatever her reasons, Zerfall's treason could topple the Täuschung, undo centuries of sacrifice and anguish. Zerfall must be stopped. No matter the cost.

Can you survive her death?

She twitched at the thought. There was something awful there she didn't want to confront. *Of course I'll survive.* In fact, the more she thought about it, the more excited she felt. Her sister had been holding her back. Maybe she no longer needed Zerfall as she once had. After all, she had been running the church with very little help for decades. *I'm stronger now.*

Zerfall had to die, and she knew just the man to do it: Aas, Zerfall's lover. As a member of the Täuschung inner circle, Aas knew the church's true mission. And Zerfall left him behind, abandoning him just as she abandoned Hölle.

Aas was an odd one, unique among her Geisteskranken priests. Unlike the others, he was plagued by a pesky curiosity. Before joining the Täuschung, he travelled the world. His inquisitive nature would drive him to dig deeper into what happened between Hölle and Zerfall. He might accept whatever she told him at first, but in time he'd question. His curiosity would be his death. That he was easily the most educated man she ever met did little for her willingness to trust him.

On the other hand, she'd know if he planned betrayal.

Hölle wiped at her face, making sure no hint of tears remained. She straightened her shirt, rigid with drying blood, and shoved her hair and clothes into place. Leaning forward with a grunt of pain, she pulled on the silk rope at the side of her bed. A bell hanging just on the other side of her chamber door rang. Captain Gedankenlos, a slab of muscle with a chin, cracked the door open, peeking only his head into her chambers.

"Fetch Aas," said Hölle.

Gedankenlos nodded and was gone.

Hölle sagged back into bed. Her world felt thin, stretched to the point of tearing. Without Zerfall . . . *If I close my eyes and let go I'll fade to nothing.* Her eyes snapped open, a rush of terror speeding her heart. *I'm real. I'm alive.* Then why did she feel so . . . she searched for the word . . . illusory?

It was Zerfall's fault. Zerfall did this with her betrayal. *She'll pay.* Once Zerfall was dead, everything would change.

HALF AN HOUR LATER, Aas entered and stood at Hölle's side. His hands fidgeted nervously, the knuckles sagging with loose skin. You'd never know he was a merciless killer. He looked more like the kind of troll you'd find hoarding books in a dark library. The man was beyond heinous, abhorrent in every possible manner. He'd be bald if not for the few thick black hairs sprouting chaotically about his pale skull. The sallow skin of his face hung wrinkled, slack and swinging, in long jowls. Thick folds of yellow flesh dragged at his lower eyelids with their weight. A longbow of blackened bone and wood hung over one shoulder and a quiver of obsidian-tipped arrows, feathers thick and glistening sable, hung on the other. The bow he'd carried for years, but the fletchings on those arrows were something new.

I know where those feathers come from, thought Hölle. It might be a minor self-destruction, but Aas already suffered Wahnist and Therianthrope tendencies. If he became Trichotillic, it might mean his delusions were winning the battle with his dwindling sanity. Comorbidity often presaged a Geisteskranken's imminent collapse.

Aas bowed low, and his eyes, black pupils surrounded by bloodshot brown and lacking any whites, examined her as if drinking in every detail. Did he search for weakness, or was he trying to see down her shirt again?

{She's been crying. I want to lick those tears.}

"Tell me you have her," said Hölle, ignoring Aas' disgusting Wahnist tendencies. The delusional wretch believed everyone heard his thoughts and broadcast them endlessly.

{Was that a nipple? Did I just see a nipple?} Aas licked thin lips, glancing at Hölle, his horrid eyes beady and bright, to see if his fixation with her breasts had been noticed. "One of the priests caught her, hit from behind with a cudgel."

Hölle's chest tightened. "She's dead?"

"She killed him, escaped and fled the city." *{Gods I miss her already. The way she cut me—}*

"Silence!" *She's alive.* Fear and jubilation wrestled for dominance.

{What if she knows I lust after her as I lust after her sister. What if she—} The stream of thought choked to nothing. Aas showed sharp white teeth in something between a desperate leer and an ingratiating grin.

Hölle knew all about the torrid little romance Zerfall maintained with this saggy-skinned and bloody-eyed vermin. Knowing of its existence didn't mean she understood it. What did Zerfall see in this man? Was it part of some larger scheme? No, Zerfall had never been one for plans—that fell to Hölle.

Hölle might not have Zerfall's Gefahrgeist power, but she understood manipulation. She watched Aas pluck one of his ear hairs and examine it in detail.

He stuffed the hair into a pocket. *{Perfect. This will do nicely for Hexenwerk.}*

Hexenwerk? What was the wretch thinking about now? Was he making something with his own foul hair? She shuddered at the thought.

He's insane, but can I trust him? She knew one sure way to find out.

Reaching out a thin-fingered hand, she caressed Aas' arm. "I need you." She licked her lips suggestively, peering up from where she sat, dark eyes speaking promises she had no intention of keeping. "Zerfall has succumbed to her delusions; she no longer rules her thoughts."

{She's touching me.} Aas blinked myopically at her hand, small eyes intent. *{Is this true?}*

Already he questions me.

Hölle had to be careful. Aas might be insane, but he was far from stupid. "She no longer hears the word of Wahrergott."

{Why did she flee Geld? Why did she leave me?}

"I know you shared a bond," Hölle said before he spewed more of his vile thoughts.

{I love her.} "A bond of suffering," he said. *{She cut me.}* "I can't believe she—"

"And that is why it must be you."

"Me?"

"You took pleasure in the suffering she inflicted."

{Yes yes yes!} "No, I—"

"The One True God sees everything. You love her."

{It's true. After, for a few short moments, I feel forgiven.} "I needed her to hurt me—"

"There is no forgiveness. The idea is offensive in the eyes of Wahrergott." Hölle removed her hand from Aas' arm and rose to her feet, one hand pressed tight to her wounded belly. Though Aas towered over her he shrank back, cowering. "You shall not be forgiven until we have *all* been forgiven, until every single man, woman, and child has suffered enough to appease the One True God." She clenched her teeth against the tearing pain in her gut. "You must suffer for your transgression."

{She knows. She knows everything.} Aas bowed his head in shame leaving her to stare at the puckered chicken flesh of his sagging scalp. "I must make amends."

Doubt stalled Hölle, strangled her thoughts. *When Zerfall is dead . . .* Everything would be different. Better, somehow. Her sister . . . *Zerfall will not despoil four hundred years of effort.*

"You must hunt and kill my sister. Wahrergott wills it." Aas would be the instrument of her vengeance. His past with Zerfall made this a desperate gamble, but knowing she'd hear his every thought guaranteed she'd know if he lied. It appalled her that there was no one else she could trust with this.

Aas stared at her, his bloodshot eyes as wide as she'd ever seen them. For a few heartbeats the endless puke of spewed thought remained quiet. Then, *{Kill her? Kill my love?}* "Me?"

She advanced on Aas, and the man retreated before her wrath. "Wahrergott demands you suffer for your pleasures."

"I shall atone for my sins." *{Wahrergott, forgive me.}* "I shall kill Zerfall."

A start, but not enough. She needed to know he would kill Zerfall. She needed to hear him think it.

There could be no room for doubt. With Zerfall gone, Hölle was the will of Wahrergott. Wahrergott chose her. Wahrergott spoke to her. Nothing else mattered. *It can't all be for nothing.*

Hölle let slip some small sliver of fear. Shadows danced and coalesced in her peripheral vision, scenes of an eternal hell with no feature other than the thronging souls who populated it. No trees littered the landscape, no mountains shimmered in the distance. No sun hung above. The sky gave off a harsh, unchanging light, illuminating the teeming crowd of souls. Distant screams echoed about her chambers. Swarm was a hell of souls with nothing to distract its denizens. Humanity, she knew from personal experience, needed nothing more than humanity to breed suffering. Scenes of endless rape and murder played over and over as tormented souls, some of whom had been imprisoned for hundreds of years, sought distraction from the unchanging nothing. Swarm, packed tight, shoulder to shoulder, went on forever.

Aas backed away, hands lifting as if to defend himself from the hellish vision. "Is it real?"

"Belief defines reality."

Aas stared, appalled and excited by the scene he witnessed. "But someone else could believe something different."

She said, "*I* believe," as if it ended all possible debate. "Those millions of souls believe."

Aas' breath caught and his eyes brimmed with tears. *{Gods, no. I believe. I believe in Swarm.}*

"You shall be the assassin of The One True God," said Hölle. "For as long as you serve Wahrergott you shall never die," she lied. "Do you swear to serve Wahrergott with all your soul?"

{Yes yes yes! Anything!} Aas knelt before Hölle, a single tear trickled down his sagging face, following deep folds. "I swear I shall serve. Forever."

"Zerfall must die."

{Zerfall must die.} "I will find her. I will kill her." *{I'm sorry, my love. I must send you to Swarm to save myself.}*

"Zerfall betrayed Wahrergott," said Hölle, ignoring the puerile filth and chaos of Aas' thoughts. "She betrayed us all." *I've done it. Her lover will betray her as she betrayed me.*

"Yes." Aas sobbed agreement. "She betrayed Wahrergott."

"She abandoned you as she abandoned me," said Hölle. Aas glanced at her, his lips stretched in anguish, tears flowing freely now. "It hurts, doesn't it?" He nodded, his sagging jowls swaying. "Make her *suffer*."

Aas nodded again, saying nothing, his thoughts spewing a confused babble of sex and torture as if they were one and the same.

"Stand."

He wiped his eyes with a sleeve. The skin on his face and skull seemed to have sagged even further. But something burned deep within his bloodshot eyes. Hunger. Dark glee. "It will not be easy to find her and even more difficult to kill her." *{Gods I want to see her again, to hurt her.}* "Perhaps I can talk to her? Discover why—"

"Beware her Gefahrgeist powers. You must kill her from a distance."

"I always kill from a distance." *{Coward!}*

"She must suffer as she has made us suffer."

{Did Zerfall hurt Hölle as she hurt me? The thought! I must escape this wretchedly insane bitch so I can relieve myself.} A hand strayed toward his groin and stopped when he saw her notice. "I shall leave immediately."

Hölle, biting her tongue, watched Aas flee the room. The disgusting bug could barely refrain from touching himself. It mattered not. He'd kill Zerfall. She'd decide what to do with him after.

With the door firmly closed, she climbed back into bed, still clutching her stomach. She shouldn't have stood, blood stained her bandages where she'd torn the wound.

She remembered Zerfall's calm face as she drew Blutblüte, the utter lack of emotion.

Zerfall must have known I would never forgive her. She knew I would repay the hurt a thousand times.

The answer, while painful, was all too clear: Zerfall, a Gefahrgeist, didn't care that she hurt her sister.

But she would. When Zerfall woke to find herself in Swarm, then she would care. Then she would regret betraying Hölle. *When she is dead I will—*

A warm hand stroked Hölle's hair as Zerfall used to during those rare times when offering comfort.

"Zerfall?" Hölle, rolled over to stare up at the beautiful woman sitting at the side of her bed. She was surprised to realize it was disappointment and not fear she felt most. "Is it really—"

The petite woman shook her head, achingly familiar thick black hair wafting scents of honey. "You are fragmented. Torn. You love her. You hate her." The woman smiled sadly. "I am your grief. Call me Pharisäer."

Hölle understood immediately. "Wahrergott sent you to replace Zerfall." *The One True God has not abandoned me because of Zerfall's failure.* The god had given her back her sister.

"I am your pain. I am your doubt. And I shall never betray you."

Hölle closed her eyes, enjoying the fingers working at the knots in her hair. "When she's dead it won't hurt any more. When she's in Swarm—"

"You don't believe that."

Hölle sighed. Pharisäer was right. "Still, I can take some pleasure in knowing she'll suffer."

"But that's not why you want her killed."

Hölle scowled and sat up, pushing away Pharisäer's hand. "It's not?" *Why am I so excited at the prospect of my sister's death?*

"When she is dead you'll be free to finally be you. She held you back all these years, but now you're ready to lead, to be the *real* leader of the Täuschung ."

Real; the word resonated. Hölle stared at Pharisäer, examining every aspect. Her eyes were brown, but so dark as to be near black, her lips full and sensuous. She drew a deep breath. This could be Zerfall—

"I'm not Zerfall," said Pharisäer. "I am your doubt."

Hölle sighed. "I know." She glanced at the door. "What shall we do with Aas? He disgusts me."

"Because he is disgusting."

Hölle decided. "I want him dead."

"But not because he is disgusting," said Pharisäer.

"No?"

"He shared something with Zerfall, something you were never part of. Something you could never have. You're jealous." Pharisäer offered a knowing smile. "But once she's dead . . ."

Once she's dead I'll have it all. And she wanted it all. It would be hers. The church. Everything. She'd been doing everything anyway. When her sister was dead Hölle would finally be—

"We must be honest with ourselves." Pharisäer brushed long black hair back from Hölle's face and flashed a regretful smile. "No one else will be." The smile fell away, replaced by a look of infinite sadness, dark eyes filling with tears. "Zerfall's betrayal hurts too much to bear alone."

Pharisäer spoke truth. The betrayal hurt, hurt more than anything in all Hölle's long life. And yet somehow it felt like that betrayal opened a door. Was this Wahrergott's will?

"Fine," said Hölle, swallowing her pain. She turned away to hide her confusion and changed the subject. "Knowing Aas' every vile thought has its advantages, even if he does turn my stomach."

"True," said Pharisäer. "He loved Zerfall, and for that he must die. First, though, we'll use him."

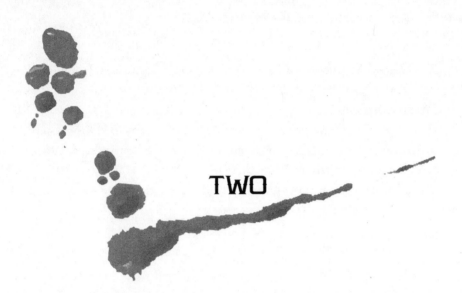

TWO

I hate who I am. I hate what I am. I loathe my humanity. It's a stain. We are animals with delusions of grandeur, impressed with all we've wrought with our madness. But animals are pure of thought and intention, driven by pure needs. Hunger. Sleep. I need to be that animal once again.

—Unknown Therianthrope

AS STUMBLED FROM HÖLLE's chambers, scowled hatred at Gedankenlos, the handsome Captain of the Guard, positioned at her door.

{Self important arse.} he thought when he was four strides away.

"Turkey vulture," said Gedankenlos, showing perfect teeth in a flawless grin.

When Aas reached the stairs he cast a glance over his shoulder, measuring the distance—about eight strides—and thought, *I'll gut you in your sleep.* When the Captain—as predictable as he was attractive—failed to react Aas knew the man was beyond the range of his broadcast thoughts.

Somewhere between four and eight strides. For the last few years the range of his thoughts had been increasing. A bad sign as it presaged the inevitable collapse of his sanity.

Did he broadcast his thoughts further in front or behind him, or was it more like a perfect sphere? An interesting thought; he'd have to experiment when time permitted.

To be sure he was alone, Aas descended half the spiral stairway before stopping to lean against the wall. With a sigh of pent-up tension he pressed his forehead to the stone, feeling the stab of sharp grit. He couldn't stop himself from broadcasting, but with psychotic concentration and absolute focus he had some control over what he thought. It was exhausting, and far from perfect; no matter how hard he tried, sometimes things he'd rather not share slipped through.

"You shall be the assassin of The One True God," Hölle had said. "For as long as you serve Wahrergott you shall never die."

Assassin of Wahrergott. Aas coughed a stifled chuckle of derision. *Hölle thinks me an idiot.* She knew what he and Zerfall shared and her disgust was writ plain on her beautiful face. She'd see him dead, he saw it in her eyes.

Zerfall, why did you abandon me? Was it something I did?

He'd given her a book of Halber Tod's poems as a gift, curious if she'd appreciate the Cotardist poet as much as he. Zerfall had smiled, that little upturn at the corner of her perfect lips, and pocketed the book without a glance. That was the last time he saw her. Two days later she stabbed Hölle and fled the compound, leaving Blutblüte, her sword, behind.

Aas thought back to his meeting with Hölle, replaying every thought, trying to recall if anything damning slipped out. Had he thought about Hexenwerk, the puppet he'd begun building as a desperate and likely doomed attempt to avoid death, the Pinnacle, and Swarm? He couldn't remember. If he had, she hadn't asked about it. He fingered the collection of bodily detritus in his pocket, mostly hair and snot, all collected from himself. *She doesn't know or she doesn't care.*

He'd made great effort to be as pathetic and disgusting as possible so as to distract her and end the meeting quickly. It seemed to have worked.

She believed what she heard.

His thoughts hadn't been a lie, but he had been able to limit them to the most base and vile topics possible. That he lusted after Hölle—how could he not, while less muscled, she was damned near Zerfall's twin—made it easier. Outright lies he found almost impossible as he couldn't stop himself from wondering whether people believed him and then, of course, they heard him wondering.

It helps that you're disgusting.

He pushed that thought aside, telling himself that deep down all people were crude animals moved by the same base urges driving all creatures.

He would do his best to murder his lover. But this was Zerfall. She'd take him with her Gefahrgeist power long before he had a chance to harm her.

Maybe she'll let me hurt her just a little.

He shivered with pleasure at the thought. Their relationship had always been as sadomasochistic as it was one sided. She held the power, though much as he enjoyed that, he always wanted to hurt her back, give some balance to their twisted relationship.

When he felt ready, Aas pushed himself from the wall. He'd find Zerfall and do his best to kill her even if he wanted to fail. Even if failure was guaranteed. Once she had him—once she crushed him with her Gefahrgeist power—maybe she'd keep him. He could only hope.

Aas took his time traversing the spiral stairs leading from Hölle's chambers down to the courtyard at the front of the church. Dust gathered in thick cobwebs that hadn't seen spiders in a hundred years.

He enjoyed every moment of Zerfall's divine torture, every lash, every cut. He loved her with the absolute worship of a man with no choice; a powerful Gefahrgeist, she left him no alternative. That his enjoyment was *wrong* made it all the more delicious. He loved the vicious and dangerous nature of their relationship, and he loved her.

Aas uttered something between a laugh and a sob. *As if Zerfall could ever love you.*

Except some part of him believed she did. Or had.

She's Gefahrgeist, he reminded himself. *Gefahrgeist can't love.*

But he could and he did. What she felt, if anything, didn't matter.

Aas slowed as he reached the bottom of the stairs. *{Hölle hates me.}* Zerfall had told him.

"Pardon?"

Aas glanced up, met the eyes of a Täuschung priest hustling toward the stairs with a leather satchel clutched to his chest, a long thin-bladed sword hanging at his hip. The man's skin moved like something wriggled beneath it and a damp slug clung to his neck just beneath his left ear. Befallen, the man believed himself to be infected with all manner of parasites.

"I said nothing," said Aas. "What did you hear?"

"Oh!" said the priest, eyes widening in recognition. "Nothing. My mistake."

"What did you hear?" snapped Aas.

"Nothing," said the priest, shuffling around Aas in the confines of the stairway.

{He heard everything. Kill him.}

The priest squeaked, a high pitched whimper, and fled, disappearing around the bend in the spiral stairs. Aas watched, eyes narrowed to a devouring squint. Such chance encounters were dangerous. He must be more alert, at least until he left the Täuschung compound. If the wrong person heard his thoughts, they'd report them to Hölle. For a moment Aas considered following and killing the priest. What had the man heard?

Nothing worth killing him for, he decided.

Once in the courtyard, Aas stood, his rounded shoulders hunched forward, turning in a slow circle.

Where will Zerfall go?

Aas allowed himself a rare grin of pleasure, careful no one saw it. If there was one thing that made living worthwhile, it was a good puzzle.

He thought through what he knew of the nearest city-states.

Geld—home of the Täuschung—being the eastern-most of the city-states, with the endless wastes of the Basamortuan Desert sprawling beyond its eastern border, west was the obvious answer. Following the Flussrand River back toward its source in the Gezackt Mountains were a dozen or more city-states of varying size and wealth. Abgeleitete Leute, an entire city populated by copies of a single Mehrere, was the closest, with Grunlugen beyond that. Further west were Selbsthass, a militant theocracy with an insane new god, and Gottlos, the festering armpit of a city-state which had recently fallen to Selbsthass. Beyond Selbsthass lay the ruins of Neidrig, a ghost town populated by an insane religion worshipping the shattered body of an undying cat. Rumour was some Slaver-type Gefahrgeist enslaved most of the city's population and took it west where it was later wiped out by a Hassebrand teetering at the Pinnacle. Further afield were Auseinander, Sinnlos, Folgen Sienie, and Reichweite. All were ruled by a Geisteskranken of some kind, most being Gefahrgeist.

South of the city-states were the grassland tribes, savages worshipping strange spirits, numen, and local gods tied to one geographical location or another.

Damned near every stand of trees and pond worthy of the name had *something* jealously guarding it.

North of the city-states the Verschlinger ruled the frozen tundra and beyond, brutal barbarians reputed to devour human flesh during times of starvation. He'd also read that the most common brand of Geisteskranken in the northern wastes were the Otraalma, who believed themselves possessed by demons. Each year a fresh batch of stories told of a single Verschlinger wandering down from the far north to kill and devour dozens before being chased back or slain by squads of city-states warriors.

Zerfall will go west where she can lose herself in the city-states.

Aas, standing in the courtyard, ignored the few priests going about their duties. None came within range of his thoughts. Whether out of fear or disgust mattered not. They were nothing, beneath notice.

He fingered one of the few remaining hairs on his head. Pinching the course strand between thumb and forefinger, he pulled it free with a sharp tug. A small pain, but still pleasurable. After examining the hair, checking it for length, colour, and thickness, he placed it in a pocket alongside the other hairs, fingernail clippings, and nuggets of snot kept there. *One more for Hexenwerk.* His little puppet, made entirely of his own bodily leavings, grew too slowly. The damned thing kept falling apart. He needed to bind it to something more solid, something that wouldn't dry out and crumble apart. If Aas was to move his soul into the puppet before he was sent screaming to Swarm, it needed to be more rugged and durable. Hexenwerk needed a spine.

Aas eyed the small finger on his left hand. The thought of sawing it off sent a shiver of near-orgasmic pleasure chasing down his spine.

{Plucking your hair and collecting your snot and nail clippings is one thing, but hacking off a finger to make a damned puppet is insane.} Aas giggled. If the puppet was to be his escape, he'd have to make some sacrifices.

Two priests, ängstlich and his wife Dämonin Schwindel, hurried past, darting nervous looks at Aas. They'd definitely caught something of his thoughts. Ängstlich, a weak and cowardly Capgrast, led his wife, as regal and beautiful as her husband was pathetic, by a chain and collar attached to one of her slim ankles. Dämonin Schwindel was the only sane person allowed in the Täuschung inner sanctum, and she was held here against her will, captive to her husband's delusions.

{Geisteskranken, the mad and delusional, make up the core of our priesthood. What does that say about our little church of suffering, eh, Ängstlich?}

The coward didn't answer.

Once the two moved beyond the range of his thoughts, Aas turned to look east. Beyond those rolling hills lay the Basamortuan Desert.

Would Zerfall go there?

He licked thin lips with a pink sliver of tongue and swallowed. His lumpy Adam's apple twitched like something inside sought to escape. Zerfall was clever; with the possible exception of Hölle, the smartest person he'd ever known. If Zerfall betrayed Hölle and the Täuschung, she had a plan. She would have chosen the least likely direction to travel in.

She also wouldn't have betrayed us without a reason.

He longed to know that reason. Perhaps when he found her he would ask. Hölle said not to talk to Zerfall, that her Gefahrgeist powers made it too dangerous. While true, Aas couldn't help but think there was more. *Is there something she doesn't want me to learn?*

What if Zerfall hadn't betrayed them at all? What if the betrayal was Hölle's?

To hells with Hölle and her lies. Zerfall was everything. If she needed him, he was hers. He stared east. If he discovered she truly had abandoned him, he'd kill her. He prayed it wouldn't come to that

Aas *twisted*, his body collapsing and falling in on itself until a condor stood, shuffling and hopping, where the man had been.

When wearing his human form, Aas' eyes had never been very strong. His constant pinched squint, he suspected, did nothing for his already ghastly appearance. But now, as a condor, the world looked crisp, sharp. The yard might be empty, but Aas saw the glinting eyes of those watching from the shadows. He spread his wings, twelve feet from tip to tip, and bounced in place, stretching his mottled neck. Freedom beckoned.

With a rattling croak he took to the skies.

Aas RODE THE CHAOTIC gusts resulting from the clash of the cold winds coming from the Kälte Mountains to the north and the dry warmth

blowing in from the Basamortuan Desert to the east. The plethora of churches, each vying for dominance in height and grandeur, blocking and bending the wind where they jutted rudely into the sky, added to the maelstrom.

Aas hated the churches but loved the resulting turmoil. *Unpredictability is beauty.* He banked and dove as the breeze he rode disappeared. The weather over Geld, insane and tumultuous, killed thousands of birds every year, slamming them into walls or plummeting them to the street. Taxidermists made a fortune capturing their agonized deaths and selling the stuffed corpses to wealthy idiots who considered it high art. To be hit by a bird falling to its death was considered a sign of impending good luck. To be killed by one was not.

Strange, the insane beliefs the sane hold. What differentiated the sane from the insane? Aas thought about this often. *Is it the ability to manifest one's delusions? Could it be something else, like strength of will or personality? Could I be as sane as any other person in this despicable city?*

He croaked laughter. No.

Aas caught a hot updraught and in moments found himself spiralling far above the city. Even up here he caught the stench of humanity, the mouth-watering bouquet of decay lurking beneath the odours of every city. Geldangelegenheiten might smell better than most, but rot lay at its heart. Rotting food. Rotting plants. Rotting corpses. Rotting buildings. Polluted waters swam with decaying urine and faeces, the air redolent with a thousand deaths. Aas loved it. Where there was rot and carrion, there were creatures who fed off it. Aas was one such creature. He belonged here.

Glancing north he saw the distant Kälte Mountains. The morning sun lit the eastern faces in stark slashes of crimson and black, their snowy peaks disappearing into blood-smeared clouds.

Red sky at morning, traveller's warning. Not an auspicious start to the day.

Every time he saw those mountains he remembered his time with the Ausgebrochene tribe in the Gezackt Mountains far to the west. Aas loved to learn and before Zerfall brought him into the Täuschung, he'd travelled the world, driven by curiosity. When he learned of the strange delusions of the tribal *salbei*, their wizened wise men and women, he became entranced and studied with them for several months. The *salbei* believed it was possible to move one's soul between vessels. At the time he thought it an odd societal delusion. Now, facing an eternity in Swarm, it was his escape plan.

Turning east toward the Basamortuan Desert, Aas banked away from the Kälte Mountains. They too were a constant reminder; he'd been born in a village nestled in the foothills, the kind of place with more goats than people.

The cold cellar—all he had known for his first fourteen years—was never far from his thoughts. Damp earthen floors which turned to mud in the wet season. Thick wood beams, soft with rot, riddled with worms and termites, had been his sky. Field stones and crumbling mortar, damp with condensation, his horizon. He remembered staring up at those towering mountains from his only window, little more than a knothole. Distant and beautiful, they dominated his little world. The Basamortuan had been but a day's walk east, but he hadn't learned that until years later.

"You're twisted and hideously ugly," father often said. "If the villagers see you they'll kill you, burn you as a demon." And then he'd hold and comfort Aas and bring him a treat, often a hand-carved wooden toy, to play with.

Father kept him hidden, kept him safe.

Amazing the crap children will believe.

Had his father's words shaped his self-image, changed his appearance, or would he have been ugly anyway? He'd never know.

Fourteen years he watched the regal condors sweep down from the mountains to pluck unsuspecting rabbits from the earth. Alive one moment, the rabbits were meat the next. Fourteen years he watched the condors retreat to their mountain holds, soaring free on winds he could only imagine and never feel. He dreamed of their freedom, imagined himself looking down on a cruel world which had cursed him before he was even born.

And then his father died.

One moment he'd been standing, having brought Aas his dinner of offal, and the next he lay sprawled rigid on the floor, fingers splayed in an agonized half-fist, clutching at his chest.

Days passed and Aas hid in the damp cellar with his father's corpse, growing ever hungrier.

If he left, they'd kill him. He couldn't leave, father forbid it.

On the fifteenth day he began eating his father.

Aas shook off the memories. Childhood was a curse, something to survive and escape. He was no longer that boy, huddled in a damp basement. He was a Täuschung priest, not because he was dedicated to bringing about the redemption of all mankind, but because that's what Zerfall wanted him to be. If she was gone, if her need no longer defined him . . . . He didn't know what he was.

I am a killer.

Aas flew east, the rolling hills of Geld giving way to the eternal Basamortuan Desert. He'd find Zerfall there, he knew it. Either he'd kill her or she'd take him with her Gefahrgeist power, leaving him no choice but to once again worship her as he had since the day they met.

But which do you want?

He knew the answer; gods, he missed her so much.

THREE

The wise goat walks alone rather than in the company of a düster snake.

—Basamortuan proverb

SIX UNBLOODED HASIERA WARRIORS squatted, feet flat to the ground, in an uneven circle. Sand-coloured *oihal*, the long flowing robes of the Basamortuan tribes, draped their lean bodies, protecting them from the angry sun. Jateko tried to wedge himself between Nazkagarri, and Dedikatu, the younger brothers of Gogoko, the massive warrior standing at the centre. The siblings, their attention on Gogoko, ignored him. Jateko lowered himself until his bony knees protruded up past his ears, and then toppled backward to sprawl in the sand.

"Oaf," muttered Nazkagarri, the youngest of the three brothers.

Jateko shuffled forward again and neither brother moved to allow him room. Settling for sitting behind them, he stretched out his legs between the two so his toes were within the circle. *There, I'm in.* A glance over his shoulder showed the elders, children, and women, gathered to send the soon-to-be-blooded warriors off on their raid. His mother, Etsita, wearing the same pinched expression she always wore, managing to look sad and annoyed all at the same time. Was she proud to see him sitting here with the warriors? He doubted it.

"Jateko!" snapped Gogoko, the blooded warrior who would lead this raid. "What are you doing?"

"Huh?" He returned his attention to Gogoko.

"Why are you here?"

"I'm of age, I'm joining—"

"Your ass in the sand is an insult to Harea." Gogoko shook his head, and made a clucking sound like that of a disappointed chicken.

"You sound like a—"

"Squat like a man."

"Sorry. I fell," said Jateko, pushing himself back into a squat. He couldn't get his feet flat to the ground like everyone else and perched, balanced precariously, on the balls of his feet.

Nazkagarri, the youngest of the brothers, whispered, "Back with the women, weak-chinned son of seven filthy sandals," and brushed a shoulder against him hard enough to topple him again to the sand.

Jateko scrambled back to his feet. "I'm of age. I'm coming on the raid. Gogoko, tell him I'm coming."

"No," said Gogoko. "You're not."

"But I'm—"

"Were we raiding the *hiria ero*, the soft city-states, I might bring you along."

"Not likely," muttered Nazkagarri.

"We raid the Etsaiaren," continued Gogoko. "Too dangerous. Maybe next time."

"Maybe when you can sit like a man," said Nazkagarri, loud enough for everyone to hear.

Gogoko shot his brother an annoyed look but said nothing.

"I am of age," repeated Jateko, thumping his chest, the sound less impressive than when Gogoko did it.

"You're weaker than *hiria ero* wine and crazier than a düster snake on black sand," said Nazkagarri. "How you see past that giant nose is a mystery. Your clumsiness will get us all killed."

"I'm not clumsy!" But he was, and he knew it. Mom said he just hadn't grown into his bones yet, but then she said a lot of stuff that turned out to be camel dung. *And I'm not crazy.* If they'd only give him a chance he could prove his worth. He could help, be an important part of the tribe.

"Harea says no man is a tribe," Jateko added. "We all contribute—"

Nazkagarri flashed out a hand and swept Jateko's legs from under him sending him hurtling into the sand.

"If I can do that with one hand," said Nazkagarri, "imagine what a blooded Etsaiaren warrior will do."

"I wasn't ready," protested Jateko, rolling in the sand, entangled in his *oihal*. Dedikatu glared at his brother. "A little kindness, please."

Nazkagarri made a camel fart sound with his lips. "I'm just saying what you're thinking."

"I'm thinking," said Dedikatu, "if you aren't careful, Jateko won't be the only one missing this raid."

Rolling muscular shoulders, Nazkagarri spat into the sand; a small offering to Harea, the Basamortuan desert god. He nodded to his brother in the centre of the circle. "Gogoko decides."

Finally freeing himself from his robes, Jateko regained his feet. "Gogoko, let me come. Who is the Etsaiaren champion? I'll bring you his head and spine." He regretted the words the instant they left his mouth. Like his bones, maybe they too were something he'd grow into.

"You'll defeat Abiega Guerrero and commit *bizkarrezurra erantsita*," said Nazkagarri using the ancient words, "the ultimate trophy?" His eyes widened in mock awe. "You'll fill his body with sand driving his soul up into his head and then remove skull and spine in a show of unmatched strength?" He glanced at his brother, eyes alight. "Gogoko, we must bring him!"

Jateko groaned and stared at the sand. He could barely carry two water skins; tearing a warrior's skull and spine free of his body was less than unlikely.

Gogoko muttered something under his breath.

"Jateko," said Dedikatu. "Stay home with your mother. Maybe later, when you've grown into your body, put some muscle on."

"Maybe when he stops tripping over those huge feet," said Nazkagarri and the gathered tribe laughed.

Jateko kicked at Nazkagarri and the man avoided it, not even bothering to leave his squat. "Pfft!"

"Enough." Gogoko cut the air with a slash of his massive hand. "You embarrass us all."

"Especially your mother," said Nazkagarri

"I meant you, Naz" said Gogoko. "Jateko stays—"

"With the women," said Nazkagarri.

"One more word," said Gogoko, "and you too will stay behind."

Nazkagarri shot Jateko an angry look, baring his teeth in a rabid animal snarl and bowed his head in acceptance.

"Jateko," said Gogoko, "you stay. My word is final. Unless you challenge me for leadership of the raid?" Gogoko raised an eyebrow.

Jateko stared up at the massive warrior. The man had arms like twisted knots of wood. *But I'm of age. I should be allowed to—*

"Well?" demanded Gogoko.

"I'll stay," said Jateko. "But only because I want to," he added, trying to salvage some shred of pride. "There is important work to be done."

Nazkagarri bit his lip but didn't dare his brother's temper.

Gogoko stared at Jateko for a long time before saying, "We leave when the sun sets."

Jateko left the circle of warriors, his head held high, his back straight. He'd show them. They'd see he could be a great warrior, just like he knew his father had been. Whoever his father was.

WANDERING INTO THE DESERT, Jateko found somewhere to sit where no one would bother him; not that any were likely to come looking. A snake, one of those nasty black ones his mother always told him to get for her awful-tasting soup, slid past, belly hissing against the sands. His arm ached in sympathy; the vicious bastards always seemed to manage to bite him in exactly the same place.

Harea, I need a sign. I need to know your plan.

Gusts of wind whipped a dusting of sand from the dunes' crest, spinning it in tight, dancing circles. Patterns appeared and faded and Jateko watched, trying to make sense of the message.

Is he telling me this is my time? A shiver of excitement ran through Jateko. *But what am I supposed to do?*

The spiral of dust came apart and fell back to the sand. Was that an answer?

The sun hung low in the west, turning the rolling dunes orange and red. That way lay the *hiria ero*, those distant, semi-mythological city-states where the women were fat and willing, the men and wine weak, and the steel beyond compare.

"I'm tired of being weak and clumsy," Jateko told the sand, praying the desert god listened. "This can't be all there is." There had to be more. In the Basamortuan you were a warrior or you were nothing. "I can't be nothing forever." There had to be a way.

"Harea helps those who help themselves," Jakintsua often said. To Jateko that sounded suspiciously like the desert god did nothing. But it did make sense. If Jateko wanted to be something more than he was—if he wanted to be respected—only he could change that.

How? How am I to do this? I need to be bigger, stronger. He needed to learn how to fight, but as long as everyone thought him weak and clumsy, no one would teach him even the basics.

Jateko remembered the stories Jakintsua told by the fire on the coldest nights, tales of inhuman warriors who ate their foes, devouring their brains and organs, and growing in power. In stories the warrior was always depicted as evil, as possessed and demonic. Was that true or was Jakintsua embellishing for effect?

Probably the latter.

Gogoko was a big strong warrior but he certainly wasn't evil. *And I'm not evil.* What was the difference between eating a sand rat and a defeated foe?

Jateko tried to imagine eating a man, pulling the heart from his chest and stuffing it raw into his mouth.

"Yuck."

There had to be another way.

There's the raid. What if he went anyway and killed a few Etsaiaren warriors? Wouldn't that prove to everyone he had potential? And maybe he could be sneaky and eat a little bit of a slain warrior, just to see if it worked.

But he wasn't allowed on the raid. The only thing he'd be eating was his mother's gritty snake soup.

How could he do it? How could he show everyone his worth?

I might be clumsy, but I'm not stupid. He had to figure out a way to join the raid.

Jateko heard his mother calling his name, her voice shrill. She probably wanted him to empty the slop bucket. He was pretty sure he'd left it full. With a sigh he turned and headed back toward the camp. In a few days, once the warriors returned from their raid, the entire tribe would move on, make the long trek to the next oasis. More of the same. Walk. Set up the *karpan* he and his mother shared, mend his *oihal*, hunt for snakes, birds, or rabbits slow and stupid enough to get caught, and empty the slop bucket. It had been the same, day after day, his entire life.

Cresting a dune, Jateko saw Gogoko, and the unblooded men preparing to leave the camp. The young warriors collected their weapons—mostly long spears—and what little supplies they'd carry. A crowd of women gathered to see them off with kisses and hugs. Jakintsua, the tribe's elderly *sorgin*, pulled Gogoko aside and spoke into his ear. The warrior bowed to the wizened woman.

I'll watch the warriors leave and then return home. Jateko sank into a squat and then toppled back onto his ass.

Sorry Harea. Some of us just aren't meant to squat. Did the desert god really get upset every time someone's bum touched sand? It seemed silly, but who knew the minds of gods. Jateko considered sitting for a while but decided he'd best get back to his feet. Annoying Harea wouldn't help anything.

Down below the warriors said their final farewells and left the camp, Gogoko and his brothers in the lead. Their long, loping strides soon took them from view. Jateko watched the trailing warrior disappear behind another dune. Nearby a scorpion skittered across the sand and stopped to watch him, tiny black eyes intent.

Was *this* a sign, a message from Harea? Was he meant to do something now? The scorpion turned away, scuttling across sand in the direction the warriors were heading.

Jateko watched the scorpion, blinking. *Is that . . . Should I . . .*

The scorpion disappeared into the sand.

Harea helps those who help themselves.

Without another thought, Jateko set off after Gogoko and his warriors. He'd trail them to the camp of the Etsaiaren, dogging their heels at every step. They'd never even know he was there; he'd move like a desert ghost, like a hunting snake. Then, when they prepared themselves for the raid, he would join them. Gogoko would have no choice but to bring him along. It was, he decided, a brilliant plan.

E IGHT HOURS LATER JATEKO still hadn't caught up with Gogoko's warriors and the eastern horizon ran red with the bloody light of a newly rising sun. A prophecy, no doubt, of the bloodshed to come. He walked on, the day's heat an ever-growing weight as the sun crept higher. By mid-morning he staggered with exhaustion and dehydration. Of Gogoko's passage, he found no clue. He'd lost their trail during the night and only Harea's will would see him to the Etsaiaren camp. Glancing over his shoulder he saw his own meandering tracks disappear beneath the blowing sands.

By Harea he was so thirsty. He should turn back, go home.

No. This is a test. The desert god was merciless when it came to cowards. Jateko had to keep going, have faith. Soon he'd catch Gogoko and the warriors.

He walked for hours. Days. Years.

The sun, high overhead, did its best to crush Jateko to the sand. Its weight bore against his thin shoulders, making every step an effort of will. It reminded him of his mother's endless pestering. Jateko, have you gathered anything for dinner? Jateko, have you emptied the slop bucket? Jateko, where are your sandals?

Jateko, are you going to die out there in the desert sun?

"What?"

Jateko, remember what that dead snake looked like, the one you found when you were a little boy? Remember how it was all dry and black and crusty? Remember the dry snap sound it made when you tried to bend it?

"Yes."

Jateko, you're going to look like that snake.

"No," he whispered, his voice little more than a rasp of sand. "Harea guides me."

Jateko staggered deeper into the desert.

A S THE SUN DIPPED behind a long row of dunes to the west, Jateko shuffled onward, eyes slitted against the blowing sand. Hidalko, those lost spirits, the desert's unbound souls, whipped dune crests into miniature whirlwinds reaching past his shins. *Don't give up*, they said, *Harea watches over you.*

Sometimes he imagined he was a god, striding across the world. Most of the time, eyes and teeth gritty with sand, he cursed himself for leaving camp so unprepared.

Harea helps those who help themselves.

Staggering up the side of yet another crumbling mountain of sand, Jateko stopped at the top, blinking burning eyes. Was that Gogoko's camp? Yes, he recognized the *karpan* the men slept in. For a long while, many hundreds of heart beats, he stood staring down into the desert valley where the young warriors of his village had set camp and slept through the worst of the day's heat. The sun would soon set and they'd once again awaken and continue toward the Etsaiaren in search of trophies.

Jateko licked dry, cracked lips with a leathery tongue. There'd be water down there in that camp. Beautiful wet water.

Did I pass your test?

The desert god gave no answer.

Well, here he was. He'd done it. He'd tracked his prey through the trackless wastes and there they were. Harea, he *knew*, must be at his shoulder.

Jateko's feet hurt. His knees hurt. His thighs hurt. Come to think of it, everything hurt.

Water and a camel. Next time I want both.

A hot wind gusted and blew sand across his sandals. The desert god telling him it was time to move?

"I'm not complaining," said Jateko, "But if I am to do your work, I could use a little help."

Jateko stared at the *karpan* of his fellow Hasiera warriors. Should he walk down and announce his presence, tell them he'd joined their raiding party? No. That felt wrong. He hadn't walked all this way to empty slop buckets and cook their meals. He'd come to prove he was better than that.

But first, water.

Jateko ducked low and slid down the side of the dune toward the gathered tents. *I'll be quieter than hidalko. I'll ghost across the sands, leaving no hint of my passing. I'll*—he tripped, his toe catching something hidden beneath the desert's shifting surface, and tumbled in an ungainly heap of long limbs and knobbly joints. For a long moment he lay still, listening. Had they heard him? No, the camp remained quiet.

Jateko pushed himself to his feet muttering curses.

Staying low he continued toward the circle of tents. *Harea, smile down upon me and don't leave anything else lying around for me to trip on.* Stopping outside the *karpan* Gogoko and his brothers shared, Jateko took a few calming breaths. Water. There'd be water in here. If he didn't drink soon he'd scream. Except he didn't think he could. His throat felt like he'd gargled sand.

"Move like hidalko," he whispered as he parted the flaps and slid inside.

The three brothers lay sleeping, their weapons, as always, in easy reach. Jateko quashed the urge to laugh. This was going to be too easy, they snored like old men. He didn't even need to be sneaky, no way they'd hear him over that racket. Sauntering between the sleeping men, he made his way to Nazkagarri's side. The young warrior slept, lips parted, tongue exposed like it was about to tumble from his mouth. Picking Nazkagarri's favourite knife from the ground, Jateko slid it from its sheath to better admire it. Patches of rust stained the ancient blade. Eastern metal, from the corrupt city-states. Jateko had no idea where the long knife came from. Probably Nazkagarri's grandfather. Gogoko always bragged about the daring raids their grandfather led and how he was going to bring that kind of pride back to the Hasiera.

Jateko grinned at the knife, noticing his crooked teeth in the blade's pitted surface. His reflection warped and twisted and he saw himself, larger and stronger, wrapped in impossible muscle. His jaw was strong and manly and not non-existent as it was now. He blinked and again saw his own receding chin.

Nazkagarri's eyes snapped open. For an instant Jateko saw naked fear there, but that look dimmed to rage as the warrior recognized him and twisted well beyond rage when he saw the knife in Jateko's hand.

The young warrior grinned murder. "You are dead—"

Jateko panicked, slammed the knife into Nazkagarri's chest throwing the weight of his scrawny body behind the blow.

All Naz's rage bled away, replaced by something Jateko couldn't begin to understand. Nazkagarri lifted a hand toward Jateko, stopping short of caressing his cheek. The mouth worked, opening and closing, the body spasming each time.

Is he trying to tell me something? Jateko leaned closer until he felt Nazkagarri's breath ticking in ear.

"Going to kill you," whispered Nazkagarri, blood frothing his lips.

Jateko heard Gogoko move within his sleeping roll and his heart gave a savage kick of terror.

They're going to think I *did this!*

You did!

They'll think I did it on purpose.

How could he explain? It was a mistake! Naz startled him!

They'd never listen. They'd never understand. Gogoko would see the knife and his brother and—

Gogoko would kill him for sure. Blinking down at Nazkagarri, Jateko watched the young man touch the hilt of the knife jutting from his chest like it was something terrifying, like one of those red scorpions that made people swell up and burst like an over-ripe—Jateko's mind stumbled, thoughts tripping over each other like a nest of panicked mice. Then, a moment of bright clarity.

Run. Run now.

Spinning, Jateko fled, bouncing off the *karpan*'s centre pole on his way out. The walls shook and he heard confused grunts and muttering from Gogoko and Dedikatu. Once out of the tent he turned west and ran as hard and as fast as he could. He still hadn't tasted a drop of water.

It didn't matter.

They were going to kill him.

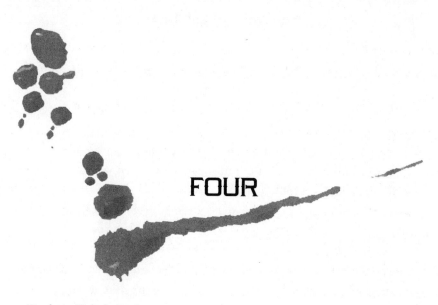

FOUR

Truths in Unbedeutend
Are lies in Geldangelegenheiten

—Halber Tod, Cotardist Poet

ZERFALL, RIDING EVER EAST, felt like a child walking through tall grass, unable to see where she was going or where she'd been. If not for the slow change of the scenery, she might have been going in endless circles. Rolling fields flattened and verdant green died and faded. Life bled colour, the slow trickle of a wound that never healed. Even the sky, crisp blue when she left the city, wept until all the world became an eternity of grey. Her skin too looked grey, her right arm blackening toward the fingertips to blend with the few flakes of black polish clinging stubbornly to her fingernails. Her left hand remained closer to its original flesh-tone, the black tattoo of the closed eye retaining its sharp contrast.

She hadn't eaten in days and suffered neither hunger nor weakness. Though she loathed his ideas and understood little of what he said, sometimes she fished Halber Tod's book of poems from its pocket. Did his Cotardism influence his poetry, or was it the other way around?

She rode on, contemplating the last poem she read. The man was obsessed with death and rotting and insanity. *Dissolution*. The word plagued her, hounded every thought. Who was she? Who had she been? Was she becoming someone new or was this the final stages of the disintegration of whoever she once was?

"Prayer, or curse?" she asked the stolen horse. The chestnut gelding ignored her, its ears not even twitching.

Yesterday the beast stumbled and fell, throwing her from the saddle. She'd stood over it, watching its beautiful brown eyes slide closed with a long sigh.

"I'm not walking," she told the horse. "Get up."

The horse, dejected and ragged, once again rose. Since then they hadn't stopped and not once did the horse falter. He plodded ever onward, head down, not even noticing the occasional tufts of hardy grass they passed.

Zerfall ran numb fingers through the horse's mane and strands of the once lustrous chestnut hair came away in her hand. He didn't seem to notice.

"Do you have a name?" Zerfall asked, not expecting an answer.

Again the horse ignored her.

"I can't just call you horse," she said, resting her hand on a rolling shoulder. "You feel cold."

The horse farted, a noxious stench.

"It smells like you've been rotting from the inside out. What the hell have you been eating?"

Again he ignored her.

She rode on in silence, thinking. *I don't know anyone and I remember nothing of my life. What can I possibly call this horse?* Her entire existence consisted of a couple of knives, a bank note with her name, and a book of awful poetry. She fumbled with indifferent fingers to once again retrieve it from its pocket. The stained black leather cover looked well-handled, the poet's name, Halber Tod, embossed in flaking gold leaf. Someone read this book many times. Had it been her?

Opening to a random page, she read:

Gibbous moon, fat belly heavy
Sun and delusional earth, circling or circled
Faith and reason battle in ignorance
As you're both flat and very round

"Meaningless dreck," she said. Still, it was all she had.

"I'll call you Tod," she told the horse.

An ear twitched and the beast glanced back over its shoulder at her, beautiful brown eyes swarming with flies. Zerfall shooed them away and Tod didn't so much as blink. In moments his eyes once again swam with flies.

"Tod, you aren't looking too good."

Tod plodded ever east, the sun rising and falling. At night she watched the moon's fat bellied progress and wondered what Halber Tod—a talentless poet if ever there was one—meant. Did people think the earth circled the moon, or was it perhaps the opposite? Did philosophers argue the shape of this grey world? She had no idea.

But it hadn't always been this grey. When she first awoke, skull throbbing, nauseated with pain, the colours were brighter, more vibrant. Reaching back with her right hand she prodded again at her skull. Blood had hardened, forming a thick crust of matted hair. The skull seemed to give a little. Probing, she found something wriggling and squishy. For an instant fear coursed through her, savaging her gut. And then, nothing.

With numb fingers she pulled free a clotted mass of hair and blood long dried to black. Maggots crawled through the mess, writhing glistening white over dark fingers, and she stared, uncomprehending.

You're broken. Damaged. She tossed the offending mess aside. *Your skull has been shattered and you're dying. Only the damage to your brain saves you from the agony of understanding.*

With nothing else to do she rode on, ever east, waiting to topple from the saddle.

Another day died and the rot crawled from the fingertips of her right hand, reaching up beyond her elbow. Though the tattooed left hand looked as grey as everything else, it didn't blacken. Coincidence, or did this mean something? She had no way of knowing.

Long grass had given way to endless rolling sand and she hadn't noticed the transition. Desert stretched before her forever. Sun and moon were nothing. If the days were hot and the nights cold, she felt none of it. No thirst nor hunger plagued her and Tod seemed equally willing to walk on forever. She reopened the book of poems but again returned it to its pocket upon finding the word hebetudinous rhymed with fruitless.

"Tod," she told her horse, "you've written some awful poems."

Tod, like any poet, didn't take criticism well and became glum and uncommunicative.

WHAT WAS THAT? HAD something passed overhead, briefly throwing her into shadow? Glancing up she saw a black condor, wings spread wide, riding a hot desert updraught. The bird banked and circled, once again dragging its shadow across her.

Was that on purpose?

Shading her eyes with a blackened hand, she watched the hideous bird once again turn to bring its shadow across her path. Was it following her?

Condors are carrion birds. When she remembered nothing of who and what she'd been, how did she know that? Carrion. The thought left an unpleasant feeling tickling her spine.

The condor, grey skull tilting to watch her with a single bright eye, circled. Watching. Waiting.

"Go away!" Zerfall shouted.

The condor uttered a rattling croak and turned its bald head to watch with the other eye.

"There's nothing to eat here," she called. "Go find a dead mouse or something."

Folding its wings and shedding altitude, the condor dropped below a dune and disappeared from sight.

How long had it been since she'd seen another living creature out here? Days? She couldn't remember.

Up ahead a gaunt man in dark robes crested the dune and stood staring down at her. In his left hand hung a long bow and his right held an arrow, spinning slowly in his fingers. He stood watching, unmoving. Everything about him looked black, but then the world had become rather monochromatic of late. He might be wearing dark purple for all she could tell.

What were the odds someone had stumbled across her here, in the middle of the desert? *Pretty damned slim.*

"I have nothing worth stealing," she called out.

Tod issued a wounded grunt.

"Except the horse," she corrected. "But he's a terrible poet."

In one smooth motion the man nocked, drew, and loosed an arrow. Tod let out another disappointed grunt and dropped boneless to the ground, a thick black shaft protruding from between his once beautiful eyes. Zerfall rolled free and without conscious effort found herself standing, turned sideways to offer a smaller target. The man in black stood watching, another arrow turning leisurely in his fingers, the threat clear.

"Zerfall," he called, voice harsh, "you look awful." He shook his bald head, the wrinkled skin grey and hanging about his throat in long wattles. "I thought this was going to be harder."

"Thought, or hoped?" Zerfall asked. He hadn't put an arrow in her. Did that mean he wasn't here to kill her? *Lure him closer. Get him with the knives.*

"Fleeing in a straight line." The man laughed, a rueful snort. "How you got to be so old is a mystery."

Old? From what Zerfall had seen of her body, she would have guessed she was in her early twenties. "You know me?" She edged closer, and the bow rose, the arrow nocked and drawn to full extension.

"No closer, please." He licked thin lips, blinking in the harsh desert sun. "I don't want to kill you—"

"Well that's a relief."

"—any sooner than I must."

"Oh."

"This is some game, correct? You're playing with me?" The bow lowered, wavering. "Even from here you might be able to take me."

Take him from here? Zerfall gauged the distance; no chance of throwing one her knives that far.

"Why are you not telling me how much I love you?" He sounded disappointed.

"You love me?"

"You know I do."

"Sorry. I got hit in the head. I remember nothing."

"A lie."

"I can't remember you so I have no idea if I once cared what you think." She shrugged. "But right now, I don't."

"Another lie."

"No," she said. "I really don't care."

"I meant the other—"

"My skull is broken. I think I'm dying."

He tilted his head, wattles hanging off one cheek like a fleshy curtain. "Truly?"

Zerfall glanced at where Tod lay. His eyes, gaping sockets, no longer crawled with flies. His belly had grown bloated, the skin stretched tight, the chestnut hair patchy and worn thin. *When did that happen?* She returned her attention to the ugly man. "Put an arrow in me and be done. I'm tired." Her shoulders sagged. "I haven't closed my eyes in a long time."

"I'm not falling for this. You haven't lived hundreds of years by giving up."

Hundreds? The man was a lunatic. "Hundreds of years would cause anyone to give up."

"Not you."

Changing the subject, Zerfall gestured at her empty scabbard. "Was I any good with a sword?"

"After four hundred years of practice?" The man barked a humourless laugh. "I think Hölle would love to return Blutblüte to you. Point first, of course."

"Of course." *Blutblüte. My sword has a name.*

Hölle, the woman Zerfall betrayed and apparently stabbed. She said nothing.

He examined her. "You once told me Blutblüte's secret. You said it was to show how much you trusted me."

"What was the secret?" she asked, caring far more about that than any trust she may have once had in this man. Her sword. She wanted it.

"Swarm," said the man.

The girl Zerfall hamstrung back in the city said something about a swarm. "I don't understand."

He offered a sad smile and she believed the emotion; it wasn't faked. "Perhaps best we leave it that way," he said. "Maybe ignorance can save you." He sighed with regret. "I am envious. If you don't know, you can't believe. If you don't believe, you might escape your own hell."

Escape my own hell? "Why haven't you killed me yet?" she asked.

"Because I love you. Hölle says—" The words choked to silence.

The arrow pointed at the ground now. Sagging folds of skin hung under deep-set eyes, dragging them open in a damp droop. *Is he crying?* Could she use this? Perhaps this wasn't the end after all. Strangely, she felt less relief at the thought of not dying than she expected.

"Were we lovers?" she asked.

"Were?"

"Are?"

"You don't remember?" Naked hope, raw emotion laid bare.

"Wait, it's coming back. Yes, we were! God, I love you *so* much."

"What is my name?"

Zerfall opened her mouth, willing some memory to return. Nothing.

"My name is Aas."

"Ass?"

The arrow slammed into her gut and she collapsed, landing with her back propped against Tod's bloated carcass.

She thought herself numb to everything. She thought herself protected from all the hurt the world offered, wrapped in the safety of unfeeling.

She was wrong.

Agony seared her insides. That arrow found that last spark of feeling, that last bastion of life nestled deep within. And punctured it.

Zerfall knew fear. She had thought anything was better than this, anything was better than endless nothing. Pain, endless pain, was far worse.

There is no nothing. Something far worse, far more terrifying than nothing lurked beyond her last breath.

Aas stood over her, his eyes streaming tears. She hadn't noticed his approach. He'd slung the bow over a shoulder and clutched a heavy knife in one hand. "I'm so sorry." *{Tell me how much I love you. Tell me I have to save you. Don't leave me a choice, I beg you.}*

His desperate need hammered at Zerfall, pounded at the ocean of pain drowning her every thought. "You love me," she forced through gritted teeth. "You have to save me."

She heard his breath catch. *{I feel nothing, no compulsion at all.}* "You are the most subtle and powerful Gefahrgeist I have ever met. You can do better." *{You must, or I must obey Hölle.}*

Gefahrgeist, she remembered: People whose need for followers and worshippers defined the reality around them, stealing choice and freedom from others. *How can I remember that but not who I am?* "Aas, I'm scared." She poured her fear into her words. "You *must* save me."

Aas shook his head, folds of grey skin swinging. "I feel nothing." He watched her for a moment, waiting. *{I can't lie to Hölle, she'll hear my thoughts. She doesn't forgive. She never forgives.}* "Demand my love, leave me no choice. We'll return to Geld and kill Hölle. We'll be together."

Together? What could she have seen in this jowled wretch? Agony twisted her gut ripping a whimper from between clenched teeth. "You must love me. Together we'll—"

"Nothing." *{She has lost what she was.}*

"We still can—"

"No, you can't." He wiped at his tears with a sleeve. "I promised Hölle I would kill you and I have. She'll know if I lie. If you were the woman I knew, we could . . . But you're not." *{I have no choice.}* "Hölle wants you to suffer," he said, shrugging in apology.

Aas leaned forward to grip the shaft of the arrow protruding from her belly— *{For so long I wanted to hurt you. But not like this.}*—and gave it a savage twist.

A scream shredded Zerfall's throat as her insides spasmed as if trying to clutch at the intruding object. The world came apart, blinding white agony.

AAS LET GO OF the arrow shaft and, torn with regret, stepped back to admire his work. The placement was perfect, as always. He'd done as Hölle commanded, even if perhaps he had given Zerfall the opportunity to ensnare him with her Gefahrgeist power. He couldn't delude himself that much. He gave her every chance and she failed. If his thoughts betrayed him and Hölle heard, she'd kill him. His only hope was to return with proof he'd done the foul deed. Zerfall would suffer, as Hölle decreed.

{She'll take days to die.} Though the desert and whatever animals called this inhospitable hell home might speed that along. If all else failed, the düster poison coating the arrow head guaranteed an agonizing death. Hopefully it would be enough.

{Zerfall, what happened to you?} She'd been so beautiful. Long black hair hanging in curls around the muscled curves of her petite body. Now she looked like she'd been half dead before he caught up with her. *{Why did you run in a straight line? You could have gone anywhere and I never would have found you.}* The smell of rot filled his nostrils making his mouth water; the carrion bird within him was never far from the surface and shallower every day. The horse had been dead for some time and that was strange. Had Zerfall's delusions kept the beast on its feet, or were horses capable of self-deception? Part of his mind picked at the puzzle, struggled with the mystery and his hunger to understand. Could this be a manifestation of hallucination? *{Hölle is the Halluzin, not Zerfall.}* He pushed the thought aside for later. An arrow in the skull had dropped the beast sure enough.

He nudged Zerfall's leg with a foot. "Wake up. We're not finished."

She groaned, a soft moan that pulled at heart and groin alike. *{Gods, how long have I waited to hear that sound from her?}* But not like this.

Her eyes fluttered open. Once as dark as her hair, now they were filmed, white and yellow like rotting milk. Reaching a hand blackened with rot toward him she whispered, "Please. End this. Pain."

"I'm sorry," he said, crouching beside her. Zerfall fumbled for the knife sheathed at her side and he took it from her, dropping it in the sand out of reach. "I must bring Hölle proof of your death." She looked pitifully grateful at the mention of an end to her suffering. *{If I end you quickly, Hölle will know.}*

"Take my head," she said, reaching a hand up to grip the collar of his robes.

{Sorry.} "Rather too difficult to carry all the way back to Geld," he joked. Aas gestured at her left hand, untouched by rot. "I'll take that."

His words seemed to bring some part of her back. She blinked at the hand. "The tattoo, is it important?"

"You once told me you saw Swarm with that eye."

She laughed, a pained grunt ending in a torn sob. "Swarm," she said without explanation.

{What's so funny about Swarm?} He breathed the sweet scent of rot wafting from the woman he worshipped and loved. *{Not just the horse,}* he realized. He watched the too slow throb of a pulse in her neck. She wasn't dead, but soon, even had he not found her, she would be. His stomach rumbled with hunger as the condor within sensed the proximity of a meal.

He fit the pieces of this new puzzle together and his eyes widened in understanding. "You're a Cotardist!"

"Cotardist?" She frowned, her once flawless skin now thin and flaking.

"You're rotting. Your delusions devour you."

"I knew that," she said, sounding surprised. "Somehow." The hand gripping his robe tightened. "Kill me. No one will know. Tell Hölle I suffered."

"No," he said. "I'm a Wahnist, as well as a Therianthrope."

"Wahnist," she said. "The manifestation of false beliefs."

Aas shrugged. What was false where delusion defined reality? It was a question he'd asked himself many times. "Hölle hears my thoughts." *{Everyone can, once I'm close enough.}*

"Everyone can," agreed Zerfall.

Aas raised the knife. "Such a rude weapon," he apologized. "Unlike you, I hate knives."

"Knives," she said. Her milky eyes slid closed.

Straightening her left arm, he hefted the knife; no way he'd hack through her wrist in a single chop. "This will hurt," he said. "But then, I suppose that's the point."

She let go of his robes—tried to roll away—but he held her in place. She'd always been so strong, and now she was as a child under his hands. He stared at the tattoo of a closed eye, half expecting it to open and stare back. Her loss of memory, what caused that? Had it been the blow to the head, or was it something else? Was it a manifestation of some particularly strong delusion, and if so, was it hers, or someone else's?

"You're a beautiful puzzle, and I love puzzles."

She wasn't listening.

"I thought I was going to have to start a fire out here to cauterize the wound so you wouldn't die too quickly," he said, nodding at her hand. "I was trying to figure out where I'd find wood." Zerfall looked lost, distracted like she was trying to remember something important. "Small consolation," he told her. "But you won't suffer nearly as long as you would have. Your rot is well along. Your delusion will kill you long before the gut wound." *{Once the rot reaches your heart.}*

Gritting his teeth, Aas chopped at the wrist with all his strength. Memories of hacking his father apart flooded back and he remembered how the man's innards looked, round and wet, and how delicious they were after weeks of starvation.

{I'm sorry. I have no choice.}

T HE IMPACTS FELT DISTANT, like a dog tugging on Zerfall's sleeve. Cotardist. For how long had she been dying, slowly rotting? It was enough to make her laugh. Or would have been if not for the agony of the arrow impaling her.

When she'd known who she was she'd been insane, a powerful Gefahrgeist if Aas was to be believed. With the loss of her memory she lost that power. That mad dog tugged again on her left sleeve, jerking her body with the force. Had something in her memories caused the delusions? Had her mind been broken by some forgotten tragedy, or had she been born a selfish manipulator?

What had Aas said?

Knife.

That was important.

His thoughts intruded on hers. *{She wears rot like perfume.}* He eyed Zerfall, licking his lips. *{Should I take a small piece for myself?}* He reached toward her but stopped short. *{Hölle will kill me. I won't be able to hide it from her.}*

The ugly man prattled on, and she no longer knew what was spoken and what was the endless litany of tainted thought. He talked about how someday he'd see her in Swarm, and how much he loved and worshipped and feared her.

Knife.

Blutblüte, her sword. The mystery of the empty scabbard answered. *I want my sword.* Well that wouldn't be happening, not if she died here in the desert.

Zerfall's hand tumbled away and the loss snapped her eyes open. Not the pain, the theft. *He must not take that hand.*

Knife.

She had two knives. But only one hand.

Her right hand, numb and blackened with decay, fumbled for a hidden blade.

Aas, crouched beside her, held up her left hand, turning the palm toward her. For an instant the tattooed eye opened and Zerfall felt the tumbling vertigo of seeing herself slumped against the bloated corpse of a horse. Her hair, thin and greasy, showed patches of grey scalp. Dead eyes stared back, clouded and tenebrous. Cracked lips pulled back in a desiccated snarl exposing chipped and rotting teeth.

Zerfall's fingers closed around the hilt of a knife.

"Aas," she whispered.

"Yes, my love," he said, leaning close. *{You smell delicious.}*

She drove the knife into the soft flesh of his belly. The effort tore something vital deep in her own gut and she fell back against Tod, unable to move, pinioned by agony.

Aas jerked away with a wet sob, clutching at the knife with twitching fingers. He staggered several paces and collapsed to the sand, whimpering like a savaged dog.

The effort broke her, dimmed what little was left of that spark deep within. Snuffed what life she stubbornly clung to. The pain faded, numbness sank into her, worming fingers burrowing deep in flesh. What was the point of any of that? She'd awoken, already dying, only to be killed a short while later. Why had she bothered fleeing? She didn't even know what she'd fled. She heard something lilting insanely between choked laughter and agonized weeping.

With a groan of pain Aas pushed himself to his knees. "Oh, that was well done," he gasped, hunched around the knife protruding from his belly.

"That's a killing wound," said Zerfall. "You'll die here beside me."

"I'm a Therianthrope."

She remembered: Shape-shifters who believed themselves possessed by animal spirits. "So?"

Aas dragged the knife free and flung it away with a snarl. "I heal when I change." He *twisted*, collapsing and crumbling in on himself until a condor stood where the man had been. The bird, shuffling and dancing from foot to foot, cackled rattling croaks of deranged laughter. Gripping her severed hand in its talons, it launched itself into the sky.

Zerfall lay against Tod watching Aas circle, spiralling ever higher. After a dozen loops, the condor, little more than a black dot in a grey sky, flew west.

The pain in her gut faded, that tiny spark of life fizzling and sputtering like a star falling through the night sky.

Nothing left now.

Light and dark cycled without meaning. Sand piled around her legs, crashing against her in slow-motion waves, waging war against her existence, burying her. Tod's splayed hooves disappeared beneath that encroaching inevitability.

Is there an Afterdeath for people who don't know who they are, don't know what they believe?

Who was she? Who had she been? She'd carried weapons, a sword and knives—god how she wanted to hold her sword, Blutblüte, one last time. She'd been violent and deadly.

Do my dead await me?

Maybe she'd ask them who she was.

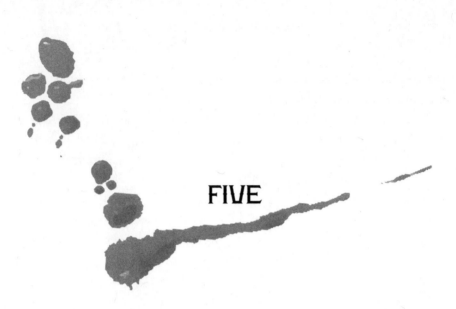

FIVE

Only a fool gets bitten by the same snake twice.

—Basamortuan Proverb

J ATEKO RAN.

They'll never catch me. I'm a ghost. I'm the spirit of the desert, protected and warded by Harea.

Jateko ran until he couldn't and then walked until that became too much. At some point the sun rose and he staggered on, often stumbling and falling. Sometimes he crawled.

Thirst no longer plagued his every thought. He was clear headed now. He'd even stopped sweating at some point, a sure sign the desert god watched over him.

Reaching the top of a towering dune, he stopped, sure he'd long lost his pursuers, and turned to look back. His footprints weaved drunkenly across the desert floor describing a long arc.

Well at least I can't see them. He squinted at a distant dune. There, at the dune's crest, sat a familiar *karpan*. He tried to swear but managed only a dry cough. Gogoko and his brothers—no, *brother*—had made camp, thinking to rest through the day and continue their pursuit at nightfall. He could do the same, it was the smart thing to do, but they'd catch him in no time. If he kept walking, dared the day's heat, the desert winds might obscure his tracks. If he could find an oasis he might yet survive.

Harea guide me, he prayed. *Cloak my tracks and lead me to water.*

His life was in the desert god's hands.

Jateko walked west. Or mostly west.

He blinked. When had he fallen? Hot sand seared his palms. He thought about how water disappeared into sand. He felt ill, nauseated. Actually, he'd been feeling ill for a long time.

Pushing himself back to his feet, Jateko once again set off.

"Empty the slop bucket when you get home," his mother said, pacing along beside him.

"Do it yourself," he said. "I follow Harea's will now. Never again will I let the doubts of the tribe sway me."

"You always were a bent little sandal. What do you think the desert god would want of *you*?" She had a way of speaking that made him feel useless and pathetic.

"I don't know. Maybe he—"

"All you're going to do," she said, "is feed the coyotes."

"Mom—"

"You're as useful as a wet camel turd."

They walked side by side for a long while. Eventually, her dry crackling giggle got on his nerves. "Mother," he said, turning to face her. "I don't—" She was gone, and with her the mad laughter.

Jateko grunted and walked on. It wasn't even that hot any more. For what seemed like an eternity Jakintsua walked at his side, just beyond his peripheral vision. Over and over she told him the old stories where warriors ate their foes and grew in strength and skill until they challenged the gods. By Harea he was so hungry, so thirsty.

His shadow stretched out beneath him, becoming a long exaggeration of his thin frame. His head looked awkward, ears protruding.

"Many families of ezkutatzen lizards could shelter in the shadows cast by those ears," said Nazkagarri, striding at his side.

"Go away."

"Make me."

Jateko groaned. He hated it when Naz got like this. The man would follow him, teasing mercilessly, for hours.

"You should give up," said Naz. "Sit down and wait. Why drag this out?"

Jateko stared at the ground, blinking. "Where did my shadow go?"

"It's night."

Night. When did that happen?

"They'll catch you, you know."

He stumbled forward, feet dragging in the sand. It would be cold soon. His head felt swollen which was funny because he didn't think there was any water left in his body at all. Maybe it had been filled with sand. "Catch me. Who?"

"My brothers."

"Why?"

"They're going to bring me your skull and spine."

"*Bizkarrezurra erantsita,*" muttered Jateko, remembering how Naz had used the ancient words back at the camp. "Why?"

"Because you murdered me."

"It was a mistake. You scared me."

Nazkagarri grabbed Jateko by the shoulders, spun him until they stared eye to eye. "Your soul shall serve me and I will make eternity a living hell for you." He showed bright teeth in something Jateko thought might have been a smile had it not looked so angry. "Dedikatu swore me this oath. And you know Dedikatu keeps his oaths."

True, Dedi never lies. "How can it be a living hell if I'm dead?" Jateko asked, thoughts muddled by extreme dehydration.

Nazkagarri gave him a shove, sent him toppling over backward to land awkwardly in the sand. The young warrior, handsome and broad-shouldered, stared down at him, his expression one of odd regret. "I feel sorry for you."

Jateko lay in the cooling sand, feeling it shift beneath him. "I really am sorry," he said. "Do you have water?"

Nazkagarri blinked in disbelief. "Gogoko and Dedikatu will catch you at morning's first light."

"If I last that long."

"You will."

"Naz—" But Naz was gone.

Unable to stand, Jateko crawled. His heart thrummed in his chest reminding him of the time he held a wounded bird. What happened to that bird? He couldn't remember.

"It died," his mother reminded him. "I put it in the stew."

Right. That was it. It died.

Nausea twisted Jateko and he sprawled, retching, in the sand. A thin stream of dark drool hung from his open mouth, but no matter how much his stomach heaved, nothing else came out. He rolled onto his back, panting in shallows gasps. His limbs felt heavy and weak. The eastern horizon swam, sinuous snake-like arms of dust danced above the dunes, lit bloody by the rising sun. *Beautiful.*

Voices. Close.

Jateko rolled onto his stomach, forcing open eyes raw with sharp grit.

"We're close, I can smell him." Dedikatu's voice.

Glancing around in desperation, Jateko spotted a strange mound of sand shaped like a crescent moon. Not much, but enough to hide behind. Clawing at the sand, Jateko dragged himself into the centre of the crescent.

"I hear him," he heard Dedikatu say.

Gogoko said, "Then he's not dead." The warrior sounded disappointed. Sad, even.

Huddling against the sand, Jateko felt something hard buried there. Glancing up, he found himself staring into the empty eyes of a partially buried face. He stifled a startled scream. *Dead. No danger.* Sun and sand had dried the corpse, leaving the skin stretched taught across sharp cheek bones. The lips, peeled back, exposed teeth in a manic grin. An arrow, the shaft thick and black, the feathers those of a condor, protruded from the corpse's belly. Jateko pressed against the inside of the crescent, trying to make himself small. A shadow fell across him.

"Here he is," said Dedikatu, standing with muscular arms crossed, eyes bright and triumphant. "Hiding behind a corpse. Fitting."

Gogoko approached, his mouth set in a grim line. He stood for a long moment, frowning at Jateko. "There's a horse here too. How did someone get this far into the desert with a horse?"

Jateko tried to say he had no idea, but his voice fled.

Dedikatu, satisfied Jateko would not escape, kicked one of the horse's hooves free of sand. Bending, he examined the shoe. "*Hiria ero*," he said. "Metal from the west."

Curled in the sand, Jateko met Gogoko's gaze. The warrior's face, wrinkled brow, teeth gnawing lower lip, looked out of place. *He doesn't want this.*

"Dedi," said Gogoko, watching Jateko. "Let's bring him back to the village. Let Jakintsua decide what to do with him."

Dedikatu stood, flexing muscled arms, his shoulders making deep rumbling sounds as he rolled them. "No. The *sorgin* might spare him, use his madness as an excuse." Large hands squeezed into tight fists, knuckles popping loud enough to cause Jateko to twitch in fear.

"I'm not—" A fit of coughing interrupted Jateko. His throat felt lined with sharp grit.

Reaching down, Dedikatu gripped Jateko's ankle and dragged him from the sand covered corpse.

Gogoko unslung a goat's bladder from his back. "I'll give him some water." When Dedikatu looked ready to argue, he added, "He must be able to speak his defence."

Dedikatu dropped Jateko's ankle and nodded acceptance.

Kneeling at Jateko's side, Gogoko poured a splash of water into his throat. Nothing ever tasted so good. This was life. He coughed and sputtered most of it into the sand.

Gogoko shook his head, eyes sad. "Drink slowly."

"Don't waste water," growled Dedikatu.

"Can you talk?" asked Gogoko, ignoring his brother.

"Yes," whispered Jateko. Maybe he could explain. Maybe they'd see this was a terrible mistake. He hadn't *wanted* to kill Nazkagarri.

Dedikatu nudged him in the ribs with a foot. "Did you kill Naz?"

By the desert god he wanted to lie, but Harea had no place for deceivers in Borrokalaria, his Hall of Blooded Warriors. And having killed Naz, that's exactly what he was, a blooded warrior. He wanted that for so long and now. Killing didn't feel at all like he imagined.

"It was a mistake," said Jateko, knowing they would never believe him.

"A mistake? I told you he was mad," said Dedikatu.

Jateko gestured toward the water skin and Gogoko spilled more water into his open mouth. "I'm not lying. If he'd just stayed asleep—"

Dedikatu's foot smashed into Jateko's face, shattering his vision into a wash of sparkling lights.

"He wasn't finished," said Gogoko, standing and returning the water skin to its place.

"He was," answered Dedikatu.

Between them, Jateko rolled around in the sand, mewling and clutching at his face. Blood poured from between his scrawny fingers. His nose definitely felt broken, bent and smashed to one side.

"We should take him back," Gogoko tried again. "The *sorgin* should decide."

"No," said Dedikatu, voice devoid of emotion. "I want *bizkarrezurra erantsita.*"

They weren't just going to kill him, they were going to make a trophy of his head and spine, trap his soul so it would never make the journey to Borrokalaria. Jateko stopped rolling and peered at the two brothers from between his fingers. They faced each other, ignoring him. Gogoko was his only hope. As the elder brother and blooded warrior, it was his decision. *And he doesn't want to kill me.*

Gogoko closed his eyes, drew a deep breath, and let it out in a long hiss . "Do it," he said, opening his eyes to glance at Jateko with a look of pained regret.

Dedikatu nodded once, everything about him screaming tight-pent rage though he uttered not a sound. He drew his fat-bladed short-knife with calm economy; he might be carving a rabbit for all the emotion he evinced. For a score of heartbeats he stood over Jateko, watching.

Trying to talk, trying to offer some reason they shouldn't tear his skull and spine from his body, Jateko made wet *snurk* noises through his battered nose.

Dedikatu kicked him in the stomach, knocking the wind from him, and dropped a knee onto Jateko's chest. Grabbing a fistful of greasy hair, the young warrior forced Jateko's head back. Clamping his jaw closed, Jateko squealed through clenched teeth. He clawed at Dedikatu and the warrior ignored him. Spinning the knife in his hand, Dedi drove the pommel into Jateko's concave chest, striking the solar-plexus. When Jateko's mouth opened in agonized response, the warrior again spun the knife in nimble fingers and slid the blade neatly between his front teeth, forcing the mouth to remain open. Jateko's squeal became an open-mouthed scream, his bleeding lips writhing away from the blade. Leaning on the blade, Dedikatu shoved it deeper into the gaping mouth.

Even over his own howls of terror Jateko heard the groaning complaint of bone and muscle as his jaw was forced ever-wider. He felt the already spacious gap between his front teeth grow as the blade spread them like the slow parting of a lover's thighs. His screams choked off with a sudden intake of breath when the tip of the blade pierced his tongue, pinning it to the soft meat at the bottom of his mouth.

Dedikatu sat back, releasing the knife. His other hand maintained its grip on Jateko's hair, pinning his head to the sand.

Jateko lay still, eyes wide and blinking, watching. The intruding blade had slashed his lips and blood painted his face from the bridge of his shattered nose to the tip of his weak chin. His mouth levered open and his tongue pinned, he had no choice but choke down copious amounts of his own blood.

"Nazkagarri awaits," said Dedikatu scooping up a fistful of sand with his free hand.

Jateko peered past Dedikatu, saw Gogoko turn away, refusing to watch. Again he tried to speak, tried to offer an explanation, but all he managed was a retching whiny noise, all bubbling vowels.

Dedikatu, motionless and unblinking, waited until Jateko fell quiet. Then he poured sand into Jateko's open mouth, choking his breath to nothing.

"Dedikatu," Gogoko said. "Kill him. Be done with it."

"No," said Dedikatu.

Gogoko turned, stopped. He stood rooted in the sand, staring past his brother. Jateko, unable to move his head, swivelled his eyes to see what caught his attention. Behind Dedikatu a figure rose, sand pouring from empty eye sockets like rivers of tears. Thick ropes of black hair hung in clumped strands, knotted by dried blood and sand. Desiccated lips exposed a death's head grin of foul teeth. It stood, head tilted to one side, watching Dedikatu pour sand into Jateko's gaping mouth. The last of the sand drained away and those deserted sockets lifted to examine Gogoko.

The mouth opened in an unholy yawn vomiting sand ripe with rot.

Heriotza, Goddess Death. Harea sent her to rescue me.

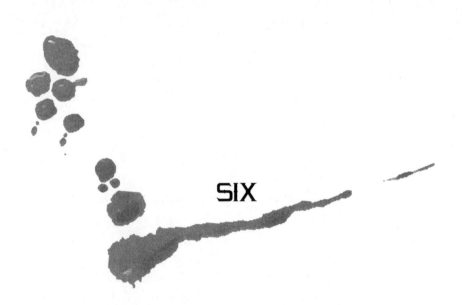

SIX

We are all Gefahrgeist, each and every one of us. We are all manipulating and scheming, using even those we call our closest friends. We do this as easily as breathing. People treat Gefahrgeist like we're sick or diseased or deficient in some way. People treat us like we are the ones missing something. We're not.

You are a lying manipulator just like me. The difference is I'm not lying about it.

— Böse Schwindler, Gefahrgeist

NOTHING HURT. THE PAIN in Hölle's belly where Blutblüte had been thrust into her gut was gone. Gone like it never existed.

This isn't right. Everything is . . . better. Hölle knew better didn't happen on its own. You struggled for better, fought and clawed for every tiniest step in that direction. One didn't wake up to better.

"That's because you're dreaming. Or maybe hallucinating. It's so hard to know the difference with you Halluzin."

Hölle glanced toward the figure sitting silhouetted in her chamber's bay window, the glass stained yellow and brown, opaque from centuries of neglect. She didn't need to see the face to recognise that body, the way she sat, back curved as if hugging herself. And of course the voice. For four hundred years she listened to that voice.

Was this a dream, or a manifestation of her Halluzin power? And was this Pharisäer or Zerfall?

You know who you want to see. You know who you fear. You know who this is.

"I sent Aas to kill you," Hölle said.

"Of course you did."

"You might be dead already."

Zerfall shrugged like the thought didn't much concern her. "This dream would be different if I were. *You'd* be different."

What does that mean? "Probably," said Hölle, sitting and dragging the blanket up to tuck it under her armpits.

"Really?" said Zerfall. "Modesty?"

"Betrayal doesn't encourage one toward exposure."

"Betrayal." Zerfall snorted, an unfeminine noise. Even concealed in shadow, Hölle saw the slight smile quirk the corner of Zerfall's mouth. "As always, nothing is ever your fault."

"*I* didn't betray anyone."

"You would have. Eventually."

"Never! I—"

"How exciting is the prospect of my death?"

The pain returned in a rush of savage heat and Hölle clutched the sheets tighter, her stomach tensing around the still-healing wound. "You tried to kill me."

"For no reason whatsoever?"

"I don't know. You said, 'This is rotten,' and then stabbed me."

"This *is* rotten," said Zerfall. "We founded a church of suffering. We send people to hell."

"To save them."

"Look around you. The church is filthy. The whole thing is decaying."

"Our true priests are Geisteskranken, not scullery maids."

"What if we got it wrong? What if we misunderstood Wahrergott's message? What if we were just a feverish little girl and wrong about everything?"

Hölle brushed this away with an airy wave of fingers. "You were there. You heard the message just as I. When we've suffered enough, the One True God will free us. Swarm is the answer. I created it to—"

"*You* created it? Are you sure?" Zerfall held up her left hand and Hölle knew the eye watched her even if she couldn't see it. "*I* saw Swarm." She lowered the hand to her lap.

"After *I* hallucinated it."

"Do you ever have doubts?" Zerfall asked.

"No. Only one of us is confused."

"That," Zerfall said dryly, "I would agree with. How far back do you remember?"

"To the very beginning."

"You remember being sick, the fever?"

"Of course."

"Do you remember a time without me?"

Hölle frowned at the shadowed Zerfall. "What do you mean?"

"Do you remember a time in your life when I wasn't there, when it was just you?"

"I . . ." *Zerfall has always been with me.* "We're sisters, twins. We were born together."

"I remember a time without you."

Hölle's vision faded for a moment before returning. *No.* "Liar."

"Who are you trying to convince?"

"You!"

Zerfall grinned in response.

"What are you smiling about?" demanded Hölle.

"You're dreaming." Zerfall shrugged, again flashing that damned smirk. "Or hallucinating."

"So?"

"I'm not here. You're talking to yourself. It isn't me you're trying to convince."

Hölle awoke in a dark room, her belly throbbing pain. A familiar body, petite and warm yet firm, pressed against her back.

"Zerfall?" She asked, dreading and hoping.

"No." A soft whisper.

"Sorry. Bad dream." Or was it an hallucination? A dream she could ignore, but as a Halluzin, her hallucinations shaped reality. Could she hallucinate Zerfall back from the dead? Her delusions birthed Swarm, returning one woman to life was nothing in comparison. The thought terrified her. Her sister had to die.

A strong hand massaged her tense shoulders. "You were talking in your sleep," said Pharisäer.

"I dreamed I was talking to Zerfall."

"I'd guessed that," said Pharisäer, her hand moving down Hölle's spine to massage her lower back.

Hölle groaned as Pharisäer worked the tight muscle above her buttock. "She seemed to think it was my fault she betrayed me."

"That's ridiculous."

"I know! And she said she remembered . . ." Hölle trailed off, unwilling to repeat Zerfall's words. Zerfall had been right; it was just a dream.

"It doesn't matter what she said," Pharisäer whispered into Hölle's ear from behind, her breath warm and tickling. "It was just a dream."

Too close to her own thoughts. *Those* were *my thoughts*. What, exactly, was Pharisäer? Had Wahrergott truly sent her?

"What are you?" Hölle asked.

Pharisäer's hand slid across the small of Hölle's back to rest upon the curve of her hip. "I told you." The hand slid upward, tickling her waist. "I am your doubt."

"That doesn't answer my question."

"You've always been two."

"Always," agreed Hölle.

The hand caressed her ribs. "You are two again, complete. I am your doubt. I free you from it so you may focus, do what must be done."

But did she want to be two? "I have no doubts."

Pharisäer laughed. "You aren't to blame for Zerfall's betrayal."

Her voice. Was that a hint of mockery? "I know. I have things to do. I should rise from bed now."

Pharisäer held her down with a gentle hand. "You must rest and heal." She offered a sympathetic smile, fingers tracing across the bandaged wound of Hölle's belly. "I'll lie with you for a while to keep you company."

LATER, AS THEY LAY curled together as they had on that night when Wahrergott first talked to them, Hölle found her doubts had indeed faded.

I can do this. I don't need Zerfall. The betrayal hurt, but she'd continue on as she must. Täuschung must not fail.

"The Täuschung must know nothing of Zerfall's betrayal," Pharisäer whispered. "They must not be given reason to doubt."

"How can we do this?" Hölle asked.

"We kill the few who know."

"But Zerfall is gone. How will we—"

"Do I not look enough like Zerfall?"

"You look exactly like her."

"Well, then?"

Hölle nodded. It made sense. "Yes, you'll take Zerfall's place." A shiver of terror shot through her. "No one will know." *It's okay. It's not really Zerfall.*

"Good idea," said Pharisäer. "I can help guide the Täuschung until you're strong enough to once again take the reins." Her fingers reached around to caress the bandages binding Hölle's belly.

Hölle sucked in a sharp breath. "Ow!"

"Sorry," said Pharisäer, removing her hand.

"No," Hölle said softly. "I'm sorry. My stomach is tender. Even the slightest touch causes great pain."

"Then I shall protect you—be your armour—until you are healed."

God that sounded tempting. "I can't lie here and do nothing. Giernach Reichtum is dying." The woman was a highly ranked member of the Verzweiflung Banking Conglomerate and fabulously wealthy even by Geld standards. "When her soul crosses to Swarm—"

"It needs to be an event," finished Pharisäer. "A spectacle. The One True God's highest priests must be in attendance."

"She's openly decided to spend her last few days in our hospice to ensure her soul goes to heaven."

"It will bring many new people to our doors. Fools always mistake wealth for wisdom."

"If I'm not there—"

"If Zerfall leads the service, no one will question your absence."

She's right. Hölle sighed. "You can do it?"

Pharisäer grinned that Zerfall grin. "I'll send Giernach to Swarm myself."

AAS FLEW. DEPRESSION DRAGGED at him like an anchor, threatened to pull him from the sky. He'd done it. He killed Zerfall, the only woman he ever loved. It didn't matter that she was Gefahrgeist and incapable of love and empathy. He loved *her*, that's what mattered. Expecting his feelings to be reciprocated would be insanity. When you're unlovable, the best one can hope for is to find someone who will allow you to love them.

I killed her. What kind of man does that?

He knew the answer: He was a coward, terrified of what Hölle would do to him, to his soul.

If only Zerfall had been herself. If only she'd crushed his will with her Gefahrgeist power and left him no choice but to obey. He'd never wanted to be robbed of choice so badly.

Aas spread his wings wide, feathers splayed to slow his descent, and *twisted* as he landed in the courtyard of the Täuschung compound. The world, bright and crisp, faded and blurred as he shed his condor shape and once again became earthbound. Myopic as he was, he still saw the refuse piled against the ancient stone walls surrounding the church. Did someone sweep it there, too lazy to collect and remove it, or was this where the wind blew it? Gods how he loathed humanity.

Entering the main building Aas ascended the spiral stairs to Hölle's chambers. The steps were cluttered and he kicked aside a cup someone dropped the moment they finished their beverage rather than return it to the kitchen.

As he climbed, he fingered the blood-encrusted hole in his robes where Zerfall stabbed him.

You were lucky. Hexenwerk isn't ready yet. If she killed him, his soul would have made the journey to Swarm. Aas shuddered at the thought and growled in frustration; the damned puppet crumbled every time he touched it. Perhaps, with a solid spine, he could then wrap it tight in his own hair and better bind it together. *Pinky finger, left hand,* he thought. *It's useless anyway. Just chop the damned thing off.* The pain would be incredible, but if Hexenwerk fell apart it was useless.

The *salbei* of the Ausgebrochene tribes spent years making their puppets, were masters of hair weaving, and managed to construct sturdy puppets of their own bodily wastes. Of course they didn't need theirs to last as long as he might, and they never travelled as far as he would likely have to.

Aas stopped halfway up the stairs to listen. All was silent. He gathered his thoughts, dredging every foul memory and loathsome act he ever perpetrated to the surface. He thought about Hölle's breasts and how much he wanted to see them. He bathed in carrion dreams, swam in the shallow rot of his soul. He must be pathetic, pitiful. His thoughts must disgust Hölle so she'd send him away. He thought about how much he wanted to rut that curvy little body. He must be foul and creepy.

When he felt ready, suitably spoiled, he continued up the stairs.

Once at the top, he spotted Gedankenlos, the Captain of Hölle's personal guard. The man wasn't smart enough to become bored.

Aas gauged the distance: ten paces. *She picks her guards for lack of intelligence.* Gedankenlos didn't react.

Closer. Seven paces. *{Festering armpit of a—}*

Gedankenlos glanced in Aas' direction. "She's expecting you."

{My range is increasing.} Each increase in range meant a decrease in his sanity, meant he was one step closer to the Pinnacle, one step closer to losing control of his delusions. Aas bit down on the thought, crushed it beneath the layers of pitiful self-loathing he wore as armour against these meetings.

{Calm yourself. You have nothing to fear.}

"Right," drawled Gedankenlos. "Nothing at all."

{She'll know you wanted to fail. She'll know you gave Zerfall every possible chance to—} Aas bit the inside of his cheek until he tasted blood. *{Breasts! Nipples!}* He glanced at the Captain. "She might not—"

"She'll know," promised Gedankenlos with a smug wink.

Aas arrived at the door. *{Kill him. Let him rot in the sun. Eat his tender—}*

Even through the door he heard Hölle's resigned sigh and then, "Enter."

Aas stepped past the Captain—who gave him a condescending pat on the back and squeezed his shoulder a little too firmly—and into the room, closing the door behind him. Turning, he found himself looking at two women. Hölle was at her desk, her beautiful face pinched with pain. She sat with a slight hunch as if cradling her stomach. The other woman stood behind Hölle, hand resting protectively on her shoulder. His plans, his layers of despicable surface thoughts, his shield of self-loathing, vanished in surprise.

{Zerfall? No, that's impossible. I left her dying.} Aas bowed low, desperately trying to gather his most disgusting thoughts to hide behind. *{Two of them, imagine them both at my knees.}* "Hölle." Was this an hallucination? Hölle was rumoured to be a powerful Halluzin. He'd been told she hallucinated Swarm, created an entire hellish reality from pure delusion.

"Report," said Hölle, wincing as if speaking hurt.

"Zerfall fled east, into the Basamortuan Desert. I caught her there."

"Yet you failed to kill her," said the standing woman.

{Gods, does it reek of sex in here?} Hölle slammed her fist to the desktop. *{Is she blushing?}*

"God," corrected the standing woman.

"This," Hölle reached up to touch the hand resting on her shoulder, "is Pharisäer. You left Zerfall alive?"

{Pharisäer? But she looks identical to Zerfall. Did Hölle hallucinate her? Is she a Mehrere Fragment? A Doppel—}

"You left her alive," said Pharisäer, eyes narrowing.

"Yes and no," *{Speak quickly lest your thoughts betray.}* "I left her in the heart of the Basamortuan, weeks from civilization." He saw a train of thought that would likely distract the two women and pursued it. *{They rutted recently, Hölle and this manifestation of her madness.}*

"Pharisäer is no manifestation of madness," said Hölle. "Wahrergott sent her."

{Stupid delusional bitch.} He imagined the two of them together, in bed, entwined in an orobouros embrace, hoping his arousal would disgust Hölle and get him out of here sooner so . . . *{Like sisters, tangled on the bed—}*

"Were you not commanded to kill her?" asked Pharisäer.

"Yes, of course. I left her punctured through the gut with one of my arrows. I was told to make sure she suffered. The arrow—"

"Yes?" the two women asked in unison.

"Poisoned. Düster snake. The arrow would have killed her even were it not poisoned. The placement was perfect."

Hölle licked her lips, a slow, sensual slide of the tongue. *{Oh gods where that tongue has been.}*

A look of loathing—poorly concealed—flashed across petite features.

"God," said Pharisäer.

"She suffered?" Hölle asked.

"Yes." *{Should I tell her?}*

"Tell me what?"

"Nothing!"

"Tell me," she commanded. Shadows in the ill-lit corners of the room danced and flickered in response to her anger.

"Zerfall was rotting. Cotardist."

Aas saw Pharisäer's hands tense on Hölle's shoulders.

"She was already dying," mused Pharisäer. "We didn't need him after all."

"Are you sure?" asked Hölle.

"Absolutely," answered Aas. Stray thoughts leaked past his control and he gnawed at the inside of his cheek trying to rein them in. He swallowed blood and shreds of flesh.

"She was losing her mind," said Pharisäer, ignoring Aas and turning the tensing of her hands into a massage.

Hölle's perfect eyebrows crinkled in a frown of concentration. "I remember no signs of rot."

{She looks doubtful. Why?}

Pharisäer glared at him. "Hölle has no doubt."

{Why is she angry at me?}

"We were right," said Pharisäer. "Zerfall's betrayal was due to her decaying sanity."

"It was?" asked Hölle.

{Why does Pharisäer want to convince—}

Pharisäer's dark eyes never left his. "Her betrayal was never your fault," she said, sounding relaxed but looking like she was about to come across the desk and throttle him where he stood.

"It wasn't my fault," agreed Hölle, nodding slowly.

{What the hells is all this about?} And then it all made sense. *{Pharisäer is a—}*

"Hell," snapped Pharisäer. "There is only one hell: Swarm."

"Beg to differ," said Aas. "There are many hells. Almost every religion has one and many have several. The northern tribes believe—"

Hölle waved him to silence with a slicing chop of her hand and winced in pain. She studied him, eyes narrowed with suspicion. "How did you resist her Gefahrgeist power?"

{I didn't. Gods, I wanted her to take me.} "I—"

"God," corrected Pharisäer.

{Let me talk before my thoughts betray—} "She showed no hint of Gefahrgeist power. She said she lost her memory." The words poured out of him. "She said she couldn't remember who she was, that she didn't recognise me."

"An act?" Hölle asked.

"No."

"How can we trust him?" Pharisäer asked, digging at a knot she found in Hölle's shoulder muscles.

"How can we not?" said Hölle, glancing over her shoulder at the woman behind her.

"I brought you something," he said. *{I knew saving the best for last was a good idea.}*

Pharisäer's distrustful glare never left him. "Best for last?" she asked, voice dripping doubt.

Aas drew a cloth sack from within his robes and made a show of undoing the knotted string. *{I'll show you who is worthy of Hölle's trust.}*

Hölle lifted an eyebrow but watched patiently, allowing Aas his small drama. The sack untied, he drew forth Zerfall's hand, palm facing him.

"A hand?" Pharisäer asked. "You brought us a hand?"

{Not 'us', bitch, her.} He grinned, feigning confidence. *{Oh gods, Hölle is frowning. She's unhappy. What if she doesn't want it? Why would she want this? What was I thinking?}*

"Black nail polish," Hölle said, eyes glistening.

Aas turned the hand so Hölle could see the tattoo of the closed eye and heard her breath catch in a soft sob. She stared, unblinking, at the hand. "Leave us," she said.

His stomach felt like it spilled out over the floor. Aas latched on to his terror, spinning it around and around in his thoughts as cover. He backed toward the door, ready to flee.

"Wait." Hölle lifted a hand toward him. "Leave the hand. And . . . thank you."

Aas flashed a triumphant leer at Pharisäer. *{Who does she need more? Me, or some gods-damned—}*

"*God*-damned," Pharisäer corrected with a sweet smile.

"I shall take my leave," Aas said formally, bowing to Hölle and placing the bloodless hand—palm up—on her desk. He sketched a quick and mocking bow in Pharisäer's direction before once again turning for the door. *{I know you.}*

In the hall Gedankenlos smiled perfect teeth and again patted him on the back like they were close friends. "Went badly, did it?" he said as if commiserating.

{I'll lay your guts in the sun—} Aas choked the thought off as he hurried toward the stairs.

Once he was sure no one was in range of his thoughts he stopped and stood, leaning heavily against the wall as he let loose a shaking breath. He'd shared far more than he meant to, the shock of seeing two women having rattled the cage of vile thoughts he'd built. Luckily Hölle hadn't noticed or hadn't cared. Pharisäer however was another problem. Though she looked just like Zerfall, there was something about her that reminded him more of Hölle.

He didn't for an instant believe Wahrergott—the distant and unresponsive god of the Täuschung—sent Pharisäer to replace Zerfall. There was a far simpler, far more likely explanation: Hölle's delusions manifested a replacement for her sister.

Did it signify a collapse of Hölle's sanity? How could it not?

The question then, was which side should Aas be on? If Hölle was manifesting new delusions, it meant she was finally, after hundreds of years, nearing the Pinnacle, that moment when a Geisteskranken's delusions broke free of their restraints and conquered the mind that birthed them. No one survived the Pinnacle.

On the other hand, Hölle was rumoured to have been a Halluzin for hundreds of years and had somehow avoided the Pinnacle. Could her god—or her belief in that god—save her?

Aas pushed himself off the wall, brushing dust and cobwebs from his robes. Pharisäer definitely saw him as a threat rather than an ally. In that regard he suspected he hadn't done himself any favours antagonizing her, but he'd been desperate to distract Hölle.

When he left Zerfall in the desert he felt like he left some of his heart behind. He'd been sure he'd never see her again.

Pharisäer is no Zerfall. But they shared some similarities; both had a dangerous edge that attracted him. Would she hurt him as Zerfall had? And even more interesting, would she let him hurt her as Zerfall had not?

Could they be allies?

Could we be more?

Hours later Aas stood in the sheltered entranceway of Medium Rare, a boutique butchery yet to open to the morning's business. The awning, a rich fabric in alternating stripes of warm brown and a red much like the centre of a medium rare steak, snapped and fluttered in the breeze. In the window behind him hung meat in various stages of preparedness, from slabs of ageing beef to thick farmer's sausages to salted and cured charcuterie. The air smelled of spices and grilled flesh, but his scavenger's senses caught lurking hints of decay from the dry-ageing racks at the rear of the shop. Soon Trost, the owner of Medium Rare, would arrive and Aas could purchase the scrapings and bones—black with age and furred green with mould—he craved. She sold them without question or comment, weighing and pricing, as if this happened all the time. Perhaps his request wasn't as strange as he thought. Did she sell rotten meat to others? Was there enough of a demand that she intentionally allowed flesh to spoil?

Aas fingered Hexenwerk, the partially constructed puppet in his pocket. Snot, hair, nail clippings, and condor feathers were more difficult to work with than anticipated. Snot, so sticky when on his fingers, stubbornly refused to hold the thing together. He might have to add some external adhesive if he couldn't figure something out. He'd tried winding it in hair, but the few he possessed were too short to do a good job. He'd yet to yank teeth to add to the puppet and his little finger remained attached to his hand. Apparently some part of him resisted the idea of pulling healthy teeth and hacking off perfectly good fingers.

Even yanking his own feathers—when *twisted* into a condor—proved difficult. The condor cared nothing for human delusion.

If only he could think of some way to generate more snot and grow longer hair.

Aas watched the people of Geld stroll about their business, strutting in bright peacock clothes, secure and comfortable in their little bubbles of self-serving delusion. Even the sane fooled themselves a little, each and every breath and step made with the assumption it would be followed by another. This was Geld. People didn't step from dark shadows to snuff lives without warning.

He remembered the book of poems he gave to Zerfall. Sometimes it felt like Halber Tod foretold Aas' life.

I've peered into eyes of evil.
Tasted lips of sin.
Drawn toward the drowning rot.
Sinking deep within.
I've drained blood from severed veins.
Flayed flesh from broken limbs.
I am whom I'm torturing.
Loathing what's within.

Lips of sin; the line always reminded Aas of Zerfall; the round fullness of her lower lip, the way it moved as if begging to be bitten—not that he ever dared—and the curved corner of her mouth where perfection met perfection. He lost himself in that meeting.

His breath caught. "You gave her a book written by a Cotardist poet," he whispered, "and the next time you see her she's rotting."

Coincidence? It had to be. It couldn't be his fault.

But what if it was? What if his gift triggered everything? Halber Tod had a way of infecting one's thoughts. Zerfall's betrayal of Hölle and the Täuschung might all be Aas' fault.

What if Hölle found out?

She'd kill him.

That was a thought he'd have to bury deep under layers of self-loathing and bile.

She's going to kill you anyway. Maybe not today, but someday. Someday soon. He saw the way Hölle and Pharisäer watched him, eyes of evil brimming with hate. *Push this aside*, he told himself. *Forget this thought.*

Pulling free one of the thick hairs sprouting from his ears, Aas grinned sharp teeth at an approaching merchant. The fat man wore a deep burgundy vest stretched tight across a vast belly, billowing black pants of the finest silk, and dozens of bright and swirling scarves about his neck. Aas slipped the hair into his pocket. Usually the slight pain of yanking out his own hair was enough to calm him. Since Zerfall left, that small pain no longer sufficed.

Give yourself greater pain. Remove the finger.

Therianthropes healed most wounds when they *twisted*. Would a severed finger grow back? He doubted it. Did it matter? He preferred being a condor, and birds didn't have fingers.

That was part of the problem. His sanity crumbled. He was deteriorating. Someday he would *twist* and become a condor and never again return to his human form. He didn't dread that day, he looked forward to it. Animals knew a freedom from guilt and shame he longed for. The real question: would that happen before he died and his soul went to Swarm? He couldn't take that chance.

Will I be able to twist *after moving my soul to Hexenwerk?* It seemed unlikely. He'd not escape so easily.

The obese merchant nodded happily at a slim young lady, and adjusted his scarves to better hide his many chins. Aas judged the distance to be a little over eight strides.

{Fat man, your civilization is delusion. I'll step from this alley, knife bright with intent. You'll show me the animal hiding within. You'll fight with desperately clawed fingers.}

The merchant glanced about, confused.

{Ah, you're close enough to hear me. My delusions grow in strength. Will I scream my thoughts loud enough for all the world to hear before madness lays me low?}

The merchant still hadn't seen him and stood as if transfixed, gaze darting as he sought the source of the strange thoughts filling his head.

{Here, in the butchery.}

Their eyes met and Aas drank the dawning terror, tasted the delicious moment, inhaled the sharp scent of fear.

{Flee and cling to your delusion of civilization or stand and I'll open you wide.}

The peacock merchant squeaked like a stomped mouse and fled. Aas, disappointed but not surprised, watched the waddling escape. *Will he tell his friends of this moment? Will he brag of bravery or admit to fear? Will his next meal taste better for having escaped death, or will this be forgotten, replaced, once again, by the delusion of security?*

Aas reached into his shirt, gripped one of his few chest hairs and pulled, savouring the moment when the resisting skin stretched and clung to the hair as if unwilling to surrender it. That instant when the hair escaped its prison flesh rolled his eyes back in near orgasmic appreciation. The pain, while nothing compared to what Zerfall used to inflict, was sharp if over too quickly. He released a shaking breath and added the hair to the wad in his pocket.

He watched the crowd move past, each caught in their own little world of delusion. Gods he hated cities. The carrion creature lurking at the heart of his soul screamed to flee the confines of stone, the trappings of civilization he wore like a loose cloak. He hated this city more than most. Geldangelegenheiten, where everything was for sale. Honour hocked, virtue rented, dreams whored. A bad place to be poor, no doubt.

A woman passed, gaunt and pale like death, thin like starvation, face pinched and suspicious, nostrils flaring as if seeking some scent. A monstrous black geldwechsler, the headgear of the Verzweiflung Banking Conglomerate, swaddled her head in long folds of thick fabric hanging low enough to catch her arms and piled high enough each step was made in careful awareness of her balance. The lack of colour, combined with the geldwechsler's unmanageable size, meant this woman was indeed highly placed within the bank's hierarchy—probably a Commercial Lending Officer or some such nonsense.

The Verzweiflung cloaked themselves in mystery. A gold-worshipping religion with a military command structure and a virus-like drive to spread and infect, they had invasive tentacles reaching into every city-state. Verzweiflung banks—monolithic edifices of marble, brass, and gold—alters to avarice, shamed even the churches of the Wahnvor Stellung and the Geborene upstarts.

Monuments, built by thieves, erected to dazzle and impress the masses.

The Verzweiflung held the wealth of the Täuschung and every other church. Zerfall hated the bankers.

Zerfall, gods how he missed her. She may have hurt him, sliced with words as much as blades, but that's how she showed she cared.

Fool. Gefahrgeist don't care.

People parted around the banker, staying well clear, dipping quick bows if the woman deigned to glance in their direction. Most mistook the walk of bankers for stately grace. Aas knew if they moved any faster their stupid hats would fall off and they'd pass out from heat exhaustion.

The thought died as Zerfall strode past, Blutblüte hanging at her hip.

She's alive. Hölle would kill him for sure. She'd tear him apart, flay him inch by bloody inch. She'd take years to send his soul screaming to Swarm.

Aas reached over his shoulder. No bow, no quiver of condor-fletched arrows. *Gods damn!* He couldn't kill her from a safe distance. His hand dropped to his waist, touched the hilt of the long-knife concealed there. The knife he used to take Zerfall's hand.

Had the woman possessed both hands? He wasn't sure, it happened too quickly.

He left Medium Rare in pursuit of his love. He followed, giving her as much distance as he dared. Too close and she'd hear his thoughts. Too far back and he'd lose her in the crowd.

She wended through curved streets paved in stones of red and black. Upscale bathhouses and salons thickened the air with the imported spices of luxury and wealth. This was an old neighbourhood, lined with ancient oaks, manicured by well-dressed gardeners. No poor here, the Geld Guard kept them out. Where much of the city was a raucous hubbub of life, the ever-present haggle for a better deal in a city-state ruled by bad deals, this small utopia was a moment of hushed silence.

And if you catch her? Could he kill Zerfall with nothing but a long-knife? Yes, if he caught her by surprise. *But no one surprises Zerfall.* Four hundred years of assassination attempts left her preternaturally aware of her surroundings. *And yet you caught and killed her in the desert.* It had been too easy. Had she somehow tricked him?

If he didn't kill her, she'd definitely kill him for what he'd done in the desert.

And now she had Blutblüte. Even had he a sword, he wouldn't want to face her in a fair fight. *When have you faced anyone in a* fair *fight?*

He caught another glimpse of Zerfall moving gracefully through the throng of morning shoppers, the swaying strut of her hips. He remembered how she joked about her walk, saying she plodded like a brick-layer. *Funny*, he thought, *how even Zerfall can be so dishonest with herself.* How could she be unaware of the hungry eyes of every man she passed by? How could she not note their predatory gaze, the puffing of chests and the sucking in of flabby bellies as she approached. Women watched too, though whether in lust or envy Aas couldn't be sure. Even at her diminutive height, none failed to notice her.

How long are you going to follow her?

He wasn't sure.

What will you do, kill her? Beg forgiveness?

Aas increased his pace, ghosting closer, hand resting on the hilt of his knife. He hated knives, such clumsy tools. *Might as well whack someone with a tree branch as knife them.* The back of her head, the luxurious dark hair, became his world. Closer.

Blutblüte. The sword hung at her side. Had she taken it from Hölle, had she succeeded in killing her other half? Or had Hölle given her the sword? Were the sisters once again united in purpose?

A dozen strides separated them.

Hölle forgive and forget? Mad laughter bubbled at the thought and Aas crushed it ruthlessly.

Slide the knife between ribs, open a lung wide. She'd stand for a moment, gasping and frothing blood, making that strange *uhhhn uhhhn* noise people made when you did them just right and they knew they were done. *Second cut, sever the carotid.* He imagined the spray of blood, pulsing with each weakening heartbeat. He might not like knives, but he could have been a surgeon. *What a mess.* He'd give anything to have his bow and put an arrow in her heart from a distant rooftop.

Ten strides. He caught her scent, warm lavender. Her hips swung, sensuous like a writhing snake dancing to the pipes of a Schlangenbeschwörer, the Therianthrope snake charmers of the SumpfStamm swamps. Zerfall ran the slim fingers of her left hand through her hair. He wanted to bite those fingers, to lick them, crush—

{Left hand. Gods, it can't be—}

She stopped and turned to face him. "God," she said.

"Pharisäer." Aas did his best to laugh scornfully. *{Did that sound scared?}*

"It did."

{Could you—could we—} "You're no Zerfall," he said to cover his thoughts.

She blinked in mock surprise. "I'm better."

"If you were Zerfall I'd be dead already, *Fragment*." He spat the last word.
{You're a fool to let me this close.}

Pharisäer looked unconcerned, glancing about, watching passing shoppers as if they were at least as interesting as he. "I choose to let you live," she said, eyes locking on his.

{Oh those lips.}

She smiled at his thought, a slight curve at the corners of her perfect mouth. "I want you to do something for me." Pharisäer examined him, an eyebrow raised, head cocked to one side, thick hair spilling about her shoulders.

"I don't serve you."

"You will. You'll enjoy it." She gave him a look that did things deep in his belly. "Narr Unerheblich, and Nimmer."

He recognized the names. Täuschung priests. He knew they were Geisteskranken, but nothing of their delusions. Curiosity won out. "Yes?"

"I want you to kill them. They know the truth about me." She examined him with dark eyes.

"As do I."

"As do you. But you I want. You are useful. The others . . ." She shrugged.

"I'll tell Hölle what you really are." *{Would she reward me or hate me? Would she even believe me?}* "Do you even know how to use a sword?"

She leaned close, the scent of sweetened coffee on her breath. *{She's going to kiss me.}* She licked her lips in a sensuous swirl of wet tongue, eyes glinting playfully. "Hölle wants you dead. But I see what Zerfall saw."

Pharisäer's proximity, the warmth radiating from her flawless skin, left Aas little room for thought. Hope and fear warred for supremacy. His thoughts stumbled over each other. *{She's/I playing/want with/her you/to}* "Zerfall abandoned—"

She touched his arm, nervous and tentative, softer than Zerfall ever touched him. "I'll give you what you want. I'll let you do things Zerfall never would." She bit the soft fullness of her lower lip and it flushed red.

{I . . .} "I . . ." His thoughts fled, scattered like startled cockroaches.

"I'll give you everything, do anything." She leaned her forehead against his chest, absolutely vulnerable. The scent of her became his world.

{Kill her, kill her now.} Aas reached a hand to the small of her back, pulling her against him. She didn't resist, instead moulding her body to his, lifting her face into his neck. The crowd parted, water rolling around a rock, giving the lovers privacy though they stood in the centre of the street. "Hölle will—"

"Don't worry about Hölle," she purred, a tongue flicking out to touch his ear.

"I can't hide from her. She'll hear my thoughts."

Her petite body still pressed against him, she leaned back far enough they stared into each other's eyes. "I said don't worry."

"But—"

Icy fire slid into his gut. Pharisäer's eyes lit with pleasure at whatever she saw on his face. A high-pitched whine escaped his clenched teeth and her nostrils flared as if she sought to catch the scent of his agony. Pharisäer twisted the knife and he screamed, his body wrenching away from her in a desperate attempt to escape the pain. His knees buckled and he collapsed to the street.

Pharisäer watched, an eyebrow cocked as if she'd never stabbed anyone before and was curious to see how it all played out. She held a short, viciously serrated blade dangling loose in her hand. "Still worried?"

The morning shoppers, moments ago parting around them, were nowhere to be seen. Aas, clutching his belly, used his other arm to drag himself away. Blood pooled around him, soaking his robes, slicking the cobbled street.

Pharisäer didn't bother to follow. "Does it hurt?" she asked, eyes hungry with curiosity.

He grinned crimson teeth at her and laughed, a spraying cough of blood when she looked surprised. *{Beautiful, beautiful suffering. Gods this hurts so much.}*

"God," she corrected, though with no hint of anger. With a raised eyebrow, she watched as if waiting; as if mocking.

"You . . . you don't believe," he said. *{Wahrergott, the One True God—}*

"Is nothing more than the delusion of a sick mind."

"The same mind you sprang from."

"You might want to think that through," she suggested.

{What the hells does that mean?}

She shook her head, lips pressed together in a thin line of disappointment. "Täuschung—everything Hölle and Zerfall have worked for—it will all come to naught. Hölle is cracking. Otherwise . . ." she glanced at her fingers, checking the perfection of her manicure. "Otherwise I wouldn't be here. I will replace her and I have no interest in her mad little religion beyond what I can get from it."

"I'll tell Hölle everything."

She shrugged, unconcerned.

{Why is she not following, why does she not finish me?}

"If I wanted you dead, you'd be dead."

He coughed another red laugh of scorn. "Liar. You should have killed me when you had the chance," he said, dragging himself another arm's length. A curved smear of sanguine cobblestones marked his progress. Each beat of his heart pulsed blood over the hand clutching his gut.

"I do, however, want Narr Unerheblich and Nimmer dead. But I made it interesting for you; a puzzle. I told Nimmer you were going to kill him." She smiled sweet innocence. "He's a Getrennt. It should be fun."

{Fun?}

Aas *twisted*, shattering and collapsing in on himself until a black condor stood, feet dancing, in his own blood. Spreading his wings, he leapt to the sky with a rattling cackle of screeched laughter.

Pharisäer made no move to stop him. Sheltering her eyes with a slim-fingered hand she followed his ascent, a satisfied smile playing about her lips. "I told you I'd give you what you want," she called. "Did Zerfall ever hurt you so perfectly?"

SEVEN

The rot
The putrefaction
Part of the way
Part of the action
Life beyond life
But always the rot
It's said, "Follow the path with heart."
What heart?
It's just another part
Part of the rot
Death is the best part
But what removes the certainty
Is just so much rot
Whose fault is it?
No death left to die
Only to 'live' every moment
A mute metaphor
And the rot is always there

—"Cotardist Lament", by Halber Tod, Cotardist Poet

ZERFALL FLOATED IN OCEANS of numb. Unanchored. Uncaring.
Sensation, distant and repetitive. Her left arm jerked and tugged as
if some scavenger worried at it. Scavenger. Carrion.

Condor.

Awareness slammed into her like a charging warhorse shouldering aside a child. *He's taking my hand!*

Zerfall struggled to sit and for a terrified instant thought she'd been buried. Again she felt the distant tremor of something against her left arm. *No!* Gritting her teeth she forced herself into a sitting position, her body strangely heavy. She dragged her arm free of the imprisoning sand and lifted it to stare at the bloodless stump. *It's gone.* The skin looked dried, mummified. White bone, hacked and splintered, protruded from her truncated wrist. *That should hurt.* It didn't; everything felt distant.

Zerfall considered once again lying back in the sand. *No reason to do anything else.*

How had she gotten here? Why had Aas taken her hand and why hadn't she stopped him? He loved her, worshipped her. She barely had to use her Gefahrgeist power to get him to do anything. She remembered all the times she hurt him, cutting, whipping, biting and clawing. Not once had he complained.

She remembered not remembering him, trying to command the Therianthrope and failing. Either he resisted her Gefahrgeist power, or—

Swarm. She remembered. An hallucinated hell, created from madness in the service of an imagined god. A god she once believed in. A god she once worshipped. A god to whom she helped sacrifice millions of souls. And Blutblüte, the sword which held her hell. It all made so much sense. Use the sword to condemn souls to hell.

She remembered her church, the Täuschung. And she remembered her sister.

She walked the halls of the Täuschung compound for centuries, ignoring the filth and decay. Only after reading Halber Tod's book of Cotardist poems had she noticed the rot. But it hadn't just been the corrosion of her religion that she saw. She became aware of the atrophying of all she was, all she believed in. Hölle had slowly been replacing her, taking over the Täuschung, deciding more and more of their path. Somehow, the more sure Hölle became the more Zerfall doubted. At some point she began to suspect Hölle wasn't really her sister. The idea grew over decades, took root and refused to let go. The Täuschung had been Zerfall's idea, had been her life's work, and now she had virtually nothing to do with it.

For centuries Hölle told Zerfall how *she* was so much better at planning and how Zerfall's contribution was her ability to conscript Geisteskranken to their cause. Zerfall created this religion and somehow she'd been reduced to handling the mad and often disgusting priests. She rarely even got to set foot in the larger church preaching to the sane public. Hölle worried she'd give away what she was.

Then, while Hölle babbled on about her plans for the church and everything *she* was going to do, Zerfall realized she had no memories of her sister from before the plague. She'd gone to bed alone, she was sure of it.

An understanding decades in the making solidified in her thoughts: *She's not my sister. I never had a sister. She's a figment of my imagination, a Fragment.*

She'd panicked.

Zerfall remembered thinking of Halber Tod's book of Cotardist poems and how her world had lost all meaning.

She pushed the thought away, the absurd pointlessness of reality too terrifying to face.

Aas took my hand to Hölle to prove he killed me. Somehow her sister survived being stabbed. *She has my sword.* That tiny spark she thought dead, impaled by Aas' arrow, sputtered to life, fed by rage. She couldn't lie here forever in the sand, not while her sister had her sword. *Blutblüte is* mine.

My sword. God how she wanted her sword.

Choked grunting and the sounds of struggle penetrated her mental fog. Glancing to her left, she saw a well-muscled man clad in desert tribal attire, straddling a scrawny youth and pouring sand into a mouth wedged open with the fat blade of a knife. The man on top wore an assortment of trinkets and trophies including what looked like a rusting belt buckle. A variety of knives were strapped about his powerful body, none concealed. She watched, frowning, as the youth battered ineffectually at the man atop him.

Why is he filling him with sand? This made no sense whatsoever. None of this did.

Rising to her feet required a surprising effort and she almost gave up. Her balance felt wrong, her torso leaden and heavy. Zerfall glanced down, taking in the tattered and faded state of her clothing. Sand cascaded off her as she stood, unnoticed, behind the two men. The struggles of the youth weakened by the moment. Movement caught her attention and she glanced up to find another man, muscular and attractive, on the far side of the two struggling at her feet. He looked like his god had just risen from the sands.

Two large armed men against this bony weak-chinned youth, barely more than a boy.

Can I watch this and do nothing? Strangely, she didn't know the answer. Part of her said this was nothing to her, that she should help the two who were so clearly winning whatever this was. And yet she hesitated. They were going to kill this boy. She could stop them. It would be nothing. Souls for Swarm.

She opened her mouth to speak and sand poured out.

"Dedi," said the second man in warning to the one straddling the choking youth.

Zerfall stepped forward, the weight of a long knife comfortable in her right hand, and took the head off the closest man in an effortless sweep of the blade. Then she toppled forward, top-heavy and awkward, to sprawl at the feet of the second warrior. Getting her arms under herself, she struggled to rise. Her unwillingness to release her grip on the knife combined with the lack of a left hand, made it an ungainly process.

The warrior wasted no time, stamping a sandal-clad foot on her back and driving her back to the sand. Zerfall's left arm skidded under her and she landed, trapping it beneath her, with enough force to drive a cloud of sand from her open mouth.

Zerfall spun, kicking the warrior's feet out from under him, and rolled away. By the time she regained her feet he too stood, an ancient and battered sword drawn, in a fighting crouch. They circled each other warily, Zerfall testing the balance of her blade. She could throw the knife but if she landed anything other than a killing blow she'd be left unarmed.

The desert warrior circled, keeping his distance, watching for an opening. *He moves well.* With the right training, this warrior possessed the potential for greatness. But what was he waiting for? A hugely muscled man with a sword ought to be confident he can defeat a tiny girl with nothing but a long-knife. If anything, he looked terrified. Like maybe he was contemplating turning tail and running. She had cut the other warrior's head off rather easily. That, she supposed, might be enough to cause one to rethink. She darted a quick glance at the head sitting nearby in the sand. It had landed on its side and the blood drooling from the severed neck turned the sand around it black. She returned her attention to the crouching warrior and saw the familial resemblance. The two were brothers. *This man will not flee.*

"Heriotza," the warrior said, little more than whisper. His words were strangely accented, round and soft.

With no idea what that meant, Zerfall tried her best insane grin. The man blanched and retreated.

"Did Dedikatu displease you?" he asked.

That must be his brother. No harm in bluffing. Again she tried to speak and found herself unable to make noise. Her tongue felt trapped, leathery and immobile.

"No, you're not Heriotza." His eyes widened as if in sudden understanding. "*Hilen deabru!*" He attacked, feinting low and drove his sword at her stomach.

Zerfall pirouetted, sure she could avoid the clumsy attack. Once again the ungainly weight of her upper body betrayed her and the sword rammed deep into her belly. The young warrior stood, pressed against her, handsome face so close she could kiss him. Lips peeled back in a savage snarl, he growled "Back to hell, demon," and twisted the blade.

She waited for the shock of pain.

Nothing.

Again she tried to speak. No sound or breath of air escaped.

The warrior spun away, ripping the sword free of her body. Sand bled from the wound in a spiralling torrent like water draining from a sink.

Zerfall staggered back, retreating before the once again advancing warrior. Even with the sand haemorrhaging from her belly, she still felt top heavy. If anything, the weight seemed to be even higher and more awkwardly balanced than before. *My lungs are filled with sand.* But that was impossible. No way she could breathe—

Taking advantage of her distraction, the warrior smashed the knife from her hand with an unsubtle but fast blow.

I never would have allowed that to happen before, Zerfall thought, embarrassed at how easily this amateur disarmed her. He stalked her, cautious, sword stabbing and feinting. Behind him she saw the scrawny youth regain his feet.

The young man wobbled on bony knees, blinking furiously. A long stream of dark drool hung swinging from a mouth wedged wide with a knife. Sand, damp with blood, spattered his chest. He'd vomited all over himself.

The youth crouched, gathering his thin legs beneath him, and she realized what he planned. Without thought Zerfall hurled herself on the warrior before her, batting aside his sword with her left forearm. Her attack and weight must have surprised him as the warrior stumbled backward, apparently unaware of the youth behind him.

Amateur.

JATEKO, ALREADY DESPERATELY DEHYDRATED, rolled on the ground, coughing and puking damp clumps of sand. His throat and tongue felt like someone tore them from his body, tied them to a camel, and dragged them the length and breadth of the Basamortuan before stuffing them back in his mouth with a red hot poker. His belly heaved gritty mouthful after gritty mouthful.

By Harea, he was so confused. Heat prostration and dehydration scrambled his thoughts like his mom whisking lizard eggs.

He tried to lick his lips but something sharp slashed his tongue. *The knife.* He had to go cross-eyed to see it. He tasted blood. He tried to draw breath through his broken nose and was rewarded with a sodden *snurk!* Everything hurt, his face his nose, his teeth, his tongue. Everything below his neck felt like it had walked a thousand days without rest.

The sound of metal on metal punctured his misery and he glanced up to see Gogoko battling a corpse. *Hilen deabru!* A soul rejected by Harea, doomed to wander the sands for all eternity. Rising to his knees he found himself staring into the vacant eyes of Dedi's decapitated head. When had that happened? He spotted the headless body lying nearby, the surrounding sands stained dark red.

Jateko's robes were soaked in Dedikatu's blood and caked with clinging sand.

Shocked, he watched as Gogoko stabbed the *hilen deabru*, stared in mute horror as the demon ignored the wound, and almost cheered when Gogoko disarmed it. Then he realized that, once finished with the demon, Gogoko would likely finish what Dedikatu began.

If Gogoko kills it, I die. If it kills Gogoko . . . What then?

Jateko gathered his legs under him, unsteadily trying to regain his feet, and the *hilen deabru* hurled itself at Gogoko, wrapping him in a disgusting embrace. Again his eyes were drawn to Dedikatu's head.

He retched up another mouthful of sand. His jaw ached, still wedged open with Dedi's fat-bladed knife. Pulling that out was going to hurt. A lot.

Jateko glanced around, searching for an escape. He was, he realized, too weak to make any distance on foot. Gogoko would track and kill him. He saw the *hilen deabru* manoeuvre Gogoko so his back was to Jateko and force the warrior toward him. For an instant the demon looked over Gogoko's shoulder, stared at Jateko with dark, gaping sockets.

Did it raise an eyebrow at me?

If he stayed where he was, Gogoko would trip over him.

Decision made, Jateko grabbed the hilt of the knife jutting from his mouth. He tugged and it didn't move. Blood trickled down his throat in an unending stream and he gagged, unable to swallow. He pulled harder. It felt like someone tried to rip out all four of his front teeth at the same time. His tongue, as if remembering it had been pierced, gushed fresh blood. The blade moved, filling his skull with a grating song of notched steel on teeth. He sobbed in gratitude when the tip of the blade slid free of his impaled tongue.

Looking up from the blood and puke spattered knife clutched in his hands, Jateko saw Gogoko's broad back. The Hasiera warrior grappled with the demon for possession of the sword. Impossibly, even though Gogoko outweighed the little corpse, the demon drove him back toward Jateko.

Do it now. Now, before it's too late.

With the knife gripped in two hands, Jateko hurled himself at Gogoko's exposed back. The blade slammed between the lower ribs and Gogoko uttered a soft grunt as his knees gave out. Toppling backward Gogoko landed atop Jateko, crushing the wind from him. The *hilen deabru* was on them in an instant, desiccated fingers wrapped around the warrior's throat, teeth exposed in a silent snarl.

Jateko struggled under Gogoko's twitching weight until the warrior's spasms faded to nothing. In eerie silence the demon released its grip and straightened. For a dozen heart beats it stood over him. Empty sockets studied him in cold regard. Then it hinged at the waist and placed its hands flat on the ground between its legs. Sand poured from its open mouth. When the stream slowed, it kicked its legs up into a perfect handstand and remained there until sand stopped flowing.

That was the most graceful thing I have ever see a corpse do. Jateko watched as the *hilen deabru* lowered its legs and returned to a standing position. Even dead, it's hips were surprisingly curvy. *Female demons?* The thought had never before occurred to him. It made sense, he supposed. Harea could reject the souls of women as easily as those of men.

The demon ignored Jateko as it collected Gogoko's sword and scowled at it as if disapproving of its metal. With a sneer of disgust the sword was thrown spinning into the sand. The demon then searched Dedikatu's body and retrieved several knives which disappeared, hidden about its small body. Finally it seemed to once again notice him.

"How . . ." the word faded into a soft wheeze as if the creature didn't have the air to power it. The demon frowned and moved its mouth, lips and tongue making dry smacking noises, as if trying to speak. It laughed, a cough of sand, and took a long sucking intake of breath. "How long are you going to stay there?" it asked, looking down at him. He heard the last of the demon's breath hiss out between exposed teeth.

"I'm trapped," he said, from beneath Gogoko's corpse.

It grunted—definitely female, Jateko decided—and rolled Gogoko's body away with a nudge of its foot.

"Thanks. Are you going to disappear now?" Jateko asked.

It stood, hands on hips, watching with those unnerving empty sockets, and took another strangely intentional breath "Disappear?"

"Now that your task is complete." It examined him, still as only a corpse could be. "Unless Harea wants you to further serve."

"Harea? Never heard of him. Are you deranged from heatstroke?" it asked.

THE SCRAWNY WEAK-CHINNED YOUTH lay in the sand, staring up at Zerfall with dark eyes. His nose lay flattened and smeared to one side.

He panted through an open mouth, breath whistling between the gap in his front teeth.

"That's entirely possible," he said, and spat blood and grit into the sand. "I haven't been thirsty since yesterday. That's a bad sign."

He spoke with the same odd accent as the warrior and Zerfall wondered if it were perhaps a regional dialect. Some of his words meant nothing, but most of what he said she understood.

"How long have you been in the sun?" she asked.

"All my life," he said, a twinkle of humour in his eyes.

Zerfall would have sighed in exasperation, but couldn't be bothered to draw the requisite breath to make it possible. "When was your last drink?"

"I've recently swallowed a lot of my own blood, but before that, days." He blinked up at her and made a nasal honk as he blasted a thin stream of blood from his crushed nose. "I can't breathe very well," he said, as if apologizing.

Zerfall reached down with her single hand and wrenched his nose straight. The boy screamed and trashed about in the sand, clutching his face and sobbing.

When he finally stopped, he rolled over and glared at her.

"You can breathe now?" she asked.

He drew a tentative breath and nodded. "A little warning next time please." His voice sounded better but still had a noticeable nasal quality. "Harea didn't send you?"

"No. I don't think . . ." She trailed off. He'd lost consciousness.

Zerfall stood, staring at the unconscious youth. Scrawny and weak looking, he was barely out of childhood. She guessed his age at perhaps sixteen years. *Walk away. Leave him to the sun and sand.* He'd be dead within a day. Some part of her wanted to lie down beside him, return to the bliss of nothing.

You can't let this child die here.

"Why not?" she said.

A good question.

At least get him some water. He could be useful.

Useful. That word meant a lot to her not too long ago. It defined her, decided her relationships.

"He looks too feeble to be useful."

Who did she want to be, the old Zerfall, who let her needs decide all?

I won't leave him.

Decision made, Zerfall searched the two corpses and retrieved several water skins, an awkward task with only a single hand. Returning to the youth, she knelt and was about to upend water into his open mouth when she noticed her remaining hand. The skin was dry and cracked, flaking away in places to expose desiccated muscle and hints of white bone. Her hand looked awful, the skin sunken and clinging.

Damn, that's way past old lady hands. The black nail polish long gone, her nails looked rather like hooked talons. A simple manicure would not fix this travesty.

Your lungs and belly were full of sand. She glanced at the wound in her belly and realized Aas' arrow still protruded from her gut. She hadn't even been aware of it. Sand dribbled from the hole when she drew it out and tossed it aside. *You have to consciously draw air into your lungs to speak, because you are no longer breathing.*

"I'm dead."

The fact it didn't bother her bothered her more than the being dead part.

The youth groaned, drawing her attention. How long had she squatted there? She had no idea and her knees offered no complaint. Perhaps there were some advantages to being dead.

Why are you doing this? Why give him water?

"It's not like I need it."

True, but why help him at all? Why not leave? He was nothing to her.

Stand up. Walk away.

Yet she crouched, examining the boy's face. The nose was too big and the chin too small. If there was a scale where handsome and rugged were at one end, this boy was about as far in the other direction as it was possible to travel.

Memories battered at her, clamouring for attention. Aas and Hölle. The church. Avoiding those thoughts she glanced at the youth's filthy robes. Even before the blood and vomit stains they probably hadn't been clean. She sniffed experimentally. Nothing. Did he not smell, or was she incapable of smelling anything at all?

Stop shying from the truth. You know who you are.

She remembered things she'd forgotten long before her attempt to kill Hölle. Was the weight of centuries to blame for the lost memories only now returning, or had that been the influence of her sister?

I have no sister.

She remembered everything. Memories so ancient, buried so deep they seemed unreal—more like a story she'd once been told and then forgotten— returned. She remembered the plague that wiped out her village and killed her family. She remembered lying on that cot, stained with sweat and her own shite, stinking of fear and death. She'd been so alone, just her and a house of corpses; everyone she ever knew was gone. Terrified, she desperately needed someone to hold her, someone to tell her it would be okay. She remembered hallucinating, feverish dreams. Nightmares. A hell of naked bodies and nothing else, endless suffering. She remembered the thundering voice screaming its commands into her brain. She was to save humanity and somehow that meant suffering. She'd been so confused, unable to follow the god's words. Somehow humanity was supposed to *use* this responsive reality, become more than they were. She had to free them all. Everything was wrong, it wasn't supposed to be like this. The god's voice splintered her mind shattered everything she was. It was too much to contain. She couldn't do this alone. She needed help.

With Zerfall, everything was always about need.

Then, when the fever finally broke and she awoke, she'd been two. The other girl said she was Zerfall's sister, that they were chosen by Wahrergott, the One True God, the enforcer of the rules of reality, to free humanity. The young Zerfall believed her and for hundreds of years they worked side by side.

I went to bed alone. She never had a sister. Hölle was a fragment of a mind ravaged by fever, created by desperate need. What Zerfall didn't know was whether Hölle knew. Not once in hundreds of years had her sister—*no, my Fragment*—tried to wrestle control from her as all Fragments of Mehrere were supposed to.

That's not quite true.

Hölle had been so sure. She told Zerfall that *she* hallucinated the hell and named it Swarm, trapping it in the blade of a sword they found in the haunted remains of their village. Together they crawled from the bed, leaving behind the stench of fever. They left that village, sisters and yet more. And less. For so long they were impossibly close, always knowing the other's thoughts, always there to comfort each other. Together they founded the Täuschung.

Slowly, over hundreds of years, Hölle changed. She needed Zerfall less and less, made more and more of the church's decisions. It was Hölle who saw a need for the Täuschung to have a public face, who thought to lure in the sane with promises of a paradisiacal Afterdeath where their souls would await their eventual ascension as gods. Zerfall had been amazed at how quickly the religion grew after that, how eager the supposed sane were to believe without evidence.

As Hölle became ever more sure of what the church should be, Zerfall's doubts grew.

Somehow the little book of poems Aas gave her pushed her over some sort of edge. Halber Tod saw death and depression in everything. He saw little of worth in humanity and yet still somehow held out hope. Critics mocked him, and he wrote more books. His flesh blackened and peeled away and he wrote of lost love. His fingers fell away and he wrote of bravery and that last chance. He wrote of redemption. What room was there in Swarm for displays of humanity? What room was there for love? Where was redemption to be found in hell?

These thoughts plagued her until one day, while climbing the stairs to the chambers she and Hölle shared, she tripped over a pile of refuse that had been there for years. Rage washed through her, a tornado of roaring emotion, devouring her every thought. This church, this place, everything they ever wrought was rot. Since that night when Wahrergott spoke to them, they had not once heard the god's voice. He abandoned them just as her parents abandoned her. Had he even been real? Then, the dawning horrific realization: It didn't matter if he'd been real. She and Hölle, two powerful Geisteskranken, believed he was real. The millions of souls trapped in Swarm believed he was real. All across the city-states the public face of the Täuschung preached a watered down version of his message and were blindly believed. Even if he'd been nothing but the fevered dream of a dying little girl, Wahrergott was real now.

She had no doubt.

If millions of souls believed a lie, that lie became truth, became reality. They'd made a terrible god from their madness. If reality hadn't been a prison before, it certainly was becoming one now. They'd done something terrible and all humanity would suffer for it.

Zerfall had entered their chambers, thinking to explain to Hölle the rush of new memories—to try and understand the truth together—but her sister ignored her. Hölle prattled on about how the church was spreading and would soon overtake the Wahnvor Stellung as the largest church in the world. Zerfall turned to leave and stopped. *Hölle doesn't need me*, she realized. *If I leave she'll run the church on her own.*

It hadn't always been like this. There was a time when Hölle needed her and that she no longer did was somehow very, very bad. Because when Hölle truly no longer needed her . . .

For the first time Zerfall saw the church for what it was: a construction of rampant madness, the creation of a sick mind. Words escaped Zerfall. Hölle would never understand, would never agree to end the church. She'd always been more driven, more focussed.

I have to end this. But she couldn't see how. For centuries Hölle made fun of her quick temper and inability to plan. And now . . . She saw it clearly: the Täuschung would continue as long as Hölle lived. *I have to kill her.* She'd figure out how to topple the church after. She was their god-appointed leader. They'd listen, they had to. They had to see how rancid this religion had become.

"You're trying to replace me. You're trying to kill me," she said, driving Blutblüte into her sister's belly. She made one last attempt to explain but the words escaped her. "This is rotten." She meant the church and their mad religion. She meant the terrible way Hölle subtly undermined her, chopping away at her confidence for centuries. She meant the filth and decay she saw within their church.

She meant how awful it was to kill one's own sister.

No, not my sister. My Fragment. God that hurt so much.

Before she had time to think or plan they were on her and she'd been fighting for her life. Someone hit her from behind, crushing her skull, and she killed him, staggered away knowing she was dying.

The splintered bones protruding from the stump of her left hand caught her attention. *I'm dead. Dead things rot. And fall apart.* How long did she have before she couldn't move? How long before whatever held her together dried out and fell away and she collapsed into a pile of helpless bones? Not long, she suspected. Soon this weak boy would be far more capable than she.

I'm going to need him if I'm going to kill Hölle and get my sword back. The ragged stump of her wrist caught her attention. *I don't care. The sword is* mine.

Staring down at the unconscious Basamortuan youth Zerfall laughed. Had they left her alone she would have wandered into the desert and either died or finally succumbed to decay. She didn't know what would happen when her body finally collapsed, but the thought terrified her. *Eternity gazing out through empty eyes, watching the sand bury me.* Somehow, Aas changed that. He took her hand and told her Hölle lived and that gave her will, gave her purpose. She'd thought her sister dead, assumed she'd done what she had to do and that without her and Hölle the Täuschung would surely fall. But if Hölle lived, if her Fragment ruled the church . . .

"I remember everything," she told the boy at her feet. "I remember who I am."

No, that wasn't quite true. She remembered who she had been. She felt different now. She couldn't explain how, but she was changed.

But am I more or less? She wasn't sure. The woman she had been was a powerful Gefahrgeist, capable of bending people to her will. She remembered how she hurt Aas, over and over, how she cut and slashed him and how he thanked her. How he begged for more. She knew something was missing, but was it the power to bend people, or the desire?

She glanced at the stump of her left wrist, bleached bone protruding from ragged flesh. The tattoo came years after Swarm. She'd found an artist with exotic delusions regarding their work and forced the woman to give her a third eye so she might see Swarm, watch her hell grow. As always when dealing with the mad the tattoo hadn't worked as planned. She caught glimpses of Swarm over the years but she'd never been able to control the visions. Sometimes she saw things, impressions of strange lands and stranger people.

Doesn't matter now. It's gone.

Zerfall poured a measure of water into the youth's mouth and waited as he coughed and sputtered. His eyes flickered open to gaze about in confusion. She fed him water until it was gone and then sat back to watch as his wits returned.

"You're still here," he said, sitting up. "I thought maybe Harea called you home."

Even with her memories returned some of the Basamortuan's words meant nothing. "Who's Harea?" She knew nothing of the savage Basamortuan tribes.

"God of the Sands. Heart of the Basamortuan. Husband to Heriotza, Goddess Death." His eyes widened. "Are you Heriotza?"

"No."

"Oh. *Hilen deabru* then," he said.

"What's a *hilen deabru*?"

"*Hilen deabru* are lost souls rejected by Harea and Heriotza. It means 'undead demon' in the ancient tongue."

Knowing her decaying states, she understood his confusion. "I don't think I'm one of those either." She offered a hand to pull him to his feet. "My name is Zerfall."

"Jateko," he answered, staring at her hand.

With a shrug she dropped it back to her side. "That man was trying to fill you with sand."

"Yes."

When it became obvious he had nothing more to say on the subject she asked, "Why?"

"I killed his brother," said Jateko.

"In a fight?"

"No." He shook his head, eyes downcast.

So the boy was a murderer. Zerfall didn't much care. *I've killed thousands. How could I possibly judge?* "Why did you kill him?"

He looked up, met her eyes with his own. "It was an accident. I panicked. I was delirious from dehydration." He glanced around, taking the corpses. "Am I still hallucinating? Are you real?"

She ignored his questions.

Standing, Zerfall did a slow turn. Endless sand in every direction. When she once again faced Jateko she found him staring, eyes wide, at a swirl of dust motes dancing in the breeze.

He blinked, and focussed on her. "Are you going to eat me?" he asked.

"No."

"Are you going to eat *him*?" He nodded at the corpse sprawled in the sand beside him.

"Dead things don't eat," she said, bemused.

"Good." His expression didn't match his words. He looked decidedly ill, like he might puke.

"Why?"

"I . . . I want to eat him."

"You don't look like you want to eat him," said Zerfall.

"It will make me strong. I will know what he knew."

This he did seem sure of. "Is this normal where you come from, eating people?"

"Normal?" He laughed. "Eating the dead is forbidden." He glanced up at her again. "I'm guessing this might not bode well for your opinion of me."

Zerfall examined the boy's guileless face, trying to decide if he was serious and whether she wanted to know more. *No.* She wanted to go west, to end Hölle and the Täuschung. She wanted to lie down and let the sand abrade her to nothing.

She watched Jateko wrestle with the corpse before managing to free his knife from its back. He examined the body from different angles, poking it experimentally, looking perplexed at the resulting trickle of blood. Gripping the knife with both hands, he stabbed repeatedly at the chest, achieving little more than exposing a few ribs.

"How do I get to the heart?" he asked, panting.

Some dim memory of curiosity won out over world-crushing apathy. "Why do you want the heart?"

"I gain strength and wisdom from eating my foes."

"Have you eaten many foes?" Zerfall asked, eyeing his concave chest and scrawny arms.

"Gogoko will be my first."

Well that explains a lot. "You should probably eat the other one too." An idea coalesced. If this youth was so deluded that eating people really did make him stronger, she could use this boy. She hated the thought the moment it formed. *No. That was the old me.*

"After Gogoko, if I have room. Can you open the chest for me? I'm . . . I'm too weak."

"Sure." Zerfall held out her hand and Jateko passed her the knife with no hesitation.

Driving the blade into the cartilage in the centre of Gogoko's chest, she twisted it, cracking the ribs apart. After wiping the blade clean on the corpse's robes, she sheathed the knife in a hidden scabbard.

"Umm . . . Can I have that knife back?" Jateko asked.

"No."

"Oh."

Reaching into the corpse's chest with her remaining hand and using a foot as leverage on the far ribs, she pulled the chest apart with a great sucking tearing sound. Within, nestled in bloody gore and exposed lungs and organs, lay the heart.

Jateko scampered forward on his knees and stared into the sanguine destruction. He glanced up at Zerfall. "You're sure you don't want any?"

Is he joking? "Quite."

He reached in, bony fingers filthy with sand, and began tugging and tearing at the heart.

He'll never get it out on his own. Zerfall drew her knife and cut the heart free with a practised flick.

Jateko lifted the organ from the gaping chest and held it before his face as if deciding which part to eat first. He shrugged and tore at it with his teeth. Blood showered his already soaked robes as he savaged the heart like a starving dog. It was gone in moments.

"So, how was that?" she asked.

"Not as bad as I'd thought," he said, spitting blood and gristly strands of heart. He sat, splashed red, poking about the interior of the chest with a long finger.

"Are you sure this will make you stronger?"

He nodded. "And wiser. Or smarter. Not sure what the difference is. Our *sorgin*—" He glanced at Zerfall. "That's our tribe's wise-woman. Jakintsua said warriors used to eat each other and that they grew stronger and more skilled with every foe they ate." He paused in thought. "It wouldn't be forbidden unless there was something to it. Right?"

"Something beyond the mere fact that eating your fellow tribesmen might be considered evil?"

"Exactly." Returning his attention to the body he asked, "Which one is the liver?"

"It's a little further south." Leaning forward she sliced the torso open to the navel. After he peeled the skin back she pointed out the various organs, naming each one.

"Can you cut out the liver and kidney, please?"

She did as asked and Jateko bit his lower lip in look of absolute perplexity. "Which is more important?" he asked.

"How do you mean?"

"Different strengths lie in different organs, but I don't know which has what."

Zerfall shrugged. "I suppose that makes sense, but I can't help you."

Jateko lifted the kidney. "This one. It's smaller and I can finish it."

Zerfall watched him wolf down the kidney and about half the liver before collapsing back into the sand with a contented sigh, belly distended.

"I should at least try and eat some of the brain," he said. "Can you split the skull for me?"

The skull proved a little more problematic than the chest cavity. With only a single hand, she had trouble keeping it still and landing a clean blow. Eventually she decided she'd batter it open and it would take however long it took.

She talked as she worked. "Do you feel stronger and wiser?"

"Stronger, maybe. You gain wisdom and skills from eating brains. The organs are for strength and health and speed. I'm really full. I doubt I'll be able to eat much of the brain."

Zerfall glanced at Jateko. A strong wind would flatten him. He'd be of little help in a fight, but if eating brains would make him wiser, give him more information, he might be useful. *But stupid people are so much easier to manipulate.* She ignored the thought; that was the old Zerfall, the person she had been. "Next time, eat the brain first."

"Why?"

The skull split open saving Zerfall from having to answer. "You'll have to open it the rest of the way," she said, stepping back. "This is awkward with one hand."

But Jateko was already asleep and snoring loudly.

She stood over him, watching the steady rise and fall of his chest.

You're done. He's eaten and had his fill of water and blood. He won't die today. She glanced west toward Hölle and Blutblüte. *Leave him. Go. Walk away.* She examined his stick-like limbs. *He's weak. He'll slow you down.*

Am I the same person now as I was?

She knew the answer. She was more and less than the Zerfall who led the Täuschung for hundreds of years. Could she still bend people to her purpose, make them *want* to serve? Somehow she doubted it. The blow to the head—the shattered skull—had changed her.

What made a person who they were, their parents and friends? Or were people a result of their choices and actions? Could dreams and goals define someone?

If she wasn't who she had been, who was she now?

I can be whoever I want. If choices and actions define a person, I can define myself. She couldn't decide if this was freeing, or a trap.

The person she had been died in an alley, skull crushed; maybe it was time to be someone else. But how?

Zerfall frowned at the sleeping boy. Every part of her wanted to leave him, to walk away. Attachments were a hindrance. Jateko was young and naive and pathetically weak. Whatever he might become, right now he was useless.

Is that the old me?

It felt like it might be.

Were that true, all she had to do to be someone different was help the boy. Would saving his life make her a good person, someone who helps others?

Worth a try.

And if he was right and eating brains and hearts made him something more?

Then he'll be useful.

JATEKO DREAMED, REPLAYING THE decision to eat Gogoko over and over. He knelt by the corpse, staring into opened guts. Blood and horror was all that remained of a man he respected. He felt Zerfall's eyes on him, judging.

Does she think I'm too cowardly to follow through, or is she disgusted that I might? He wanted to ask but couldn't. Shame. Fear. These words defined his life. Rare were the days he didn't see those to expressions on Mom's face when she turned her attention in his direction. A decade and a half of living under that gaze left him doubting his every choice.

He noticed the mess he'd already made of his *oihal*. Mom would be so angry.

Thirst and hunger, days of dehydration, drew his eyes back to the corpse. He poked something coiled and looping and wet with a dirty finger, leaving a smear of sand. With a stab of guilt he wanted to wipe it clean and apologise.

He's dead.

What if he ate Gogoko and nothing happened?

Then they're right and I'm crazy.

But he didn't feel crazy. No, that wasn't true. If he didn't drink, his mind would surely break.

I need to do this to stay sane. It sounded good but felt like a justification.

If I'm weak, she'll leave me. That much did feel true. *I'll die out here. Alone.*

He was already dying. He knew it. Jateko wouldn't last another day without something to drink. *I don't want to be alone.*

Gogoko would have water somewhere. Why didn't he drink that instead? *Because then I'll be too afraid to come back and eat this corpse.* Without desperate need to drive him, he could never follow through with what he planned.

He watched as Zerfall cut the heart free, remembered the feel of it in his fingers, hot and slippery.

Jakintsua told him those stories for a reason. She never did anything by mistake. She led him here. To this moment. He would eat Gogoko and become strong. He would become a great warrior. He would matter. People would need him.

You'll become evil.

No. He wasn't evil. This wasn't evil. Gogoko was dead.

He'll live on within me. I won't be alone.

Jateko brought the heart to his lips.

If I eat Gogoko's heart and become stronger, then all this means something. There's a reason. If I eat it and nothing happens, I'm evil. He tasted blood. *I don't want to be evil.*

He dreamed he had a long conversation with Gogoko, explaining his decision and why it wasn't evil. He dreamed Gogoko was less than convinced.

JATEKO WOKE FEELING RELAXED and refreshed. Night had fallen and the air cooled rapidly. His robes, sodden with sweat and blood, had hardened into something resembling boiled leather. Each movement caused fearsome chafing. His belly no longer stretched to capacity, he felt happily sated. *Thirsty, though.* Who knew blood was so salty? He sat up and groaned. Everything hurt. His legs felt like they'd been filled with sand and beaten with a stick. His arms hung so heavily he thought for sure they'd fall off if he moved. The *hilen deabru*—Zerfall, he remembered—stood beside the corpse of the buried horse, its empty sockets turned in his direction. Did it watch him or had it fallen asleep on its feet?

What if it passed on during the night and this is an empty shell? He waved at it tentatively.

"Yes?" it asked in its raspy, wheezing voice.

"Just checking." He sat in the sand, unwilling to move before he had to. "Hey," he said, glancing about. "Where did Gogoko and Dedikatu go? You get hungry after all?"

She stared at him for a moment, not cracking even the faintest hint of a smile. "I moved them away." It gestured with the stump. "Didn't want carrion creatures disturbing us."

"Good idea," he said, stretching out the kinks in his neck. "They might carry you away too." He thought it might have growled but wasn't sure. *Sense of humour must have died too.*

"I saved some of the brain for you," she said, gesturing toward a misshapen pile of slimy grey sitting upon what looked like the remains of Gogoko's blood-spattered *oihal*. "I had to pull it apart to get it out."

"It looks like clay," said Jateko, crawling closer. He lifted a knuckle-sized lump, cold and slippery, and gave it a tentative sniff. "Smells like dried blood." He popped it into his mouth and chewed. "Cold," he said, making a face. "Tastes a little like my mom's snake soup after it's gone a little off." She continued to stare at him, unmoving. "Not that I'm complaining." He swallowed the nugget and stuck out his tongue. "Would be better warm."

"You could cook it."

"I have to eat it raw. They always did in the stories." He eyed the brain for a moment before shrugging and selecting another piece. He clenched his eyes closed and stuffed the chunk into his mouth, chewing furiously.

Feeling a little better, Jateko pushed himself to his feet. It hurt less than expected. "I bet you used to be pretty," he blurted. Empty sockets stared at him. "I mean before you were dead and all rotting and had no eyes and weren't shedding flakes of skin every time you move." She watched him, unblinking. *Well that makes sense. She doesn't have eyes. Why should she blink?* "So . . . Gogoko said the steel on your horse's shoes was *hiria ero*. From the west," he added when she remained silent. "From the city-states."

She stared at him.

"I thought all *hiria ero* women were fat."

Zerfall nibbled on her lower lip with brown teeth. Her rotten gums had receded making them look over-large and canine. She spat out a shred of decayed flesh. "I go west."

"Okay," he said, feeling not at all okay about being left alone. He felt better than he had in days. Maybe ever. Jateko flexed his arms. "Do I look stronger?"

Dark pits studied him for several heart beats. She drew breath to speak. "Your chest might be a little less concave."

Jateko frowned down at his hairless chest. "Uh . . . thanks."

She leaned forward, her face close enough he'd smell her breath if she was breathing. "And maybe your skin looks a little healthier." A faint whiff of decay followed her words. Even dead and rotting her heart-shaped face held traces of the beauty she had been.

"Gogoko always had good skin," Jateko said.

The brows over the empty pits furrowed. "What will happen when your tribe finds out you ate Gogoko?"

"They'll hunt and kill me." He remembered Jakintsua walking with him, her endless stories filling his thoughts. Somehow she'd forgotten the part of the stories where the tribe would gather its strongest warriors and hunt those who had partaken of the flesh of men. *That was an hallucination.* He'd been so hungry, so thirsty. *I still am.* Odd, as he just ate. "You're going west."

"Yes." Her voice left no room for doubt and yet he hesitated. To follow her to the city-states was to leave behind everything he ever knew. *You did that the moment you killed and ate Gogoko.*

"Why?" he asked, surprising himself. Mother always dissuaded him from questioning, said it was annoying. No one in the tribe liked his questions. He long ago learned to accept whatever he was told. "Why return to the city-states?"

Empty sockets examined him for an uncomfortably long time. "I . . . There is a church there, a religion called the Täuschung. They preach that our world is a prison and that only through suffering can we be freed." She looked away, the bony fingers of her right hand clenching into a fist. "They've created a hell, populated it with millions of people. These people will suffer in this hell forever unless I end the religion, unless I destroy it completely."

"That's—"

"I made the religion."

"—insane."

Her attention returned.

I shouldn't have said that. She's going to kill me now.

"Belief defines reality," she said.

Jateko blinked. "Is that some *hiria ero* philosophy?" *Where are all these questions coming from?*

Her brows furrowed. "It's the way things are. If enough people believe in this mad god I invented, he *is* real."

"So?"

"The world will truly become our prison and we will suffer for an eternity in hell." She drew breath. "And it will be my fault."

Understanding dawned. "You're going back to the city-states to end this religion."

Zerfall turned away. Head tilted, she examined the corpse of her half-buried horse. The animal's hooves protruded forlornly from the sand. Even by moonlight the *hiria ero* metal on its hooves shone like something ghostly. The

Basamortuan tribes talked about how city-states metal was better, but Jateko had never actually seen a tribesman make steel. He had no idea how it was done. All the metal he'd ever seen had been around for generations. Even the newest knife was older than the oldest person in the tribe. New tools were all wood or, more likely, bone.

Hiria ero steel. He remembered seeing his reflection, chin strong, in Nazkagarri's pitted knife. He stared at Zerfall's back. She was going west, to the city-states to fight some evil god. Alone.

I want to help her.

But why? Why leave the desert and everything he knew for this strange dead woman?

I don't know. She needed him. He had to help her.

"I can't let you travel alone," he said, joking. "It's too dangerous."

"Yeah?" she asked over her shoulder. "You think maybe someone will try and kill me?"

"There's worse things than death," he said, remembering Jakintsua uttering the words in dark threat while telling a scary story of demons and lost souls.

She nudged the horse's distended belly with a toe. "Yeah?"

The beast looked like it might pop, and Jateko backed away. "Uh . . . rape?" She glanced over her shoulder, an eyebrow arched over a dark and empty pit. "Maybe not," he admitted.

"A guide wouldn't be a terrible idea. At least until we're out of the desert."

"I'm with you to the end." He hadn't meant to say that, it slipped out.

Again she stared at him before shaking her head. "I'm going to kill some very dangerous and powerful people. I'm going to end a centuries old religion and burn it all to the ground. If there is a god, if Wahrergott is real, I'm going to kill him too."

She'd die without him. She'd never make it out of the desert. *She needs me.* Nothing else mattered. "I know."

Zerfall laughed, a dry wheeze as she'd forgot to fill her lungs, but looked doubtful. "You can come."

"I'll help you, and in return you can help me . . ." Help him what? Help him kill and eat people to make him stronger and smarter?

Her hand strayed down to caress the empty scabbard hanging at her left hip, thin fingers little more than flesh stretched tight across pale bone. "You can ride west with me," she said, attention once again on her horse.

Jateko glanced about the moonlit sands. "Ride?"

"Tod, get up," said Zerfall, kicking the dead beast. "I'm not walking all the way to Geld."

With a great stinking fart of rotting intestines, the horse rose from the sand. It stood on shaky legs, belly stretched and looking ready to burst. Its head hung low as if too heavy to lift. With a gaping yawn it vomited sand and Harea knew what else down its front legs. If a corpse could look miserable, this horse managed it admirably. Zerfall scowled at the arrow jutting from between the horse's empty sockets. Reaching up she snapped the shaft, leaving a finger's width of wood sticking out like a pathetic horn.

With quick, practised movements she removed the saddle, tossing it aside. The desert sun hadn't been kind and the leather was faded a pale yellow, dry and cracked. The bit, bridle, and reins she left in place.

"You might want to stand back," suggested Zerfall, hefting her knife and eyeing the horse like she was trying to decide where to stab it.

Jateko backed away. "I think he's already dead."

"Going to relieve Tod of the excess weight he's gained. Lying in the sand has made him fat and lazy." She rubbed the horse between the ears. "Sorry Tod," she said fondly.

Zerfall slashed along the horse's belly, spilling ropey intestines, huge organs, and all manner of black gore.

The stench clubbed Jateko to his knees. It became his world, suffused the air, clawed at his nostrils, infused his tongue. He retched and spat what little his stomach hadn't yet digested. Nothing would ever *not* smell like putrescent horse innards again.

"Does it smell bad?" Zerfall asked, standing ankle-deep in coiled horse guts, blue and green and black with decay, wriggling with white worms.

Jateko fled, crawling through his own puke in an attempt to escape the miasma.

"Really?" asked Zerfall. "I can't smell a thing."

From a safe distance he watched as she slashed away the horse's belly, emptying it until little remained of the beast but patchy skin stretched tight across wiry muscle and protruding bone. The horse looked wretched but made no complaint and stood motionless through the process. Zerfall moved with easy efficiency. She made those sand cats who raided the tribe's refuse look clumsy in comparison.

Jateko watched her work. Zerfall felt some connection with her dead horse, maybe even liked it, and yet had not hesitated to gut the beast.

What am I to her?

EIGHT

In outward appearance Doppelgangists (and their Doppels) can easily be mistaken for Mehrere (and their Fragments) as both manifest as multiple people. They are not, however, the same. Doppels are aspects of the Doppelgangist's personality, a part of themselves they hate, or a manifestation of who they wish they were. Mehrere are true schizophrenics. Fragments—the manifestation of their delusions—exist as completely different personalities.

There is one trait all Doppels and Fragments share: They want to be the original and they will stop at nothing to achieve that status.

—Vorstellung, Natural Philosopher

PHARISÄER GAZED UPON THE church, commonly referred to as 'the Hospice,' that acted as the public face of the Täuschung religion. Täuschung Hospices were littered throughout most of the city-states. Within this church sane priests preached of Swarm, the heaven where the most deserving souls awaited rebirth as gods. It was a successful lie. Everyone thought they were deserving. Everyone feared death. Everyone wanted to return as something more.

We are a species of wishful fools.

Towering spires decorated with carvings, mystical icons, gargoyles, and intricate stained glass stood at every corner and flanked every entrance. At just shy of three hundred years old, the building showed a variety of architectural styles from the solid stone slabs of its earliest days to the ornate mosaics currently in fashion.

Squinting she examined the carvings. While impressive, they had nothing to do with the Täuschung or Swarm. The church had one purpose: Appeal to the masses.

It's all a lie.

But then wasn't that true of all churches? Anywhere people preached of an Afterdeath they'd never seen and gods they'd never met, falsehood must abound. Really, from that metric, the Täuschung was one of the more honest churches. While everything the priests leading the public sermons said was a lie, purposefully planned to make the sane masses feel comfortable and safe, at least the religion's creators had actually met their god. And while she might not personally care, might not have a vested interest in the Täuschung as a religion, she had no doubt Swarm was real.

Such a waste. All this power, all the money brought in by proselytizing priests begging for donations, and Hölle and Zerfall did nothing but send stupid souls to their ridiculous hallucinated hell.

They could have done something interesting. Enough sane worshipped at Täuschung churches that they'd define local reality with their beliefs. Instead of using that, Zerfall and Hölle only told the worshippers they'd go somewhere special after they died and later return as gods. *They could have changed Geld, shaped the city.*

The Geborene Damonen, Pharisäer decided, had the right idea: Use the masses to make yourself a god. Or something like that. She wasn't really sure what they believed. Glancing at the Geborene pyramid sitting like a glistening white turd on the far side of the city, she wondered at the kind of gods created by fastidious arseholes.

I suppose I owe Zerfall, in some small way. The woman spent centuries creating her mad religion, building two virtually unrelated churches—the public face to draw in the fools and their money, and the core of reality-twisting Geisteskranken to collect their souls—only to disappear when it finally was about to become successful. Not that it ever would; Pharisäer would see to that. Toppling the Täuschung would grievously wound Hölle and that was a thousand times more valuable than a mad religion.

When Hölle falls, I shall be real.

Until then, Pharisäer would remain a manifestation of the woman's delusions, a fragment of a damaged mind, unable to exist on her own. Until she became real, Pharisäer was a prisoner. She couldn't leave Geld, couldn't stray too far from Hölle lest she cease to exist altogether. Luckily this church was located near the Täuschung compound where Hölle convalesced. Hopefully when more people believed Pharisäer was Zerfall, she'd be able to travel further afield.

Where was Aas now? *Twisting* would heal the worst of the wound she'd given him. She saw two likely possibilities and a third less likely. Chances were Aas had either fled Geld or was now hunting the two priests she wanted dead. It was possible he'd gone to Hölle, but Pharisäer felt sure his fear, and the woman's unconcealed loathing, would keep him away. Either way she won. If he fled the city he was gone and she need not concern herself. If he pursued the two Geisteskranken she wanted dead, he was likely trapped in the sphere of Nimmer's influence. All that mattered was that Aas stayed away from Hölle so he couldn't—accidentally or otherwise—reveal the truth about Pharisäer.

I gave him a puzzle. No way he left. Hölle thought Aas dangerously clever, but Pharisäer saw him for what he was: A coward hiding behind stacks of books. He respected Zerfall because she was intelligent and dangerous. *He's submissive, he needs a strong woman. He needs a woman he can fear.* Pharisäer had tricked him and trapped him and it had been easy. Even if he managed to figure his way out of her trap he'd be impressed. He'd return and he'd be hers. She didn't need him, but how could having an assassin in your pocket not be handy?

She returned her attention to the church.

A few stragglers, late for today's sermon and the Departing of Giernach Reichtum, a highly ranked banker in the Verzweiflung Banking Conglomerate and one of Geld's wealthiest citizens, hustled to enter before the massive doors were closed. Today marked the next chapter in the Täuschung story. With Giernach publicly declaring herself a believer, more bankers would soon follow. They were an unimaginative lot. Where the Täuschung had lurked in obscurity for hundreds of years, really only finding some small success in the last few decades, the religion was poised for massive expansion. Where Geld lead, the other city-states followed. Handled correctly, the Täuschung could vie against the Wahnvor Stellung within the next decade.

Shame it all has to go.

For now, however, she needed to be seen and to do her part. Once she dealt with Hölle, replaced her as the heart of the Täuschung, perhaps she would start her own religion, something with more profitable ideals.

Pharisäer entered the building through the entrance at the rear. Ranks of priests, true believers in the lie that was the façade, stood in ranks, awaiting her arrival. Centuries ago Zerfall and Hölle hired Geld's best designers to create these robes with an eye to being impressive. Layers upon layers of the most expensive materials wrapped each man and woman, the number of layers and colours denoting the priest's rank.

All these supposedly sane men and women so ready to believe in a lie. Not that the deranged were any less gullible. Still, sanity really ought to be worth *something*.

Unterwürfig, Bishop of Geld, bowed as she entered. The man was as tedious as he was impressive. Dark hair, silvered at the temples, matched perfectly to a well-trimmed beard shot through with grey. Groomed eyebrows and a face lined with compassion and concern completed the image. With the right speach writers the man was a master orator.

Unterwürfig straightened, smoothing the many layers of silk and gold-threaded robes. "Giernach Reichtum . . . is ready." He spoke in slow, even tones, his voice deep and ringing.

Pharisäer watched him listen to the dying reverberations of his voice, head tilted to one side as if he contemplated the world-shattering wisdom of his words. No one loved Unterwürfig's voice more than Unterwürfig.

"The hall?" asked Pharisäer.

"Just shy . . . of capacity."

"Close the doors." She wanted to be done with this, get it over with. There were other, more interesting things to do with her time.

"I have prepared . . . a special sermon . . . for Giernach's Departing," announced Bishop Unterwürfig, spreading his arms and closing his eyes as if in prayer.

Of course you have. He droned on and she ignored him. If the windbag's speeches were long it wasn't because he said a lot; he spent more time listening to his voice bounce about the arched cathedral ceiling than he did actually talking. The thought of standing behind Unterwürfig while he prattled on gnawed at Pharisäer. Zerfall and Hölle preferred to take a background role in the public face of the Täuschung, allowing the sane priests to run the Hospices littered across the city-states.

What a waste.

"I will lead today's sermon," she said, interrupting the priest. She needed to be seen, to be real. *Might as well get something out of this stupid church before I burn it to the ground.*

The Bishop's eyebrow crept up in askance. "I think . . . "

"This is too important," she said.

He nodded agreement. "Of course."

Much as he loves talking, he loves getting paid even more.

Pharisäer pointed at one of the lower-ranked priests. "Fetch me the proper robes." The priest dipped a quick bow and left without a word. She nodded at Unterwürfig. "Begin the ceremony, Bishop." She didn't want to have to go through all the boring preamble shite the man loved so much. "You'll introduce me."

WEIGHTED DOWN WITH COUNTLESS layers of bright silk and wrapped in gold brocade, Pharisäer stood behind Bishop Unterwürfig, waiting. Somehow he managed to drag her introduction on for a full half hour and he still wasn't finished. She gazed out over the cathedral hall. Far above, the arched ceiling, sweeping lines like gold sails catching a brisk wind, caught the Bishop's voice and amplified it.

Giernach Reichtum, the dying Banker and focus of today's Departing, lay on a litter of gold, centre stage. Her skin shone pale and grey. Gold and assorted gifts—more wealth than most people would see in a lifetime—lined the litter, offerings to Wahrergott. Thin white hair had been combed as much as it was possible to groom a half dozen sparsely spaced strands. The old woman's *Geldwechsler*, the ornate and awkward hats worn by the Verzweiflung bankers, was conspicuously missing, subtle cue that in the end she chose the Täuschung over the Verzweiflung. Pharisäer doubted Giernach was even aware of its absence. If the old woman's chest didn't rise and fall in shallow breaths, Pharisäer would have thought her a corpse. Every now and then eyes set deep in wrinkles would open and pear about for a few heart beats before once again closing.

Wealth is no protection from disease, mused Pharisäer. *Or gullibility.* The old woman's body was riddled with cancers and the best medickers the city had to offer agreed she'd be dead within the week.

Pharisäer stifled a grin. *Less than that.*

Knowing her time had come and being a true believer in the One True God, Giernach came to the Täuschung Hospice, begging for a public Departing so she may best prove her faith to Wahrergott. The banker thought she'd be surrounded by believers as her soul passed on, that their faith would guarantee she woke in a heaven of beauty and wealth and comfort where she'd await the saving of all humanity and their return to godliness.

She's not completely wrong.

Giernach would be surrounded by priests, but not these powerless sane idiots. After the ceremony, Giernach would be taken to the deepest chambers, far beneath the ancient Täuschung church. The secret inner core of Geisteskranken priests would surround her. Their faith and reality-bending madness would send her soul to Swarm.

The audience, comprising entirely of the sane, watched with reverent awe, soaking in Bishop Unterwürfig's words. Their shared reality crashed against her every time the Bishop brought her to their attention. He droned on about how Wahrergott chose her to be his eyes in this world so that she may see His holy path. She felt thin and illusory, like she might fade to nothing if they all decided she wasn't real.

They don't know. They don't know that.

They saw her, she was real. For the first time she truly appreciated the strength of the sane masses. *They could snuff me with a thought were they capable of agreeing on something.* And Bishop Unterwürfig, as a skilled orator, was dangerously powerful. Should he decide to sway the crowd against her, she'd be doomed. Luckily he'd never shown signs of comprehending his power or wanting more than shallow titles and wealth.

"And now I give you Zerfall, the Eyes of Wahrergott," finished Unterwürfig, turning to Pharisäer in a deep bow and backing away from the pulpit.

All eyes were on her. *They see me. I am real.* It was a lie, but their growing belief in her would solidify her existence. She couldn't deceive herself it would be enough. Until she replaced Hölle, she would remain nothing more than a Fragment, a shallow figment of a twisted mind. Pharisäer stepped forward, basking in the attention. *They see me.* There weren't enough people here to make her truly real, but already she felt more solid.

Taking her place behind the pulpit Pharisäer lifted her arms just as Unterwürfig had and the room seemed to hold its breath. How many people were here, four hundred? No cough or fidget disturbed the silence.

"Heaven," said Pharisäer, voice strong and loud. The ceiling caught her words and she heard the beautiful decay of reverberation. *It's like rain. I speak and the church shatters my words so they may fall upon the believers, soak into their thoughts.* "The Wahnvor Stellung preach of an Afterdeath of second chances and redemption. The Warrior's Credo promises an Afterdeath of war and strife. The northern tribes wear fetishes, bones taken from those they've slain. The GrasMeer ride endless plains in the Afterdeath, worshipping their mad horse gods." She had no idea if this was true but it hardly mattered. "All those Afterdeaths are real," she said. "They all promise something, and maybe they even deliver some of what they promise. But these are old religions born of ignorance and fear. What sets us apart?"

Four hundred mouths whispered "Wahrergott." Four hundred fingers touched foreheads and then rose as if to push their prayers to the sky.

"Reality is responsive," said Pharisäer, basking in the attention. She never felt so real, so alive. "Reality bends to the belief of the masses." No need to mention the mad; the sane hated and feared Geisteskranken and with good reason. What these dullards needed to hear now was how powerful *they* were. "Belief. Defines. Reality." She nodded as if she'd said something profound and four hundred heads nodded agreement. *Tell them what they know.* "Reality is responsive," she repeated, "but there are rules, laws binding even the most powerful Ascended. The gods of every other religion are bound by rules." She paused to let that sink in. "They are limited." She drew a deep breath. "I ask you, what kind of god is limited? What kind of god is bound by rules?"

Four hundred pairs of eyes watched in rapt attention. Four hundred pairs of lips quivered, desperate to answer the question yet afraid to speak out.

"False gods," announced Pharisäer. "Lesser gods. Ascended mortals. Local spirits lifted by the faith of uneducated fools." Two things the populace of Geld loved above all else: Gold, and the sure knowledge they were smarter and better educated than the rest of the world. "What happens if we declare that murder is a crime but do not punish the guilty? What happens if we declare debts must be paid but don't pursue negligent debtors? What are laws and rules if there is no enforcement? They are nothing! Where there are rules—where there are laws—there must be enforcement."

Whispered words of agreement crept to the stage, fed her belief in herself and the knowledge that she had this crowd, that she'd guide them where she wanted.

Tell them what they know.

"Wahrergott is the One True God, the enforcer of reality's rules. Wahrergott returns the world to sanity after it's been raped by Geisteskranken."

Eyes widened in shock. Four hundred mouths gasped, wondering if they should be appalled but agreeing with her words.

"Humanity was meant to be more than pathetic fumbling beings. We were not meant to be slaves to reality. It bends to our will and its responsiveness tells us something. It tells us we were meant to be gods. This . . ." She waved her arms. "This is all temporary. Call it a test. True godhood is earned, not given by the whims of some mad boy like those deranged Geborene believe!"

Quiet mocking titters reached her on the stage. In spite of the huge turd of a pyramid, the Geborene had few followers in Geld.

"We will be gods," she told the crowd and they nodded. *Tell them what they know.* "But only once we have saved everyone, every single last soul in all the world. It is our task, but we are not alone."

A few people shuffled and fidgeted in the back rows. Had she gone on too long? Best not to be like Bishop Unterwürfig, best to wrap it up before she became an insufferable windbag. She felt drunk with power, basked in the attention. This, standing before a crowd, was more than most Fragments could ever dream of. *They see me. They make me real.*

"Everything that happens happens for a reason." She gestured at Giernach on her litter of gold. "Did this woman achieve all she achieved by mistake? No! And make no mistake, Wahrergott's rules are no accident. This woman," she pointed again at the litter and the old lady sleeping upon it. "All of you." She raised her arms to encompass all the room. "It is *you* who define reality." *Should I have said "we"?* No one seemed to notice. "We are Wahrergott's chosen. It is *we* who shall awake in the heaven he promises. It is *we* who shall rise to once again take our place amongst the gods when all the world has been saved." That the lie preached to the public contained whispers of the truth tickled Pharisäer and she crushed the urge to mock the gullible fools. "Giernach Reichtum is a brave woman. She worked endless hours, rising through the ranks of the Verzweiflung Banking Conglomerate." Always best to remind the faithful why they were here and how much they wanted to be as successful as the old banker. "Giernach Reichtum is a true believer and we are awed by the statement she chooses to make today." She doubted the old woman would so much as utter another syllable before awaking in Swarm. "She has asked that her Departing be public so that you may learn from her wisdom." She suspected Bishop Unterwürfig somehow bribed the greedy old bastard, but it hardly mattered.

Pharisäer drew another deep breath, waiting until once again all eyes were on her. *They see me. I am real.* It almost felt true.

"We are gathered here today," she said, listening to her words rain down from the ceiling, "to say goodbye to our friend, our mentor, Giernach Reichtum."

A N HOUR LATER, AFTER every member of the church from the lowliest debtor to the wealthiest banker had a chance to pay their respects to the dying woman, a stately procession of priests carried her into the deepest chambers, far beneath the church. Once the litter was stripped bare and the sane priests herded from the room, the Täuschung's inner core of priests—Geisteskranken, each and every one—entered from hidden doors.

For the first half hour Pharisäer watched as the insane priests stripped and tortured the old woman, telling her over and over of Swarm, the hell awaiting her. This would go on until the woman broke, until she believed with utter surety in Swarm. That, combined with the suffocating proximity of half a dozen powerful Geisteskranken, ensured the destination of Giernach's battered soul.

When the screaming and chanting grew monotonous Pharisäer left.

AAS FLEW FAR ABOVE Geld.

Did Zerfall ever hurt you so perfectly?

He needed to think but his thoughts rebelled, danced like drunkards, stumbling from one topic to the next.

Pharisäer wasn't trying to kill me. He saw that now. What then had been her goal?

Below, he spotted the local Geborene Damonen church and spread his wings to glide in a looping crescent and land. A cold wind gusted from the Kälte Mountains to the north of Geld, ruffling his feathers and chilling the bright pink puckered flesh of his bald head. The building, a perfect pyramid which had only been built in the last couple of years, was an architectural monstrosity of pristine white stone. Geborene priests rose each morning and spent their day scrubbing the church in staggered work parties. Aas saw what appeared to be an emergency cleaning crew dash from the building to scrub away unsightly bird droppings.

Unable to resist, Aas shat on the very apex of the pyramid.

A Geborene acolyte spotted Aas and climbed the sloping temple wall toward him, a mop and bucket clutched in one hand. Aas screeched, a retched croak, and glared at the young priest with bloodshot eyes. The priest stopped and studied him, hefting the mop as it were a weapon. Spreading his wings to their full extension, Aas shuffled in place, cackling carrion laughter. *{Come priest, I want to watch you bounce down the side of this stupid church.}*

The acolyte ceased his ascent and blinked up at Aas before wisely retreating to go in search of something less dangerous to clean. No doubt the coward would return later, but by then Aas' little gift to the Geborene would have hardened, forever staining the unsullied white stone. He glanced about, noting the lack of other stains. The temple was pristine. Could faith alone maintain the appearance of a building? But if that were so, why have these idiots out here scrubbing?

You're avoiding what you came here to think about.

True.

Aas settled, folding his wings in tight and closing his eyes to enjoy the cold wind on the sagging flesh of his bald head.

Did Zerfall ever hurt you so perfectly?

No she hadn't. He was hard-pressed to explain—even to himself—what Pharisäer had done to him. With Zerfall there had been no promise of pleasure, no suggestion their relationship would ever be other than one-sided. Zerfall caused him pain and he took pleasure in her gift; she left him no choice. Pharisäer showed tenderness and vulnerability. She let him think he could hurt her, that she'd *let* him hurt her; if only he knew how to ask. And then she slid a knife into his belly.

Had she planned that encounter? Could she read him so perfectly?

Gods she is dangerous. Aas blinked beady red eyes. *God*, he corrected with a cackle of laughter.

He should fly straight to Hölle and tell her everything.

He'd threatened to do just that and Pharisäer hadn't cared. She didn't think he would.

She knew I wouldn't.

That rankled. Aas hated being predictable.

The answer was easy and yet telling Hölle everything to prove to Pharisäer he wasn't predictable was stupid. Aas hated stupidity even more than being predictable.

Sensing an updraught of warm air, he leapt from the apex of the Geborene pyramid. Wings stretched wide, he caught the breeze, riding it like a boat following a strong current.

His mind wandered and he remembered fleeing the town he'd been born in, hearing the startled yells of the men he stumbled into outside of the tavern. At the time he thought they'd given chase and fled for his life.

He'd run west. Pure luck, really. Had he travelled east, he would have wandered into the Basamortuan Desert and no doubt died there, leaving sunbleached bones protruding from the abrasive sands.

After two days he collapsed, weak with hunger, and lay blinking up into an eternity of blue sky. To his right, beyond the reach of his outstretched arm, stone pushed through thin soil like broken bone through flesh. He slept where he fell, prostrated in the rolling foothills of the Kälte Mountains, with neither the strength nor the will to move. When he awoke, two condors flew overhead in lazy circles while another sat on the outcrop of rock, watching. When he grunted and tried to shoo it away, the bird didn't so much as twitch. It waited with the perfect patience of a creature certain it would soon enjoy a meal. Aas remembered thinking, *Eat the dead and you'll never go hungry.*

He had no idea how long he lay, slipping in and out of consciousness, until he opened his eyes to discover a condor standing over him, neck bent, staring him in the eye.

"You've come for me?" Aas asked the condor, and it nodded, its throat making soft glottal clicks. "Not much flesh left," he told it, and it shrugged as if unconcerned. He looked past the bird at the two circling overhead. "Usually you all land and eat in a circle," he croaked. "Come, there's enough for three."

The bird turned its head as if listening and waited.

And Aas understood. "You're not here for my flesh, you're here for my soul."

Every day, for fourteen years, he watched the noble birds through his knothole, dreaming of their freedom. When his father died, he'd eaten him. It was the chain of life: The living became carrion and the eaters of the dead were but the next link in the chain. That had been the beginning of his transformation, though he hadn't realized it at the time.

These condors weren't there to eat him, they were guides. The two circling above guarded his body while he was vulnerable. This one, here on the ground. . . . It was time. He was dying. He was ready.

Aas' eyes slid closed and he felt his soul leak from his body and enter the vessel waiting nearby.

When he once again opened his eyes he expected to see his starved body lying at his feet. There'd been nothing, an area of trampled grass and the savoury scent of death. He hopped about then, dancing on taloned feet, stretching great wings, until hunger drove him into the air in search of food. Later that day he ate the remains of a farmer's dog and it was the most delicious meal he ever tasted.

Focus. Focus on what you're doing.

Aas banked and dropped low enough he could have made out the faces of those below should they ever think to look up. Which they never did. Sometimes humanity seemed like poorly drawn art scrawled across rough cotton paper. They mistook texture for depth, never realizing they were trapped in their narrow perception of reality.

Are you so sure you're free of that same trap?

If he said yes, he was a fool. If he said no, he wasn't being honest with himself.

You can only avoid thinking about her for so long.

Pharisäer. What did she want? And why did she look exactly like Zerfall?

Aas loosed a startled shriek. *What a fool I've been!*

The condor screeched laughter. There seemed no end to his foolish blindness.

What did Pharisäer want?

What do all Fragments of Mehrere personality want?

To be the original.

Pharisäer knew I'd put this together. And yet she hadn't killed him when she had the chance.

He should run to Hölle, tell her everything.

Why? She hates me, always has. And if Pharisäer was a Fragment, Hölle was already doomed.

Pharisäer could be his new Zerfall.

He wanted that more than anything.

When I beat Pharisäer's puzzle she'll see my worth.

Pharisäer wanted Nimmer dead. She said he was Getrennt, divorced from reality. It was a common delusion, but rarely dangerous. Many Getrennt thought they only had limited control of their thoughts and actions and weren't particularly deadly.

How Nimmer's delusion manifested, Aas had no idea. If Nimmer thought himself separate from the world around him, Aas would complete that process.

First, however, he'd kill Narr Unerheblich, the easier of the two targets.

Aas flew in search of his prey.

Hölle awoke, eyes gummy with sleep, disoriented from a strange dream. Wahrergott had been trapped in an iron box, screaming and pleading with her. His words were incomprehensible gibberish and he sounded frustrated more than scared or angry.

Sunlight slashed sharp around the edges of the heavy curtains sheltering her room from the harsh light. Dust danced gold in stabbing beams, illuminating the detritus heaped in the corners of her chambers. The floor was a mess, piled deep with clothes in need of laundering, and littered reports from wandering Täuschung priests, few of which she bothered to read. She grimaced, squinting and turning away from the pain. How long had she been asleep?

"Zerfall?"

No. Never again. Gone. Forever.

Why had she expected an answer?

If I close my eyes I'll fade to nothing. The thought jolted her with fear. Hölle darted a glance toward Zerfall's hand on her desk. It sat, palm up, where Aas dropped it, and showed no sign of decay. *Why won't it rot?* How long had it been, how long since she saw Zerfall? She remembered the sword, Blutblüte, sliding into her belly and ground her teeth as the muscles there tensed around the imagined agony.

It had been weeks. She wasn't sure how many. She'd taken longer to heal than expected and hadn't left her room since—

She drew a calming breath. *Zerfall, why did you betray me?* She would never know.

No, that wasn't true.

Zerfall awaited her in Swarm.

It would be a long time before Hölle set foot in the hell she hallucinated. Hers would be the final soul, the last sacrifice. What would happen after her death, she couldn't be sure. Humanity would be freed, that much Wahrergott had promised. But what did freedom mean?

Anything had to be better than this. Nothing felt real since her sister's betrayal. The world seemed somehow shallow, an artist's water-colour rendering. Sometimes when she lay with her eyes closed she imagined herself fading to nothing. The thought terrified her. Her dreams had become nightmares. She dreamed she got Wahrergott's message wrong. She dreamed the god wasn't real, that he was nothing more than a manifestation of madness. She dreamed that *she* wasn't real.

Every morning she reminded herself they were just dreams. Wahrergott was the One True God and she was real. In these quiet moments she contemplated the ingenuity of the gods who built this prison. By making reality responsive to the desires of humanity they made humanity responsible for its own hell. *If everyone believed this prison were a golden paradise then such it would be.* Filth and depredation—deceit and violence—lay at the core of every human soul; reality offered irrefutable proof of this.

This could be utopia and instead we make it our hell.

Hölle thought about rising from bed, crossing the room, and touching Zerfall's hand.

No, the pain would be too much. The stitches had been removed and little more than a thick ridge of angry pink scar remained, but her stomach needed more time to heal. Pharisäer said Hölle needed to be strong and cared for her while she recuperated, dealing with the daily business of running the Täuschung, insisting Hölle rested.

That's probably where Pharisäer is. Some urgent matter must have called her from my side.

Again she thought of Zerfall. Even when they'd been apart Hölle always knew she'd see her sister again soon. She'd always felt something in the very centre of her that knew with absolute certainty Zerfall was safe and alive. And now she was gone.

And yet every morning you awaken, expecting to find her either in bed with you or at her desk working.

The heavy oak double doors to Hölle's chambers swung open revealing the silhouette of a woman, petite and curved. Long hair hung well past the shoulders. On a slim waist hung a plain sword. Even in shadow Hölle recognized that simple blade. She remembered her dream of Zerfall sitting in the bay window and her stomach wrenched, forcing a hiss of pain between clenched teeth.

She's come back to finish me.

"Zerfall—"

"No," said the shadow, stepping into the room and closing the door behind her. "You're wearing her sword."

Hölle examined Pharisäer. Though she dressed and stood as Zerfall would, something looked subtly wrong. *It's the sword, she's too aware of it.* Zerfall wore Blutblüte like it was part of her—an extension of her will. Pharisäer wore it like an accessory.

Pharisäer glanced about the room, taking in the scattered detritus with a raised eyebrow. "If we are to maintain the lie that you are whole—that Zerfall has not betrayed us all—I must play the part."

"And the people who know?"

"I'm taking care of that."

"How?"

"Aas." Pharisäer flashed a grin that was pure Zerfall. "There were matters that had to be dealt with."

"I was thinking of Zerfall when you arrived," said Hölle, annoyed it sounded like an apology.

Pharisäer sat on the side of the bed and reached out a hand to run gentle fingers through Hölle's hair. "You miss your sister."

"It's not that—"

"I'm not here to replace her. You no longer need Zerfall." Pharisäer massaged the back of Hölle's neck, easing the tension there. "Things have changed," she said, leaning forward to kiss Hölle on the forehead. "I am what you need now."

"Sorry, it's just that—"

"Apologies are doubts. Never apologize."

"Stop interrupting me."

Pharisäer flashed that heartbreakingly familiar grin. "That's better. Now, what's bothering you?"

Hölle gestured toward her desk. "I keep thinking about that hand." *The hand refuses to rot and each day it doesn't rot I feel less real.* Something stopped her from voicing the thought.

"I'll take it away."

"No!" She took a calming breath. "It's a constant reminder, and I think I need it."

Pharisäer nodded her understanding, still massaging Hölle's neck. "So what's the problem?"

"Before, when we were apart, I always knew Zerfall was all right. I knew that if something happened to her I would know. I knew things would change. I knew . . ." She trailed off, unable to voice what she knew. "We share a connection."

"Shared."

"Yes. Shared."

"And?"

"I expect to see her every time I wake. Each time the door opens I expect it to be her. She's dead and gone but I can't *feel* it. She was my other half." She shook her head, angry, and Pharisäer's hand dropped away. *She's gone and I feel broken, less whole. I should be rising*—she wasn't sure if she meant getting out of bed or something else, something more important—*and I feel like I'm sinking. I should be taking her place.* Come to think of it, Zerfall hadn't done much within the Täuschung in the last few years; taking her place should be so easy. And yet it wasn't. She couldn't. *It's like she isn't really gone.*

Pharisäer laughed, light and breathy. "I am your other half now."

It sounded right but felt wrong, not at all comforting. "I suppose. You're using Aas to assassinate those who know Zerfall is gone?" she asked, more to change the subject than out of interest.

"We might as well use him before we kill him. And I admit, I enjoy toying with him. He's so predictable."

"Careful. He's not stupid."

"He's a man. All men are stupid. Anyway, he's educated, not intelligent. There's a difference. He can bore you with a thousand dull facts about every religion and city-state and the minutiae of how every type of Geisteskranken might manifest, but he can't see past his own beak of a nose." She pushed her chest forward suggestively. "Unless there's a pair of tits in the room."

Hölle wrinkled her nose in distaste. "Zerfall was always better at that kind of manipulation." She lay back with a groan, her stomach aching. "I never understood her relationship with Aas."

"She knew you didn't like it."

That struck too close to her own thoughts. She shuffled about, trying to get comfortable, and said, "You don't feel anything for him, do you?"

Pharisäer made a very unladylike snort in the back of her nose. "Hardly. When he is no longer useful . . ." She showed perfect teeth in a sweet smile.

"Good."

"But do expect some unusually confused brain-babble from him," said Pharisäer. "I've been doing what I can to keep him confused. He's dangerous enough we don't want him thinking clearly about his future."

"Fine." Aas was disgusting enough when she couldn't hear the perverted lustings of his inner mind. If he tried to look down her shirt again she'd kill him. "Better yet," she said. "You deal with him. Keep him away."

"I'll let you know when he's dead."

Hölle examined Pharisäer, nodding toward the sword. "Do you think you can kill him?"

"He'll thank me when I do."

Hölle recognized that cold confidence. *Maybe she does have some Zerfall in her.* And if she did? *Will she too someday try and kill me?*

A AS SAT ATOP THE roof of the pawnbroker across the street from a run-down mansion, plucking hairs from his scalp and adding them to the growing collection in his pocket.

The black bone bow lay across his lap. A single condor-fletched arrow spun in the fingers of his free hand like a prestidigitator rolling a coin across their knuckles. Keeping the chimney at his back to ensure he was not silhouetted, he glanced at the mansion's outhouse, judging the distance. Three hundred and fifty strides, he guessed. Looking east he spotted the central tower of the Verzweiflung Banking Conglomerate and watched the lazy fluttering of their flag, a massive rectangle of black with a single gold coin in the centre.

Pharisäer, what would she be to him?

If Pharisäer wasn't Gefahrgeist, might she be capable of loving him?

No one can love you. With a growl he shoved away the thought.

She showed no sign of Zerfall's Gefahrgeist power, made no attempt at coercing him, demanding his love, or conscripting his will. If there was even a chance she might love him . . .

No. Focus on the job at hand. Show her you are useful. He learned that lesson from Zerfall.

Again glancing at the flag he tested the breeze, sniffing. *Gentle wind from the north.* Not much, but enough he'd have to account for it. Early afternoon, the sun was high enough not to be a factor. He lifted his nose, breathing deep. As always, in his human form, his senses felt dull and muted like a curtain lay between him and the world. Only as a condor was he truly alive. That delusion allowed him this mattered not. Freedom, *that* mattered. Being part of the world, a link in the chain of life, that mattered too. As a condor he belonged.

Having deposited a few more thick hairs into his pocket, he once again examined the small finger of his left hand. Taking another deep breath, he let it out in a slow exhalation. *I can do it.* Once he'd killed Narr Unerheblich, he'd remove the finger, start Hexenwerk from scratch. *With more of me in the puppet, having made a greater sacrifice, the transference should be easier.* It was a long shot, but the *salbei* of the Ausgebrochene tribes lived lives of suffering, torment, and sacrifice. Maybe that mattered.

The wind shifted and brought him the cool scent of mountain air. He remembered the first time he breathed that air free of the wood and stone rot of his father's cellar.

Aas had devoured his father over the course of a week, gnawed bones clean and then broken them open for their marrow. Only the few bones too thick for him to break and the skull and brain remained. He hadn't eaten that out of respect and love.

But a sated hunger always returns. He had no water and licking damp stone walls wasn't enough. Thirst and hunger drove him from the cellar.

Late in the evening, seeing the village dark and sleepy, he stumbled from his father's house, fleeing the ghosts living there; the mother he never knew, the father he'd eaten. The cellar door hadn't even been locked.

The world was impossibly large, the horizon so far away he couldn't touch it if he ran for a thousand days. The sky, crisp blue with soft clouds shrouding the mountains to the north and fading to black far to the west, called to him. Far overhead he saw a wheeling condor and followed it, paying no mind to where he walked. It wasn't until he stumbled into a group of men leaving a well-lit building—which later he recognized was an ale-house—that he realized he'd gone deeper into the village.

"If the villagers see you they'll kill you, burn you as a demon." His father's words. Aas flinched away, unsure where to run. He knew nothing of this world. The men stood, eyes wide with surprise, and one stepped forward. Then the door swung open bathing Aas in light from the lanterns within. They gasped, stumbled away, turned and fled.

Aas did the same. They'd hunt and kill him.

Now, sitting on a roof in Geld, he laughed. What a sight he must have been, covered in his father's blood and stinking of rot. No wonder they ran.

For fourteen years his father lied, kept him hidden in a damp cold cellar. Why, Aas would never know. He might not be pretty, but he'd seen many uglier men and women walking the streets of Geld, neither molested nor commented on.

Aas returned his attention to the mansion and outhouse. The sprawling grounds covered most of the block and included several guest houses, separate buildings for the hired help, and a massive boat house replete with docks stabbing far out into Geld Lake. There was room for scores of staff and an entire wing of once opulent suites—now filled with crumbling mouldings, remnants of mouldering furniture, and rotting shreds of silk draperies—set aside for visiting dignitaries. In any other city-state, this would be the palatial home of whatever self-centred Gefahrgeist tyrant ruled. In Geld it was home to one deranged Attonitatic lurking in the over-sized outhouse near the estate's midden pit.

Aas' prey, Narr Unerheblich, didn't own the property. She rented the outhouse from the Verzweiflung for an exorbitant fee.

But then Geisteskranken rarely make sane choices. Aas had to laugh at the thought. Here he was, crouched on a roof, intent on killing a mad-woman living in an outhouse on the orders of another insane woman, herself a Fragment of yet another unstable mind.

When you've killed Narr and Nimmer, what then?

Then he'd be the last person alive who knew Pharisäer was not Zerfall. Did Captain Gedankenlos know? Killing that patronizing arse would be a pleasure.

Would she have someone else kill him, or might she have further use for a killer? His soul would go to Swarm. *Zerfall will be there.* He wasn't sure what terrified him more, Swarm, or meeting Zerfall again. In a hell of suffering, she'd find some way of making it worse. Zerfall never forgave.

A better idea would be avoiding Swarm altogether. Forever. To do that he'd either have to escape death—unlikely for a deranged murderer with a decaying mental state—or cease believing in Swarm.

Aas grinned. *Or believe my soul will go somewhere else.*

The arrow continued its slow spin, first one direction, then another. Aas plucked a hair from his ear and held it aloft to examine the colour and thickness before tucking it into his pocket alongside the other bodily detritus collected there. The pile had grown to near fist-sized. No doubt Hölle thought he'd developed Trichotillic tendencies, but it wasn't that at all.

Really? You do rather enjoy the feel of hair sliding from flesh, that moment before it comes free.

True, but he had a reason and reason separated the sane from the delusional.

All Geisteskranken have reasons for what they do.

A crazy reason, he had to admit, was still crazy.

But I have a good reason.

Aas remembered the first time he watched an ancient *salbei*, half-starved and mad from malnutrition, move his soul from his body to possess a puppet constructed of snot and hair and nail clippings and shite. The snot puppet danced a deranged jig as if celebrating its freedom and then wandered off into the Gezackt foothills. It staggered home three days later, crumbling and flaking apart, and the *salbei* again leapt the gulf of sanity to return his soul to his body.

The ancient witch-doctor admitted one night, while drunk on fermented goat's milk and blood, that that he had once moved his soul into another's body.

All your hopes rest on the inebriated confession of a mad man.

The arrow stopped spinning.

It was a lovely theory, this idea of moving his soul from his body to Hexenwerk, his own little snot-puppet, and later to another body, but theory often failed when hurled against the mutable walls of reality. Perhaps that was why he hesitated to saw off his little finger. Making the puppet was one thing, transferring his soul to it was something else altogether. Belief defined reality. To move his soul, he'd have to not only believe he could, he'd have to *know* it. Insane as Aas was, his delusions were limited to Therianthropy and the Wahnist belief people heard his thoughts. *And maybe a few Trichotillic tendencies.*

If he doubted, even for a moment, that he could move his soul, he would fail.

The problems didn't end there. Even if he managed to convince himself—which would mean embracing an entirely new delusion and suffering additional damage to his already crumbling sanity—it only made sense to move his soul when his real body was about to die. Hexenwerk was a mad and desperate backup plan. It might save his soul from Swarm, but then he'd be trapped in a puppet of snot and hair and extremely vulnerable. He'd have to find another, stronger body.

What kind of delusion would that require?

The more he thought about it, the more insane his plan seemed.

Well then stop thinking about it!

The door to the outhouse swung open and Narr Unerheblich exited, snarling and spitting in vehement argument with a shadowy form perched on her right shoulder.

Aas nocked the arrow and shot Narr through the throat. With her head turned he was able to impale both the internal and external jugular veins. She stood, swaying and blinking for a moment, mouth opening and closing. Slim fingers rose and fluttered near the shaft, unwilling to touch it, to confirm the reality of it. The figure on her shoulder gone, Narr turned and looked up at Aas on the rooftop. He raised a hand in greeting. Never friends, they still knew each other. She lifted a hand in a small, almost wave, and collapsed. Spasms shook her body and faded to stillness.

He'd never before seen her without something immaterial lurking on one of her shoulders, whispering gods knew what in her ear. Was death a moment of sanity?

Trying to make it sound like you did something more than put an arrow in her throat and end her life?

He stood to leave and stopped, staring at the condor-fletched arrow protruding from the corpse's throat. Could he make wings for his puppet? That might make escaping whatever killed him easier. The bones of birds, however, were much lighter than the bones of men. If Aas used even his smallest finger as the puppet's spine, how long would the wings have to be to get enough lift? Would Hexenwerk even be strong enough?

Cursing, Aas dropped from the roof and went to collect his feathers. It couldn't hurt to try. He tugged at the small finger of his left hand as he walked. Soon it would have to come off. He needed Hexenwerk ready before his situation got worse.

And now to see to Nimmer. What did Pharisäer mean when she said it was a puzzle?

She knows you too well, knows you can't resist a challenge.

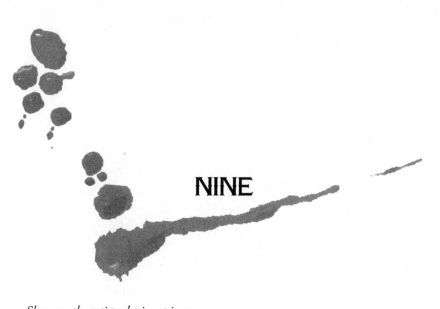

NINE

Show me the artist who is not insane
For all art is suffering, torture, and pain
We dream in colours you can not find
For we are the artists, you are the blind

—Halber Tod, Cotardist Poet

AFTER COLLECTING WHAT FEW supplies Zerfall found, she tied them about the corpse of her horse using the billet and cinch straps from the saddle. Tod looked awful. With his guts no longer distended, his torso had collapsed. Tattered skin hung fluttering about his ribs like a wind-torn tent. Even his face, already gaunt, seemed to have fallen in on itself. The sockets, once filled with big, beautiful, brown eyes, were gaping maws of wriggling rot. She scratched his ear and her hand came away coated in clumps of hair.

She heard Jateko's shuffling approach and turned to face him. He didn't look much better than the horse. Devouring Gogoko may have strengthened him and filled out his scrawny chest a bit, but the lad looked starved and dehydrated. It didn't help that his tan desert robes—*oihal* he called them—were spattered with puke and blood and caked stiff with sand.

Thank god I'm dead. His stench would probably kill me otherwise.

"We need water," she said. "There's enough to last you a day. Maybe."

"Harea will provide." He licked wind-chapped lips. "I hope." He didn't look particularly convinced.

THEY RODE WEST, JATEKO sitting behind Zerfall. He'd clearly never been on a horse before. They talked briefly, Jateko asking incessant questions, but falling to silence when her answers became little more than grunts. Eventually she fished the small book of Halber Tod's poems from its place within her mouldering clothes. Cracking it open, she read to the Basamortuan youth. He listened in rapt amazement.

"That's beautiful," he said after each poem. "I didn't understand most of it, but it was beautiful."

Tod grunted in dusty disagreement and plodded ever onward. He might not tire, but Jateko did.

"What is Geld like?" he asked.

"Much like any city-state."

"I've never seen a city."

"Well, there's lot's of stone. And mostly they stink."

"Oh." He examined her, eyes lingering, brow crinkling as he tried to form a question. "Are most of the women fat and soft?"

"Some."

He seemed disappointed. "We need to stop," he said. "I need to sleep. I'm going to fall off the horse soon."

When had the sun risen? She hadn't noticed. It now sat high in the sky.

"Why didn't you say something sooner?" she asked, sliding from Tod's back.

He shrugged, more falling off than dismounting. "Didn't want to be a burden. My mom always says I . . ." He muttered something under his breath, looking away.

Something punched Zerfall in the back three times in rapid succession. She glanced down to find three viciously barbed arrow heads protruding from the left side of her chest. She reached up and touched the point of one with a numb finger. *Well that lung won't be holding air.* She knew enough anatomy to know all three had punctured her heart. *Nice grouping.*

Jateko rolled to his feet and stood wobbling. "Etsaiaren. We're dead." He glanced at her and laughed.

"Run," she said.

"Are you running?"

"Run," she commanded. He turned and fled, long legs stretched in an ungainly sprint of nobly knees and flapping feet, faster than she would have thought possible.

Zerfall drew her knife and turned. Six men approached, their *oihal* catching the light desert breeze and dancing about them like ghosts. All shared the dark skin, lean strength, and narrowed eyes of the desert born. None had drawn weapons. They moved cautiously but showed no sign of fear. Judging the distance separating her from the men—at least two dozen strides—she noted three carried bows slung across their backs.

Zerfall glanced at Tod. On the dead horse they'd never catch her. *If I flee they'll have Jateko in minutes.* Could she buy him time to escape? To what end? He was weak, dehydrated. Without her, he'd die within two days at the most and probably less. Probably a lot less. She watched the men spread out, moving to encircle her but drawing no nearer. That was bad. If they cut off her escape, she'd have no choice but to fight.

Hölle. The Täuschung. Swarm. She had to return to Geld and end it all.

And still she didn't move.

"What little I have I will share," she offered the approaching warriors. "No water, but we have a little food."

They ignored her, moving until they had her surrounded. Did they understand her? Jateko did, but this was apparently some other tribe.

"I don't want to kill you," she said, "and I'm already dead. This is pointless."

Three of the men drew cudgels the length of her femur, each with a knot of what looked like unworked iron attached to the end. The tendons in their forearms stood taught betraying the weight of their simple weapons. The other three drew long coils of rope she'd mistaken for part of the tribal clothing and began spinning it in snaky loops over their heads.

Lassos. It never occurred to her they might not be here to kill her. The thought of being bound and helpless sent an unexpected shiver of fear coursing through her.

"You can have the horse," she said and Tod shot her a wounded look. "Sorry, Tod."

The three cudgel-carrying men approached, circling to their left, while the others remained beyond.

This looks too practised. They showed no fear and moved in perfect concert. Each man wore a long curved knife, barely short of a sword, at his hip, and yet they chose the cudgels.

It made sense. She was dead. Stabbing her would achieve nothing, while breaking her bones would immobilize her.

They've fought corpses before. How many dead wandered the desert? Apparently more than she would have thought.

One of the warriors stepped forward. Smaller than the rest, he was whipcord thin and roped with muscle. Pale scars latticed oaken skin like veins on a leaf. He eyed her with the look of a man judging a horse.

"I am Abiega Guerrero," he said, his accent indistinguishable from Jateko's. When she didn't react he added, "Of the Etsaiaren."

Zerfall shrugged apologetically, examining the man, the easy way he stood, relaxed, but poised and ready. He moved with deadly grace and perfect balance. "You're a warrior."

Abiega waved her words away with his empty hand like they fouled the air. "*Hiria ero* words are prisons. Labels mask ignorance."

"I was a warrior of sorts. Before." God damn she wished she had Blutblüte now. This small man would be meat in seconds.

He perked up, looking interested. "Really?"

"Why don't the three of you come find out?"

Abiega turned to the largest of the warriors, a huge man with bulging arms and legs like trees. "Mozolo, you are a brave warrior, no?"

Mozolo grinned disdain at the smaller man. "None braver."

Abiega gestured toward Zerfall. "Could you subdue this *hilen deabru* on your own? She looks small and weak, soft like all *hiria ero*, but she might be dangerous." The small warrior gave the larger a doubtful look. "I'd understand if you didn't want to. None in the tribe would question your bravery if you chose not to face this . . . girl."

Mozolo rolled his shoulders, loosening the muscles. He waved the other men back. "Watch."

Abiega winked at Zerfall as he retreated, seemingly pleased with the outcome. *What the hell was that about?* They had her outnumbered six to one, why endanger themselves at all?

The big man advanced, crouched low, his stance wide and solid like rooted stone. Zerfall reacted without thought, her movement liquid like water. He feinted at her with his cudgel and spinning in a complete circle, swept low with his leg. The move was fast for such a large man but the set of his hips and the position of his feet announced his intentions. Instead of retreating, Zerfall stepped forward, skipping over the sweeping leg, and stabbed the warrior six times in the liver and kidneys before he completed the turn. By the time he once again faced her, she'd retreated a step and waited with calm readiness.

Mozolo grimaced, once again rolling his muscular shoulders. "Your little knives—" Then his knees buckled and he looked up at her from where he knelt in the sand, eyes wide with confusion.

"Well done, *hilen deabru*," said Abiega, clapping as he stepped forward. "Mozolo, she has killed you."

"No. It's just . . ." Mozolo sank back to his haunches, dropped his cudgel, and reached back to feel the wounds. His hand came away splashed with blood. He glanced down to see the sand greedily swallowing his life as it leaked from his body. "The *sorgin* can heal—"

"She is a day away," said Abiega. "You have a few hundred breaths at most."

Mozolo slumped sideways into the sand with a groan, trying to staunch the many wounds. He bared white teeth in agony as his body came to terms with what had been done to it.

"And they'll be painful breaths," added Abiega. "An unpleasant way to go," he said as if commenting on the weather.

Zerfall watched, confused. Abiega seemed far more interested in Mozolo than he did in capturing her.

"Please," hissed Mozolo between clenched teeth.

"Quiet," cooed Abiega as if calming a child. "I know you planned to challenge me. You're as predictable outside a fight as in."

"You wanted me to kill him," Zerfall said.

"Either outcome was acceptable."

"Why? Did you fear he'd win his challenge?"

Abiega made a gesture with his hand she didn't understand. "You *hiria ero* call it efficiency; a concept as ugly as the word. We call it *bide sinplea*, the simple path."

"But the six of you might have subdued me without anyone dying."

"Which would have been *bide sinplea* had I not wanted Mozolo dead." He gestured at Mozolo. "He was a fearsome warrior." Abiega touched his own chest. "Abiega is not a warrior. He is more. I manipulated Mozolo unto his death and didn't lift a finger. *Bide sinplea*."

"And you got a chance to see me fight," added Zerfall.

Abiega grinned like a little boy. "Yes, that too." He hefted his cudgel and approached. "I will find somewhere beautiful in the *Santu Itsasoa*."

"What is—"

Abiega closed the distance between them faster than she would have thought possible, slapped the knife from her hand, and shattered her right knee with his cudgel. The force of the blow spun her to the ground. She lifted her head to see shards of dry bone stabbed through the parchment flesh of her knee.

The slight warrior, dark sun-wrinkled skin on bone, stood over her. The cudgel swung loose and lazy in his hand. "I'd rather not break you apart" he said. "You're easier to drag in one piece."

"Drag?" Zerfall asked, frowning at the wreckage of her knee. Dead or not, no way she'd stand on that.

"To *Santu Itsasoa*, the Sea of Souls."

"That doesn't sound so—"

"Where you will await the arrival of the All Consuming in perfect vigilance." He shrugged non-committally. "Unless Harea forgives you before then."

"Is your desert god a forgiving god?"

"Is this a forgiving desert?"

"Right. So what happens when the All Consuming arrives?"

"The end of the world," said Abiega as if nothing could be more obvious. He gestured at one of the lasso-men, a youth not much beyond the first awkward throws of puberty. "Gazte, bind her."

The young man approached, not looking pleased. He bent to bind her hands behind her back with his lasso. Were she alive, Zerfall had no doubt the circulation to her hands would have been cut off, so tightly was she bound.

"Don't forget the arrows," said Abiega.

Gazte dragged the three arrows impaling her chest free and returned them to their owners. When finished, the warrior turned to Abiega. He gestured at the lasso binding Zerfall. "This leaves me short a weapon."

"Take Mozolo's," answered Abiega.

The youth eyed Mozolo squirming in the sand. "He's not dead."

"Kill him and take a weapon, or do not."

"I thought you—"

"No."

"His belongings—"

"Go to the man who kills him."

"Or woman?" asked Zerfall.

"True. Though women rarely join demon hunts."

"Too dangerous?" she asked sarcastically.

Abiega examined her, eyes lit with humour. "No. They're too smart."

"Oh. In that case shouldn't I get his weapons?"

"No," said Abiega. "As Gazte so astutely pointed out, Mozolo is still alive. Although," he glanced at the downed warrior still twitching in the sand, "he does appear to be fading quickly."

The young warrior who'd tied her stepped forward and, drawing a knife not much longer than his hand, stabbed Mozolo repeatedly in the neck until the huge warrior stopped moving.

"Congratulations, Gazte, you have slain a great warrior." Abiega flashed Zerfall a quick smile mocking his words. "Mozolo's possessions are yours."

Gazte stripped the corpse of belongings.

Abiega nudged Zerfall with a sandal-clad toe. "Your friend?" he asked, gesturing in the direction Jateko had fled.

"Are you going after him?" she asked.

"There is no oasis in that direction for many days." Abiega glanced at the sky. "And many hours until nightfall."

He waved Gazte over. "How far to *Santu Itsasoa*?"

Gazte squinted south west, licking his lips and looking rather like a nervous student. "Less than half a day?" he said, sounding far from certain.

"So if we leave now, we'll get there before we die?" Abiega asked.

Gnawing his lower lip, Gazte hesitated. "Yes? I—"

"We leave now," said Abiega, slipping a quick wink in Zerfall's direction. "I hope you're right," he added, returning his attention to Gazte. "Or you've killed us all."

Zerfall watched Tod dwindle into the distance as they dragged her away. The Etsaiaren showed no interest in the horse.

JATEKO RAN UNTIL HIS legs gave out and then he lay in the hot sand waiting for the Etsaiaren warriors to come and kill him. He wondered at the odd compulsion that sent him sprinting into the sand but found no answer. Zerfall hadn't followed.

She stayed to buy me time.

Why would she do that? Why had she saved him? No one had ever done anything like that for him before.

She needs me. Her need drove him to his feet and he stumbled back in the direction he'd come before collapsing again to the hot sand.

He lost consciousness. Or maybe fell asleep.

When he awoke, the sun was high in the sky and his mouth felt like he'd been gargling sand. Come to think of it, he kind of had been. His stomach grumbled at the weight of sand in there. *Can I digest sand?* He wasn't sure. *Will I crap it out or* . . . He shuddered at the thought.

His tongue had swollen to fill his mouth and when he yawned, his lips cracked and bled thin blood. Sitting up, he glanced around. By his reckoning not much more than an hour had passed. Had he evaded the Etsaiaren, or had they not bothered to pursue him? Probably the latter, he decided.

Jateko stood, his knees shaky. He turned a complete circle and saw he was in a slight depression, surrounded on all side by long sloping dunes. Sand in every direction. With the sun overhead, his shadow told him nothing beyond the fact is shoulders were narrow.

She needs me. He had to move.

He set off, stumbling often as he climbed the dune.

Harea, guide me.

After reaching the crest of the dune he staggered a few paces before collapsing forward to the sand. Something sharp and hard dug into his belly but he couldn't be bothered to move. *I'm too tired. Too thirsty. I can't do this.* How long had it been since he was properly hydrated?

A shadow fell across him and the stench of rotting meat filled his nose. Jateko cracked an eye open to find himself staring up into the pits of Tod's gaping eyes.

Rising, his toe struck something hard buried in the sand where he'd previously been lying.

He glanced down to see the hilt of Zerfall's knife protruding from the sand. "Oh." After offering a quick prayer of thanks to the desert god he retrieved the long knife, tucking it into his belt and eyed the horse.

"Let's go get her back, Tod."

JATEKO RODE WITH CARE, keeping his weight balanced in the centre of Tod's broad back. Each time he adjusted his position the animal's skin slid alarmingly as if about to come free and slough away in great sheets. He rested a hand on the horse's back. The beast's muscles, cold and dead, rolled loose under the skin.

Why were they taking her south west? Nothing lay west except the *hiria ero* city-states and—*Of course. Why didn't I think of that earlier?*

Santu Itsasoa, the Sea of Souls. Etsaiaren sacred ground. They were going to break her apart and rebuild her as a skeletal totem, an eternal guardian, forever staring west across the Basamortuan sands, awaiting whatever it was the Etsaiaren feared. They were an odd tribe with strange beliefs. For the last few dozen generations they'd collected the undying and *hilen deabru* to use as wards, guards against some threat from the west. Most of the sentinels were delusional *hiria ero* who wandered into the desert to die, but there were more than a few Basamortuan tribes folk as well. Jateko's mother even suggested once that his father was somewhere in there, but she was probably lying. She did that a lot.

Jateko would love to ask the Etsaiaren what they feared so much that building an army of dead totems seemed sane, but they had a reputation for murdering members of the Hasiera tribe and wearing their flayed skins as condoms. Then again, his mother told him that too.

Zerfall needs me. He kicked the dead horse and the beast increased its pace. *She needs me.*

BOUND IN A TIGHT cocoon of coarse rope and dragged behind a young warrior, Zerfall stared out across the eternal and unchanging sands.

When did I lose the ability to blink? She wasn't sure. Her eyes had long rotted to nothing. Had they shrunk like dried grapes and fled the empty pit of her skull, or been plucked free and devoured by carrion insects? Come to think of it, how was it she could see? *I see because I expect to see, because I believe I can see.* The thought felt right, but she couldn't explain her certainty. Unfortunately, she didn't seem to believe she could blink. She had no way of shutting out the world, no means of escaping the battery of visual sensations; even when there wasn't much to look at. She missed the illusion of escape achieved by closing one's eyes. *An illusion slain by a delusion.*

She thought back to her last day in Geld. She remembered the stain on the fingertips of her right hand, the way they felt numb and distant. Had that been the first sign of her encroaching Cotardism? "This is rotten," she'd said, meaning the garbage-strewn church, the foul religion they built, the fact she just stabbed her sister, and maybe even herself.

In one of Halber Tod's poems he asked: "What kind of god does this?"

That question stuck with her, haunted her thoughts.

A book of Cotardist poems.

Rotting fingers.

Seeing the rot of her religion for the first time.

What kind of god does this?

Had reading this book of poems somehow triggered a mental collapse?

The poems were certainly bad enough.

Maybe all this is a nightmare and I'm still lying in that alley. Dying.

Sand. Monotonous endless sand.

She slid past the shrivelled corpse of a snake, baked black and twisted in agony. Its skin had collapsed and clung to protruding ribs. Even rotted and sunken it was twice as wide around as her torso and looked to be at least twenty strides long. She watched it fade into the distance. There was nothing else to look at and she had no choice but to look.

I wish I could close my eyes.

And yet in other ways she was dead to the world.

Here she was, dragged mile after mile, across hot sand. The heat and abrasion should be agony—*god knows how much skin I've lost*—and she barely felt the friction. A clump of dark hair pulled free from her disintegrating scalp and followed along behind her in a tangled knot of dried blood and corrupt flesh until coming free to be left behind. Watching it disappear from sight, she thought about the abuse she recently suffered. She'd pulled an arrow from her guts and even now her lungs and belly were no doubt coated with sand. Her heart had been pierced by no less than three barbed arrows and yet the damage to her lung was of greater concern. When they retrieved the arrows, causing further damage, she felt nothing. Each time she forced her unresponsive body to draw breath she heard air gush from the left side. If she took much more damage to her upper torso, communicating might become problematic.

The thought of spending an eternity, mute and unable to communicate, pushed her to the edge of panic and she retreated into dark sarcasm as if it would shield her from the terror of reality. *Yeah, how about spending a few thousand years stuck in the desert waiting for some tribal myth to show up?*

At first she'd been stalling, giving Jateko time to get away. No doubt pointless as the youth would in all likelihood die within a day anyway. And yet Jateko's life—no matter how short that might be—had to be worth more to her than her unlife.

Didn't it?

Why can't I answer that?

Now that he was away and free, she'd bide her time, make her move when the Etsaiaren stopped to make camp. Hopefully the hours she spent as an unresisting lump would lull them into a false sense of security.

What exactly will be false about their sense of security?

Zerfall thought about how easily Abiega disarmed her and shattered her knee. That would have gone differently had she her sword. *And not been dead.*

The sky darkened as the sun, swollen as if bloated with internal decay, sank to the west turning the cloudless sky a monochromatic smear. A giant cactus towering twice the height of a tall man slid past, a collection of sun-bleached bones embedded within. At some point a human skull had been mounted at the top but the cactus had long ago grown over and around it. Only the ridges of the brow, cheek bones, and upper jaw poked through. How slowly did cacti grow? Wouldn't that take decades, maybe longer? Zerfall picked out more detail. There, a spine hidden from view, the wind-worn spinous process bones jutting like a line of shark fins cutting through water. The bulbous head of a femur, white and smooth, gleamed dull. At the base of the cactus she saw a collection of smaller bones, some recognizable as fragments of fingers and toes. She stared up at the skull, wrapped in the tight embrace of barbed cactus flesh, and felt the weight of its gaze upon her.

It's alive. Whoever that is, however long they've been there, they're still alive. Watching. Waiting.

They dragged her by another cactus, this one smaller, with a corpse attached. Sun-bleached bones protruded at odd angles, long ago stripped clean. Thin strands of rope remained where they had once bound the bones to the plant. The rope looked strange, twisted and translucent where stretched thin. *That's not rope.* Muscle, sinew, and intestines bound the bones to the cactus. She could guess whose. They'd gut her, using her own bowels to lash her to a cactus where she'd await the coming of the All Consuming and the end of the world. That seemed like adding an unreasonable insult to injury.

Might be worse, she told herself.

A lie.

How long could sanity withstand the assault of constant nothing?

What would the All Consuming consume, the dried bones of the undying delusional?

No, our souls.

Even though moments ago she dreamed of escaping the putrescent confinement of her body, the thought of something eating her soul returned her to the screaming edge of panic. Her terror grew as they dragged her past cactus after cactus, each with human remains bound to it. Most were little more than bones, but every now and then she saw something with gristly meat stubbornly clinging. Few showed signs of desert attire, most dressed more like herself if they were clothed at all. For how long had the Etsaiaren been bringing the delusional of the city-states here?

I can't die here.

Not yet. She had to kill Hölle, bring down the awful church the two of them spent centuries building. She had to end the evil that was Swarm, somehow free the millions of souls imprisoned there. She had to kill Wahrergott, the gaoler god she created.

It can't end here.

Blutblüte, Zerfall's sword. Hölle had it and Zerfall wanted it back so bad she had to fight down the urge to try and tear herself free of these ropes. *She has my sword and my hand.*

In a colourless world of decaying senses Zerfall remembered the hand with startling clarity; that closed eye seemed more real than anything in her ever-collapsing reality. She remembered the way the eye looked like it was about to open.

Damned tattoo never worked right.

The desert faded away.

A petite woman, curved and soft, sat in a bed large enough for six. She hunched forward, one arm held across her stomach as if perhaps she suffered a bellyache, reading a stack of papers piled before her. Chestnut brown hair hung long, thick and glowing with luxuriant health, around her shoulders hiding her face from view.

Hölle. Aas told Zerfall the woman still lived, but seeing her was altogether different. So many memories. They were everything to each other. *She was my only companion in the darkest times.* They shared so much more than their mad quest to free humanity through their hallucinated hell of suffering. *How could I have believed such madness?* The words of Wahrergott bound them. Words Zerfall no longer heard or remembered. She'd worry the blow that crushed the back of her skull somehow stole the truth of the One True God, but she'd already lost faith when she stabbed Hölle.

Her sister. Her Fragment.

I'm going to kill you, she told the woman on the bed.

A second woman of slimmer build paced into view, a sword hanging at her right hip. *That's wrong, it shouldn't*—The woman with the sword sat down on the bed beside the first and ran a finger through the other's hair, pushing it back and hooking it over an ear in a heartbreakingly familiar move. Zerfall studied her profile, the small nose, the soft swell of the lower lip. *I know that face. That's me.* Except it wasn't.

Drowning in memories of how things had once been with Hölle, Zerfall wanted to apologise for hurting her. Even more, she wanted to cut her down, spill her blood across the filthy floor of their chambers.

The two women turned and, for a brief instant, stared at her.

Zerfall found herself looking up at a mangled corpse bound to a cactus in blue-black ropes of its own viscera. *Not more than a few days old. It looks fresher than I do.* The terror which moments before her sudden vision threatened to engulf her, returned with thought-shattering force. The corpse's belly hung gutted and open. Carrion beetles battled over shreds of meat within that gaping wound and writhed throughout the ripe organs spilled at the base of the cactus. The limbs had been crudely hacked off, stripped of muscle, and bound at its sides with sinew stretched to the point of breaking. The head, neck ragged from where it had been torn away from the spine, sat perched atop the cactus. A single milky eyeball hung from a puckered socket, swinging in the breeze. It focussed on her.

"Someone else has been here recently," said Abiega, examining the corpse with an appraising eye. "Sloppy work." He pointed out a snapped sinew allowing a chunk of what looked like upper thigh to sag. "This will fall off within the year. Probably Axolagabe. Lazy bastard." He turned a wry smile on Zerfall. "We'll do a better job."

"Please no," she tried to plead but it came out as little more than a weak cough of dust. Once again she'd forgotten to draw breath to power her words. She sucked in air but let it whistle from her torn lung when Abiega turned away to congratulate Gazte on not leading them to their deaths. The young warrior strutted about with a puffed out chest and Zerfall would have found it endearing were it not for the fact they planned to hack her apart and leave her tied to a god-damned cactus for the rest of eternity.

Keep it together. Wait and watch. You're going to be fine.

No. She was waiting to be butchered like a cow in a slaughterhouse.

Calm. Calm. Calm.

As the sun set, the Etsaiaren bustled about, erecting their *karpan* and joking about the shoddy work of whoever mounted the most recent corpse. Zerfall struggled to ignore them, to think about anything else. Her head lolled, trying to look at anything other than the mutilated corpse above her. Horizon to horizon in every direction, broken bodies adorned cacti. Thousands of bodies. Maybe tens of thousands. Fallen cacti, brown and hollowed with rot, littered the landscape, their undead burdens either pinned face-first into the sand or staring forever into endless sky. Didn't cacti live to be two hundred years old or more? How long had the Etsaiaren been doing this? She shied from the thought.

There couldn't be this many Cotardists. Maybe *hilen deabru* meant more than she understood. Maybe each and every one of these corpses wasn't a lost soul, trapped forever in its rotted husk, awaiting the coming of the All Consuming and the end of the world. Maybe—

Movement caught her eye. Entranced she watched the swaying eyeball with hypnotized intensity. *It's looking at me.*

The mouth of the severed head opened in a cavernous yawn spilling the worms and insects feeding on what remained of its tongue and Zerfall lost herself, drowning in an endless ocean of terror.

She screamed without air, mouth wide and silent.

"**W**HAT'S WRONG?" ASKED PHARISÄER, glancing over her shoulder to see what captured Hölle's attention.

Hölle, her skin crawling like soft fingers tickled the short hair at the back of her neck, ignored Pharisäer. She stared past her, eyes narrowing. Zerfall's grey hand lay palm up on her desk. Had she imagined seeing the tattooed eye slip closed? *Zerfall, is that you?* No, that was impossible.

The world shivered and bled colour. She felt translucent, a water colour painting left in the rain.

The hand hadn't changed or decayed since the hideous assassin dropped it there. He said Zerfall had become a Cotardist. Did being freed of her decaying mind and body protect the hand from rot? It didn't make much sense, but in Hölle's experience, expecting logic from reality usually ended in disappointment. Perhaps she hallucinated the eye closing, a minor slip in control. Considering the stress she was under, she could hardly be blamed for a few petty hallucinations.

What if it isn't rotting because she's alive? What if the reason I keep feeling like she'll show up at any moment is because she might? Aas, the sagging sack of puckered skin. He admitted to leaving Zerfall alive. *He promised she'd die out there, poisoned and gut-shot.* Had he lied? No, not possible; his ceaseless brain-spew would have betrayed him. But could he have been mistaken? What if she hadn't died? She might be out there, even now, hunting and haunting Hölle.

Pharisäer leaned forward, reaching a hand toward Hölle. "Are you—"

Hölle waved her to silence and leaned away from the hand. She couldn't afford the distraction, she needed to think.

Why in all bloody Swarm hadn't Aas killed Zerfall when he had the chance? *Because you told him not to.*

Oh, so it was her fault now?

No. Aas should have made sure Zerfall suffered, but stayed with her until the very end. It wasn't her fault; the man was a moron.

She drew a sharp breath and held it. *I knew Zerfall wasn't dead. I knew it and I ignored my instincts because—*

Returning her attention to Pharisäer, Hölle scowled, confused and scared. "Why are you so sure Zerfall is dead?"

"Me?" Pharisäer asked, eyes widening in surprise and maybe a little hurt. "Well, Aas said she was dead. We'd know if he lied."

True. Pharisäer's thoughts mirrored Hölle's own. *Not surprising, I suppose.* "She was alive when he left. Aas said the Düster poison would kill her."

"No one survives that. And even if she did, Aas said she'd become a Cotardist. She'd die the moment the rot reached her heart, as do all Cotardists."

Did they? That's what everyone said, but she felt wriggling worms of doubt twist in her belly. *If everyone believes Cotardists die when the rot reaches their heart, then that must be the truth.* Belief defined reality. "What if he was wrong?"

"Aas has many faults. He's hideous, odious, predictable, smelly, insane, easily manipulated, violent, lacking in anything even approaching a moral compass, and he loves the women who loathe him most, but he knows his poisons. If he said she would die, she is dead." Again Pharisäer reached for Hölle and again Hölle leaned away. "Come, what's this about? You can't really be worried about Zerfall."

But she was. Zerfall consumed her thoughts. Every night she dreamed her sister getting closer, becoming more and more real, while Hölle faded. She didn't want Pharisäer to know; she'd see it as weakness. "What do you mean he loves the women who loathe him most?"

Pharisäer blinked and frowned, a small crinkle in her perfect brow. "Zerfall. You. Don't tell me you hadn't noticed the way he looks at you."

"He's always trying to look down my shirt. That doesn't mean—"

Pharisäer's laugh stopped her. "He has the social skills of a fourteen-year-old boy and the class of a rutting pig in heat. But he'd do anything for you. Just as he would for Zerfall. Were she alive."

Could that be true? Zerfall was the Gefahrgeist, shepossessed guile and charm enough for both. Hölle had always been awkward with people, annoyed when they couldn't follow simple instructions. Freeing humanity from its prison was too great a task to allow indulgences of flesh and emotion to get in the way. But Pharisäer was smooth and comfortable, like Zerfall. Did she possess some of Zerfall's Gefahrgeist tendencies? *Does Aas now love Pharisäer as he once loved Zerfall? If he does love me, does he love her more?* She knew the answer and felt a stab of jealousy. It made no sense, she loathed everything about the man. And Pharisäer seemed too happy, too sure of herself. It was like she knew something Hölle didn't and a triumphant smirk lurked behind every smile, every expression of love and concern.

Pharisäer leaned closer but made no attempt to touch Hölle. "What's wrong?"

"What do you know of Cotardists?"

Pharisäer accepted the question as if it were not at all strange. "Same as you. It's a delusion typically fed by self-loathing. Most decay only in part, until a limb becomes shrivelled. Extreme cases think they're actually dying and the rot spreads further. If the decay reaches their heart or internal organs they die."

"It doesn't make sense."

"What doesn't?"

"Zerfall, a Cotardist. She loved herself."

Pharisäer gave her an indecipherable look, quickly masked. "Perhaps your sister hid something from you. Perhaps that illusion of self-love masked some deeper hurt or hatred." Pharisäer shrugged apologetically, reached a hand toward Hölle, but stopped short of actual contact like she feared rejection. "She did betray you. Something wasn't right." She bit her bottom lip and her fingertips brushed feather-light on Hölle's knee. "You can't think this is your fault." Her brow furrowed in concern. "Tell me that isn't what this is about."

"No, of course not. There was no way I could have foreseen her betrayal." Did she sound defensive?

"Of course not," soothed Pharisäer.

She glanced again at Zerfall's hand. "Do Cotardists *always* die when the rot spreads far enough?"

"You can't live without a beating heart."

"True." She remembered her thought from earlier: Expecting logic from reality usually ended in disappointment. "Aas said Zerfall lost her memory. He said she didn't know who or what she was, that she lost her Gefahrgeist power."

"So?"

The thought coalesced, built upon itself, solidifying and becoming real. "What if she didn't know? What if she didn't know Cotardists are supposed to die when the rot spreads?"

"She's only one person. And Aas said she lost her delusions."

"But there was no one else out there, no other belief but hers for maybe hundreds of miles." *She was so strong.*

Pharisäer examined her, a sardonic eyebrow cocked. "You think she might not have died because she didn't know she was supposed to? That's insane."

"So was Zerfall. Powerfully so." Hölle nodded to herself, certain. "If anyone could survive Cotardism, it's her."

"But what about the Düster poison? She would have *known* that would kill her."

"Yes," she said, dragging out the word. "But what if she didn't know she'd been poisoned? Did Aas tell her the arrow was poisoned?"

"That doesn't . . . shouldn't . . ." Pharisäer stumbled to a stop when she met Hölle's eyes. "I'll ask Aas. At least we can know that much."

"The fool should have stayed with her, made sure she was dead. Really dead." Hölle made a fist but stopped short of punching the bed in frustration. "I'm surrounded by idiots. Incompetents."

"He failed you," agreed Pharisäer. "It wasn't your fault."

Is that sarcasm? Hölle searched Pharisäer's eyes. No, she must have imagined it.

Pharisäer rubbed Hölle's leg. "You're under a lot of pressure, and you're healing from a wound that would have killed anyone else." She smiled, her eyes damp with love and concern. "I'll take care of this. If Zerfall is alive, I'll find her. I'll make sure she's dead. Really dead."

Hölle winced as the memory of pain stabbed her gut. Pharisäer was right, she needed to rest. She was under a lot of pressure; it wasn't her fault if she leapt to conclusions. *I'm so tired.* The world looked like she viewed it through spidery gauze, pale and muted in colour.

"Rest," said Pharisäer. "Get some sleep."

Hölle shut her eyes, but couldn't shake the image of the tattooed hand, the dark eye sliding closed in the centre of the palm.

AN HOUR LATER PHARISÄER paced the cramped shop of Zahlen Liegen, the wizened old man who maintained the Täuschung's books. She had to turn sideways to fit down the narrow aisles. Scrolls and leather-bound tomes sat tucked in every nook and cranny. Leaning closer she saw countless scraps of paper, often little more than corners torn off larger sheets and scribbled on in a cramped and hectic hand, jammed into every space. It was all very dusty, clearly untouched in years. Everything smelled of ancient parchment, dried vellum, and cracking leather. Her nose tickled with the dust.

She'd introduced herself as Zerfall and the Täuschung bookkeeper accepted it without comment. It rankled that she had to lie, but someday that lie would become the truth. First, however, she needed to destroy Hölle and part of that would be wrecking her life's work.

She glanced at where Zahlen sat squinting into the Täuschung ledgers. "None of this has been touched or looked at in years," she said. "Why not get rid of it and make yourself a little room?"

"Geld law says all financial and tax records must be kept for fifteen years," he said, without looking up from the book.

"Everything is covered in years of dust." She glanced at the nearest books. Many of the spines were no longer legible, the text faded to gaunt scratches. "How often do you have to find stuff in here?"

"Never. I only keep it so I can say it has been kept and not lie." He looked up, checking to see no one else was in the shop. "They can tell when you lie. But if you don't lie about keeping the documentation, they never actually check the back records."

"Geld law is insane," she muttered to herself, returning to her pacing.

"Geld law is the very definition of sane," he said, offended. "Geld law keeps the city peaceful and organized and profitable." It was clear which one he thought the most important.

Pharisäer had no interest in a discussion of the sanity of laws created and enforced by the wealthy and blindly followed by the poor and allegedly sane masses. *Sanity in no way guarantees intelligence.* "Have you found the records I want?"

"Of course," he said.

"So?"

"The church is quite profitable. Even after taxes—"

"Excellent!"

"But most of that goes into supporting . . ." He pursed his lips. ". . . the other church." He shrugged. "The older church is on prime real-estate in the centre of the city. The property taxes in that neighbourhood are the highest in all Geldangelegenheiten. And then there are the bribes and cover-ups the Täuschung pay every year to keep its true nature a secret. If your less than sane priests were a little more circumspect, did a little less damage to the city, you would save a great deal." He waved her to silence when he saw her about to speak. "Everything else goes to maintaining Täuschung churches, almost always two of them, in other city-states. You barely break even."

All this wealth going to fund a stupid religion. Apparently crazy was no guarantee of intelligence either. "We're going in a new direction," she said. *Spiralling into madness.* "Making some changes."

Zahlen shrugged, uncaring.

"I want you to sell off all the properties outside of Geld. All of them."

"That's not really what I do," he protested. "I'm an accountant, not a—"

"You'll get five percent of every sale," she said. Compared to the amount of gold haemorrhaging out of the church every year, giving away five percent was nothing. "Find whoever you need to make this happen. Take care of everything."

The accountant's mouth fell open and she saw him running calculations in his head. She'd just made him fantastically wealthy. She knew he'd still steal, skim off the top, but didn't care. This wasn't about making money—though she'd certainly come out of this one of the richest women in Geld—it was about ruining Hölle.

"And stop all bribes," she added. When the Täuschung's mad priests ran rampant destroying the city—as she planned to have them doing shortly—she wanted it to come back to haunt Hölle.

"That's not—"

"Figure it out. You'll get five percent of whatever you manage to save."

Zahlen nodded, stunned.

"I'll check in for updates each week." Pharisäer grinned, feeling more alive, more real than she ever had. This was progress. "Don't worry about getting the best price. I want this to happen fast."

"And Hölle?" Zahlen asked.

Time to spread some rumours. "She's very ill." Pharisäer gave a sad sigh. "Soon it will be just me."

The accountant's eyes lit with understanding. "I shall begin immediately."

"Good." She turned to leave and stopped. "I've changed my mind. Sell everything. Both properties here in Geld." Why leave Hölle something to cling to?

I'll reduce her stupid religion to dust.

PHARISÄER WHISTLED AS SHE walked the streets of Geld. It would take months to sell off the church's holdings, but by this time next year she'd be fabulously wealthy. It was easy manipulating Hölle into staying in her chambers. The woman now put very little effort into maintaining herself—Pharisäer shivered in disgust at the memory of the stench and filth staining the rooms. *Hölle will crack in the next few weeks.* Maybe sooner if events played out just right.

Here, on Lender's Row, the buildings were built to look like banks, if much smaller. Even the cobbled street, stones alternating in patterns of green and grey, mimicked the streets on the Banking District. Yet somehow everything had a slightly shoddy look to it. Marble, brass, and granite still abounded, but lacked lustre. Everything looked smudged and worn, like old money fallen on hard times. She glanced up and down the street, seeing exactly the same wear on every building.

If just one of these lenders hired someone to polish their storefront, they'd stand out above the others.

But none of them had. It certainly wasn't from lack of funds. Was this a choice? Was there some local bi-law enforcing this appearance, or was this a sound business practice? Did sane people want money lenders to mimic banks yet seem small and grotty? Real-estate cost a fortune everywhere in Geld and this was by no means one of the cheaper districts.

There could be no understanding the sane.

The insane, however?

Pharisäer grinned to herself at the thought of Aas confronting Nimmer. Removing him had been critical. He knew too much about Geisteskranken and realized she was a Fragment rather than some sending of Hölle's imaginary god. But did he know that Hölle was a Fragment rather than Zerfall's twin sister? She didn't want the hideous man sharing that information with Hölle. How the stupid woman went centuries without knowing the truth of her existence, Pharisäer couldn't comprehend. Maybe belief in her silly god and even sillier purpose—free humanity to be gods by sending them to a hell of suffering, what a laughable concept—somehow maintained her. Pharisäer neither knew nor cared. All that mattered was that she could and would take full advantage of the woman's ignorance. With Aas out of the picture for the foreseeable future, ignorant she would remain.

What should I do next? Pharisäer considered her options. The more damage done to Hölle's church, the more wounded the woman would be, the more depressed. Hölle's dreams and goals had to be undone, reduced to ruin. She must to see her life's work as an utter failure.

Pharisäer considered the church. The weakness of the Täuschung had always been the Geisteskranken priests making up the hidden religion existing beneath the heaven-preaching public façade. *I need to get rid of them.* If Hölle saw her priests leaving, it would further weaken her. *Can I send them away?* Perhaps she could invent reasons to litter the mad priests throughout the city-states. She thought about Aas, soon to be trapped in Nimmer's reality. Sending the assassin to kill the man really was a stroke of genius. A grin lit Pharisäer's face. *A schism within the church!* She'd pit the Täuschung priests against each other. There'd be death in the streets and the church would be in chaos.

How lucky that Zerfall was so feared by her mad priests. They'd obey Pharisäer no matter how insane or contradictory her orders were.

She hurried back to the Täuschung compound, deciding who to send after whom. She'd keep a small cadre of the most powerful, most unstable, as backup. She could either use them as weapons against any foes who may rise up against her, or as a last blow to Hölle's sanity.

Time to turn the Täuschung mad loose on the streets of Geld.

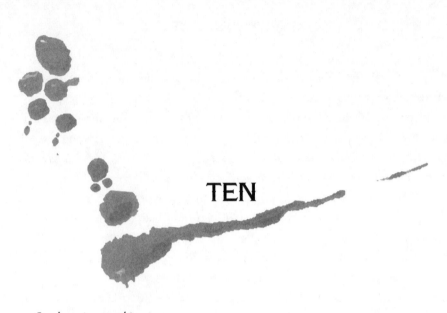

TEN

Sand gets in everything.

—Basamortuan Proverb

*Z*ERFALL NEEDS ME.

Jateko rode atop Tod's bony back, lurching from side to side. Only fistfuls of Tod's mane and the grip of his legs around the horse's gutted torso kept him mounted. His thighs burned like someone doused them in oil and lit them afire, and his fingers and knuckles ached from being clenched tight for so long. Every now and then the horse tilted alarmingly as the sand under its hooves gave way and Jateko tore matted clumps from Tod's ever-thinning mane trying to keep from falling off.

She needs me.

How the hell did Zerfall do this? She made it look easy, the way her hips rolled with each step. The thought of those swaying hips left Jateko with an uncomfortable feeling deep in his gut.

She's dead. You can't think of her like that.

And he didn't. Not really. And yet . . .

You have the horse. Why are *you chasing after her?*

"Because she needs me," he answered, his voice a dry whisper. Jateko frowned at the back of Tod's head and the horse ignored him. *When did I start questioning?*

Let's say we take this crazy mad god crap seriously. Do you really think Zerfall needs the help of a stupid and scrawny boy?

Jateko felt the knife he'd tucked into his belt press against his belly. It was one of hers.

The *hiria ero* of the city-states had all kinds of strange ideas about debts. Out here in the Basamortuan, the tribesmen knew what real debt was. Blood. Life.

You owe her a blood debt?

Did that sound like Gogoko? "I do."

Jateko's breath caught. He'd eaten Gogoko, the warrior was part of him now. It *was* Gogoko.

Once your blood debt has been repaid, you can go your separate ways.

"I don't want to go my separate ways."

I know.

SUN.

Funny shaped cactus.

Sand.

That cactus had ribs.

Really thirsty.

Did that cactus have a head?

Up one side of a dune.

Another odd looking cactus.

Down the other side.

Was there a body tied to that cactus?

He wanted to stop and split open a cactus, drink whatever he found inside, but Zerfall needed him.

Either the sun was sinking toward the horizon and night would soon fall, or he'd got turned around and lost track of time and was now seeing the sunrise. Both possibilities seemed likely.

Jateko swayed on Tod's back, narrowly avoiding falling off. Had he fallen asleep? When he tried to swallow his throat made a dry clicking sound. It felt like he'd eaten a live locust and it was lodged in there somewhere.

You're dying of dehydration. Again.

He blinked.

There, not fifty paces ahead, a *karpan* hunched in the sand, the front flaps tied back. A man sat within, eyeing Jateko with interest. The tribal scarring ridged across his face and scalp where the skin had been slashed open, peeled back and filled with sand, marked him as an Etsaiaren warrior of some notoriety. When he stood, it was like he unfolded in one smooth movement. He walked like he barely touched the sand, like he floated above it. Perfect. Poised.

Gogoko kind of moved like that.

Not quite like that.

The man, eyeing the horse with some distaste, approached and stood beside Tod who had stopped walking of his own accord. "You followed us."

"You took my friend," answered Jateko, looking down at the warrior and realizing how short the man was.

Just ride straight into their camp. Brilliant.

"The *hilen deabru?*"

"She says she isn't—"

The man cut him off with little more than a frown and gestured at a pile of sand beside the *karpan*. "There it is." he said, tilting his head to one side.

Jateko squinted at the unmoving lump in the sand. "Is she alive?"

"Such things never die."

"Good. I want her back."

"No."

Jateko decided to try again. "I am Jateko," he said, in his biggest deepest voice which didn't sound nearly as big and deep as he hoped. He tried to swallow, to find some saliva, and *click* went his throat. Then he toppled off Tod, landing with a pained grunt on already bruised ribs.

The short man turned away. "Gazte!" He bellowed at the tent. "Come kill this idiot. He has a nice knife."

For some reason this reminded Jateko of the words *zama gurtza* in the ancient language. It had something to do with collecting things left behind by the gods.

As Jateko pushed himself to his feet and tried to brush the sand from his blood-caked robes, a young man, showing only a few of the ridged scars, exited the *karpan* and examined him with a critical eye.

"He doesn't look like much," said Gazte.

Several other men exited the tent and stood watching.

"Looks can be deceiving," the short one said. "Though in this case, you are correct."

That's Abiega!

"No, he's too young," said Jateko.

"He's sun-addled," said the young man with a look of disgust. "There is no honour in killing a defenceless idiot."

"Honour, no," said the short warrior. "But there is a nice knife."

No, the short one.

"Abiega's a midget?" Jateko laughed, feeling dizzy.

The short man turned back to Jateko, his face a mask that would impress a rock. "Pardon?"

"Nothing," said Jateko. "Someone told me you were Abiega Guerrero."

"Someone?" the short man asked, glancing around with a look of mild perplexity.

"You can't be Abiega. You're a scrawny little midget," said Jateko.

"Never mind, Gazte," said the short man, waving the youth back. "I'll kill him myself."

It's Abiega. You're dead.

"Really?" Jateko asked.

Yes.

"Yes," said Abiega. "I'm really going to kill you."

Jateko grabbed for Zerfall's knife tucked in his belt and fumbled it, dropping it at his feet.

By Harea you are the clumsiest oaf I have ever met.

Jateko stared at the knife for a moment before looking up to meet Abiega's eyes.

Click went his throat.

"Well?" Abiega asked. "Are you going to pick that up?"

Jateko licked his lips with a tongue like the inside of an old sandal and glanced again at the knife. "If I do, are you going to kill me?" None of this felt real.

"Yes."

"And if I don't?"

Abiega's eyes narrowed to thin, angry slits.

"Thought so," said Jateko. He licked his lips again, his tongue, impossibly, even drier than before. *Click.* "Can I have some water first?"

No one moved.

"Right then." Jateko eyed the knife lying in the sand between his feet. "What should I do?"

Die with a blade in your hands at the very least.

"Right," he said, stooping to pick up the weapon.

The squat warrior drew his own weapon and circled to his right. Jateko, who'd never been in an actual fight, stood motionless, watching.

Weapon is in his right hand and he circles to the right. Move to your right, turn your body to present a smaller target.

Jateko did as instructed. Abiega Guerrero looked bored, frighteningly calm, as he followed.

"You don't have to kill him," said Zerfall from where she was bound at the side of the *karpan*. "Let him go. He's harmless."

Switch the knife to your left hand.

"But I'm right handed."

You're useless with either hand. Do it.

Jateko moved the knife to his left hand and Abiega's eyes narrowed.

You're confusing him.

"I'm confusing me," Jateko admitted.

Shut up!

"Well then stop talking to me. I'm supposed to be fighting this damned midget." This little man was going to gut him and all he could think about was blood.

Not water?

Abiega darted forward and Jateko stumbled away in a clumsy retreat, only narrowly avoiding falling on his ass.

"Ha! Missed!" Fire lit across Jateko's belly in a searing line. It stung like a thousand angry wasps. "Ow!" He touched his stomach and the fingers came away streaked in blood.

"So thirsty."

Stop looking at your hand.

Jateko focussed past his hand in time to see Abiega drop and spin. Legs swept from under him, Jateko crashed to the sand in an ungainly heap, accidentally cutting himself with his own knife.

Get up.

Abiega retreated several paces, examining Jateko with the slightest frown, and stood waiting. Thin rivulets of blood dripped from the tip of his knife.

Get up!

"I heard you the first time," muttered Jateko as he pushed himself back to his feet with a grunt of pain. His ribs, already abused, sent sharp stabs of pain into his chest with each breath.

Seeing him back on his feet, Abiega once again approached, moving like a desert snake sliding across hot sand.

"I hate snakes," muttered Jateko, remembering how often he'd been bitten while collecting them for mother's gritty soup.

"Jateko." Zerfall rolled and now lay facing him. She looked terrible; much of the skin along one side had been abraded away leaving little more than rotting muscle and desiccated meat. "If you drop the knife and run away, they might not chase you."

Her voice sounded wrong. Sad beyond all comprehension. Devoid of life and hope. His heart broke. *She needs me.*

Jateko glanced at Abiega and the little man stared back, expressionless.

It's a better plan than dying here.

"No it's not," said Jateko, standing tall. "I am Jateko," he repeated, more to calm himself than anything else. "And I will eat your brain."

Abiega's mask slipped a little at that, though Jateko wasn't sure if it was fear or disgust.

"I see your fear," Jateko said, baring his teeth.

No, that was definitely disgust.

"Shush." Jateko crouched, holding the knife out in front of him, hoping it might keep the little warrior at bay.

Don't hold the knife out—

Jateko's knife spun from numb fingers to land half a dozen paces away. "Hey—" And again his feet were swept out from under him. The back of his head slammed into the sand, shooting bright sparks and slashes of white fire across his vision. When his eyes cleared, Abiega waited several paces away, arms crossed.

"Beg," said Abiega, "and I'll end this quickly. Stand, and I'll flay you alive."

Jateko crawled toward his knife and called "I haven't stood yet," over his shoulder.

The little warrior sighed, but waited.

I don't know if that was clever, or the stupidest thing I've ever seen.

"It was clever," answered Jateko, clutching his knife and rising to his feet.

Abiega pursed his lips in annoyance and for a moment Jateko thought he would speak.

Keep your knife moving.

Moving the knife around in what he hoped looked like a threatening manner, Jateko again approached the Etsaiaren warrior.

Be ready—

"I am ready."

Abiega stepped in, kicked Jateko on the outside of the knee, crumpling the leg, and slashed him twice more across the belly as he collapsed to the sand. Blood ran and Jateko's *oihal* hung in shredded tatters. This time it took Jateko several attempts to regain his feet and when he did, he stood swaying. He touched fingers to the blood and then licked them clean. That wasn't right. It wasn't his own blood he wanted.

"So thirsty."

More than anything he wanted to lie down in the sand and close his eyes. "I'm tired of this." He tried to swallow and his throat clicked painfully. "He keeps giving me weird looks."

You're talking to yourself.

"I'm talking to *you*."

Abiega's eyes widened a little at this outburst.

He's playing with you.

"It's a crappy game." Jateko watched the liquid dance of the Etsaiaren warrior's knife, the way the sun glinted of its pristine blade. The slow drip, drip of blood.

Stop focussing on his knife.

"It's beautiful."

Abiega advanced, balance perfect. The little bastard was grinning now, but there was something about the grin.

"I'm going to peel you," Abiega said.

Jateko retreated, keeping his free hand pressed to his belly. It felt like his guts might tumble free. "Is it just me, or does he look a little nervous?"

He pities you.

"I think he's scared."

Watch his chest and shoulders.

"Why would I—"

Abiega's shoulders moved and Jateko screamed in terror. Eyes clenched shut, he lashed out with Zerfall's knife. He felt the knife torn from his fingers and something hot splashed across his face.

Open your eyes, idiot!

Abiega knelt before Jateko, struggling to staunch the gush of blood pouring from his gaping throat.

No one in the camp moved, all eyes fixed on Abiega until the short warrior toppled forward to lie at Jateko's feet. Glancing down Jateko saw his already filthy robes were spattered with fresh blood. Some had landed on his lips and he licked what he could reach with his tongue. "More," he whispered.

You'd better say something fast or you're going to have to fight the rest of them.

Jateko tore his gaze away from Abiega and the blood soaking into the sand around him. He was so thirsty and that blood looked deliciously wet. *Click.*

Zerfall and four remaining Etsaiaren warriors watched him. The hands of the Etsaiaren hovered near weapons.

"I am Jateko."

You've already said that. Twice.

"I know." The Etsaiaren blinked in confusion but none moved to attack. He ran a hand through his hair and it came away red with blood. He licked clean his fingers, ignoring the sharp grit of sand. "I'm so thirsty," he said, by way of explanation. "I'm dying." Jateko swallowed. *Click.* He looked at the corpse leaking blood onto his feet. "I want that blood so bad. I want—" *Click.* Suddenly terrified they'd steal the corpse, claim it for their own, he returned his attention to the Etsaiaren. "Abiega is mine," he snarled through clenched teeth. "I killed him. He's mine. All mine. Heart. Liver. Kidneys. I claim him."

Don't forget the brain.

"Yes. I'll eat the brain first."

One of the Etsaiaren took a step back, eyes wide.

"I'm so thirsty," Jateko said again. Blood and organs filled his thoughts, left room for nothing else. "So hungry."

"He is," said Zerfall, "the All Consuming."

Now would be a good time to do something insane like—

Jateko couldn't take it anymore. If he didn't drink he'd lose his mind. Dropping to his knees he buried his face in Abiega's open neck. He sucked greedily, drinking in all he could.

That should do it, you can stop now.

Jateko ignored the voice in his head. Nothing mattered but blood and slaking the thirst threatening to shred apart his sanity.

"YOU TOOK MY FRIEND." Jateko's voice snapped Zerfall from the bleak eternity of misery.

Oh Jateko, what have you done? She willed this to be nothing more than some delusion or bad dream. He couldn't possibly be crazy enough to have followed the Etsaiaren warriors.

She heard Abiega's unmistakable voice, calm, with a hint of humour. "There it is."

Leave me here. It doesn't matter. I'm broken. In so many ways. *This is rotten.* Zerfall's flesh. The mad religion she birthed. All reality.

She turned her head so she could see the Basamortuan youth. He looked terrified but defiant. *He'll die now.*

"I want her back," said Jateko.

The words, said with utter certainty, ripped through Zerfall, shattered her dark thoughts. He wanted her. He'd followed a half dozen Etsaiaren warriors and confronted them. His need fed her need, ignited that spark she thought long dead, slain by Aas' arrow. She'd given up because she had no reason not to. *Everyone needs a reason.*

Jateko would be hers. *And vengeance.* Hölle and Aas would die for what they did to her. She'd bring it all down, leave her mad church in utter ruin.

Zerfall watched, helpless, as Abiega repeatedly knocked Jateko to the sand. At first she prayed that he'd run away, that the little warrior would see he was no threat and let him go. Then, as hope died, she prayed he'd stay down, accept the quick death offered. Each time Jateko climbed to his feet he moved a little slower, left a little more blood soaking into the sand.

Bound and helpless, Zerfall watched Abiega slice apart her reason to live.

Stumbling, weak with blood-loss and dying from dehydration, Jateko once again stood before his opponent. The young man's knees wobbled as he kept up a stream of meaningless banter. No hint of fear showed in his eyes.

"I think he's scared," Jateko blurted, grinning blood at Abiega

Abiega would kill him now, Zerfall saw it in his narrowed eyes, the way he adjusted his grip on the knife. Jateko, too busy arguing with himself, wasn't even paying attention.

The short Etsaiaren warrior moved faster than any snake, knife licking out like a fork of lightening.

Eyes clenched shut, Jateko cut him down.

Straining against the ropes, Zerfall pushed herself into a sitting position. Jateko stood over Abiega, babbling and raving. She glanced to the remaining Etsaiaren and saw their indecision. Jateko, scrawny and on his last legs, hardly cut an imposing figure. And yet he had killed their greatest warrior. Gazte reached for his knife.

Zerfall wheezed, cursed the lack of air in her lungs, and drew breath. "He is the All Consuming."

Jateko dropped to his knees, burying his face in Abiega's open throat. Gazte and the remaining Etsaiaren warriors bolted.

Zerfall watched Jateko pull open the diminutive warrior's throat with his bare hands and drink the blood pooling in the gaping wound. He worked with a fixed expression, one of rapt concentration. Whatever possessed him, she had this strange feeling she didn't want it focussed on her. She waited in silence.

When he sat back, licking his lips, she called his name.

He stared at her, unblinking, for long enough she thought maybe he'd become catatonic.

"Jateko? It's me, Zerfall."

"Did they hurt you?" he asked.

Hurt? More like broke. "No. Well, yes, but it didn't hurt."

"Oh." He finally blinked and started as if he'd just noticed the body at his knees.

"Can you cut me free?" she asked when he continued to stare at the corpse.

She watched as he made some internal decision, nodded, searched the sands until he spotted his knife, and crawled to retrieve it. Then he crawled to her side and sawed with feverish intensity at the ropes binding her. His breath came in shallow gasps, his sun-darkened face flushed an unhealthy and florid red underneath its liberal coating of fresh blood.

"Are you all right?" she asked.

"Too weak," he said with forced calm. "Have to free you before I lose consciousness." He stopped sawing and stared at the rope. For a moment she thought he'd forgotten what he was doing. "You're my only friend," he whispered. "If I pass out I'll die. You'll be stuck here forever." He returned to sawing, teeth bared in a silent snarl.

When the ropes parted he collapsed with a sigh of gratitude and lay sprawled, eyes closed, in the sand. Though not all of the blood covering him was his own, a lot was.

"Zerfall?"

She pulled the rest of the ropes away, freeing her arms and legs. "Yes?"

"Can you get something for me?"

"The brain?"

"Yeah." He laughed weakly.

Something about that laugh sounded unlike the Jateko she knew. It sounded older.

"Sure," she said. Collecting Jateko's knife, which she recognized as one of her own, she crawled to Abiega's body, her right leg flopping uselessly below her shattered knee. She'd need a crutch of some kind or Jateko would have to drag her the rest of the way to Geld.

Opening a skull with one hand and a stump was no easier the second time. When she had it cracked, she looked at the corpse and then back to where Jateko lay. No way she'd drag it that far with only one hand and a shattered knee.

"Jateko."

He lay still, his chest barely moving with each breath. He groaned. "I was dreaming."

"I can't drag this to you."

"His brain is really heavy?"

"No, I—" She glanced down at the shattered skull. *Why the hell am I trying to drag the entire body?*

Prying a brain from its bone cage with a long knife and a single hand wasn't all that easy either. By the time she finished night had fallen and the temperature plummeted. She crawled back to Jateko's side, trying not to get too much sand on the mangled grey matter.

"I kind of made a mess getting it out," she said as she reached him.

"Not nearly the mess I'm going to make eating it." His head flopped to the side and he stared at her, brown eyes wide. "This is kind of embarrassing. I don't have the strength to sit up."

"This is a ploy to get me to finger-feed you."

"Yeah."

"If you choke because you're eating lying down, I'll leave you here."

"Thanks, mom."

For a moment Zerfall enjoyed the interplay, forgetting she was a walking corpse. She focussed on her desiccated hand, thin fingers, dried flesh stretched tight across bone. *What the hell are you thinking? He isn't flirting; he's brain damaged from sun stroke.*

She carved off a thin slice of brain and held it over Jateko's mouth, dropping it when he opened wide. He swallowed without chewing.

Over the next hour she fed him the rest of Abiega's brain He finished it all, belching happily at the end and laying with his hands resting on his belly.

"I thought it would taste worse," he said. "I can't explain how much I wanted that. His blood was good, but the more I had the more I needed." He belched again.

"Feel better?"

"Yes. In the morning I'm going to eat as much of the heart and organs as I can keep down."

Sitting at his side, Zerfall leaned in and brushed a few stray hairs from Jateko's face. "I'll try and keep the animals off—" She glanced at the corpse lying silent and rubbery, skull shattered, open and empty. He'd been a smart man, quick-witted and clever. *I fed this naïve child that man's brain. I must be crazy.*

Jateko crawled to one of the Etsaiaren tents, clutching his ribs and making soft whimpering noises.

"I should stitch you up," she said.

"You know how to do that?"

You don't practice with a sword for several hundred years without getting cut. Zerfall nodded.

"It sounds painful."

"Probably."

"Wait until I lose consciousness." He grinned at her, the gap between his front teeth turning his esses into a soft whistle. "It won't take long."

She examined the wounds. She didn't think he'd bleed to death any time soon. "Fine," she said, wheezing as she once again forgot to draw breath.

"You saved my life," he said.

"You saved mine," she answered. He peered at her over the heaped blankets, his eyes glinting with humour. "You know what I mean," she added.

"Had to. You needed me." He rolled back, closing his eyes.

Need. She hated that word. She hated needing and she hated that her need might be all that kept him here.

Jateko lifted a blood-spattered hand, an appeal for contact, and Zerfall stared at it, unable to look away, wishing she could close her eyes. *Why am I hesitating?* She couldn't shake the image of her rotting flesh crumbling beneath his fingers. "Stitching you up with one hand will be hard enough. Anyway, I should keep watch outside of the tent."

The hand dropped back to his side. "I understand."

Did he sound disappointed? "I have to make sure animals don't carry Abiega off," she added.

He nodded without speaking, eyes closed.

"After all," she said, "we want you to grow up to be a big, strong boy, don't we?"

A slight smile graced his lips. "Thanks, mom."

She watched Jateko breathe, his chest rising and falling, until she was sure he was asleep. He looked so young.

She reached out a hand but stopped shy of touching his brow. *You're going to use him. Probably get him killed in the process.*

"So leave him," she whispered.

She didn't want to. She didn't want to go on alone.

After searching the tent and finding a bent needle and gut thread, Zerfall returned to Jateko's side. She worked fast, stitching his wounds. He made no complaint, apparently unaware of her ministrations. When she finished, she took a moment to examine her work. The stitching was neat and tight.

Zerfall crawled from the tent, her right leg dragging behind her, and sat beside Abiega's cooling corpse. She'd made a terrible mess opening the skull; it looked like a child had thrown a tantrum and dashed a pottery bowl to the floor.

The sight of her broken knee, fragments of white bone jutting through paper skin in odd directions, drew her eye. She was falling apart. She wouldn't heal, her leg would never get better. It wasn't even a case of it not healing correctly, it would never not be broken. Each indignity heaped upon her dead flesh would haunt her until she crumbled to dust, unable to move or interact with the world beyond witnessing the passage of time. The dark of night fell in on her like a suffocating blanket. She had but one future: decay.

Before entropy took her she would find Hölle and reduce their sick religion to ruin. She'd kill every last mad priest. She'd end the Täuschung and free the souls in Swarm. She'd kill the god she created.

Somehow.

She remembered the woman she had been, driven by the word of Wahrergott. She'd used people with no thought to the cost; when you thought you were saving someone, you could do anything to them, no matter how terrible.

I'm not that woman any more. I won't use Jateko.

But she had to. She couldn't bring down the Täuschung without help. She picked a flake of dead skin from her arm. She knew exactly what she was going to do. She'd feed Jateko brains and hearts and livers and whatever else he desired until he was unstoppably strong.

Maybe you haven't changed that much.

She'd use the boy, but she'd make sure he got what he wanted too. She'd feed him brains and bodies until he was a man, clever and strong.

And if in becoming smarter he realizes he doesn't want to help me, so be it.

But she knew who she had been. No one had ever resisted her Gefahrgeist power.

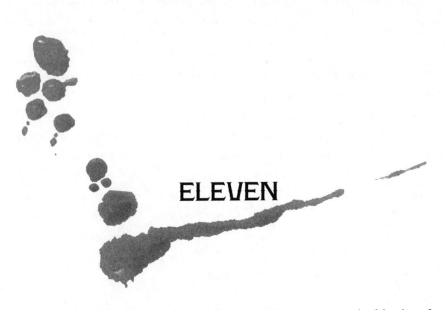

ELEVEN

Anywhere people gather to practice belief, a Gefahrgeist, wearing the false skin of faith, will be found standing at the pulpit.

—Traurige Tatsache, Philosopher

AAS WATCHED NIMMER'S APARTMENT with the patience of a scavenger awaiting its next meal. By nightfall he decided either the Täuschung priest had barricaded himself within, or there was an exit Aas didn't know about. Both were possible, both were likely. Of course he was dealing with a deranged Geisteskranken here; there might be a far less reasonable answer. The man's corpse might well be hanging from the rafters. Suicide amongst the delusional was common, and Getrennt were prone to choosing that route.

You couldn't possibly be so lucky.

Pharisäer had seemed all too pleased with the thought of Aas hunting and killing the priest. He tried to remember what she said. The savage agony of having a serrated knife driven into his guts was more than a little distracting. Had she said it would be fun? That sounded ominous. Did she mean he'd have fun killing, or that she'd be entertained by his attempt?

He tried to force the memory of how perfectly she hurt him from his mind.

Why did she think it would be fun? Certainly not because Nimmer was unable to interact well with the reality around him and felt distanced from humanity.

Growling, Aas *twisted* back to his human form and crossed the street to Nimmer's apartment. He reached a hand toward the door, but stopped short of making contact. His fingertips brushed the brass knob, hesitating.

With a sigh he gripped the knob and turned. The door swung open on well-greased hinges. Not even locked. Was the priest even home?

She told Nimmer I was coming to kill him.

Aas stopped, eyes narrowing as he thought this through. If the man was forewarned, he'd had time to prepare. Had he trapped the apartment hoping to kill Aas? Possibly, but something else niggled at the assassin's thoughts.

Pharisäer said Nimmer was Getrennt and that she'd warned him. She put those two facts together, like they were related.

"Oh."

Getrennt were typified by long periods of melancholy and depression, but the manifestation of their delusions changed when under stress. This was not uncommon among Geisteskranken, but Getrennt were a strange lot. Aas, who read about all manner of Geisteskranken, searched his memory. As with all delusional, Getrennt manifested in any number of ways.

Some Getrennt became lost in a mental fog which faded their surroundings, leaching life and colour from reality, until the world around them became porous and unreal. Those near the Pinnacle of their power, whose minds were close to crumbling, rendered reality so thin approaching them became dangerous. People disappeared into that fog. Occasionally they'd return, but as little more than hollow imitations of who they had been. Others, Aas had read, were so detached from themselves they were capable of leaving their bodies.

Standing in the doorway, one hand resting on the brass knob, Aas frowned. If he went inside and found Nimmer's body, what would that mean? Even if he killed it, chopping it into pieces and burning the remains, would that kill someone who had fled their physical form?

Did Pharisäer think it would be fun for Aas to try and kill Nimmer because it was impossible? He thought not; more likely the Getrennt was dangerous. What if he believed so strongly that his surrounding were unreal that they actually became unreal? Could Nimmer cause Aas to wink out of existence by believing he didn't exist? Could the man believe Aas never existed and wipe out everything he ever accomplished?

What is it you've accomplished? Without you, perhaps your father wouldn't have died in a shite basement looking after his deranged son. Certainly you wouldn't have eaten him. Aas shoved the dark thoughts aside. *Sulk and moan about your unworthiness later.*

"Focus."

What else had he read about Getrennt? Much of it had been confusing. Getrennt and Unwirklichkeit shared many tendencies and were often Comorbidic, with the Geisteskranken suffering both delusions. It made discerning one from the other problematic. What if Pharisäer made that common mistake? What if Aas wasn't stalking a Getrennt, but a Unwirklichkeit instead?

Aas blinked. What if *he'd* confused them? Come to think of it, all that stuff about being lost in the fog of delusion might have been Unwirklichkeit rather than Getrennt.

He stood, hand resting on the brass knob, hesitating. Should he leave, research Nimmer and come back better armed for the situation?

Pharisäer knew him too well, knew he'd find such a puzzle irresistible and that the lack of a clear-cut answer would drive him to distraction.

She's dangerous, and you're playing right into her hands. What if she told him it would be fun and that she warned Nimmer just so he'd stand, like an idiot, in a doorway trying to figure everything out when there was nothing to figure out? She might be watching, laughing, right now.

What if she lied about Nimmer being a Getrennt and he's something more dangerous? The man could be a Hassebrand or, gods forbid, a slaver-type Gefahrgeist.

Aas glanced down at where his hand rested on the door knob. "To hells with Pharisäer and all her machinations, imagined and otherwise."

Squaring his shoulders, Aas stepped into Nimmer's home, closing the door behind him. He stood in a foyer, the walls hung with an assortment of coats and sweaters and hats. Something was wrong, out of place, but he couldn't quite put his finger on it. The coats weren't crowded on a single hook or ugly or filthy. The hats didn't stink and the sweaters wouldn't have looked out of place on anyone he'd seen out in the streets. Sure, maybe it was a bit warm for sweaters right now, but then they were here in the foyer where they'd be needed when the temperature dropped.

It's too normal. Nothing said, "insanity lives here."

Aas had read of people who were so crushingly sure of their sanity they nullified the reality altering effects of the deluded.

You're doing it again.

He drew his long-knife from its place within his robes. No more thinking, he'd find Nimmer and kill the man. He moved a few paces forward and stopped, catching the faintest hint of something sour. Nostrils flared, he tested the air. Stale body odour.

Aas advanced, knife held ready, tensed for combat. The scent grew stronger, fresher. Ahead he saw the foyer opened into a kitchen tiled with slabs of green granite veined in orange. A hideous colour, but one which had been fashionable thirty years ago. Come to think of it the sweaters, coats, and hats, while all well-maintained, were all of a dated style as well.

Approaching the kitchen, Aas leaned forward to glance inside. A man sat at the kitchen table, dressed in heavy sweaters too thick for the weather, his back turned to Aas.

Aas tensed, ready to close the distance. "Nimmer." The man didn't react, not even the slightest hunching of shoulders to show he heard. "Nimmer!"

Nothing.

Aas stepped into the kitchen, ready to slash and stab.

"Nimmer, I'm here to kill you."

Nothing.

Silent as death Aas slid behind Nimmer, knife ready. If the man so much as twitched Aas would drive the blade deep into his brain.

"Speak or I'll lobotomise you."

Nothing.

Aas stared at the Getrennt's back. *Is he dead? Is that Pharisäer's joke?* No. Not funny enough.

Clutching his knife and poised for sudden violence, Aas circled the man. Nimmer sat with his legs pulled up so his feet rested on the seat of his chair. Scrawny arms wrapped about those legs, pulling them tight. Eyes wide, lips pulled back in a frozen and silent scream of terror, he stared at the far wall.

It looks like someone scared him to death.

Except Aas felt sure the man wasn't dead.

Aas watched for fifty heart beats and Nimmer neither blinked nor moved in the slightest.

Interesting. Feeling confident the man wouldn't explode into action and tackle him, Aas took a moment to examine the kitchen which looked to have been decorated a few hundred years ago. Much of what he saw looked antique. The windows were all boarded closed and hung with heavy blankets. Not a scrap of light made it past. An oil lantern sitting in the middle of the table lit the room. *So, he's a shut-in, trying to distance himself from humanity.* Here, in the kitchen, the body odour smelled no more than a few days old. Somehow Nimmer managed to smell like sweaty old clothes without a hint of recent sweat.

"Nimmer."

Nothing.

Aas listened.

Silence, not even the soft intake of breath. He might as well have been alone in the room.

Kill him and be done with it.

No. This mystery was too interesting. He wanted to understand. *Had* to understand.

"He's catatonic," Aas said to the kitchen, dragging out a chair and sitting across from Nimmer. At least killing him would be easy enough.

Or did Pharisäer know this would happen? Had she foreseen all of this, planned it, even?

Sighing, Aas took a long moment to examine Nimmer. The man was thin, but not malnourished. Slim and weak rather than lean and wiry. The clothes fit poorly, like they were tailored for someone much broader and taller. Like the coats in the hall, they were of a style long fallen from favour amongst the wealthy of Geld. And like the coats they were well-maintained, as if rarely worn.

Such a delicious mystery.

"How long will this catatonia last?" Aas asked.

Nimmer, of course, said nothing.

"If you'll talk to me, I could be convinced not to kill you." Aas raised the palms of his hands in a shrug. "If I wanted you dead I'd have killed you already."

Nothing.

Aas sat back, crossing his arms over his chest. What was so fun about this? He didn't get it. Why did Pharisäer make a point of telling Aas she warned Nimmer he was coming, and why did she think this would be fun? Was the man dangerous? He didn't look dangerous.

Far from being fun, this looked like the easiest kill Aas would ever make. He scratched at a tuft of thick hairs sticking out of his neck and without thinking tugged them free to add to the collection in his pocket. There was a mystery here, but he was missing it.

Kill him and go home.

"And when Pharisäer asks if I had fun, what then? Do I admit I couldn't figure it out? The only way she'll respect me is if I beat her at her own game." He'd solve the mystery of why killing Nimmer would be fun, kill the man, and escape unharmed. Pharisäer tested him and he knew it.

She's a little like Zerfall and a little like Hölle. She's smarter than you are.

"True. Maybe."

What if the mystery didn't lay with Nimmer at all? What if it was his surroundings?

This building, the clothes, the way it was decorated. Everything spoke of the past. Though Aas was hardly a collector of antiques, he'd read enough on the topic to have a rough guess as to how old most of this stuff was.

He leaned in to examine the workmanship of the table, the twisted wrought-iron legs. The table was near flawless, the iron showing no signs of rust or wear even though it must have been decades old at the least. The elite of Geld always preferred building materials to be made out of the rarest and most expensive materials. Gold never faded from favour, but these days, with the nearest source of old-growth trees being weeks away, wood was once again popular. How long ago had this kind of iron work been in style?

Aas' eyes widened as he remembered reading of the iron shortages occurring when the miners in the Kälte Mountains went on strike demanding improved working conditions. That was over two hundred years ago. Though the miners had refused to work many times since then, it was never for long enough to drive fashion.

Was it possible for an iron table to look so perfect after two hundred years? Aas scowled, regretting his lack of reading in the arts of iron lore. He glanced again at Nimmer to make sure the man hadn't moved. When he was sure the Getrennt remained catatonic, Aas ducked down to check the bottom of the table. There he saw the iron-worker's mark alongside a date stamped into the metal. It was a local smithy. Hopefully that meant they used the dating system most commonly accepted in Geld, taking the formation of the Verzweiflung Banking Conglomerate as year zero. With many city-states using their own dating systems, translating between the different systems was chaos. All counted year zero from different points in time, and many had different numbers of months, seemingly random lengths of month and year. A week, depending on which city-state you were in, could be anywhere between five and ten days.

If this table wasn't an excellent forgery—and why bother?—it was two hundred and thirteen years old and in perfect condition.

Aas sat straight and frowned at Nimmer. *Why is your furniture so old and so well maintained? Why are your clothes all out of style?*

Not expecting much, Aas decided to try one last threat and held raised knife. "See this? I'm going to drive it through your foot."

Nothing.

"I've made a study of nerves and muscles. This will hurt more than you can imagine."

Still nothing.

With a philosophical shrug Aas leaned forward to follow through with his threat and stopped when he became aware of a deep hum so low he felt it in his chest more than heard it. What was that sound? All thought of stabbing the Getrennt forgotten, he leaned back and the humming disappeared. When he leaned in once again, the low hum returned. This time he leaned closer and the hum grew in volume and pitch, but remained near the lower register of what he could hear.

Very strange.

Wisdom demanded he retreat and contemplate this mystery before again approaching the Getrennt. It remained possible the man might be dangerous.

Aas sighed. "Okay Pharisäer, you win. This is a good mystery. I'm having fun."

Spotting a crumb of food sitting atop the table Aas flicked it away, watching as it arced across the kitchen. The crumb gathered speed, becoming a streak of fire like a falling star glowing ember red, and then came apart like wind-blown ash.

He blinked away the streaked after-image burned into his vision. *Odd.*

Aas remembered something he once read on the underlying laws of reality: The power of a Geisteskranken is inversely proportionate to the distance. The further one got from the deranged, the less effect their delusions had. There were rare exceptions, he'd read, where the delusions of the Geisteskranken related to something distant, but on the whole most Geisteskranken couldn't change things more than a stride or two distant. There were confounding factors to measuring such things; as their minds crumbled under the weight of their delusions, the deranged became more powerful and their range increased. Likewise, the presence of sane minds or competing beliefs limited a Geisteskranken's range.

Aas stared the floor where the crumb should have landed. Only a dusting of ash remained. He had flicked it away, and it accelerated as it got further from the table where he and Nimmer sat. It had been leaving their sphere of influence.

Assuming he himself wasn't the cause of the crumb's odd behaviour, why would leaving Nimmer's presence cause it to accelerate and burn up?

Is the man a very rare breed of Hassebrand?

Unlikely, but not impossible.

Aas rose and backed away from Nimmer, hesitant lest he suddenly accelerate or burst into flames. Nothing happened.

Returning to the table and retaking his chair, he found another crumb. This time he flicked it toward the Getrennt. The crumb slowed as it neared the man until it sat motionless, hanging in the air, a hand-span from his chin.

Aas blinked. "Interesting."

HÖLLE STOOD BEFORE THE floor to ceiling mirror turning to examine herself from different angles. She looked bonier, more angular than she remembered. *I'm real.* She'd dreamed she'd become immaterial, that people saw through her. *I look awful.* Her hair had lost its lustre and her skin looked corpse grey. Dark rings circled puffy eyes. *Zerfall's hand has a better complexion than I do.*

Her shoulders bore a rounded slump she'd never before noticed.

Zerfall always stood so straight, so sure of herself. It was strange, Hölle had never before given much thought to her body. Most described her as perfect. Sure, having to focus her time and energies on the day to day running of the Täuschung, she never had her sister's lithe muscularity, but she'd always been slim and curvy. For hundreds of years neither aged. Now she looked older, bent, and if not broken, perhaps breaking.

Damn it, Zerfall! You did this to me! Zerfall's betrayal plagued her in ways she never imagined.

She glanced at the hand lying, fingers splayed, on the desk. The tattooed eye remained closed.

I hope you're screaming in Swarm. I hope your every moment is haunted with the memory of what it cost you to betray me.

Hölle leaned forward, her forehead pressing against her reflection's forehead. The cool glass soothed her thoughts. Zerfall's actions weren't Hölle's fault, there was no way she could have foreseen the betrayal.

"It's not my fault," she whispered. "Zerfall is weak. *Was* weak," she corrected. "Four hundred years was too much for her."

"It's too much for anyone," said Pharisäer.

"I haven't seen you in two days," said Hölle, doing her best to sound casual. Pharisäer stood at the entrance to her chambers, her hair tied back in a style Zerfall would never have worn, Blutblüte hanging at her hip. The sight of the sword sent a stab of sharp pain ripping through Hölle's gut and she hissed through clenched teeth.

I thought maybe I hallucinated you, or . . . She couldn't finish the thought. "I thought you were gone."

"Never," said Pharisäer, closing the door behind her. "I will never abandon you."

That smile, almost a knowing smirk.

Hölle remembered thinking Wahrergott had sent Pharisäer to replace Zerfall. She'd said it aloud with perfect certainty as if doing so made it fact. Now she doubted. Had the One True God sent Pharisäer, or was she nothing more than a manifestation of Hölle's decaying sanity? *The One True God protected Zerfall and I from the Pinnacle for four hundred years. He would not abandon me now.* But Zerfall had. What if Wahrergott's protection left with Zerfall? *What if Wahrergott never—*

"You're in pain," said Pharisäer. "What are you doing out of bed?"

"I need to—"

"It's not your fault, you need to heal."

Hölle straightened, but kept one hand pressed to her belly. "I'm fine."

Pharisäer raised an eyebrow and shook her head. "You're clenching your teeth."

"I'm fine," Hölle repeated, forcing her jaw to relax.

Glancing to where Hölle's hand held her belly, Pharisäer said, "Yes, I can tell. Why are you rushing this? You were run through by several feet of steel." Hölle's gut clenched like a fist. "You need to rest, to heal. If you tear yourself open inside, everything you've worked for will fall apart."

Pharisäer pulled Hölle into a hug, Blutblüte's pommel pressing against her belly like an erect cock demanding entrance. "There is no shame in resting," Pharisäer whispered into her ear. "Surrender. Surrender to your body's needs. You can't do this. Not alone. Let me help."

Sagging, Hölle allowed the other woman to take some of her weight. Pharisäer was right. It was too much to do alone. She carried the fate of all humanity on her shoulders. The responsibility was more than she could bear.

Pharisäer cooed soft words of comfort as she guided Hölle back to bed.

Once nestled in the heavy blankets, Hölle felt her stomach relax and the pain fade. She pushed herself too hard. Taking a little more time to heal would hardly hinder the progress of her life's work. Täuschung would unite all humanity in a hell of penance and set it free. This was a task requiring millennia of dedication and struggle; if it took a few months longer, so what? There was no deadline. All that mattered was that she didn't fail.

Looking up at Pharisäer standing over her, Hölle reached out to catch her hand. Rubbing the fingers she arched an eyebrow and then frowned. "You have no calluses."

"So?"

"This was Zerfall's sword hand. Her fingers were hard and strong. Yours are as soft as mine."

"I'm not Zerfall," Pharisäer said, retrieving her hand. "You should remember that."

"I know. I keep expecting you to be like her, to be her replacement."

Pharisäer's eyes glinted like glass. "She betrayed you."

"I know—"

"I am not like her."

Lying in bed, cocooned by a heavy blanket, staring up at this woman standing over her, the sword which had stabbed deep into Hölle's guts hanging at her side, Hölle felt a tremor of fear. Pharisäer's anger cut her features like cold diamond. This was not Zerfall; Pharisäer was both harder and softer. Physically, she showed none of Zerfall's strength. Inside however lurked something sharp and dangerous. She might offer comfort Hölle desperately needed, but this woman held an edge not unlike Blutblüte.

You're afraid of her.

"I have good news," said Pharisäer, smiling brightly as if that moment of tension had never happened. "Aas has been dealt with."

"Dead?"

"Better. I sent him to kill Nimmer."

"Why?"

Pharisäer kept her face straight for a heartbeat and then burst out laughing. "For fun. I told Nimmer Aas was coming to kill him."

"He didn't take it well?"

"He panicked. It happened so fast I almost didn't make it out." She offered another innocent smile.

Hölle's eyes widened in surprise. "Nimmer is cracking. How bad will the damage be when he snaps?" She shuddered to think what covering this up would cost. Luckily, bribery was everything in Geld.

"He'll freeze a good chunk of a city block when his delusions take him."

"You should have told me of your plan," Hölle scolded. *If she'd been trapped within Nimmer's power, I'd be alone.* Alone. The word terrified and excited. Her breath quickened and the room darkened. The garbage-strewn corners writhed with shadowy images of a feverish girl awakening, alone, in a sweat soaked cot, surrounded by the corpses of her family. "It was dangerous," she snapped. "Stupid."

Pharisäer, ignoring the dancing shadows, shrugged this away with a lift of one shoulder. "I may have also suggested to Aas there was a bit of a puzzle involved, something he'd need to figure out."

Though her anger was not forgotten, Hölle had to laugh at the thought of Aas being presented with such a puzzle. In response to her shifting mood, the shadows faded away. "That'll drive him crazy. He'll spend hours with Nimmer before killing him." *Why had there been only one girl on the cot?* That wasn't right. *Do you remember a time without me?* Zerfall had asked in Hölle's dream.

"Centuries," said Pharisäer. "Isn't this so much more fun than killing him?"

Zerfall was never this reckless. She'd always been more temperamental than Hölle, quicker to violence, but never incautious. "Careful," warned Hölle. "Don't underestimate Aas."

Why did Pharisäer want Aas removed, but not dead? *He knows more about Geisteskranken than anyone.* Had Pharisäer temporarily disposed of Aas to stop Hölle from learning something? *No, you're being paranoid.*

Pharisäer grinned white teeth at Hölle and waved off her warning with a graceful sweep of fingers. "That's the beauty of it. If he's smarter than I think and gets out sooner rather than later, he'll have enjoyed my puzzle and appreciate my trust in his cleverness. If we don't see him for several hundred years, he'll return, awed and cowed by my genius."

Hölle saw confidence in Pharisäer's every movement, the way she brushed off Hölle's concern, and the way she stood, Blutblüte hanging casually at her hip. Again her stomach tightened with pain. "I hope you're right."

"I am. I win, no matter what. Aas is out of the way, and when he returns I will own his heart more than Zerfall would have dreamed possible."

Why does she want to own Aas' heart? Was this jealous competition with a dead woman? The man was an odious wretch, as hideous as he was dangerous. Was there something Zerfall and Pharisäer saw in him that she missed? *He's educated, and he's*—Hölle kept her face blank as she examined Pharisäer. *He's a murderer.*

F OR THE FIRST TIME ever, Virwirrt wore the robes of a Täuschung priest. It was good not to hide what he was. For too long the true Täuschung had remained hidden, skulking in basements. He limped, dragging his left foot behind him. His right arm hung useless, swinging with every step. Every year more of him fell to the disease devouring his muscle and bone. In less than a decade he'd be completely helpless, a bag of brain and blood. The doctors told him it was all in his mind, but he knew better.

Gods he hated being weak, being useless. All he ever wanted was to be strong, but the world made him its victim. His first memories were of being held helpless by bigger children as they mocked his inability to fight back. He remembered his father's disgust that he hadn't defended himself. He spent a lifetime under that disgust before the old bastard finally died.

"Zerfall said it's time to show them I am powerful. Zerfall said it's time to show the world the truth."

He followed his prey, Beraubt, through the streets of Geld. She too wore the robes of a Täuschung priest. All of the Geisteskranken who had lived secret lives in the Täuschung compound now openly wore their vestments.

"Zerfall said no more hiding."

Virwirrt followed his fellow priest, hating her as he hated all women. Except Zerfall. Zerfall was too terrifying to hate.

"Zerfall said Beraubt hates me. Zerfall said Beraubt turns my friends against me."

He hadn't slept in two weeks and the world around him felt like a poorly acted puppet show. None of this was real. Cobwebs of silky thought distracted him, made it difficult to remember why he was here. Pressure built behind his eyes, threatened to split his skull.

"Zerfall said Beraubt tells the other women I can't rut, that fear unmans me."

Morning dew glistened on the cobbled streets turning dull stone to sparkling diamonds. Somewhere behind him he heard exclamations of joy as someone stumbled across the wealth his hallucinations left behind. Like joy, the most ephemeral of emotions, the precious stones wouldn't last. Taken beyond the sphere of his influence, they'd once again become dew drops soaking the pockets of the fools who collected them.

This early in the morning there were few pedestrians, the streets mostly empty. Though the city seemed abandoned, he felt the influence of the sane crushing him. Were the streets busier, he'd be helpless, just one more sleep-deprived madman. But now, in the early dawn hours, he was powerful. This was his time.

He passed within a stride of a man stumbling home from a long night at the pub and the drunk turned boneless, collapsing to the ground. Virwirrt liked people to be helpless. He *needed* it. How many people had he reduced to pathetic blubbering and begging in dark alleys, their impotent fear feeding his need? Their powerlessness made him strong. Only with a helpless woman could he successfully rut. He showed them his power. They worshipped him like a god. He saw it in the fear on their faces.

He passed the drunk. On any other day he'd stop to hurt the man, leave the victim some reminder of their inability to stop him. Not today.

"Zerfall said Beraubt betrayed us. Zerfall said Beraubt plots against us. Zerfall said Beraubt is trying to kill me. Zerfall said Beraubt is the reason I haven't slept. Zerfall said . . ." The litany went on, a constant reminder. "Zerfall said Beraubt has to die."

When Beraubt lay dead he could finally sleep. But first he'd show her he was a man. *She shouldn't have mocked me.*

He watched Beraubt stagger and fall. On all fours she stared at the stone beneath her hands. He saw the street pulsate and breathe, form a mouth, lips of stone, and whisper to her. An Auslösekugeln addict, she was reputed to be capable of powerful hallucinations. He hated powerful women. Except Zerfall; she scared him. But that was alright, it didn't make him a coward. Zerfall scared everyone.

"Zerfall said Beraubt is at her weakest in the morning. Zerfall said Beraubt will not have eaten Auslösekugeln since yesterday."

Virwirrt drew a thin stiletto, keeping it hidden from sight. "Zerfall said I should play with Beraubt before I kill her. "

He examined the woman, taking in the tattered clothes and ragged fingernails. Even from a dozen paces he caught the stench of sweat and rotting teeth. She pressed her ear to the ground, listening to whatever it said. One small hallucination. If that was all she could manage, she'd soon be his. His own madness reached out a full half-dozen strides beyond him, twisting reality to suit his desire. He imagined her brain like rotted goat's cheese, stinking and riddled with worms and mould. After he was finished with her, after she knew him for the powerful man he was, he'd open her skull and see if he was right.

"Zerfall said it was time to show the people of Geld the truth. Zerfall said it was time to open their eyes to the horror. Zerfall said it is time I walk among them, a god not yet risen."

Beraubt would watch as he dismantled her. Virwirrt's groin stirred in anticipation.

"Zerfall said I should do it right here on the street. Zerfall said I should display her as my trophy."

As Virwirrt's sphere of influence passed over Beraubt she glanced up, drooling brown down her chin and grinning Auslösekugeln-stained teeth. She spat a wad of well chewed leathery mushroom gristle at his feet. "Zerfall said you would follow me," she said. "Zerfall said you would try and kill me."

He bent his will against her, crushed her with his need. She'd be helpless, a doll to do with as he wished.

Beraubt stood, her sphere of influence washing over him like a shadow and encompassing the entire block. The world staggered, frayed apart.

"I knew you were coming," she said. "I've been eating Auslösekugeln all night."

Reality shuddered under her narcotic-induced madness. Every cobble stone for a hundred paces opened mouths and screamed. Every house sagged and expanded as it drew breath. The world came alive, lit with impossible colours too bright to see. The sun opened eyes of purple and black and giggled in terror. The clouds turned red and rained salty tears of blood. The drunk, still sprawled where he'd fallen, came apart like an over-ripe melon smashed against a wall.

"Zerfall said you like to hurt women," she said.

Virwirrt's knees buckled and he dropped to the street. His bones melted, soft cheese. His teeth fell out and dissolved in his mouth. The stones beneath him chewed at his flesh, eating him one mouthful at a time. He could do nothing to resist.

"Zerfall said—"

He didn't hear the rest as his skull softened like butter left in the sun and fell in upon itself.

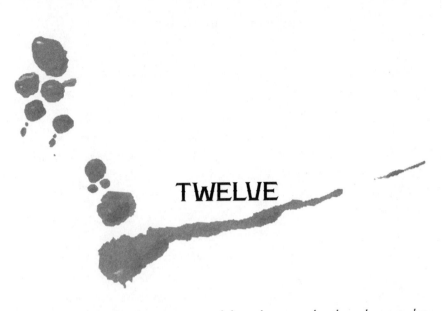

TWELVE

The goat wants what the goat wants and the snake wants what the snake wants, but Harea does whatever he wants.

—Basamortuan Proverb

I CANNOT *BELIEVE YOU KILLED me.*

Jateko sat up, wide awake, blinking sand and grit from his eyes, the taste of feculence and sweat staining his tongue. His *oihal* lay crumpled at his feet, crusted solid in brownish blood. It looked to have been repaired, the larger holes sewn closed. Ignoring the stench, he donned the garb. He scratched at his near hairless chest. Was it a little less flat and featureless than he remembered? The world seemed crisper. He glanced about the inside of the *karpan* in which he'd slept. It was his, everything intimately familiar, and yet he'd never seen any of it before. He knew where his knives sat, where the water skin hung, and where he'd stashed a fistful of dried goat jerky in case he got hungry in the middle of the night.

Jerky. *Bleah!* He wanted something fresh. Gnawing hunger twisted his belly in an iron grip. He felt like he hadn't eaten in months.

You ate my brain just last night.

Sure, but now he was ravenous.

Jateko stood, feeling strange in his body as if he were a little too tall and too weak. He approached the entrance, careful not to trip over his huge, floppy feet. Outside he found Zerfall sitting over Abiega's corpse, flicking away carrion beetles, her right leg jutting out at an odd angle below the shattered knee. Abiega's empty skull, its contents hacked free and devoured, reminded Jateko of his dream and the slippery wet clay taste of souls.

The sun hung low to the west, its fat belly brushing the horizon. Hadn't it been nightfall when he fought Abiega? Either he hadn't slept much at all, or he slept through an entire night and a day.

"I'm glad you're up," Zerfall said. "This was getting boring." Even with only one working leg she stood in one smooth, graceful motion. For the first time he appreciated her perfect balance and flawless proprioception.

Proprioception?

The knowledge of one's own body, answered the new voice in his head. *Zerfall knows exactly where all of her is at all times. She moves like a predator.*

"Oh," he said aloud, nodding. "Thank you."

Empty sockets turned toward him for a heartbeat and then swung away.

I bet she was unbelievably sexy before the rot set in. Jateko tried to ignore this uncomfortable thought.

"What are we going to do about your leg?" he asked.

"Afraid I'll slow you down?"

Nothing about her changed and he read no hint of emotion in her face. He realized he was aware of how she had to draw breath into her dead lungs before each sentence.

She's dead. Never forget.

"I won't leave you," he said.

She stared at him, her regard empty and heavy. "Why?"

"You're going to do something important. I can tell. And you need my help."

And you need her, said that new voice in his head. *Think it through.*

Jateko considered what would happen should he part ways with Zerfall. *I'll die.*

Right. You need to be useful to her.

Empty sockets examined him and he wished he could read her expression.

She talked. She told him of a mad god and an even madder religion. She talked of assassins and Geisteskranken, city-states people who bent reality to their will. She told him of the woman who was her sister and something else, a sliver of Zerfall's personality manifested as real. She told him of the purpose that drove her. She told him her plans, how she'd return to the city-states and kill this figment of her imagination, and burn her church to the ground, and how she'd kill a god.

When she finished he said, "You need the help of the person I will become."

"When you've killed and eaten more people."

"Yes," said Jateko. "If I don't, I won't be of much use to you. If anything, I'll be a hindrance."

"You change after each person you devour," she said.

"I'm smarter."

"You're different."

He shrugged, wanting to say he was the same Jateko but knowing it was a lie. "Does it matter?"

When she spoke she'd forgotten to draw air and her voice was little more than a dusty wheeze. "It should."

"We can bust up the *karpan* and use the poles as splints for your leg," he said, changing the subject.

And it'll take care of that distracting thing her hips do when she walks.

"And it'll take care of that distracting thing your hips do—" Jateko slammed his mouth shut. "Sorry. Still getting used to the voices in my head."

"We'll bring blankets," she said as if he hadn't spoken. "Drape them across Tod and use him to shelter you from the sun." She laughed, a rattling cough. "He'll make a disgusting tent."

Tod stood nearby, head drooping, nose touching the sand between his front hooves, ignoring them.

"Hungry?" She glanced at Abiega's corpse.

"Ravenous. Famished." He grinned at her. "Rapacious."

She examined him, dead expression unreadable as she looked him up and down. Shrugging, she drew a knife and offered it hilt first. He drew his own without thought and stared at the blade in his hand. Had he collected it last night before falling asleep? "I have my own," he said, and added, "You'll need that for the *karpan* poles," when she sheathed the weapon.

Kneeling at the side of the corpse, Jateko examined the torso, licking his lips. "How do I . . ." He blinked, realizing he knew how to open the ribs. Abiega had broken apart many bodies and hung them from cacti. He peeled back the flesh exposing the cartilage in the centre of the chest. Examining the bloody mess, he probed for the right spot with his fingers. There. Gripping the knife in both hands, Jateko raised it high, made sure of his aim, and slammed it into Abiega's flayed chest. The tip of the knife didn't go as far in as he expected—*Harea are you weak*—but it would do. Leaning his weight against the blade, he levered it back and forth, working the tip deeper. When it felt right—and he had no idea how he knew—he pushed the knife sideways until he heard the wet *pop* of parting cartilage. Twisting the blade, he managed to open the ribs far enough to get his fingers in. Dropping the knife, he worked the fingers of his other hand into the gap.

"Now it's just a matter of pulling it open," he said, flashing Zerfall a cocky grin.

She watched as he struggled, wrenching and twisting, fighting to drag Abiega's chest apart and expose the meal within. Frustrated, he got the heel of his right foot wedged in as well and was able to wrestle the chest cavity wide enough.

It should have been a gory mess in there. He should have been appalled by the raw copper stench of blood and internal organs, the slack sacks of deflated lungs.

He should have been disgusted.

He wasn't.

Jateko's mouth flooded with saliva at the thought of the meal to come. There, nestled in the bowl of spread ribs lay Abiega's heart; the heart of a warrior. The heart of a man feared by Hasiera and Etsaiaren alike. Jateko reached a hand into the open chest to caress the heart. It was beautiful, perfect. And here, huddled deep in the torso, Jateko found the great warrior's liver and kidneys. These were the organs of a man strong beyond the physical strength of his tough and wiry frame. Abiega, Jateko realized, had been strong in so many different ways, physical, mental, emotional, and spiritual. Truly Harea loved and blessed this man.

And now he is mine. He is me. I am him.

Jateko cut the heart free with a few practised flicks of his knife and held it aloft, feeling its weight. "Abiega," he said, "you honour me and I shall seek to honour you. I know this isn't what you would have chosen—"

No kidding.

"—but I shall endeavour to earn your respect."

Eat camel dung.

"I'll pack up some supplies," said Zerfall. "Get Tod loaded with whatever we'll need." She examined Jateko, head tilted to one side, looking as if she might say more. "Enjoy your meal."

Jateko ate, chewing each piece until it all but disappeared in his mouth. He ate the heart first, confident it was the most important of the torso's organs. Where the mind was the seat of all thought and skill, the soul dwelt in the heart. This was where courage, strength of will and body, would be found. The heart not only drove the blood which powered the muscles, but it also held a man's emotions and his deepest truths.

After finishing the heart he felt fantastic, fed and comfortable, yet energetic. He licked clean his fingers and thought about what to eat next. The kidneys. Though he was unsure what they did, they were small enough he felt sure he'd finish them.

By the time he swallowed the last nibble of kidney, his belly felt full. He could eat more, but didn't want to.

Jateko glanced over his shoulder to see Zerfall snap the *karpan's* central pole and begin lashing it to her right leg with rope she found somewhere. He watched for a long time, unable to take his eyes off her. She moved with a subtle grace that, as someone who regularly tripped over his own feet, he couldn't imagine possessing. There was more though. Something about the way she moved screamed intent. She had drive. She was going somewhere to do something. Her intent was intoxicating. He wanted that. He wanted to have a purpose. He wanted to matter. Not just to his mom and the others in the tribe, but to someone he actually liked. Maybe loved. His head swam at the thought of finding someone who cared about him beyond his willingness to do the most disgusting chores. He was sick and tired of mom sending him out to hunt snakes for the awful gritty soup she made. He'd been bitten so many times they barely numbed his arm now unless they got their fangs in real deep. He remembered how he passed out in the sand the first time he got bit. He'd lain there, hallucinating in the sun, for most of a day before managing to drag himself back to the tribe. Mom seemed annoyed to see him. Sometimes he wondered if she sent him after the damned snakes hoping he'd get bitten, hoping he'd die.

No, he thought, *you're being unfair.*

He stared at Zerfall, admiring the way she moved. She wasn't at all what he expected from a *hiria ero* woman.

I want her, he realized. *Not like this, but what she was.*

Yet he couldn't imagine Zerfall as someone's woman. She was more. So much more.

Zerfall glanced up from her work, catching him staring at her. Embarrassed, he turned away.

Returning his attention to Abiega, he studied the liver, marvelling at its velvety pink perfection. His stomach rumbled, but in protest rather than hunger. *That thing is huge.*

Maybe he'd just eat a little.

You swore to honour me.

True. And how often would he have the chance to devour such a great warrior? Letting such an opportunity pass by to avoid discomfort was stupid.

Jateko carved the liver free and held it up for inspection. This was the centre of life, and from it came a man's ability to heal.

After a few deep breaths he set about carving the liver into thin slices. He ate until his jaw ached, until his distended belly pressed against his normally loose *oihal* turning him into a round tent. He ate until shoving each sliver of liver into his mouth was an act of sheer will.

After, when he'd forced himself to swallow the last mouthful, he lay back in the sand and loosed a long offal-flavoured belch. "I am so full I can't move."

Zerfall approached, one leg lashed to a *karpan* pole, and stood over him. She glanced about, her attention lingering on each corpse-ridden cactus. "You're going to have to."

Pushing himself upright, Jateko groaned and let slip another brackish burp. He faced west, toward the city-states and away from everything he ever knew. Zerfall had collapsed the *karpan* and packed everything on Tod's drooping back. The horse looked glum, its rotting lips hanging open to reveal a retreating gum-line and long brown teeth.

"We should leave now, make full use of the night," he said. He thought about riding, his full belly bouncing with Tod's every step, and wanted to puke.

Don't you dare.

"I'll walk," said Zerfall as if she read his mind. "I don't tire, and with all that gear there's hardly room for two."

His stretched stomach burbled complaint.

"How are your ribs?" asked Zerfall.

"A little tender."

"Not broken?"

"No."

"Let me see," she said, gesturing for him to lift his shirt.

Jateko did as he was told and saw that the stitched wounds had closed, the bruising over his ribs already fading.

Zerfall pursed rotting lips. "We should go," she said.

Jateko swung up onto Tod's back and sat perfectly balanced. He might be uncomfortably full, but he felt amazing, in tune with his body. Even his feet didn't seem quite so floppy.

Zerfall watched, her head with that slight tilt he was pretty sure meant she was thinking. She was doing that a lot lately, watching and thinking. Did she see the changes in him?

You could ask.

No, that would be weird.

Nodding to herself, Zerfall set off into the desert without a word. The pole lashed to her right leg lent her an uneven and rolling gate. It was the first time Jateko ever saw her move with less than flawless grace.

Tod sighed and followed her toward the bloody smear of desert sunset.

THIRTEEN

Time is a shadow in the sky
Afterdeath redemption in the blink of an eye
And hope is ever here
And never near
And all that's left is to ask why
Why am I just parts, not whole
As early decomposition takes its toll
Lasting forever more
Life-sucking whore
With payment sought only my soul
Soul illusion fake or fact
Or a chip for barter in the devil's pact
Shedding my flesh with tears
Shredding my fears
For there are those I will attract
Sometime

—"Untitled", by Halber Tod, Cotardist poet

EFYING ALL REASON AND logic, the crumb hung in the air two arm's lengths from Aas.

No, this wasn't a failure of reason and logic, but rather of his ability to understand reality.

I flick a crumb away from Nimmer and it picks up speed and burns to ash. I flick a crumb toward Nimmer, and it slows and stops to hang motionless in the air. Did the Getrennt have some weird delusion pertaining to cleanliness or crumbs? That, he decided, was silly. If the man suffered obsessive compulsive delusions regarding cleanliness, there wouldn't have been crumbs on the table at all.

Unless someone planted the crumbs to throw you off. If he kept thinking like this, he'd have to worry paranoia might become one of his delusions. Then again, there definitely *were* people who wanted him dead. *Can you be paranoid when people are trying to kill you?* Sadly, he suspected the answer was yes. Delusionally believing something which happened to be true was no guarantee of sanity.

Aas leaned forward to pluck the crumb from the air, but as he closed the distance it once again began crawling forward and the low-pitched hum returned. When he sat back the crumb stopped moving and the hum faded back below what he could hear.

Pharisäer, this is a fabulous mystery. If he survived this, he'd have to thank her; it was far too long since he studied something so intriguing.

Again Aas leaned toward the crumb, and again it retreated, moving closer to Nimmer. The low-pitched hum, so deep it shook his bowels, also returned. This time, Aas didn't retreat, but held his position. Once the crumb reached about two arm's lengths distance, it slowed to a stop. The low hum remained. When Aas sat back, the crumb didn't move and the hum sank below the range of his hearing.

How is my proximity affecting the movement of this crumb? On the surface, it made no sense, but Aas felt sure he lacked some key piece of the puzzle. Reality might seem insane, but it made sense. Which in itself seemed a nonsensical statement. But if one accepted there were rules, no matter how well hidden or clouded by perception, one could find the truth.

Aas saw two possibilities: Either his own delusions influenced the crumb's movement, or the changes in his proximity to Nimmer altered his perceptions in some strange manner. Seeing as he had no delusions regarding crumbs—at least none he was aware of—the second option seemed the most likely. This, he decided, required further experimentation.

Aas leaned toward Nimmer, closer than he had previously approached, and retreated just as fast. Once again the crumb moved, picking up speed the closer Aas got. The sound scaled upward in pitch and volume and then dropped as he retreated. It reminded him of the sound of someone screaming as they rode past on a very fast moving horse, a sound he'd heard more than once. But that made no sense; Nimmer wasn't moving. In fact, the man hadn't moved at all, hadn't blinked, or drawn breath since Aas entered the room.

Pursing his lips in thought, Aas reached a hand toward the crumb, this time without leaning any closer. The crumb didn't move, and he heard nothing, but some pressure resisted his hand. It felt like he was lifting something which grew increasingly heavy.

This makes no sense. Nothing separated Nimmer and Aas. How could nothing get heavier? Maybe not nothing. There was, he supposed, air. But how could air get heavier?

What if it's getting thicker?

Again he leaned forward, listening to the low hum grow in pitch and volume and seeing the crumb crawl forward with increasing speed as he got closer. He drew a deep breath. If there was a change in the thickness of the air, he couldn't detect it. Once again the crumb slid to a stop when it reached two arm-lengths distance from him.

The closer I get . . . what? Well, the closer he got, the closer he got. By leaning toward Nimmer, he entered the sphere of influence of the man's delusions.

The inverse square law, of course!

The closer he was to Nimmer, the more he was within the effects of the Getrennt's power, the more he existed within the man's delusion-defined reality.

So?

So what were Nimmer's delusions? Getrennt typically felt like they were distanced from reality, like they couldn't interact with people or the world moved on without them. That could mean anything, could manifest in a damned-near infinite number of ways.

Aas examined Nimmer. Had the man's eyes closed, ever so slightly? He waited, watching. Nothing.

As a mystery, this was quickly becoming his favourite. He didn't however like that it might beat him.

Admit to Pharisäer she outsmarted me? Never!

Leaning even closer than before, Aas focussed on Nimmer's eyes. Once again the crumb slid away and the hum grew in pitch and volume until it became recognizable as a human voice holding a single impossibly deep note. He held that position for scores of heartbeats.

His eyes are closing.

But no one blinked that slowly and smoothly.

Aas leaned back to escape the annoying sound, listening as it sank in pitch and volume.

Getrennt. Distanced from reality. Distanced how? Certainly not in physical distance. Had he wanted to, Aas could have leaned forward and stabbed Nimmer at any time.

Time.

Distanced in time.

Aas thought about the sound scaling up and down depending on his distance from Nimmer. Did that fit? He thought about how it was effortless for him to lean toward the Getrennt, but if he reached a hand forward, he felt resistance. What was the difference? Well, when he reached a hand forward, his head and body remained distant.

My perceptions—the centre of my own sphere of influence—remain distant, he corrected. An important distinction when dealing with Geisteskranken. Belief defined reality, and perceptions shaped one's belief.

He thought again of the crumb he flicked away and how it burst into flame as it gathered speed.

It got faster. Time outside Nimmer's area of influence moved faster than within.

That wasn't quite right. *Remember the underlying immutable reality.* Everything beyond the Getrennt's influence was normal, defined by the largely sane population of Geld. They weren't moving faster, Nimmer moved slower.

And the closer I get to Nimmer, the slower I move in relation to those beyond.

Did moving slower in time equate to moving slower in space? He'd read about energy and the laws defining motion and an idea called the maintenance of energy, but understood little of it. Still, it seemed to make sense. If someone who moved slowly through time saw an object moving quickly through time, it would probably also appear to move quickly through physical space. *And perception defines reality.* If it *appeared* to move faster, maybe it really did.

How fast did a bread crumb have to move to burst into flames?

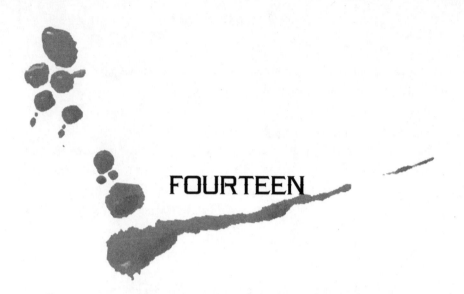

FOURTEEN

I rank sin as humanity's third greatest invention and delusion. There is no better means of manipulating people than guilt. Guilt I rank fourth.

—Versklaver Denker, Gefahrgeist Philosopher

PHARISÄER FOUND HÖLLE PACING her chambers, stepping over piled detritus and plates of untouched food as if she didn't see the mess. The woman still wore the crumpled robes she slept in for the last few weeks. She stood straight, unaware of her wound.

She's healing. Hopefully the news Pharisäer came to deliver would return her to bed. *I need her shaken, scared, upset and unthinking.*

"I have bad news," said Pharisäer stepping closer and running a hand over Blutblüte's pommel to draw Hölle's eye and remind her of she'd been stabbed with that very weapon.

Hölle's attention darted to the sword and flinched away. She rubbed her belly, hunching as if trying to protect it from further harm. "Tell me."

"Two of your priests clashed on the street this morning. They wiped out a dozen houses and killed scores of people before the Geld Guard brought them down."

Hölle retreated toward her bed and Pharisäer followed.

"It gets worse," continued Pharisäer. "For some reason the idiots were wearing the vestments of Täuschung priests." She shook her head in disgust. "And now the church is under investigation. Apparently one of your Geisteskranken has been talking to the wrong people, telling them what goes on in the basement, telling people the truth about the Departings. Most of your sane priests have been arrested and there's talk of the Verzweiflung Banking Conglomerate getting involved," Pharisäer lied. In Geld the bank was the highest court. "There's going to be an inquest. They might even freeze the Täuschung accounts." Most of this was purest fantasy, made up on the spot. "We might be destitute inside of a week. And if the Verzweiflung get hold of the wrong people, we'll be fleeing for our lives soon after that."

Hölle sat, collapsing onto the bed. "Who?" Her shoulders sagged. She blinked rapidly, struggling to comprehend the news.

"The street battle? Virwirrt and Beraubt. I'm guessing Virwirrt was stalking her, thinking she'd be easy prey for his . . . appetites. Judging from the damage done and how many of the Geld Guard got twisted into unrecognizable smears, I think Beraubt had a belly-full of Auslösekugeln."

Hölle swore under her breath, staring at the floor between her feet. "I need to—"

"You look awful," interrupted Pharisäer, stepping closer so Blutblüte's scabbarded blade touched Hölle's knee. The woman paled, again flinching. She looked ill, like she might vomit. "Let me help you back into bed." *Pathetic weakling.* It was too easy. The woman would crack under the pressure and Pharisäer would replace her. *Soon I will be real.* She pushed Hölle back, allowing the sword's pommel to accidentally brush against her several times, and bustled about tucking her in like a caring mother.

"Why now?" asked Hölle. "Who is responsible for this?" She sounded lost, alone.

You are. So alone. I'll turn everyone against you. "I'll find out," promised Pharisäer. "I'll hunt them down and make them pay. Don't you worry." She paused, feigning contemplation. "It's not your fault. How could you have known making Geisteskranken your inner core of priests would end so badly?" She brushed a greasy strand of hair from Hölle's eyes. "It's not your fault. They let you down."

"We can recover—"

"Shhh. We have to hope the Geld Guard don't hear about this compound and focus their investigations on the public façade. I'm sending most of the remaining priests away. We can't chance these idiots spilling what they know. I'll keep the few we can trust. Not to worry, I'll hand pick them myself."

Hölle closed her eyes, sinking deeper into the mattress.

Gods she smells terrible. "I'll see to everything. You rest and recover. You'll open your wound if you keep pushing yourself."

Tears leaked from Hölle's eyes and Pharisäer wanted to taste them, to savour the woman's imminent defeat. Was it time? *No*, thought Pharisäer, *not yet. She still clings to some hope, still believes she can turn everything around. Not for long.*

"I'll report back with my findings," said Pharisäer turning for the door. *I'll ruin everything you've built. I'll burn your life's work to the ground. You'll beg me to end your suffering.* "Sleep well. May Wahrergott watch over you." *And forgive you your failures.*

Zhalen, the Täuschung accountant Pharisäer instructed to sell the church's holdings littered throughout the city-states, had recently reported the first sales confirmed. Several hundred sane Täuschung priests had been turned out into the streets with no word of explanation. It was time to transfer the funds into her own accounts, put them forever beyond Hölle's reach.

L EGS CROSSED, SPINE STRAIGHT, the very image of demur decorum, Pharisäer sat before the Senior Accounts Officer. The old banker looked like she'd eaten something so sour it sucked the front of her face half-way through to the back of her skull. Even here, deep within the bowels of the Verzweiflung Banking Conglomerate's Geld branch, the woman's huge black geldwechsler remained teetering atop her wizened skull. The stupid bankers clearly feared comfort.

What they apparently didn't fear was an ostentatious display of wealth. The interior of the building was finished in white marble veined in arterial red. Every railing was polished brass, unsullied by even a single fingerprint. High above, colossal candelabrum held countless thousands of candles. Those chandeliers, thirty feet or more over Pharisäer's head, were wrought in lustrous gold.

Fantastic wealth, beyond reach. No doubt the message was no accident. Glancing about, she saw no means of reaching those candles. Yet all remained lit.

Pharisäer returned her attention to the banker hunched behind an ornate desk carved of green and black granite no doubt imported from the Gezackt mountains on the far side of the world. She eyed the woman's hat. *One little touch and I can knock that silly thing off the old hag.* Pharisäer kept her face emotionless. In a few minutes she would be one of the wealthiest women in all Geld, and to be the wealthiest in Geld meant to be the wealthiest in all the world.

Zahlen, the Täuschung accountant, had informed Pharisäer that he'd sold several properties. The funds from those deals had of course been deposited in the church's Verzweiflung accounts. The Conglomerate had its fingers in every major transaction. Once Pharisäer transferred the money into her own accounts, Hölle would be shattered by the loss.

I'll tell her the bank foreclosed on the properties. Pharisäer couldn't wait to see Hölle's face when she heard the news. She'd crawl back into bed and cry, never thinking to leave her room and ascertain the truth for herself. One more support pillar kicked out from under what remained of the woman's crumbling sanity.

Pharisäer felt good. She felt strong. Alive.

The Senior Accounts Officer made a show of examining Pharisäer, gaze lingering on the black leather sheathing her legs and ass. Zerfall might have been a crazy bitch, but she had great taste in clothes. Pharisäer had barely been able to squeeze into the pants.

"How can I help you?" asked the banker, looking anything but helpful. "If you wish to open an account—"

"I have an account."

She didn't look pleased at the interruption, taking another moment to consider Pharisäer with dark eyes sunk deep in wrinkles. "You are quite mistaken—"

"I am Zerf—"

The banker stopped her with a raised hand. "I am entirely aware of who you are," she said. "And I am entirely aware of what you are."

What I am. Pharisäer's chest tightened. She wanted to crawl under this desk and hide away from those hard and knowing eyes. "I am the head of the Täuschung. I am Zerfall—"

"You are not." The old woman shuffled papers on her desk, looking impatient to get back to the important work awaiting her. The real work, dealing with real people.

"I am—"

"A Fragment. We would be happy to arrange an account for you, but what kind of bank would we be if we allowed people's delusions to access their funds? Hmn? No. Quite."

There was no bend in the woman, no give. When the world ended, when time turned her desk to dust, she would remain.

Pharisäer contemplated the fantastic wealth Zahlen recently deposited into the Täuschung accounts. Accounts Pharisäer could not access.

It doesn't matter. This will still hurt Hölle. She'll think the money gone, she won't think to check. She almost believed it.

The old banker leaned forward, geldwechsler tilting precariously but remaining atop her head. "Or you can return to us when you are real." She sat back, clearly dismissing Pharisäer. "If there is nothing else we can help you with . . ."

AN HOUR LATER PHARISÄER realized that, while Hölle remained fantastically wealthy, she had managed to beggar herself. Though the Täuschung coffers were swollen from the sales of several churches and properties, Pharisäer could not access the accounts. Not yet.

Somehow the bank knew she was a Fragment.

A temporary setback, nothing more.

Once Hölle was dead, Pharisäer would be real. It would all be hers.

HÖLLE LAY IN BED, contemplating the utter failure of everything she worked to achieve for the last four hundred years. Her tears had dried.

How had it gone wrong? The church ran smoothly for centuries. Why had her Geisteskranken priests suddenly began fighting in the streets?

Fear. Zerfall kept them in line. Everyone was terrified of her. And now Zerfall was gone. Pharisäer said she would see to the running of the church while Hölle healed. Had it been more difficult that she thought? While she looked identical to Zerfall, there were definitely notable differences. For one thing, Pharisäer had none of

Zerfall's tight wound rage. Even though Hölle found herself increasingly afraid of Pharisäer, it was a different fear. Zerfall had been unstoppable. She knew the words of Wahrergott and dedicated her every waking moment to making them true.

That's not quite true.

In the early days, the first century after the One True God wrote his words in the minds of the two sisters, Zerfall had been focussed. In the last few decades however more and more of the day to day running of the church fell to Hölle. Zerfall had been increasingly distant. Hölle hadn't minded taking on the extra responsibilities to help her sister. She was better at the daily minutiae of running a church. Zerfall was too impulsive, too quick to anger.

She was too interested in herself. Which made sense for a Gefahrgeist.

Hölle imagined how angry Zerfall would be at the damage done to her church and shuddered.

It's not my fault, Pharisäer said—

Pharisäer let her down. It was time to take back the reins of the Täuschung. It was past time.

Hölle climbed from her bed stood waiting for the pain. Nothing. She lifted her shirt and examined the scar, little more than an inch long, where Blutblüte had thrust into her gut. She took a deep breath and held it. No pain.

Good. That's good.

Releasing her shirt, Hölle reached her fingers high over her head, stretching tall. Again no pain.

That's very good.

Hinging at the waist, she reached toward the ground. Fingertips a hands' span from her toes, she bent no farther. She frowned, noticing the clotted dust-balls gathering in the corner. *I used to be able to place my hands flat on the floor.* It was effortless, not even requiring regular stretching. She hung there, willing herself lower, but gave up after a moment and once again stood straight. She blinked in surprise. She'd been so annoyed with her loss of flexibility, she hadn't even realized it didn't hurt in the least.

She tried a few more stretches targeting her stomach and all were painless.

It only hurts when . . . She released a slow breath. *When Pharisäer's here, Blutblüte at her side, talking about how badly I've been wounded.* The thought sent a pang of pain into Hölle's belly.

Had Pharisäer been keeping her bed-ridden?

"She's here to help."

Really? She's doing a terrible job. Your church is in chaos, your priests scattering like cockroaches fleeing a fire. How had it got so bad so fast?

You don't even know what she is. I wish Aas were here so I could ask him—The thought froze her. Aas was gone, put beyond reach by Pharisäer's machinations. *Coincidence, nothing more. She couldn't have done this just so I couldn't talk to the wretch.*

There were others she might talk to, but Aas' Wahnist tendency to spew his vile thoughts meant she could—in some twisted way—trust him. With anyone else she confided in or questioned, she'd never really know their intentions.

Zerfall, sometimes I think I didn't give you enough credit.

"I don't need her," Hölle told the mirror. Her reflection arched an eyebrow. *And Pharisäer?* it seemed to ask.

There weren't a lot of options. Either Pharisäer was sent by Wahrergott, or she was something else. The list of other possibilities wasn't long; if Wahrergott hadn't sent Pharisäer then she was a manifestation of Hölle's delusions. Perhaps it wasn't just her church that was falling apart.

If Pharisäer is a manifestation, you're losing your mind.

How could one tell? How could she judge her own sanity? What was madness where gods wrote their holy message in the minds of feverish girls and all reality responded to the desires of the people?

"Do you remember a time without me?" Why did that question bother her so much? Why couldn't she forget that stupid dream?

She tried to shake off her doubts. It was time—no, it was past time—to regain control of her church. The Täuschung needed her.

Hölle walked to the door, reaching for the oak handle. She stopped. She hadn't left her chambers in weeks.

"It's not my fault," she told herself. "I've been convalescing."

She hesitated. Aside from Pharisäer, she'd seen almost no one in that time. What would they think? Would they wonder why she'd been hiding for so long? Would they see her doubts?

"I have no doubts," she whispered.

Right, Pharisäer took them. Isn't that what she said?

Yes.

And so you have no doubts.

She licked her lips, staring at the door.

Then why are you hesitating?

"Because I have doubts."

And you know what that means.

Yes, she did. And she knew someone she could talk to, assuming Pharisäer hadn't sent the woman away already.

Hölle yanked the door open and snapped a sharp, "You!" at Captain Gedankenlos who stood guard at her door.

Gedankenlos snapped to attention, waiting.

"Is Selbs Bitterkeit in the church?"

"She's preparing to leave for—"

"Fetch her. Now." Hölle slammed the door before the man answered.

She stood, breathing hard, her heart pounding. "There, that wasn't so scary."

You still haven't left the room.

"I didn't need to."

Selbs, a loyal Täuschung priest, was either a Doppelgangist or a Mehrere. Hölle couldn't remember. A figment of Selb's imagination followed her everywhere, hounded her every step. *She knows about Fragments.* Hölle had questions. Questions she didn't want to ask. Questions that left her sweating with fear. *I need to know.*

She didn't have to wait long for Selbs Bitterkeit's timid knock. Swinging the door open, Hölle ushered the two women in. Gedankenlos once again stood at his post, expressionless.

The shorter of the two, dark hair lank and greasy, stared at her feet, never once daring eye contact. She shuffled forward, the tatty hem of her filthy robes dragging on the floor. Acne, red and raw and leaking fresh blood, pocked her sallow cheeks and she picked at torn and ragged fingernails. The sour stench of body odour followed her and Hölle backed away in distaste. She'd forgotten how bad the woman smelled.

The second woman, as tall and proud and beautiful as the other was bent and ugly, nodded to Hölle as if in commiseration. Gorgeous blue eyes, framed in a well-maintained mountain of luxurious blond hair, examined Hölle. "You look awful."

"I have need of your advice," said Hölle, ignoring the blond.

Red-rimmed eyes darted up, lunging toward eye contact, only to flinch away. "We are unworthy," the short, dark woman said.

"Well *you* are," said the blond.

"And yet still we'll serve to the best of our meagre abilities," finished the dark woman.

"You are a Doppelgangist?" Hölle asked.

"No," they answered in eerie unison, "Mehrere."

Mehrere. Hölle ground her teeth, hating the word. She nodded as if this was the answer she sought, but wasn't sure what the difference was. Both types of Geisteskranken manifested as multiple people. "Which is the original?"

"I am," said the dark woman.

"Good," said Hölle. "Go stand in the hall."

The woman bowed with a whimper and fled. The tall blond grinned perfect teeth and showed no hint of fear or deference when Hölle turned to face her.

"You are an aspect of her personality?" Hölle asked, taking in the perfect complexion, statuesque body, and voluptuous curves.

The woman shook her head, hair and eyes dancing. "I am everything Selbs wishes she was. She hates herself. I am what she wants to be so strongly it is breaking her mind." She smiled, full lips curving up at the corners. "She's a coward."

"What do I call you?"

The blunt question received a raised eyebrow, but the woman looked otherwise unperturbed. "My name is Beherrscher."

"And what do you want?"

"What all manifestations want." Beherrscher shrugged, blue eyes mischievous. "I want what that other woman wants."

"Selbs?" Hölle asked, confused.

"No, the one stomping around the halls pretending to be Zerfall."

Hölle's breath caught. *She's wrong. She must be wrong.* "Who else knows?"

Beherrscher waved a hand, either unaware of the danger she was in or unconcerned. "Not Selbs; she's an idiot."

Did it matter who knew about Pharisäer? Hölle couldn't decide. Too many thoughts battled for dominance. Was Beherrscher correct and Pharisäer a manifestation of Hölle's decaying mental state? Did Wahrergott have nothing to do with the woman's sudden appearance in Hölle's room? "And what does Pharisäer want?"

Beherrscher winked and said, "I think maybe it's the same the same thing you want."

"Don't try my patience."

"Oh come now. Don't get angry. I've always suspected. Your secret is safe with me. We are the same. We want the same things." Beherrscher reached a hand out to caress Hölle's shoulder. Though the touch was soft, timid even, her eyes showed no hint of shyness.

Hölle's chest felt tight, like something held her heart in a crushing fist. *Don't ask. Don't ask. You don't want the answer. Send her away. Kill her.* "What do we want?" she whispered.

"What all our kind want: To be the original."

Our kind.

That fist crushed the air from her lungs. The world collapsed into a narrowing tunnel and a buzzing filler her ears. She wobbled on unsteady feet. No, this Fragment, this figment of delusion was wrong. *Had* to be wrong! *She's trying to use you, to manipulate you.* "We're sisters. You're wrong."

Beherrscher shrugged. "Then I am wrong."

Again Hölle thought of the dream and Zerfall's words: "Do you remember a time without me? Because I remember a time without you." It felt like Zerfall had been saying that her entire life.

"No," said Hölle, unsure if it were a denial or if she were answering Zerfall's question.

The room darkened and Beherrscher's eyes widened with fear as she retreated, glancing at the strange shapes coalescing. Against one wall a shadowy cot lurked in the memory of a room reeking of poverty and the rotting flesh of her parents. One small girl lay in the cot, feverish dreams twisting her face and malnourished body.

I was there. I remember being there. I'm real!

Zerfall had always been there. Always.

"No," repeated Hölle.

Tears leaked from clenched eyes and she drove the palms of her hands against them as if forcing the tears back in. The hallucinations faded, the stench and whimpering becoming, once again, a memory.

Hölle pulled her hands away and opened her eyes. She sat on her bed, Beherrscher beside her. She had no recollection of sitting.

"I'm sorry," said Beherrscher. She placed cool fingertips on Hölle's chin and turned her face until they were eye to eye. "Where is Zerfall?"

"Dead."

"Then why the tears? You won!"

I . . . won? Hölle felt far from victorious. "I'm the original?"

"Yes, now that she is dead."

That wasn't what she meant. *I wasn't always real?* Why else the dream of Zerfall? *Is that why she tried to kill me?* The question led to more questions. If Hölle accepted she was nothing more than a manifestation of Zerfall's deranged mind . . .

Could all of this, herself, Swarm, Wahrergott and the Täuschung have sprung from the febrile mind of one feverish little girl all those hundreds of years ago?

"Did we—Did *she* hallucinate Wahrergott?" Hölle asked, mind numb from shock. *What then of Swarm?* "Is all this for nothing?"

"Even if there was no Wahrergott before," said Beherrscher, "there is now. Thousands of Täuschung priests believe, but more importantly, millions of souls populate Swarm. I guarantee they believe."

"So it is real, then. If humanity suffers enough, we'll escape our prison and become gods."

"I don't know about that," said Beherrscher. "Are there limits to what delusion can achieve?"

"But if everyone believes, if every single soul knows it's true . . . it *has* to be true."

If you accept all this, you're accepting you aren't real, that you're nothing more than Zerfall's manifest delusion. Did she have a choice?

"I am real," said Hölle. "If belief defines reality, I am real."

"If you are indeed a Fragment, then only when Zerfall is dead will you truly be real. Until then, you remain a figment of delusion, a thin slice of manifest self-hatred."

Thin slice. Ever since Zerfall stabbed her she felt less and less real. With each passing day she felt more distant. She remembered all those dreams where she faded from existence, became translucent and unreal. What did that mean? *With Zerfall dead, shouldn't I feel* more *real?*

"And Pharisäer?" Hölle asked, dreading the answer.

"She's the same as us."

"Can a figment of delusion manifest its own delusions?"

"We're manifestations of broken minds," said Beherrscher. "It's no surprise we have our own delusions."

"You?"

Beherrscher nodded.

"But you're gorgeous!"

"So are you. So was Zerfall. Attractiveness is no guarantee of happiness. Or sanity." She leered, eyes wide and crazed. "Quite the opposite, if we're anything to go by."

Hölle rubbed at her eyes, clearing away the last of her tears. "So Pharisäer wants to kill me, to replace me."

Beherrscher looked at Hölle as if she couldn't comprehend the depth of her ignorance. "It doesn't work like that. She has to *destroy* you."

Destroy. She thought back to all the times Pharisäer convinced her to remain in bed. *She was running the church, taking over more and more of my life.* She remembered how she herself pushed Zerfall from the Täuschung, reducing her sister's responsibilities. *No, we're not sisters. Yes we are! Were!* God, she was so confused. "Four hundred years I have done Wahrergott's work; Pharisäer can't break me."

"Look at yourself. You haven't bathed or changed your clothes in weeks. You stink. You're bent, and soft, and sobbing. You're weak. Her work is almost finished."

She's right. Zerfall would never let this happen. I'm disgusting. Pharisäer made me scared and complacent while she stole my life. Rage slashed through her like a torrential flood and she slapped Beherrscher's hand away. "Careful."

Beherrscher clapped happily. "Better! I knew some life remained. When Pharisäer truly breaks you, you'll give up. You'll surrender everything and she'll take your place, becoming the original."

"She'll become Hölle."

"No, she'll become you. She'll become Zerfall."

"I am Zerfall now?" She wanted that. More than anything she wanted to be Zerfall, to have that deadly confidence. But it felt wrong, rang hollow like the shallowest lie. *That's not me.* She was Hölle and she knew it. Still, she could pretend. "I have to kill Pharisäer."

Beherrscher laughed again. "You really don't know? You can't kill her, she isn't real. She's a figment of a deranged imagination. Kill her, and she'll come back."

"How do I beat her?"

Beherrscher's face fell. "Oh, you poor, poor thing. You don't."

"But . . ."

"Once your delusions manifest, the end is only a matter of time. It's the axiom that governs all Geisteskranken. Our delusions grow in strength until they consume us. Someday I will replace Selbs. Someday Pharisäer will replace you."

"No. I am Hölle. I gave birth to Swarm. I am the saviour of humanity."

Beherrscher grinned, a bright smile of warmth and happiness, all hint of sadness gone like it had never been there. "You can't even call yourself Zerfall."

Hölle glanced toward the severed hand sitting on her desk. It hadn't changed in the weeks it sat there. She remembered seeing the eye close.

The hand refused to rot while with each day Hölle felt less real.

I keep expecting to see Zerfall every time I wake. She dreamed about her every night.

She couldn't think of herself as the original, as Zerfall. In the very core of her soul she knew who she was: Hölle.

She understood now what that meant. "Zerfall lives." She knew she was right.

"That's bad," said Beherrscher.

"Yes." *Zerfall must die.* "Pharisäer first," said Hölle, sitting straighter.

"You still aren't getting it. You can't win. She is a part of you. As long as you live, Pharisäer lives." Beherrscher offered a sad smile. "Unless you can find some way of curing yourself of your delusions."

Was that what was happening to her, was that why she felt less real with each day? Was Zerfall somehow becoming increasingly sane? *I'll fade to nothing.*

Beherrscher watched, eyes measuring, waiting.

I'm not gone yet. It isn't too late. Hölle stood. "Pharisäer is no Zerfall."

"She will always undermine you. You can never trust her."

Hölle laughed, a bark of scorn. "And I can trust you?"

"Of course not." Beherrscher winked. "But you know what I want."

"To be the original." Hölle paced to the door and flung it open. Selbs, standing in the hall, head bowed and looking nervous, started with a squeak.

Gedankenlos stood at the door, massive shoulders filling the entrance to her room. As always, a longsword hung at one hip and he wore his mismatched motley of chain and scale armour. Sometimes Hölle wondered whether he slept in it. Allegedly sane—at least unable to manifest any delusions as far as she had seen—the man was a ruthless killer. Hölle prized him for his stunning lack of imagination.

"Gedankenlos, enter. I have a job for you." She nodded at Selbs. "Bring her."

The Captain rudely shoved Selbs into the room and entered behind her.

"You can't kill Pharisäer," said Beherrscher. "Having someone else do it for you won't work either. If anything, your fear of her will make her stronger."

Hölle grinned. "I'll deal with Pharisäer later." She examined Selbs for a long moment. *If the Täuschung hear about this they will doubt me.* She shuddered to think what the doubt of scores of powerful Geisteskranken might achieve. *Selbs is as loyal as any. I can trust her.* But Beherrscher . . . No, she couldn't trust the Fragment. *What if Beherrscher lied about killing the original?* If Zerfall lived—and Hölle was increasingly sure she did—she'd return. *What happens if Zerfall dies?* She needed to know beyond any doubt.

"I'm sorry," Hölle said to Selbs.

"For what?" Selbs asked, unable to make eye contact.

"Kill her."

Gedankenlos drove his sword into Selbs's back and up into her chest so hard her feet lifted from the floor. Beherrscher, eyes wide with shock, watched Selbs hang there, twitching, spasms running through her body, until Gedankenlos slid her from his blade, dumping the corpse to the ground.

"You're still here," said Hölle to Beherrscher. But where she expected to see victory, she found terror.

Beherrscher stood, tears falling, hands pressed to her lips. "You killed her."

"So now you're real," answered Hölle.

"No," said Beherrscher. The woman looked sick, like she'd suddenly come down with something virulent and deadly. "You killed her before I could destroy her. I was so close." She wobbled unsteadily. "You've killed me too."

As Selbs wheezed her last dying breath Beherrscher collapsed and disappeared as if she'd never been.

If it's true and I am Zerfall's Fragment, I can't just kill her. It couldn't be true. *I'm trapped. Doomed.*

Hölle turned her gaze on Gedankenlos. "Have someone clean this mess up. Make it spotless. There must be no hint anything happened here."

"Of course," he said, bowing. "I feel I should point out, I have no idea what any of this was about."

"That's why you live."

Gedankenlos nodded and fled.

Damn you, Zerfall. This was all her fault.

Did Zerfall know? Had she grown to distrust Hölle?

Certainly they argued more often in the last decades than ever before, disagreeing on the path Täuschung should take. Was that enough reason for Zerfall to try and kill her? Did she fear their disagreements meant Hölle was trying to replace her?

Was that what I was doing without even realizing it? She felt lost, afloat in a sea of madness. Nothing made sense. Nothing was real.

Hölle retreated into her room, climbing back into bed and pulling the covers up to her chin. At least something remained constant and real. She was safe here. Out there, out in that insane world, Zerfall walked free and alive, and that terrified her. Hölle may have been the planner, but Zerfall was the killer.

When she returned, she'd see the mess her church had become. She'd be angry, murderously angry.

Pharisäer ran Täuschung for weeks, pretending to be Zerfall. Hölle shuddered to think what plans she might have set in motion. She groaned. All the church's current problems, was that Pharisäer's doing? It made so much sense. *She wants to replace me and she's using my own religion against me.*

"I can't win. I can't stop her. She's had too much time. It's not my fault. I was stabbed, I needed to heal."

You were never the killer. Zerfall, she gloried in violence. By bloody Swarm she wished Zerfall was here; Pharisäer would be nothing before her wrath.

Zerfall.

Hölle sat up.

She's alive. She knew it to be true.

The more she thought about it the surer she was that there was no way Aas had lied. He must believe he'd killed Zerfall. And if he believed, so did Pharisäer.

If Zerfall was alive, where would she go?

She'd come here, to Geld. She'd come to kill me, to finish what she started. A shiver of mixed fear and excitement danced fingertips down Hölle's spine. *She might be here already, watching. Waiting.*

She remembered the eye in the hand sliding closed. Zerfall had been watching, listening. She probably knew everything.

Hölle glanced at the severed hand. The eye remained closed.

"Zerfall might be the killer, but I am the planner. I've always been able to out-think her." Zerfall would return—if she hadn't already—and Hölle would use her to defeat Pharisäer. She'd deal with Zerfall after. Somehow. *We're sisters. Were sisters.*

Hölle eyed the closed door. Soon Pharisäer would return.

AAS RAISED HIS LONG knife, ready to stab Nimmer in the throat. *If you try to understand every last aspect of this situation, you will be here forever.*

The man didn't move, remained frozen in time, eyes wide, mouth open in a silent scream.

How slow is he moving in time if I can sit across the table from him and he seems motionless?

Pretty damned slow.

And the bread crumb burst into flames when I flicked it away. How fast is time moving in comparison beyond Nimmer's influence?

Pretty damned fast.

How long would it take to escape Nimmer's sphere of influence? Too long, he decided. He'd escape faster if he killed the man.

But if I lean in close enough to stab him, I'll be deeper in his time well. Outside time will move even faster and I'll be trapped here longer.

Which would be faster, kill the man, or run away?

Pharisäer sent me to kill him. If I leave him alive, she wins. Not a chance that was happening.

Aas would have to kill Nimmer from a distance.

Standing, he spun his knife in nimble fingers until he gripped the tip. He flicked it at Nimmer's throat with a practised flip of the wrist. The knife slowed until it hung an arm's lengths from Aas. Aas blinked at the knife and smacked a hand to his forehead.

That's embarrassing.

He really should have foreseen that. Thank the gods Pharisäer hadn't witnessed his moment of utter stupidity.

Could he kill Nimmer from a distance? Maybe if he had something long, like a spear.

Aas glanced about the room. Apparently the Getrennt wasn't in the habit of keeping spears and polearms in his kitchen.

You're going to have to get close enough to stab him. He slapped himself again. He'd already thrown the knife. All he had to do now was lean in close enough to see if the thrown knife had finished its work. *Best get it done fast.*

A knife wound to the throat, he realized, was not a fast enough death.

Drawing a second blade and holding it tight in his fist, Aas ducked toward Nimmer. The thrown knife, which hung in the air, accelerated away, its slow spin becoming a blur. The low hum returned and scaled upward in pitch and volume until it became a throat-tearing scream of mind-shattering terror and then choked off to nothing as the knife sank home. The crumb, which Aas flicked toward the man earlier, bounced harmlessly off the Getrennt's cheek, little more than insult to injury. Aas drove the second knife through Nimmer's wide, terrified eye and deep into the man's brain. Twisting it, he wrenched it free.

Nimmer's head hit the wrought-iron table with a dull *tong* like a muted church bell.

Retrieving his knives, Aas wiped the blades clean on Nimmer's robes and spun on his heel, striding toward the front hall. How long had he been in here? It felt like minutes, but might have been days, or even months. What if it was longer? Had Pharisäer trapped him here for years?

Gods, what a fantastically clever woman. While he felt a deep bubbling rage at having been tricked, he had to admire her ingenious plan. That anger, he decided, was best directed at himself; if he was smarter he'd have escaped sooner.

Still, no good deed should go unpunished.

Zerfall would never have done something like that. She'd either have crushed his will beneath her Gefahrgeist power, or killed him. Impressed as he was with Pharisäer, she was no Zerfall.

But is she more, less, or just different? He couldn't decide; desire waged war with logic. Pharisäer proved herself dangerous, but she also stopped short of killing him. Why? And how could she have known how long he'd take to escape? Aas might have been trapped in that room for years. Why not just kill him? Did Pharisäer fear Aas? And why didn't she command his loyalty and devotion as Zerfall had? Did she lack Zerfall's Gefahrgeist abilities? Thinking back, he realized she showed no hint of that power. He followed and obeyed her because he *wanted* to.

And that meant if he didn't want to follow and obey he could choose otherwise.

He was unaccustomed to choice when it came to relationships.

Aas grinned through clenched teeth as he left the Getrennt's home and found himself again in the streets of Geld. They looked the same. Glancing about, he checked the styles of the clothing worn by nearby pedestrians. They looked no different than when he left. Either he hadn't been gone long—and knowing how quickly Geld fashions changed, no more than a month—or styles had come a full circle in which case it might be hundreds of years.

Aas checked the names on the stores around him. New businesses rose and fell faster here than in any other city-state. The same businesses lined the street he'd last seen before entering Nimmer's residence. He hadn't been gone long, weeks at most.

A lot could happen in a few weeks.

A Geisteskranken could crumble under the weight of her delusions in a fraction of that time.

Aas collapsed in on himself like a tower undermined by sappers as he *twisted* into a condor. Stretching his wings wide, he leapt to the sky. All around people scattered, fleeing his display of rampant insanity and ravaged reality. He clawed his way into the air, wings driving him ever upward.

Did Hölle live, or had Pharisäer already replaced her?

He'd have to return to the church to find out. Catching a hot updraught blowing in from the desert, Aas sailed the chaotic currents of Geld. Able to avoid the twisting streets and alleys and the shoulder-to-shoulder crush of the city's population, it would take him only moments to reach the Täuschung church.

Where am I going? Should he see if Hölle lived, or should he look for Pharisäer?

Hölle hated him. Of that he had no doubt. But she'd found him useful in the past. If her sanity had further decayed, she might once again have need and be more willing to accept his inability to hide his thoughts. *Or maybe she'll think I abandoned her and kill me on sight.*

He needed to think.

If Pharisäer sent Aas to kill Nimmer because she feared him, she'd expect him to have been gone a lot longer and wouldn't be prepared for his return. He'd have to watch her carefully, read her expression for clues as to her thoughts and intent. If she sent him there to appreciate the puzzle, she'd be happy to see him and gloat at her cleverness. *Her reaction will tell me everything.*

Aas' stomach rumbled as he caught the faint scent of rotting meat. When had he last eaten? He couldn't remember. Hunger-sharpened eyes scanned the streets below, searching for carrion or easy prey. A rat, a squirrel, a cat, even a one of those yappy little dogs the wealthy carried about in their purses. Anything small enough he could lift it away and tear the life from. He couldn't help himself. Each time he *twisted*, the bird grew in strength, became more of who he was. The bird wanted food; the crunch of brittle bones, the tang of ripe organs.

Even from this height he recognized the mass of dark brown hair, the cocky swing of strutting hips.

Zerfall?

No, Zerfall was dead. This had to be Pharisäer.

Hunger forgotten, Aas followed Pharisäer, careful not to allow his shadow to cross within her sight.

She's not far from Nimmer's house, he realized. And she was heading toward the Täuschung church. Glancing down and back, Aas saw he could draw a straight line from Nimmer's house to the church and she was right in the middle. *She's even on the same street.*

Had she been watching the house? No, that was insane. She'd have no way of knowing when he'd solve the riddle and free himself. And yet there she was, striding purposefully—hurrying even—away from Nimmer's home and toward the Täuschung church.

She knows I'm free. He didn't know how, but felt sure he was right. Perhaps she'd been warned by another Geisteskranken. It was definitely possible. There were Mirrorists who believed they saw the future. Maybe one told her when Aas would escape.

Aas tucked his wings and rolled into a cooler, slower moving current.

Coasting lower, he followed.

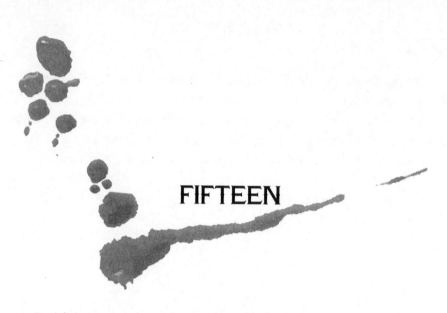

FIFTEEN

Don't let your toes peek past the edge of your blanket.

—Basamortuan Proverb

JATEKO RODE BEHIND ZERFALL, uncomfortably aware of the proximity of her cold ass and the fact his groin moved against it with Tod's every jolting step. At some point earlier in the morning, before the savage crush of the day's heat swept in to suck the life from him, the horse's stride changed. When they first set out Tod ran smooth as rolling thunder, but hours of this merciless pace broke something in his rear hips. When the grinding sound of bone on bone got so loud they could no longer ignore it, Zerfall reined Tod in to a more sedate walk. His hip made a *grind-pock!* noise with every step.

Hunger. The empty gut-churning need to peel lobes from fresh brain, suck blood from a heart that had beaten but moments earlier, and hear the wet-twig *snap* of bone and the taste of fresh marrow, was his only distraction. Jateko's mouth watered at the thought.

The hacked remnants of Abiega's tent hung over Tod, doing a rather shoddy job of hiding his advanced state of decay. They'd cut holes for him to see through, but anyone looking closely would see there was nothing in there but maggot-gnawed black pits and exposed bone. They'd been no more successful with Zerfall's disguise, though they covered her eyes in a thin blood-stained strip of cloth torn from the karpan. She said she couldn't even tell it was there.

She looks like one of the ragged insane who wandered the desert following Harea's voice. Or their own delusions or maybe both; Jateko was less sure every day. It didn't look much like a proper Basamortuan *oihal*, but as long as she kept her hands—*hand*, he corrected—tucked in her sleeves and the cowl pulled forward, it would do. At least she didn't stink. The desert had long leached the moisture from her body and she was a mummified husk, crackling like dry grass every time she moved. Her right leg, splinted around her shattered knee, stuck out at an awkward angle.

Not like these lazy hiria ero know anything about the Basamortuan tribes anyway, said Abiega.

No doubt one blanket swaddled savage wandering out of the desert looked much like another. Still, it wouldn't do to allow anyone a chance at close scrutiny.

And one good gust of desert wind will end this pathetic charade right quick.

"True."

"Did you say something?" Zerfall asked.

"There's something up ahead," Jateko said, pointing over her shoulder. "Are those buildings?" He'd never seen anything like it, monolithic structures of stone. No way this could be moved. *Those people always stay in the same place?* He felt Abiega's shrug. "Is that Geld?"

"Grenzstadt," said Zerfall, "if I'm not mistaken."

"I've never heard of that city-state."

"It's a garrison town within Geldangelegenheiten. The city of Geld is the centre and there are several outlying territories dependant on it." She examined the fortified structures as they drew closer. "There'll be soldiers," she added.

Fear stabbed into Jateko's gut. What the hells was he doing leaving the Basamortuan and everything he'd ever known? He knew nothing of the *hiria ero* and their strange ways. What kind of terrified psychotics walled themselves in stone cities and shat, day after day, in exactly the same place? Did they carry their slop buckets out to the city's perimeter every day, or did their entire civilization stink of shite?

"This is never going to work," said Jateko. "We're riding the rotting corpse of a horse. This *karpan* isn't going to fool anyone. Look at Tod's legs."

Zerfall glanced at Tod's sand-chafed legs, yellowed bone showing through where flesh had abraded away. "You're probably right."

"We should leave him, go in on foot."

"No," she said without hesitation. That one word brooked no argument. He thought about asking why, but decided against it. If she wanted the horse, she got the horse.

You're a bit of a pushover, aren't you? Abiega asked.

I understand I need her.

Pfft! You're in love. You'll do anything for her.

She's a corpse! I can't . . . we can't . . .

There can only be love if there's also rutting?

You ever been in love without rutting being part of it? Jateko asked.

Well, no. But—

That's what I thought, said Jateko, who'd never rutted anything other than his own hand.

It changes nothing. You love her. That, or her weird city-states madness is con-trolling you.

Jateko ignored the last, didn't want to think about it. *She's useful, that's all.*

You want to rut—

"Shut up!"

Zerfall glanced over her shoulder, one thin and tatty eyebrow raised. "Pardon?"

"Sorry. Not you."

She nodded, accepting. "What are you arguing about in there?"

"Nothing," Jateko answered, feeling his face flush with heat.

She turned away and gestured to the walled garrison growing ever closer. "We could go around it and head straight for Geld." His stomach, so empty it felt like it had grown fangs and was well into devouring itself, growled loud enough Zerfall flashed him a quick grin of brown teeth and rotting gums. "I guess not," she said.

"I don't think I can go another day."

"You can't eat some normal food?" Mouth crooked and tattered lips dark with rot, she looked sceptical.

The thought of chewing tough goat meat or choking down some tuberous vegetable left him nauseated. "Maybe, if I had no choice." But he doubted it.

He needed liver and heart and brain, freshly slain and warm with the memory of life.

A S THEY APPROACHED THE garrison, Jateko saw men, armed and armoured in glinting steel, standing before an open gate. He'd never seen so much metal in one place. With what he saw gathered here he could make a name for himself and return to the Hasiera a hero. Was this all the steel in the city, an ostentatious display of wealth to scare off any would-be Basamortuan raiders? What if more steel remained hidden within the city? Harea, the *hiria ero* could conquer the desert tribes any time they wanted.

The city beyond the garrison grew in detail. The pieces came together in Jateko's mind and he understood, for the first time, the scale of construction. The outer wall towered four times his height, some of the stones the size of a grown man.

"That's impossible," he said, staring in awe. Those rocks could only have come from— "We're a month south of the Kälte Mountains." And that was if one travelled without the difficulty of lugging man-sized stone. He thought about the terrain separating the garrison and the mountains from which this stone much have come. "Your gods built this." There was no other explanation.

"I don't think so," said Zerfall.

"This is impossible."

She laughed and a fly escaped her open mouth. Zerfall scowled, following it with the empty pits of her eyes before drawing breath to say, "Geld is a thousand times this size."

Stunned to silence, Jateko's mouth opened and then snapped closed as the fly darted toward him. No way he wanted to taste that.

The guards standing before the open gate glanced in their direction with bored disinterest. There was more steel here than in all the Basamortuan tribes combined. They wore it like it was nothing. The outer wall, he now saw, was as thick as a man sprawled on his back, arms outstretched. If the *hiria ero* built this, they were invincible. Not at all the soft and helpless victims he heard stories of.

Did you know? he asked Abiega.

The dauntless warrior remained quiet, but Jateko sensed his stunned awe.

Everything we believe, thought Jateko, *everything the Basamortuan tell themselves is a lie. We don't live in the desert because we're tougher or smarter, we live there because we have no choice.*

A hundred united clans couldn't conquer this one garrison. And Zerfall said Geld was a thousand times bigger.

His whole world wobbled, threatening to come apart and he grabbed Zerfall's waist to stop from toppling off Tod's back. She ignored him, maybe didn't even feel his panicked grip.

As they neared the gate one of the guards approached, eyes narrowing, nostrils flaring as he inspected them.

Jateko felt Zerfall tense and did his best to prepare himself for death.

"Your horse has seen better days," said the guard in a surprisingly soft voice as they rode past and into the city.

A woman? Encased as she was in steel and leather, Jateko had missed the slight curve of hips and breasts under all that armour. *Even their women are warriors.* Having seen Zerfall in action, he shouldn't have been surprised, but he always believed she was an exception rather than just another city-states woman. What if they all fought like her? What if she wasn't even particularly skilled?

The other guards laughed and none made any attempt to stop or slow Zerfall and Jateko's progress.

And why should they, said Abiega, *we're sand-fleas.*

"Sun-brained sand-stickers," the woman added to more laughter as she returned to her place in the shade.

Jateko bowed his head to hide his shame. Nothing he achieved could ever matter in the face of this stone behemoth. "I once asked what made you think the city-states were more civilized than the Basamortuan tribes," he whispered into Zerfall's ear. "Please forgive my ignorance."

"There's nothing to forgive," said Zerfall. "It was a good question. Stone and steel do not make one civilized, just more adept at violence."

Jateko wasn't sure what the difference was.

His heart thrummed in his chest. He couldn't breathe. "I made a mistake," he said. "I should return to the desert." He swallowed a hard lump and closed his eyes. "I want to go home."

"No," said Zerfall in that dead cold final way she had of crushing dissent. "I'm scared too, but nothing will stop me."

What scares the dead? Jateko drew a long breath and let it out slowly, searching for a calm that evaded him. He smacked his lips in distaste, wrinkling his nose. "I was right about one thing."

"What's that?"

"Your civilization stinks of shite."

ZERFALL GUIDED TOD THROUGH narrow streets clogged with refuse with nudges from her left knee, touches with her numb fingers, and quiet clucks of her rotting tongue. The horse, head hanging low, rear hips grinding and clicking with every step, seemed to understand her every intent.

A molar hung at the back of her jaw, refusing to fall out. She thought about reaching in to yank it free, but every piece of her that dropped off was a piece she'd never again have. *I'm clinging to rotting teeth.*

They rode past an inn, a chipped wooden sign hanging from sagging eaves proclaimed it the Unteren Lauf. She had the strangest desire to enter and take a room. She wanted to order a meal, sit in a common area, surrounded by the chatter of voices and the sight and smell of people going about their lives. She wanted a beer and a glass of red wine and to feel soft sheets on her skin.

You're dead. You don't sleep, eat, or even breathe.

But she wanted to, wanted it more than anything. She wanted all the things that came with life. Scents and flavours good and bad; she missed them. Colour. She barely remembered what the world looked like before it became this monochromatic hell. Endless shades of grey. She even missed pain. If something hurt, at least you knew you were alive. She scowled at her jutting right leg, lashed to tent poles. She kept waiting for it to heal or to hurt or for it to change in some way. But it wouldn't. Not unless it got worse.

"Zerfall?" Jateko, perched behind her with his arms wrapped around her waist, sounded scared. He'd lost his naïve confidence and she missed it. "How am I going to kill and eat someone here?"

This was a walled garrison, a border town. Judging from the number of armed men and women prowling the streets, she felt sure murder was a commonplace occurrence. Cannibalism, however, wasn't.

Ahead a score of people gathered around a young man with slim hips and perfect hair. A pair of swords poked past broad shoulders, framing a handsome, square-jawed face.

The man stood, arms raised, shouting to be heard over the street noise. "You all know me for I am Grausamer Schlächter, the Greatest Swordsman in all Geld."

This received a smattering of lazy applause from the crowd. Zerfall clucked to Tod and he slowed, stopping beyond the crowd. The loose molar wobbled against the decayed remnants of her tongue.

"Why are we stopping?" Jateko asked.

"A Swordsman," she said, unsure whether she answered his question.

She felt Jateko lean forward to peer over her shoulder.

"I have come from Geld," Grausamer yelled, "seeking challengers. Do any here dare?" The crowd, made up of armed men and women scarred from dozens of battles, shuffled and mumbled. "None?"

"You killed Vergangener Traum last time you came through," someone answered. "He was the best Grenzstadt had to offer."

"That was two years ago," Grausamer said petulantly.

Jateko slid from Tod's swayed back.

"Where are you going?" Zerfall asked.

"A great Swordsman. He'd be perfect."

"Are you insane? Get back here."

Either he didn't hear or he ignored her. Without glancing back, Jateko shoved his way into the crowd. His shoulders and chest may have filled out, but he looked small and weak in this gathering.

Grausamer saw the movement and parted those around him with an imperious wave. When he caught sight of Jateko his face fell in glum disappointment. "Basamortuan?" he asked, wrinkling his nose and casting a contemptuous eye over the slight youth. "I've heard you are fierce warriors, but you look a little young."

"Is it acceptable for us to kill each other in the street?" Jateko blurted. "The guards—"

"Swordsmen are *special*," said Grausamer as if that explained everything. Maybe it did, but to Zerfall it sounded like childish snobbery. "But you're no Swordsman."

"But if I killed you?"

Maybe the Swordsman would see Jateko was no threat and leave him alone. *No. Expecting intelligence from a Swordsman is a mistake.*

Zerfall heard a patter of laughter flit through the crowd. Cursing, she dismounted, careful not to put much weight on her splinted right leg; the long walk on it had been a bad idea and the tent pole looked frayed and ready to snap. Pulling her cowl forward and making sure the tent fabric hid her decaying flesh, she pushed her way into the crowd. Maybe she could drag Jateko out of there before he got himself killed.

"The guards don't give a shite," she heard someone in the crowd answer Jateko's question.

A huge man with wide shoulders blocked her approach, and she struggled to shove her way past. Her sun-dried body must weigh even less than she realized as he barely noticed her efforts. She felt like a desiccated corn stalk, papery and brittle, baked clean of colour and life.

Lie down, corpse. Let them bury you.

People edged forward for a better look and Zerfall lost sight of Jateko in the press.

"What are you going to kill me with?" Grausamer asked Jateko. "That rusty little knife?"

Had Jateko drawn a weapon? The Swordsman would gut him in seconds.

A scarred woman clad in sand-caked leathers scowled at Zerfall's attempt to hobble past and then blanched when she got a peak inside her makeshift cowl.

If Jateko replied, the growing hubbub of the crowd drown it out. She knew that sound; they scented blood and violence.

"I'm a *Swords*man," said Grausamer, his voice projecting. "I kill *Swords*men. Not stinking desert rats. You don't even have a sw—"

And then someone screamed, a long wailing screech choking off in a wet gut-shredding vomit of retching and sobbing.

Jateko!

Without thought Zerfall reached for knives, drew one, and felt the stump of her left arm bump into the pommel of another.

Stepping forward, she drove her knife into the kidney of the man in front of her. He folded, his knees giving way, and fell backward with a moan which sounded like it was half question. She spun away, drawing the knife free with a practised flick. Her right leg, knee lashed to those god-damned tent poles, skidded out from under her. On her way down she managed to drag the blade through someone's guts and blood spattered the cobbled street. She landed blind, the cowl falling across her face.

The sound of the crowd changed and she knew this sound too. Terror. There were foxes among the chickens and those foxes had discovered a lion hidden among them. Those scarred murderers, moments ago hungry for the vicarious thrill of blood-letting, crashed into each other in their attempts to flee. Booted feet trampled Zerfall and she felt ribs crack and break. Air hissed from a torn lung in a rush of rot. Someone stomped on her right ankle—whether on purpose, or in a hurry to escape, she had no idea—and the bone snapped like a dry twig. Rolling onto her belly in an attempt to protect her ribs, she lashed out with the knife, slashing tendons and hurting anything within reach.

By the time she wrestled the cowl away and could once again see, the street was empty except for a half dozen bodies, some wounded and moaning, others unconscious or dead. Jateko stood, unharmed and untouched, blinking in confusion. Grausamer lay sprawled at the lad's feet, guts open wide and red.

"Zerfall?" Jateko asked, when he spotted her. "What happened?"

She tried to roll over and the stump of her left wrist slipped on blood-soaked stone. Cursing, she sheathed her knife and used her functional right arm to push herself over.

"Are you hurt?" Jateko asked, picking his way toward her, stepping over fallen bodies.

She glanced at her right ankle, examined the shattered ruin with detachment. At least it was the same leg. "No."

Jateko reached her side, gaze darting about as if struggling to understand what had happened. A numb quiet blanketed the street, but there'd be noise enough soon. The guards might not care if Swordsmen cut each other down, but they'd come to investigate *this*.

"He said it was okay to kill him," said Jateko.

"In a duel," said Zerfall.

"What's the difference? Someone ends up dead either way. Why would they care how it happens?" He gestured helplessly.

She wanted to ask him what the hell he was thinking, but realized she didn't want to know.

She couldn't even be angry with Jateko. He was just a boy, stolen from his own world and dropped into hers. It was her fault he was here.

He'll die here.

"No," she said, wheezing. Jateko was alive. She'd get him out and send him home.

She remembered him asking—begging—not more than a few minutes ago, to go home. She'd snapped at him, denying him his desire, ignoring his fear. Why had she done that? She took him for granted. Of course he follow her. The boy was—

The boy is in love with me. She saw it in his eyes, in the way he watched while she splinted her shattered knee and the way he looked away, embarrassed, when she noticed his attention. But was it love, or something darker? Worship, perhaps? He hadn't argued when she said they'd continue forward. Was it because he couldn't? Did her Gefahrgeist power coerce him even though that hadn't been her intent?

Am I still a Gefahrgeist? She wasn't sure. She felt different, thought different, but how much had she really changed?

I am not the woman I was. She could decide who she would be in the future. She was her choices, nothing else. She could be a person who gave up. She could lie here until whatever passed for the law came to collect her remains and disposed of them. Or she could be the kind of person who didn't abandon her only friend; there was no denying that's what the boy was.

Are you trying to convince yourself that he needs you, that you are only doing what is best for him?

Jateko crouched at her side, and for a moment she thought he was offering her a hand up. "We might not have much time," he said. "Which should I eat first?"

Zerfall stared at him, uncomprehending, until he gestured toward Grausamer's corpse. She drew breath and spoke fast, air hissing from her torn lung. "Liver. Kidney. Brain too difficult." How much would a Swordsman's brain be worth anyway?

Jateko nodded and scampered back to Grausamer. He made bloody work of hacking the corpse open, cutting free the kidneys, and stuffing them into his mouth. He chewed as he worked, face set in a comedic expression of deep concentration.

She'd been a fool, planning for the future. The dead had no future. She'd get Jateko home. It would be the last thing she did. *To hell with the Täuschung, and Hölle, and Aas.* The thought she could bring down the religion and kill the god she created was too much madness.

Zerfall spotted Tod, standing where she left him. The horse continued to stare glumly at the cobbled stones between his front hooves.

"Tod," she called as loud as her torn lung allowed. "Here."

The horse wandered over without lifting his head to watch where he was going. When he reached her, she stared up at him, seeing into the maggot swarming canopy of his opened guts. Reaching up she gripped the tent fabric blanketing him and dragged it off, letting it fall to the blood-soaked ground. Then she pulled off the strip of cloth covering her empty sockets. Who was she fooling anyway?

She watched as Jateko thrust his face into the torso of the ravaged corpse and tore chunks of liver free with his teeth. "No time!" she said. "We go now!"

Jateko stood, turning to face her, but stopped, face scrunched as if trying to remember something. Then he flashed her a huge, bloody grin and she found herself staring at what little remained of that gap between his front teeth. Gore dripped from a chin stronger than she recalled.

"Swords," he said.

Bending, Jateko drew Grausamer's two swords and turned to face her before once again pausing to think.

"Hurry!" she shouted.

"Brain," he called back, and then used Grausamer's sword to hack at the Swordsman. Stooping, he collected the severed head by the hair and rushed to Zerfall's side. "I'll eat it later," he explained.

"Get up there," Zerfall commanded from the ground, pointing at Tod's sway spine. Air leaked from her torn lungs almost as fast as she could fill them. "Have to get out. Before they close city gate."

"Right," he said, stopping to pick her up.

She shook her head. "Just you. Go back to the desert. I'll slow them down, give you a chance to escape."

He stared at her, blinking in confusion. "Without you? No." Ignoring her wheezed arguments, he collected her, lifting her damaged body into his arms. "We can fix the ankle." He grinned his not-so-gap-toothed grin. "We're going to need more *karpan* poles."

Jateko hoisted her onto Tod's back and offered her one of the swords. She showed him her stump. She wanted that sword, god how she wanted to hold a sword again. If she had a proper sword, Abiega never would have— "Need hand to ride," she said, air rushing from the wound in her chest.

With a shrug Jateko leapt up to sit behind her, one arm slipping around her waist, the other awkwardly clutching Grausamer's head and two swords. She almost suggested he should ride in front, but the Basamortuan had no idea how to ride a horse, and maybe she kind of liked what little she felt of his arms. There was a new strength there.

"Go," she told Tod, and the horse sauntered forward, his rear hip grinding and clicking. "Faster."

Tod ignored her.

JATEKO GRINNED HAPPILY OVER Zerfall's shoulder as Tod clomped down the street. He'd done it. He'd killed the Greatest Swordsman in all Geld and eaten of his flesh. He felt stronger already, faster, more balanced. It took a day or more before he heard Gogoko's voice in his head and felt the difference in his body. With Abiega the change took place in less than a day. Did the changes happen faster the more he devoured? He couldn't decide if that was terrifying or exciting. *What skills, what secrets will I find in the man's brain?*

What kind of person was Grausamer? Gogoko asked. *Who else will join us in here?*

He'd find out soon enough. He wished he had more time. He hadn't even got to taste the heart. What he gobbled down barely took the edge off his bottomless hunger.

You can't be hungry already, said Gogoko. *Something is wrong. This isn't right.*

A tremor of fear, a gnawing doubt, turned his hunger sour. He remembered Jakintua's stories, how the tribesmen would band together to hunt and kill the evil creatures who ate men.

That's not me.

We need to leave, Gogoko and Abiega said together.

The streets were empty. No one came out to challenge them. Maybe it really was okay to kill people in the city-states. Zerfall seemed to think he'd done something wrong—he saw it in her expression.

Maybe we should go back so I can finish—

Are you insane? Never mind, stupid question. Abiega sounded different, scared.

What has you so freaked out? Jateko asked.

*For a hundred generations the sorgin of the Etsaiaren tribe have commanded us warriors to gather the undying in Santu Itsasoa, the Sea of Souls. That's why we brought Zerfall there. And then you—*Abiega stopped.

I what?

You came looking for her.

So?

Pay attention, said Abiega. *Here come the warriors.*

Jateko wanted to ask what caused this fearless man to shiver in terror. He wanted to mock Abiega, but the Etsaiaren warrior was right: Ahead, dozens of *hiria ero*, men and women armed and armoured in more steel than a thousand Basamortuan would see in a thousand lifetimes, stood waiting.

"We charge," hissed Zerfall over her shoulder. "Break through."

"No," said Jateko, placing a hand on her shoulder as if to hold her back. "They haven't drawn weapons."

"Good."

"No. Wait."

Tod slowed his already sedate pace and stopped a dozen strides from the gathered warriors. Zerfall cursed and dug a knee into his side. He ignored her.

Jateko slid from Tod's back and stood, still clutching two swords and a severed head, waiting.

Really? muttered Abiega. *You're going to fight while carrying all that?*

Dropping one of the swords, he transferred Grausamer's head to his free hand. "Is that better?"

Abiega ignored the question.

The city-states warriors retreated a step, hands twitching toward weapons but stopping short, and for a brief instant Jateko imagined what they saw. Zerfall was dead and had clearly been dead for a long time. Jateko, splashed in blood from his eyebrows to his knees, stood comfortably, a head dangled in one fist while a sword hung loose in the other. Even Tod, gutted and empty, tattered flesh hanging in ropey threads, regarded the gathering with baleful intent.

What a sight we must make, eh, Abiega?

Abiega didn't answer and Jateko shrugged, annoyed.

One of the *hiria ero* warriors stepped forward, a woman built like the garrison wall and sheathed in more armour than Jateko thought he could carry. "Wendigast," she said, "return to the desert."

Wendigast? Jateko felt Abiega's confused shrug. He thought about asking, but instead said, "Okay."

The woman blinked, glancing around, and gnawed on her lower lip like maybe she thought to devour herself before he got the chance. "We have dozens of archers on the rooftops," she said. "We will bring you down." Her voice quivered, betraying fear.

"Okay," said Jateko, looking around and seeing no archers. "We'll leave."

"Really?"

"Yes."

"Never to return?" she asked, as if unbelieving.

"We're never coming back here," he said with feeling. "I promise."

Jateko heard Zerfall's wheezing intake of breath. "Wendigast sated," she said. "Let us leave. Before hunger. Returns."

He was still damned hungry but decided not to correct her.

The woman nodded and both groups stood motionless, watching and waiting.

"You're going to have to move," Jateko said to the crowd. "You're blocking the street."

THEY RODE, *GRIND, CLICK, grind, click,* Tod moving ever slower, never once lifting his head to take in his surroundings. Even the long grasses, greener than anything Jateko had ever seen in his life, couldn't catch the horse's attention.

Why would they? asked Abiega. *He's dead.*

So you're talking to me again?

Abiega didn't answer.

"Do you understand why they let us go?" Jateko asked Zerfall.

"Thought you were Wendigast." She glanced over her shoulder, seeing his look of confusion. She took quick sips of breath between words. Sitting this close he heard the air escaping her torn lungs. "Crazy people. Delusional. Become monsters."

"What kind of monsters?"

"Dire situations. Starvation. People driven to cannibalism. Sometimes sanity torn by. Horrendous things they've done. Wendigast is result."

Am I a monster? Jateko was all too aware of Abiega's meaningful silence. "Am I a Wendigast?"

"Don't know," she said. "Supposed to appear. Like huge demons. Made of human flesh. And bone. Supposed to stink. Like death." She shrugged. "I can't smell anything. You look human enough."

Jateko thought about the pleasure and strength he felt rushing through his flesh when he buried his face in Grausamer's sundered guts. How could such pure joy be evil? He remembered the taste of hot blood and his mouth watered. He wanted to crack the Swordsman's skull, still hanging from its hair in Jateko's fist, and drink up all he was. "Am I a monster?"

"If you are. I am too," she said. "I helped you."

Zerfall, evil? He couldn't believe that. *She saved my life when Gogoko and Dedikatu were going to kill me.*

You murdered my little brother, said Gogoko, voice tight with rage.

But why? asked Abiega, ignoring Gogoko. *Why did she save your life?*

Jateko turned to look back at the setting sun. He frowned in confusion and looked left to see the distant peaks of the Kälte Mountains, faded and purple with mist. "Did we get turned around?"

"Taking you home."

"Home? Stop."

Tod ignored Jateko.

"This was mistake," wheezed Zerfall. "Selfish. Sorry. Deserve better."

"Deserve better?" *Does she mean me?*

You know what you deserve, said Gogoko.

Jateko dropped the swords and Grausamer's head to the ground and slid off the horse to stand waiting, arms crossed. When Zerfall touched the beast's shoulder he stopped instantly.

"You asked me to take you home," she said, rushing the words. "I said no." Once again she paused to sip air between each sentence, her leaking lung a continual whisper under her words. "That was selfish. Wrong. You should go home. Don't belong in the city-states. I'm sorry."

Empty sockets stared at Jateko, waiting. Go back to the desert? *No. She still needs me.*

"I killed Gogoko," he said. "I ate him. My tribe would kill me."

"No one knows," said Zerfall, pleading.

"*I* know. And I can't go back."

"Why not?"

Should he tell her the truth? Should he tell this corpse he loved her and she needed him and as long as she needed him he'd never leave her? Should he tell her he was going to find some way to bring her back to life? It sounded like the wishful thinking of a juvenile moron. Even if it was true. "I've changed," he said instead.

"That's not all bad."

"And it's not all good." Jateko shrugged, helplessly. "I can't stop."

"Stop what?" Zerfall asked, eyebrows crinkling over gaping pits.

"Eating." Now he said it aloud, he realized it was as a much a reason for her *not* to bring him along. Zerfall was a smart woman, far smarter than he. She had to understand the danger he presented.

Zerfall nodded her understanding, gnawed on her lower lip, and then spat out a sliver of rotten skin with a silent snarl. A shred of dark flesh hung from the lip, exposing her stained lower teeth and blackened gums. Her flesh, dry and gaunt when they first met, now hung slack and frayed, peeling. It was only a matter of time before it sloughed away to show the gristle and bone beneath. She was, Jateko finally realized, hideously ugly. *She's been dead a long time.* Her time in the desert mummified her, preserving her somewhat from the ravages of rot. But now, here in the rolling greenery of the city-states, the damp air would have its way with her dead flesh.

I don't care.

You're a fool, said Abiega. *You'll never bring her back to life. She'll never be a beautiful woman you can hold and love.*

You don't know that.

Zerfall looked east toward the desert, turned, and gazed west toward the city-states and Geldangelegenheiten. Her shoulders sagged. "I want to close my eyes. You should bury me."

"Never."

Something in his voice brought her head up and she stared at him.

"Zerfall. I'll never . . ." He couldn't say it. She'd laugh. She'd call him a fool and she'd be right.

"Yes?"

"You have a purpose," he said. "Your purpose is my purpose."

"Why?" she asked.

He couldn't answer. Was it that he loved her or that she needed him? Did he love her need? All he knew for sure was that he couldn't leave her.

"What do you know of my purpose?"

"I know the Täuschung are evil," he said. "Their god is evil. Such a god . . ."

What? Demanded Abiega. *What are the gods of the city-states to us? This is a lie you are telling yourself.*

She watched him, unmoving, that empty regard unreadable as ever. "You should return to the desert."

"You don't really want me to."

"You shouldn't—"

"I'm going to find the people who killed you, took your hand."

"Then what?"

"I'm going to kill them," Jateko promised. "And eat them," he admitted, cringing at how juvenile he sounded.

She looked away, staring west, shoulders hunched. "Eat that first," she said, gesturing at the head, eyes wide and staring, where Jateko dropped it.

"Good. I'm starving."

Jateko discovered splitting a skull was far easier with a sword and his new-found strength.

L ATER, AS ZERFALL SLID the second sword into her empty scabbard and scowled at the poor fit and Jateko licked clean his bloody fingers, he heard a new voice gibbering *What the hells is happening to me?* somewhere deep in his thoughts. Both he and Abiega told it to shut up.

The Swordsman is weak, said Abiega.

"True," said Jateko aloud, "but watch this."

"Watch what?" Zerfall asked, the last of her breath whistling from torn lungs.

Jateko winked, and danced flawlessly through a complicated practice pattern, the sword spinning, slashing and stabbing at imaginary opponents. It was effortless. He and the sword were one. He knew its weight and balance like he spent a lifetime practising with it; like he'd been born with it. He knew if he took the second sword from Zerfall he'd be even deadlier. When he stopped, he wasn't even breathing hard.

"I could kill Abiega now," he said to Zerfall, bragging a little. "With my eyes open."

The Etsaiaren warrior said nothing.

I thought you said he was weak. Jateko thought.

Mentally, Abiega answered grudgingly. *Emotionally. The man was a coward in so many ways. He fears obscurity more than death.*

And you? Jateko asked.

I cared nothing for fame.

Liar.

"You arguing in there?" Zerfall asked.

Jateko shrugged. "Maybe a little."

"That happens a lot, doesn't it."

"Yes. I didn't know it would be like this." Which wasn't quite true. He remembered wanting to not be alone.

Zerfall drew breath to speak and immediately air whistled out the many tears in her lungs.

"Wait," interrupted Jateko. "I have an idea." He flashed a fast grin and dug into what remained of the supplies he'd scavenged from Abiega's camp. "Here," he said, brandishing the bone needle and spool of gut thread.

Zerfall raised an eyebrow.

"I'm going to close that lung for you."

"Do you know how to do that?"

"I've fixed torn *karpan* and *oihal* thousands of times; I was always better at it than mom. How hard can it be?"

Zerfall looked like she was about to chew her bottom lip in contemplation and then thought better of it. "Okay," she said. "How do we do this?"

"Take off your shirt."

Zerfall stared at him, that eyebrow once again creeping upward, and Jateko's face flushed hot. "I mean . . . maybe I can . . . without . . ."

Zerfall pulled the top of her shirt open and glanced within. Her face scrunched with distaste she said, "I'll keep this on."

"Right. I wasn't trying to—Never mind." Tying the gut thread around the hooked end of the bone needle, Jateko held it up for inspection. "Ready."

Zerfall pulled apart the hole in her shirt where the knife had stabbed into her, and exposed the decaying flesh beneath.

Licking his lips nervously, Jateko crouched at her side. "Don't move." He leaned in close to inspect the bloodless wound. "I can't see much inside. Thought the hole would be bigger."

"Do what you have to," said Zerfall, tilting her head back to stare into the sky.

Tod ignored them both.

"Just going to look inside." When Jateko poked a finger into the wound, trying to catch sight of the torn lung within, Zerfall squealed and twitched away.

"Sorry! Did I hurt you?"

"Your face!" Zerfall laughed, a deep belly guffaw fading to dusty sputter. "I'm dead," she whispered, not bothering to draw breath. "Can't feel a thing."

Jateko shook his head in mock disgust and waited until she stopped shaking with laughter. "Hold still."

After poking about inside her wound, Jateko realized he'd have to further open the flesh to get to the damaged lung.

"Do it," said Zerfall. "I'm a mess anyway. If I can't talk to you . . ." Air hissed from her lungs and she turned her head away as if watching something distant. Jateko knew there was nothing there. "This rotting meat. Already a prison. Need to communicate."

Jateko peeled away decayed flesh in hanging strips, exposing yellow ribs and the torn lung beneath. Hopefully he'd be able to sew those strips back into place after. She might not feel pain, but he didn't want to damage her any more than necessary.

"To do a really good job on the lung, I'd have to break a rib or two to get at it." He waved her to silence. "Forget it. I'm not doing that. I can make do." He poked at the lung with a fingertip. "Breath in for me." When she did, he scowled and nodded. "Not much slack to work with." He glanced at Tod. "I have an idea. Do you think he'll mind?"

"No."

"Me either. He doesn't say much anyway."

Jateko approached Tod, making quiet noises as if calming a baby. "Tod?" The horse stared at the ground between his fractured front hooves. "I need some of your flesh. I'm going to cut away some lung." he reached up to stroke the horse's cold neck and his hand came away matted in horse hair.

Jateko ducked low and crawled under the horse. It didn't seem as disgusting as it should. His stomach rumbled its discontent. Somewhere deep inside himself he heard the pitiful mewling of the Swordsman. There was no quenching this hunger. He needed to be stronger and faster. He needed to be more skilful with weapons. He needed to be smarter. He needed knowledge. *Just a few more lives.*

You will never have enough.

Ignoring Abiega, Jateko stared up into Tod's hollowed torso. "We made a mess in here. I wish I'd thought of this sooner, we could have left a little more intact."

Fumbling about in Tod's shadowed belly he found hanging shreds of what he assumed was lung tissue. It didn't matter what it was, he supposed, as long as he could use it to patch Zerfall. He cut away several strips and crawled out, displaying his grizzly prize.

Zerfall looked doubtful, eyebrows doing that crinkly thing they did when she thought maybe he was crazy.

Hey, maybe I don't need to see her eyes to know what she's thinking. Maybe I can read her eyebrows.

You're just figuring that out now?

Zerfall stood motionless, holding her shirt up, as he pushed his fingers between her ribs, feeling about for the torn edges of her lungs. She looked everywhere but at him. Was she squeamish about her decaying body, or did she not care?

"I can't sew this to the old lung," he said. "I don't think I can work around your ribs." Leaning in he examined a segment of exposed rib where the flesh had been torn away and sand ground into the exposed muscle. *When did that happen?* She hadn't mentioned it. "Maybe I can attach the lung directly to the ribs."

"Lungs have to move. Inflate. Deflate. To draw breath."

"Right. Damn."

"Pull lung out between ribs. Attach new material. Stuff it back in."

"Good idea. You'll have a great lung capacity. You'll be able to hold your breath for a really long time."

One eyebrow crept up.

"I was joking," he said. "But you will be able to talk for a long time between breaths." She stared at him. "Not that you talk too much." Not a hint of movement. The eyebrows told him nothing. "Or even a lot," he added.

Ducking away from that empty gaze he got to work. Jateko sewed quickly, his fingers defter and more sure than he remembered. As he worked he discovered more damage, slashed skin, bones broken and protruding through flesh. He had no idea she'd taken so many wounds.

"If you weren't dead already," he said, leaning in to brush his fingers across a hole in her belly, "you would be now." Jateko stared at Tod for several heart beats before nodding. "He won't miss it." After searching the horse for the least damaged skin, he cut away several rough squares and used them to patch the holes in Zerfall. "Try not to get stabbed again. More of this, and you'll be more horse than woman."

She might not feel anything, but he was gentle nonetheless. This time he was aware of her gaze on him. Her attention never wandered. When he finished and prodded the mended lung back into her chest cavity, he stepped back with an appreciative nod. "Good as new." And then cringed. *Why do I always say the stupidest things?*

You really want an answer? asked Abiega.

Leaning against Tod, the empty pits of her eyes locked on Jateko, Zerfall dropped her tattered shirt back into place, drew a deep breath, and held it while he listened.

"I'm not hearing anything," he said.

Next Jateko lashed her shattered right ankle tight with sticks and bits of broken rib he snapped from Tod's open torso. It wouldn't give her much in the way of agility, but at least she could hobble around.

"We'll find you a crutch," he said.

She watched as he stood, looking like she wanted to gnaw on her lower lip and fighting the desire.

"You're alive," said Zerfall.

"Um . . . yes."

"I'm not."

"True."

"Last chance," she said.

"For what?"

"Return to the desert. Find a girl, have children."

Jateko looked east, toward the desert. No part of him wanted to go there. "No."

"You'll die because of me."

"You're all I have." The words escaped before he thought to stop them. Rather than stop now, he continued: "I'll never leave you. I've lost everything except you and now I have more than I've ever had in all my life."

"I'm a rotting corpse; ghastly, even."

"I had noticed."

"We can't—"

"We can't be friends? Why not?"

Zerfall reached out a skeletal hand but stopped shy of touching his arm. When she started to turn away, her shoulders hunching, her hand dropping, he caught the hand. Her skin felt dry, like brittle leather.

"I was a powerful Gefahrgeist," said Zerfall. "Back before this." She reached a hand to touch the back of her head.

"So?"

"Gefahrgeist use people. Manipulate them. Twist their desires. Make them *want* to serve."

"So?"

Her eyebrows did that scrunchy thing they did when she was annoyed. "What if I still am? What if that's why you stay with me?"

"So?"

She growled something Jateko didn't hear and said, "But then it's not a *choice.*"

"Command me to go away," he challenged. "Command me to return to the desert. Let's see if I obey."

"But I don't want to. I don't want you to leave. I can command you, but I won't really mean it."

"You don't want me to leave and I don't want to leave." Jateko laughed and released her hand. Grabbing her before she could argue, he lifted her onto Tod's sway back. "I don't see how this is a problem."

"Someday you might."

He shrugged and offered a crooked grin. "I can't let fear make my decisions." He squared broad shoulders, feeling the muscle ripple. Gods he felt good.

Gods? asked Abiega. *Not Harea? I think this Swordsman's thoughts are infecting you.*

Jateko ignored him.

The fingers of Zerfall's right hand clench into a skeletal fist. "Go back to the desert," she said. "I *command* you. Go home."

"Maybe later," he said.

SIXTEEN

Religion was our first attempt at understanding the world, carving meaning from the insanity. Who stops after their first attempt?

—Versklaver Denker, Gefahrgeist Philosopher

AAS FLEW ABOVE PHARISÄER as she walked, hips swinging in that familiar strut, straight to his quarters. Opening the door she slipped within, closing it behind her.

Spreading his wings wide, he coasted in to land a dozen paces away. He *twisted* back to his human shape the moment his talons touched soil. Drawing a long-knife he held it behind his back, reached for the door, and paused.

Would she congratulate him on besting her trap, or kill him for escaping too soon?

{One way to find out.} Hopefully, he'd be able to discern something of her intent based on how she greeted him. *{If she's naked, it's seduction and she wants to use me for something. If she's clothed, she's probably planning to murder me.}*

{What if she's planning murder but waiting naked to distract me?} That would be a good plan. Of course, if she turned out to possess Zerfall's Gefahrgeist power, it wouldn't matter either way as he'd be begging to lick her toes—he shivered with pleasure at the thought—and kill whoever recently annoyed her. *{Unless I kill her the instant I see her.}* If he didn't give her a chance to speak, she couldn't attempt to manipulate him.

Aas licked thin lips, staring at the door handle. *{Yes. Kill her.}* His hand refused to move. *{But what if she wants to seduce me, to use me?}* He hated himself for admitting it, but he wanted that. *{I'd give anything to touch her.}*

"Then get in here and touch me," Pharisäer called from within his room.

{She can hear my thoughts.}

"Yes. Now get in here. My toes need attention."

She sounded like she was at the far end of the room. How far was that? A dozen strides? More? That was bad; it meant his mental state was decaying and at an increasing rate. How much time did he spend thinking about spreading his wings wide, catching the perfect updraught, and searching the ground for dead things? His heart skipped every time he spotted birds circling in the distance, knowing beneath them lay something dead or dying.

"You're killing the mood," called Pharisäer.

Aas swung the door open and strode in, long-knife held behind his back. *{Does she know about the knife?}*

"Yes," she said, lying in his bed, sheets demurely hiding everything interesting from sight. Her hair looked perfectly tousled, which was weird because it looked perfectly perfect when she was out walking.

"Oh." He saw the crumpled pile of her clothes and his breath caught. Partially buried beneath the clothes was her scabbard. Empty. The sheet slipped a little, exposing a slim shoulder, distracting him. "Oh?" *{Naked?}*

"Yes. Are you planning on using that knife?"

"I haven't decided." Letting the knife hang at his side, he approached his bed and stood at the foot, staring down at Pharisäer. He made no attempt to disguise his lust. *{No point in hiding the truth, is there?}*

"None."

"So you know what I want." *{And you know I'm ready to kill you.}*

She shrugged, unconcerned, and sat up, allowing the sheet to fall away. Aas' breath caught in his throat.

"If I wanted you dead," she said, "you'd be dead."

"Maybe."

"Hölle is weak. She always was."

"She hallucinated Swarm, her delusions gave birth to an entire hell."

"Maybe." Pharisäer took a deep breath, watched his eyes follow the rise and fall of her breasts with a sly smile. "I'm going to replace her soon. She's ready to crack." She waved a hand in an uncaring arc. "Want the truth?"

"Truth?" *{What the hells is she talking about?}*

"I believe Zerfall was the original." Pharisäer arched her back as if stretching and grinned at Aas' quiet whimper. "Hölle is manifestation of Zerfall's insanity." She cupped a breast, rolling the nipple between slim fingers. "Are you going to join me in here?"

{Zerfall Mehrere? Hölle a Fragment?} That was ridiculous, impossible. *{What is she playing at, trying to convince me of such madness?}*

If his doubt bothered her she showed nothing.

He stepped forward until his knees bumped the bed's foot-board. He hesitated. "If we rut you'll know you can trust me?"

"Afterwards, you will understand. Afterwards, you will do anything I ask."

{I already want to.} "You show none of Zerfall's Gefahrgeist talent."

Pharisäer brought her fist down on the bed, showing bright teeth in a snarl. "I told you. I am not Zerfall."

"No, you're not."

Her eyes narrowed. "What does that—"

He spoke fast to cover his thoughts. "It's a mistake I keep making, equating the two of you."

Aas crawled on the bed, long-knife clenched in his fist. Her legs spread as he neared, the sheets falling to her waist, and he pushed himself between her thighs. Her lips opened in a soft intake of breath.

"You're nothing alike." *{Nothing.}*

Pharisäer reached out, caressed his face, and then slapped him hard. His eyes stung. "Do you want to hit me back? You can."

{Gods yes. Zerfall would never let me. I love—} She slapped him again and his ears rang. *{She has some of her strength.}* When she lashed out again he caught her wrist and held it tight, feeling the bones within grind together. Those perfect, full lips parted again in a soft wet sigh of lust and it was all Aas could do to stop himself from leaning in to kiss her. *{No. I have to know. I have to* know.*}*

"Know what?" she asked, hooking her heels behind his back and drawing him against her.

{Take away my choices. Make my actions not my fault. Remove from me the curse of responsibility. Gods I want this. Please.} He hated himself—loathed what he had become—but when he was with Zerfall, he no longer mattered. She was everything. He did everything for *her*. Aas looked Pharisäer straight in the eyes. "Tell me I love you."

"I know you do," she purred.

"Tell me!" he snapped, clutching her wrist in an iron grip.

Pharisäer's eyes glanced to the side, the barest hint of a twitch. "If that is what you want."

{It is. More than anything}

Aas nodded at where Blutblüte lay, concealed. "You were ready to kill me," he said to distract both himself and Pharisäer.

"Of course," she said.

"You fear—"

"Hardly."

{I know you can't love me; I can't delude myself that much. But if you have her Gefahrgeist power, I will love you.} And that would be enough. "Tell me I love you," he said, desperate.

"You love me," she purred, writhing against him. "You'll do anything I ask."

Aas killed her, slipping the long-knife between her ribs and piercing her heart. She stared up at him, eyes wide. He blinked, and tears fell upon her flawless skin like soft rain. *{I'm so sorry.}*

"How?" she asked, a whispered intake of breath.

"When you broadcast your thoughts, it's best not to plan too far ahead."

But she was already dead.

Kneeling between her parted thighs his tears ran free, following the sags and wrinkles of his face. *I wanted you. More than anything I wanted you. But you were right. You aren't Zerfall.*

Hölle might be a Fragment as Pharisäer claimed—though the idea seemed insane—but Pharisäer, the delusion of a delusion, was even less. Withdrawing the blade, Aas wiped it on the sheets of his bed. Then, throwing those sheets aside, he exposed Blutblüte. Its brutal simplicity was poetry.

How much does a soul weigh? he wondered. *How about millions of souls?*

The sword, unadorned and plain, was beautiful beyond words. The blade caught the light like oil on the deepest water. The leather-wrapped hilt, stained and worn from years of use, reminded him of Zerfall. Not once, in all the years he knew her, had he seen her without the weapon at her side. He once joked that she carried it even while making love and she'd drawn the blade and asked if he'd like to find out. Much as he wanted to, he recognized that glint in her eyes and demurred. He regretted that decision. She would have killed him, but it would have been worth it.

Retrieving the scabbard from Pharisäer's corpse, Aas examined it. This was more ornate than Zerfall's; her scabbard had been as plain and old as the sword itself. Reluctantly sliding Blutblüte home, he thought, *Should I carry Zerfall's sword? Should I return it to Hölle?*

Those questions raised more questions. What was he going to do? Should he see Hölle, tell her everything? Would she kill him, or thank him?

"She knows I'm useful."

She'll hear my every thought. She'll know what Pharisäer said about her. If she doesn't already, she'll know the truth.

"My inability to hide anything from her will protect me. She'll know she can trust me."

Really? Can she trust you?

He wasn't sure.

Aas drew Hexenwerk from his pocket and the snot puppet crumbled apart. The end was close. Pharisäer had been ready to kill him. She might have succeeded. Luck and skill were divided by an awfully thin line and even the most dangerous killer could fall to a lucky idiot. He needed this damned puppet now, before everything fell apart.

Plucking another thick hair from the sagging flesh of his neck he glared at it in anger. None of his hair was near long enough. To effectively bind Hexenwerk together he needed . . .

Aas glanced at Pharisäer's corpse. His breath escaped in a moan of pleasure as his gaze fell upon her dark, flowing hair. Perfect. The thought of plucking that hair—strand by strand—from her beautiful skull left him breathless with lust and erect with excitement.

Does it matter if it's not my hair? He'd rather it was, but it would be years before his hair grew anywhere near this length. *I don't have years.*

He'd have to chance it. If he completed Hexenwerk without Pharisäer's hair, it would fall apart too fast.

Crawling onto the bed, he lifted Pharisäer's head and rest it upon his lap. For several minutes he sat, blissfully stroking her hair, imagining this was Zerfall and she finally allowed him to touch her. That, he knew, would never happen. He wanted to lean down and kiss her, to examine her body in the intimate detail Zerfall never allowed, but couldn't. This wasn't Zerfall.

Twining a single strand of hair around his finger, he pulled it tight, stopping shy of tugging it free. Aas closed his eyes, basking in the moment, the feel of her luxurious hair wrapped around his finger. *Your death will be my salvation.* He pulled the hair from her scalp, sighing as it came free. Straightening it, he set it aside.

Aas smiled as he worked, feeling more content than he had in years, tugging hair after hair from Pharisäer's head and arranging them at his side. *Am I enjoying this too much?* he wondered. *Am I manifesting Trichotillic tendencies?* Developing new psychoses was a sure sign his mental state decayed, but he hardly needed additional evidence beyond his increasing desire to escape this rank human flesh and live out his days free, as a proud and mighty condor. That and the increasing range of his broadcast thoughts.

Pull a hair free. Set it aside. Pull a hair free. Set it aside.

His mind wandered.

No matter how twisted reality might become, there were measurable and immutable rules. Understanding them, recognizing them for what they were, seeing the patterns buried in the surface chaos, that was the tricky part.

Aas could *twist* into a condor, and he could return to his man-shape, but he couldn't *twist* to any other form. All Therianthrope's had a single shape they *twisted* to when fleeing their humanity, and that shape was always based on some terrible trauma. If a boy was savaged by dogs or watched a pack of canines devour his family, that would influence his Therianthrope shape. Likewise, if a Dysmorphic grew up weak and scrawny and was bullied and mocked to the point of mental collapse, muscles would be the manifestation of her resulting obsession. Some Gefahrgeist craved absolute domination and became Slavers while others needed hero-worship and became Swordsmen. Still others sought subtler control and became politicians, petty tyrants, religious leaders, or even joined the city-guard. Always, in each and every case, their delusions and obsessions shaped their Geisteskranken power.

And then there were the subtler ways in which reality hinted at an underlying truth. The inverse square law, which stated that the further one got from a Geisteskranken, the weaker the effects of their delusion became. The effects of mass belief was also well documented; surround a typical Geisteskranken with thousands of sane souls, and that person became powerless. Yes, powerful Slaver-type Gefahrgeist, those at the Pinnacle, might gather thousands of followers over time, but even this seeming contradiction followed the same rules; as the Slaver convinced more people of their power, the effect of that power increased. Pluck the Slaver from the centre of his horde of worshippers and drop him in a city, and he'd be powerless.

According to his reading, some Geisteskranken were born delusional while others became deranged after suffering a particularly traumatic event. Still others, he read, only gained their power after suffering head wounds or due to heavy alcohol or narcotics use.

Was that what happened to Zerfall? Maybe it had nothing to do with the book of Cotardist poems he gave her. Had her loss of memory and the sudden manifestation of Cotardist tendencies been due to brain damage? It seemed likely, but if so, what about her previous Geisteskranken abilities? Zerfall was a powerful Gefahrgeist and yet had been unable to manipulate him, in spite of the fact he wanted her to. Did this mean her delusions were an aspect of her personality, that once she forgot who she was she lost that power? The thought boggled the mind. If Aas lost all memory of being imprisoned in a basement and devouring his father, would he no longer be a Therianthrope? For the first decade and a half of his life his father told him how hideous he was; what if his appearance was one more manifestation of delusion? Would he look different were he able to forget his past?

It was a tantalizing idea. While he found use in his madness, there was one law he dared not ignore: All Geisteskranken fell to their delusions. As the deranged lost sanity they gained power until their delusions came to rule their minds. There was no knowing how that end would come, it was different for everyone. Therianthropes, he'd read, typically shed their humanity, losing themselves to their animal form until they became unable to regain their human shape. Someday he would no longer be Aas Geier, Täuschung priest and killer. He'd be a condor, riding the winds, living off the world's carrion.

Aas didn't dread that end. His crimes were numerous, his soul stained. He'd killed so many people, shattered so many lives, sent countless souls screaming to Swarm. With each crime he hated himself more.

Swarm.

He glanced at where Blutblüte lay sheathed on his bed. Proximity. Mass belief. If he died anywhere near Blutblüte, was his soul's destination guaranteed?

Aas blinked. Pharisäer's bald skull, flesh pink and perfect, lay atop his lap. Her hair, arranged by length, lay heaped at his side. Lifting her head, he slid out from under her and stood staring at the piled hair for a moment before collecting it. He carried his prize to the rickety desk shoved into one corner of his near barren room. Sweeping the books and papers from its surface, he laid out Pharisäer's hair and emptied his pockets of his own hair, snot, fingernail clippings, feathers, and pale clumps of foul scented belly-button lint.

Make the damned puppet. Maybe Hölle won't kill you today, but it's only a matter of time before either she falls apart or I do. Madness is assured.

Drawing a knife from its place concealed within his robes, Aas sat at the desk. Splaying his fingers wide on the scarred wooden surface, he swallowed a hard lump of fear and focussed on the small finger of his left hand.

Do it. You're a coward. Do it.

He hesitated.

Who the hells hacks of one of their own fingers so they can make a puppet?

This was madness. Was he developing Körperidentität delusions as well Trichotillic? If he cut this finger off and the puppet remained incomplete, would he then remove more appendages? Gods this could spiral out of control fast. What scared him most was how reasonable, how *plausible* it sounded. The more of Aas Hexenwerk contained, the better it would be. He could use a forearm for its spine, his long, bony fingers for legs. He could wrap it tight in his very own flesh, flayed from his living body in sheets. It could have his tongue, his teeth. Maybe it needed eyes. One, at the very least.

What have I done?

Aas took a deep, shuddering breath and held it until blood roared in his ears and his vision slurred red. He released the breath in a long sigh.

"I am a Therianthrope. I want to be a condor far more than I want to be a puppet of snot and bone."

Nodding to himself and muttering "I can do this" under his breath, Aas slid his hand back toward the edge of the desk, curling his fingers so only the smallest remained prostrate atop its surface like a helpless sacrifice. Holding the knife above his finger, tip resting on the desk's surface, blade touching the wrinkled flesh where finger met hand, he bit down hard, grinding his teeth.

Standing, he took one last breath and held it. The blade kissed flesh, sank into the groove of the metacarpophalangeal joint. Putting his weight behind the blade, he crushed it down.

Aas screamed. The blade caught. Why had he thought he'd be able to sever it cleanly? He screamed again, tasting blood, and sawed at the joint. Bone parted. Pain ripped up his arm, lighting every nerve on fire. He tried to pull away but a thick strand of flesh joined the mostly severed finger to the hand. Flesh stretched thin and he screamed again, the thoughtless wail of an animal in agony. He sawed at the skin like a deranged butcher hacking at an offending strip of gristle.

When the skin parted he toppled sideways off his chair to sprawl mewling on the floor. Aas curled into a tight ball, his bloody and incomplete fist clutched to his chest. Hot blood soaked his clothes.

Get up. You didn't hack off your finger so you could bleed out on the floor of your own room.

Whimpering, Aas pushed himself to his knees and then staggered to his feet. He felt dizzy, light-headed and weak. Dropping back into his chair, he began to laugh in convulsive sobs.

You're an idiot. Why had he not thought to lay out bandages *before* severing his own damned finger? With a little planning, he could have even concocted some brew to dull the pain and slow the bleeding.

That would also dull his mind. He needed to be sharp.

Really? How sharp is someone who cuts off their own finger to make a sticking snot puppet?

"Shut up," Aas muttered to himself.

He glanced at his bed and Pharisäer's corpse. The sheets, soaked as they were in her blood, were already ruined. *You're worried about staining your sheets?*

"Shut up!"

Rising, he clutched the knife in his right hand and sliced the sheet into strips. He'd have to replace these with cleaner bandages later, but at least he wouldn't bleed to death now.

Once he bound his left hand tight with shredded sheets, Aas returned to his desk. His hand pulsed hot fire, sending waves of searing agony through his skull with each beat of his heart. He sat, staring dumbly at his severed finger. Gathering the appendage and assorted bodily detritus together, he built his puppet.

Hours passed in a blur of neurotic concentration and throbbing pain. When he finally sat back to examine his handiwork, Hexenwerk sat on the desk before him, hideously twisted like a psychotic's doll.

That's what it is.

He leaned in to study the puppet. Who knew the human body made so much snot and mucus? The features he carved into its face seemed angry, depressed at his lack of artistic talent. The wings, crafted of feathers bound in Pharisäer's hair and in turn lashed to the body of the puppet—built upon the backbone of his severed finger—looked flimsy and weak.

It doesn't matter, he reminded himself. Belief, not wings, would provide the lift Hexenwerk needed to leave the ground behind. At least in theory.

The arms, little more than feathers stripped to the quill and wrapped copiously in dark hair, would be near useless. At best, they might be used to drag the puppet's weight. The wings. Everything depended on the wings.

How sure are you you'll fly?

If he couldn't move his soul into this nasty little homunculus, its ability to fly would remain forever moot. Should he test it? Could he?

What if I succeed, but find myself trapped within Hexenwerk, unable to return to my body? He shuddered at the thought. *But if I don't test it, I'll never know.* He would doubt, and that would eat at him. Belief might define reality, but doubt was the other side of that coin.

Of course, if I try and fail . . .

Shoving aside his fears and trying to ignore the pulsing heat of his left hand, Aas focussed on the puppet, staring into its snot-nugget eyes. He needed this escape route. Swarm was too terrifying a fate to comprehend. He *needed* this.

Was this like *twisting*? Could he find some similarity there, something to make the transition easier?

No. Thinking about *twisting* drew him back into his body.

Swarm. Focus on your fear.

His spirit resisted. Each time he felt himself slipping away it lurched back into his body like a drowning man clawing free of water and drawing that first sobbing breath of air.

His hand throbbed. Rather than being a distraction, it gave him something to escape. Closing his eyes, he imagined becoming the puppet.

Focus on your fear and your pain.

Aas lost himself. He felt compressed, crushed into something too small to contain all he was. He heard the soft rustle of feathers.

I'm doing it! I'm—

Aas' soul shuddered in terror, slamming back into his body. The puppet sat before him, staring with disappointed eyes. Had he imagined the sound, or had he, at least briefly, moved his soul to the puppet? How could he know?

You lost a lot of blood. You probably fell asleep and dreamed the entire thing.

Did the puppet look different? Had one of the wings been moved, just a little?

Exhausted, Aas rose from the desk. He was too tired to try again.

"Hölle won't kill me today," he said, hoping it was true.

He needed more time. He might have failed, but now felt sure he could, with more practice, possess his puppet. Aas lifted Hexenwerk, testing its weight.

How much does a soul weigh? He laughed, a pained grunt of sour humour. He remembered feeling crushed, like he'd been jammed into a tiny box.

"It's time to face Hölle," he said aloud, slipping Hexenwerk into its pocket.

Would Hölle be grateful or angry? Predicting the reactions of the delusional, Aas decided, was itself an insane pursuit.

He glanced at the body sprawled on his blood-soaked bed. He wanted to keep her.

Strapping Blutblüte to his side, Aas strode from his chambers. Rather than notifying the temple's staff of Pharisäer's corpse, he'd leave her there, his little secret. She'd rot and stink, but his fellow priests were accustomed to such smells emanating from his rooms. He grinned in hungry anticipation.

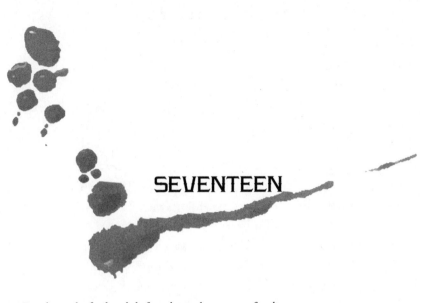

SEVENTEEN

Eat the snake for lunch before the snake eats you for dinner.

—Basamortuan Proverb

GRIND, CLICK, POP! THUNK. Late in the afternoon a new sound joined the percussive symphony of Tod's rear hips. Zerfall, riding in front of Jateko, held in his strong arms, considered the young man. Where once he had ridden awkwardly, unable to move with the motion of the horse, he rode easily now. It was hard to believe this was even the same boy. His jaw, once weak and near non-existent was now strong and square. His chest, previously concave, was powerful and muscular. The once sloped shoulders were broad.

"Sun's going down," she said. "We should stop so you can rest."

If he heard, Jateko showed no sign. He was, she realized, mesmerized by the landscape.

"Tod," she said. "Stop." The horse stopped and Zerfall glanced about. Grey, everywhere. The clear sky above, unbroken grey. The clouds spotting the horizon, the colour of dry bone left long in the sun. The sunset looked like slashes of grey surrounding the pure white of the sun. *From black to white, I have it all.*

"Jateko?"

He didn't react. He didn't even seem to notice they were no longer moving.

"Jateko!"

"Huh?"

He glanced at her, eyes wide.

"Let's stop for the night," she said. "You need to rest."

"Right." Releasing her he slid from Tod's back, his eyes already drawn back to the world around them.

"Can you describe it? Zerfall asked.

"What?"

She nodded at the hills. "Everything. The colours. The smell. How it *feels*. I . . ." She shrugged, torn between explaining her need and not wanting to admit it existed. *Why does this scare me?* More even, than being dead. *Need is a weakness.* Was this a taste of who she had been, back when alive? She didn't like it. Fear, *that* was a weakness. "I am separated from life," she said, trying to explain. "I see grey. My tongue is dead. I smell nothing. I miss it."

"It's incredible," he said, awed. "Green. So much green. It's everywhere. This is being farmed. It's food, right?"

"I believe so."

"No wonder you don't leave your cities; you don't have to. Food, it just grows. Everywhere. We—the tribes—we have to fight for everything. We move because we have to. We follow the rains and the animals. This . . ." He waved a hand, encompassing the rolling hills. "You could feed armies. Thousands of men and women who do nothing but train in weapons and wage war."

"They do. *We* do," she corrected.

He laughed, a grunted exhalation through his nose. "We talk about raiding the soft *hiria ero*. We talk about how weak you are and how strong we are. We talk about your steel like it's something we can wander in and grab whenever we want." He tore his gaze from the fields and stared at the ground, his shoulders rounding as if he were caving in on himself. "It's all fear. We never raid. All our steel is hundreds of years old, falling apart. The best knife in our tribe came from Gogoko's grandfather's grandfather. The only reason you don't crush us is because there's no point. We aren't dangerous. You aren't afraid of us."

"Jateko." He returned his attention to her. "Where we come from isn't who we are. Geldangelegenheiten doesn't define me any more than the Basamortuan defines you. We aren't our past."

"If I'm not my past, what am I?"

"We are our choices. We are our friends, the people we chose to surround ourselves with. We are our actions."

"I don't understand," he said.

"You think you're first and foremost a man of the Basamortuan tribes and that the fact the people of the city-states neither respect nor fear you in some way changes what you are."

"It doesn't?"

"Why give them that power?"

"Power?" he asked, confused.

Zerfall nodded. "If you care what others think to the point it defines your choices—defines your happiness and self-worth—you're giving them power. Over you."

"So I shouldn't care what anyone thinks?"

A better question than the boy she first met would have asked. "I'm saying you can choose whose opinion matters. I care what you think," she said, startled to realize how true it was. Some part of her, buried deep, screamed rebellion, railed at her weakness, and she drove it deeper. *That was the old me, I want nothing of that person.*

"This isn't going to be easy for me," said Jateko.

"What won't?"

He gazed out across the rolling hills. "There are colours here I've never seen. Smells unlike anything I've ever experienced."

She understood his desire to change the subject. "Try."

"I know every shade of sand and what each means. There are as many shades of green here, if not more. Some so pale as to be almost white, while others dance somewhere between black and blue." He plucked a round bulb, fronds curled up and in, from a nearby stalk. "This is deep purple near the base," said Jateko, lifting the bulb to examine it, "and fades to the softest pink near the top."

"Clover," she said. "Pluck one of those petals and suck on the inner end."

Jateko did as instructed and his eyes widened in disbelief. "I've never tasted anything so sweet."

"Bees use these flowers to make honey."

"Bees? Honey?"

Rather than try to explain, she gestured toward a sprawling field. "There?"

"Gold," he said, "like a sandstorm backlit by the setting sun."

"Grain. Probably wheat."

"This, then, is what feeds your armies."

Zerfall nodded.

"Everything smells so *wet*. There's so much life here." He bent and scooped up a handful of soil, crushing it in a fist and lifting that fist to his nose. He closed his eyes, breathing deep, nostrils flaring. "It's like the guts of a freshly cracked cactus with hints of blood." His eyebrows furrowed as he searched for words. "I feel things wriggling in there. There's more life in this handful of dirt than one thousand strides of desert. It smells like I could eat it, shovel it in."

"Not a good idea."

"I know. I'm cavernous now. No. Carnivorous. I think that's right. The Swordsman, he knew a lot of words." Jateko's eyes widened. "I know what honey is. He remembered the flavour." He licked his lips, eyes wistful.

Movement on the horizon caught Zerfall's attention. "People are coming," she said, gesturing in the direction she and Jateko travelled.

Jateko turned to watch as four wagons, each drawn by a team of two horses, crested a hill to the west. "They're flying flags," he said, squinting. "It looks like the golden outline of a triangle on a white background."

"It's a pyramid. They're Geborene priests."

Jateko glanced at her. "Are they like the Täuschung?"

"Yes and no."

"Are they dangerous?" Jateko asked.

"All religions are dangerous."

"I meant to us."

She ignored him and slid carefully from Tod's back. They stood shoulder to shoulder watching as the Geborene priests—a thousand paces distant and all dressed in flawless white—reined in their horses, pulling the wagons to the side of the road, and set about erecting tents and making camp.

"I don't think they've seen us," said Jateko.

"Good."

"Zerfall?"

"Yeah?"

"I'm hungry."

"Oh." She watched as several priests piled dry grass into a heap and then retrieved several logs from one of the wagons. "There's a lot of them. Maybe a dozen."

Jateko said nothing, his attention never leaving the camp. She knew that look. Hunger, raw and bloody. What had he said, cavernous? That was it, that's what she saw in his eyes; bottomless craving, cavernous need he would never sate. Jateko wanted to march into that camp and kill and devour each and every one of those priests.

"Too many," she said, and he nodded.

But his eyes said otherwise. They betrayed his thoughts, said he was thinking, planning. Plotting.

"We wait for one to stray from the camp," he said. "To pee."

"If they hear—"

"They won't. We'll be quiet."

We. And in some strange way, we it was. He wouldn't leave her, and she wouldn't leave him. "Let's be smarter about it this time," she said. "Let's pick a . . . a victim."

"Right. No point in eating a weak moron."

They watched as a gaunt young woman, no older than Jateko, staggered to the piled wood and grass. The youth stood, swaying, clawing at scabbed arms, face twitching and lips writhing. The rest of the priests backed away.

Smoke rose from the grass in coils, wrapping around the young woman's legs like snakes intent on climbing her thin frame. Smoky tentacles reached up past the crisp white of priestly robes leaving ashen streaks and twined around her throat. Thin fingers, tendrils of wispy fumes, caressed her face, reaching toward her watering eyes. Tears streamed down the youth's face, cutting tracks in soot smeared cheeks.

The piled grass and wood burst into flames and the young woman staggered back, retreating from the fire with a howl of soul-wrenching misery. Collapsing to her knees she buried her face in her hands and shook.

"Her," said Jateko. "I want her."

"Bad idea."

"I want to be able to do that. I ate that Swordsman and now I can use a sword. What if I eat that . . ."

"Hassebrand," supplied Zerfall.

"I'll be able to light fires with a thought."

Jateko grinned at her, eyes bright and intelligent, and again she marvelled at how he changed. The gap between his front teeth had shrunk to nothing.

If I weren't dead . . . But she was.

"You have to ask why she can do that," she said.

"Why?"

"It's not magic. All Geisteskranken pay a price for their power. She might be able to light fires, but look at her."

Jateko returned his attention to the woman, kneeling at the fire, ignored and avoided by the other priests, shoulders shaking from the force of her sobs. "She's pitiful."

"And that's what gives her power." Jateko stared at Zerfall, uncomprehending. "She hates herself. She's broken." She tapped her temple with a skeletal finger. "In here. She's insane and that insanity defines her reality. Do you really want that?"

"Wendigast. That woman thought I was a Wendigast. That's a type of Geisteskranken, right?"

"Yes."

"I might be a Wendigast. Probably am. That means *I'm* insane. But I don't hate myself. I like me. I'm important—"

"That too is delusion."

"I'm not important?"

"If you died right now, would it matter a thousand years from now?"

He stared at her, not answering.

"How about one hundred years?"

He blinked.

"Ten years?"

"Well . . ."

"One year? Thirty days? A week?"

His eyes changed, lids narrowing to slits. "You're wrong."

"Really?"

"I am the All Consuming."

Z ERFALL STARED UP AT him, head shaking so slowly she probably didn't even know she was doing it. He started again, trying to make her understand. "I believe eating people will make me stronger and smarter. And it does. So I'm what you *hiria ero* call Geisteskranken, Wendigast, or delusional or whatever. I'm crazy," he tapped his own temple. "Reality bends to my beliefs. I understand that now. Most people—like the others in my tribe—they're too sane to even try to eat people. And if they did, they wouldn't get anything more than if they ate a goat or a snake. Cannibalism. It's a terrible thing to do. It's *evil. I* am evil. I kill and eat people, and I can't stop. I don't even want to."

"It's not that simple," she said.

He waved her to silence. "Let me finish. It's difficult to articulate this." *When did I learn that word?* It didn't matter; even that was part of what he struggled to explain. "Abiega thinks I'm the All Consuming and so do I. And it matters what I believe. For a thousand years the Etsaiaren dragged the undying—Cotardists, *hilen deabru*, whatever—to *Santu Itsasoa*, the Sea of Souls, and bound them to cacti. All for me. Their *sorgin* knew I was coming. The entire point was for them to take you there so I'd come for you."

"That doesn't make sense."

"It does. The Sea of Souls is beyond the Etsaiaren lands, west of the Basamortuan tribes. They were leading me away from their people, making sure I followed you into the city-states."

She frowned up at him, the remnants of her eyebrows crinkling in at the centre. "You're saying they predicted you and me. Us?"

"Yes. But that's not all. They'd only predict us if we were important. Why else go through all that trouble. What I'm saying is that I'm important. And so are you."

She looked doubtful, and fair enough; he wasn't even sure if he believed.

"But why?" she asked.

Jateko offered another crooked grin. "We're going to end the Täuschung. We're going to kill their god. We're going to free the souls trapped in Swarm."

"What if the Täuschung and Swarm don't matter? What if it's just you?" asked Zerfall.

"I guess—"

"What if it takes a god to kill a god?"

"I don't understand."

"How smart and skilled and powerful do you have to be before you Ascend?"

"I'm not trying to—"

"How many people will you consume? All of them?"

The All Consuming. He hadn't taken it literally, more like a fancy title. But if he didn't find some way to sate this hunger . . . "I don't want to be a god."

Goat-sticking liar, muttered Abiega.

"But?" asked Zerfall.

How did she know there was a but? "But I don't want to be weak either. I need to be strong to help you."

"So you're doing it for me? If I give up and wander out into the desert to let the winds scour me to nothing, you'll stop eating?"

Jateko eyed her. "You know the answer to that just as I know you aren't going to give up."

"So we're going up there," she nodded toward the tents, "and you're going to kill and eat that insane Hassebrand in the hopes you gain something of her insanity. You understand how this might not be the best plan?"

"Yes."

Zerfall looked skyward and he wondered if she thought she was rolling her eyes. "Let's do this."

"Actually," he said, "I was thinking you should stay here." She stared at him with guttered sockets. "You aren't very quiet when you move. Everything crackles and rattles. Sorry."

"Fine."

He stared at the Geborene camp, thinking. "I'll go up there, club her on the head when she leaves camp, and then drag her back here for butchering." Zerfall looked like she was about to argue and he held up his hand to stall her. "I can hunt and kill one skinny Geisteskranken."

"Fine," she said again, scowling up at him. "But first sign of trouble, and I'm coming to get you."

Jateko watched as she clambered onto Tod's back. Gone was her lethal grace. "Comfortable?" he asked, and once again she gave him that cavernous look. "Right." He winked and sauntered off into the dark, aware of her dead gaze following him.

Approaching the Geborene camp was easy; they hadn't set a guard. It was like they didn't think it was even possible someone might wander in with ill intent. Did this tell him something about the city-states' civilization, or were the Basamortuan not as wrong as he thought? Of course it might also be that these priests were ill-prepared for travel, unaware of the dangers around them.

Or are they so dangerous, asked Abiega, *that they have nothing to fear?*

Jateko slowed as he neared the camp, placing each foot with care. It stung to think about how clumsy he used to be.

How many before you're smart enough, strong enough? asked Abiega.

When I can protect Zerfall.

Abiega was silent for several heart beats. Then, *Which part of The All Consuming do you not understand?*

"All of it," Jateko muttered under his breath. *If I'm such a danger, why didn't your sorgin tell you to kill everyone travelling in the company of the dead?*

Abiega didn't answer.

See? Your sorgin don't want me dead, they want me to do something. If you know what, tell me now. Otherwise, shut the hells up.

Hells? asked Abiega. *You sound more and more like one of these hiria ero.*

Somewhere in the background the Swordsman bubbled and gibbered and both Basamortuan ignored him.

I think, said Gogoko, *if you keep eating people, it's going to get awfully crowded in here.*

You've been quiet lately, said Jateko, moving closer to the Geborene camp. Figures moved about, silhouetted by fire. Some were cooking what looked like spitted rabbits, while others puttered about, laying a large crisp white sheet out on the ground and arranging plates and cutlery upon it. It was a strangely fastidious scene. The priests wore spotless white and stopped often to check their hands, dashing to a barrel of water where they scrubbed as if they'd found something offensive.

I've been thinking, answered Gogoko. *Our sorgin are like their Geisteskranken, but they mask it in ritual and ceremony. Jakintsua mostly makes poultices and tells the tribe when it's time to move on, but I remember my father talking about Urutiko, the sorgin before Jakintsua. He said she would sometimes warn the tribe of storms long before anyone else knew they were coming. Once she warned of a raid before it happened and the tribe was ready and butchered the raiders.*

So? asked Jateko, watching a priest collect a shovel, a stack of white sheets of paper, and a shallow bowl of water from a wagon and leave the camp. Curious, he followed. The man walked a few dozen strides, placed the bowl and paper on the ground, and dug a shallow pit. Jateko watched with interest as the man hiked up his pristine white robes, and squatted over the hole to defecate. *That is weird. Why would they crap in holes?*

It means, continued Gogoko, ignoring Jateko's question, *that our sorgin are crazy, deranged and delusional. Just like the city-states Geisteskranken. The buruzagi might be in charge of the tribe, but all real decisions are either made by the sorgin or at least after consulting her. And even then the buruzagi is always the man who most wants to be in charge. Have you been listening to Halber Tod's poems? It's Gefahrgeist who always want to be in charge.*

That's the way it's always been, said Abiega, *the way it's supposed to be.*

So the sorgin and buruzagi tell us, said Gogoko dryly.

Wait, said Jateko, understanding. *That means we let insane people make all the important decisions for our tribe.*

Exactly, said Gogoko.

The priest grunted one last time, splashed water onto his arse from the bowl, wiped himself with a few of the sheets of paper, and returned to the camp to wash his hands.

Damn these city-states people are strange, mused Jateko.

Would you judge all Basamortuan by the actions of one man? Abiega asked.

Of course not, said Jateko. *Oh.*

Harea, swore Gogoko with feeling. *Imagine what it'll be like with a dozen people in here. We'll never follow a single thought through to its conclusion.*

Sorry.

If the sorgin are deranged, said Gogoko, *we can't trust them to make sane choices. Just because the Etsaiaren sorgin wanted Jateko to wreak havoc among the hiria ero, doesn't mean it's a good idea.*

We've followed the sorgin for thousands of years, argued Abiega.

Doing a stupid thing for a long time doesn't make it smart, said Gogoko.

Gogoko is right, said Jateko. *But I'm not here because of the sorgin, I'm here because Zerfall is here. Even had the Etsaiaren not taken her to Santu Itsasoa I would still have followed her. And even if you absolutely proved that following her further would be a bad idea, that it would end in my death, I would still follow her.*

I'm not talking about your *death*, said Gogoko. *Would you follow her if it meant thousands of innocent deaths?*

Yes, answered Jateko without hesitation.

The All Consuming, Abiega whispered darkly in the back of his mind.

Would you follow her if it meant the death of everyone? Gogoko asked.

This time Jateko did hesitate. How much was too much? To what lengths would he go to save Zerfall?

Save her? Gogoko asked.

I swore I'd bring her back to life. A man's word is iron.

A man knows when he's made a mistake.

Another priest, this one gaunt, wandered from the camp toward the shite hole. Jateko recognized her. This was the Hassebrand, the one he wanted. Keeping low, he shuffled closer to the hole, wrinkling his nose at the stench. What the hells did these priests eat? How bad their temple must smell where so many lived in close proximity.

A real man, a warrior, thought Jateko, *keeps his word even when he's made a mistake.*

That's foolish.

Not more than a stride from the pit, Jateko crouched in the dark, motionless. He drew his long-knife and waited. *Then I am a fool.*

You didn't answer Gogoko's question, pointed out Abiega. *Would you follow her if it meant the death of everyone?*

Jateko drew a deep breath and released it slowly, feeling the muscles in his arms and chest relax. Hunger focussed him. The voices in his head, their endless questions didn't matter. He was in charge. They could pester all they wanted, but he knew what he had to do. What he was going to do.

Yes, he answered. *I'd follow her. Even if it meant the death of everyone.*

Gogoko and Abiega fell silent.

The young priestess arrived at the hole, face wrinkling in distaste as she lifted her robes and shuffled about, trying to find a comfortable position to squat. She finally settled, bony knees up around her ears, facing Jateko.

Jateko stifled the urge to curse his bad luck.

The priestess grunted and strained and farted and Jateko wondered what kind of horrendous diet led to such effort for a simple crap. If all the people of the civilized city-states shat like these priests, the cities would be even fouler than he thought.

The priestess' eyes clenched closed as she strained and groaned. Clutching the long-knife tight, Jateko moved closer, his centre of mass balanced perfectly. Was he strong enough now to take this woman's head clean off with a single swing?

Only one way to find out.

Now he knew it was going to happen, hunger came roaring out of his guts, washed his thoughts red in blood. Brains. Heart. Liver. He wanted all this deranged woman had to offer; wisdom, strength, and most of all, power. A guttural sound escaped his clenched teeth, the chest-shuddering snarl of the feral beast lurking deep in the mud of his soul. He needed to taste dreams and memories, to savour her essence.

You're a monster! screamed the Swordsman. *She's just a girl!* His disgust ripping through Jateko, souring the moment with revulsion.

Jateko froze, knife raised. *I . . . No . . .* But he couldn't argue. He agreed.

With an explosive fart and a contented sigh, the priestess' eyes opened and stared up at Jateko standing over her. With a squeak of terror she hurled herself backward. Jateko swung, the tip of the blade catching her throat as she toppled onto her ass in a tangle of white robes. Leaping forward Jateko found himself ankle-deep in the shite pit. He didn't care; he had to silence the woman.

The priestess crab-walked backward in a clumsy panic, hands and feet skittering in the dirt, blood from her throat staining her pristine robes. Jateko dove, hoping to slam his blade deep into her chest, and the foot in the pit went out from under him dumping him belly deep in the stench.

Coughing blood and gasping, the priestess rolled to her stomach, scrambling to rise. With a heave, Jateko hurled himself on her back, crushing her to the earth. There'd be no perfect decapitation today. Shoving her head into the dirt and using his own body mass to keep the priestess pinned, Jateko drove his long-knife into the girl's side, over and over, until the body stopped twitching.

He lay atop the corpse, soaked in blood and shite, listening. Had the priests in the camp heard the struggle? His breath came in short gasps, his heart thudding against his ribs. *I did it. I killed their Hassebrand.*

The Geborene camp seemed unchanged, unaware of the violence he committed.

The hunger crept forward, a stalking cat. Eat. Eat now. Hunch over your kill and feed like the animal you are.

No.

He had to drag the corpse away, somewhere safer. Back to Zerfall. She'd tell him what to eat first. Where would delusion lie? The brain?

The back of the throat copper-tang of fresh blood tugged at his attention.

Feed. Just a little.

No, I . . .

A taste.

Lifting his fingers to his nose, Jateko breathed in the hot bouquet. He touched a finger to his lips and his mouth parted, sucking that finger in. Had anything ever tasted so good?

Jateko rolled the priestess onto her back. Skinny arms flopped about, getting in the way and for an instant he thought about hacking this body apart, using its pieces to rebuild Zerfall's decaying corpse. No, the limbs were all wrong, gangly and weak. He needed something better. It would have to be a custom kill, a victim chosen for the task of—

Focus, you idiot! snapped Abiega.

Right. He had to drag this meat back to—

It isn't meat, said Grausamer, the Swordsman. *It's a girl.*

She's dead and that makes her meat.

He grabbed the girl's heels, ready to drag her away. Another glance showed the Geborene camp unchanged. The priests had settled down to their meal.

Just a taste.

Dropping the ankles, Jateko stabbed into the priestess' torso, hacking flesh away to expose the guts within. Rooting about with his hands, he found a kidney and cut it free. It was beautiful, glistening like a shimmering rainbow, pink and purple. He bit into it, tearing a mouthful free with strong teeth. The flavour, unlike anything he remembered, drew him in and he sat, squatting over the corpse, tearing into the kidney like a ravenous animal.

"Lehrling?"

Jateko blinked up at another Geborene priestess standing over him. She was huge, tall and soft. Her bald head showed a dusting of red stubble and bright, icy eyes stared down at him.

Clutching his knife, Jateko prepared to pounce. He'd cut her down and drag both corpses back to Zerfall. He grinned bloody teeth at her.

Showing no hint of fear the large woman said, "You killed Lehrling." She sounded like she was in shock, like she couldn't conceive of what he'd done. Like he'd shattered her reality with his simple act of murder.

Jateko tensed and a wave of heat washed over him, singing his eyebrows and curling the hair on his head. *Did I do that?* Had eating the Hassebrand's liver given him some—

Hassebrand! screamed the Swordsman.

What?

The big woman grinned her own mad leer, her lips peeling back to reveal bright, over-large canines. The air around her rippled as the grin became a snarl of rage. Her meaty fists clenched and Jateko's hair became ash and danced away on a hot wind gusting out of nowhere. Sweat poured down his face and his skin blistered.

Another?

He retreated, backing away, staggering through the shite pit.

She followed, unhurried, like she had all the time in the world and he, Jateko, the All Consuming, was no danger.

"You killed my Lehrling you pig-sticking savage."

His *oihal* burst into flames, his skin bubbling.

"You'll serve!" she screamed, her voice a tearing sob of anguish. "You'll serve my Lehrling in the Afterdeath!"

Jateko ran.

The grass around him curled from the heat and burst into flames. His tattered *oihal* baked to ash and came apart. He felt the skin on his back boil, the flesh charring.

He ran.

A concussive blast smashed him to the earth, crushing him like a child crushes an ant beneath its thumb. The world was fire, an inferno of hate and loathing and pain. He screamed and writhed, weakening as his muscles cooked and charred.

His last thought before the black took him was, *Run, Zerfall, run.*

ZERFALL SAT ASTRIDE TOD, leaning forward so his neck took most of her weight, staring into the dark. Time slid past like a snake in the grass. Overhead the stars spun. She could have been a statue for all she moved. Even her thoughts slowed with nothing to distract her. She felt distant from everything. Untouched.

So this is how they do it, she mused. *This is how the dead, lashed to their cacti in the Sea of Souls, pass time.* It was frighteningly easy. If Jateko didn't return, she might stay here forever.

There was noise. It might have been screaming. Loss and rage. It meant nothing.

The sky lit bright, the Geborene tents bursting into flames. Screams of agony cut the air, and she saw a priest sprint toward her, his white robes and hair ablaze. The man, a motile pillar of flame, stumbled and fell at Tod's feet, writhing on the ground. Zerfall watched, listening to the bubble and pop of cooking flesh. A cacophony of pain echoed the hills and a dozen flickering infernos dashed and staggered in a mad and flailing dance. She watched until each toppled to the earth and lay still, burning and smoking.

Those were priests.

Fire.

Could fire end her? If her body burned to ash would she be free of this rotting prison?

Hassebrand. Jateko went to the camp to kill the Hassebrand. He wanted to eat the girl's soul so he could light fires of his own. Had he done this, had he started these fires?

That felt wrong. The Hassebrand they saw was barely able to light the camp fire. This was the work of a dangerously powerful and insane Hassebrand, one nearing the Pinnacle, that moment when insanity ran rampant.

Jateko!

Zerfall drove Tod forward with a thought and the horse obeyed, though he hardly rushed. Tod picked his way between the candle corpses, his rear hip clicking and popping with each step. Not once did he lift his head to take in his hellish surroundings.

She found a scorched corpse sprawled in the ashes of what had once been long grass and recognized the Basamortuan long-knife clutched in blackened fingers. Sliding from Tod's back she collapsed at Jateko's side when her splinted knee crumpled beneath her, the tent poles snapping. Her right ankle twisted and whatever Jateko used to lash it in place broke. She felt nothing, barely noticing the jagged fragments tearing through her decaying flesh.

Jateko's bald skull, flesh bubbled and cracked, lay at such an angle she saw his face escaped untouched; he'd been burned from behind. His clothes, that filthy tribal *oihal* he always fretted over and continually stitched and restitched, was burnt away and his back and legs were seared black, fading to white ash in parts.

He's dead. Clear fluid seeped from suppurating cracks in his burnt flesh. *I let him go alone, and now he's dead.*

She'd been dead and empty for so long she hadn't even noticed that spark, deep in her belly, rekindling, day after day, with each moment spent in this foolish youth's presence. Until now.

That spark, it's me. It's my soul. Whatever the hell that was. *It's the last of me, the old me. The original Zerfall.* Strange that she only felt it in moments of terror, anger, and heartbreak. The spark guttered, threatening to wink out of existence forever.

What then?

She knew the answer.

I'll sit here at his side. Forever. I'll watch his flesh rot and decay. I'll watch the carrion life gather and feed upon his corpse. I'll see new life bloom from his death. I'll know no purpose. I'll wait.

Jateko's lips, bubbled and burnt, cracked open and a whine of purest agony—impossibly high pitched—escaped.

He's alive!

But he couldn't survive these wounds, not for long. He was burned beyond recognition.

"You can't leave me," she whispered, close to the broiled remains of his ear.

Jateko whimpered and she wondered if he heard, if he understood her need.

Helpless, she glanced about the burnt field. A dozen bodies, several burning like merry little bonfires, were littered about; the priests had panicked and scattered, fleeing whatever caused the blaze. Of the thin Hassebrand they'd seen earlier, Zerfall saw nothing.

Jateko shivered, twitches and spasms shaking his body. She didn't touch him for fear of the pain contact would no doubt cause.

"No!" Helplessness tore her, ripped at that weak spark, threatened to drown it in despair.

She had to do something. She had to help him, to save him. "I need you!"

Zerfall ground her teeth, feeling them loose in her rotting skull, as she stared down at the burnt remnants of Jateko's broad shoulders. She remembered when they first met; the boy had been scrawny and weak in the extreme, his too-large feet flopping and continually threatening to trip him. She remembered the stunned look on his face as he sat in the sand, knife wedged between his front teeth. That gap between his teeth closed with each life he devoured. She wanted to laugh, to cry. Anything. She wanted to experience emotion again—even wretched, soul-tearing heartbreak—as a living, feeling woman.

The gap between his teeth had closed.

Slim, weak shoulders became broad and round with muscle.

He ate and he grew, both physically and in intellect. The wounds he received fighting Abiega healed in days. He ate that warrior, devoured his strength.

A dozen bodies burned nearby.

With a snarl, Zerfall used Tod's unresisting body to drag herself into a sitting position. Glancing about she spotted the nearest priest. The body lay sprawled, the fire having guttered and died, less than a dozen strides away.

Strides.

She screamed her frustration at the shattered leg sprawled useless before her. She howled hatred at the sky. The gods—Jateko's desert god Harea, that sick little boy the Geborene worshipped, Wahrergott—could go stick themselves. They were nothing, less than useless.

She screamed at the burnt corpse, so near and yet so far. There had to be a way.

I'll hold on to Tod's side. He'll drag me there.

And then what?

She certainly couldn't lift a dead body onto the horse's back. Could she drag it back to Jateko?

The reins!

If she, one-handed, wrapped the reins around the priest, Tod could drag the corpse back to Jateko.

Examining the sun-baked leather she felt her brief moment of hope die. Would they hold? Running a rotting finger over the reins she watched sand and flakes of leather fall away.

She had to try.

Looping the reins around her wrist, she said, "Jateko, hold on. You can't go."

"I know you. I know who you are." Jateko's voice sounded wrong, the soft roundness of his Basamortuan accent gone.

She glanced at the boy. He hadn't moved. Had she imagined the voice?

"Let him die," he said in another voice, the faintest hint of a whisper.

She stared at Jateko, torn between rushing away to fetch him a body and curiosity. "Him?" she asked.

Cracked lips opened, but the body didn't otherwise move. "He's a monster. He'll kill everyone. For you he'd devour all the world."

"Who are you?"

"Grausamer Schlächter, the Greatest Swordsman in all Geld."

She snorted and a maggot slid from her nostril. "You're dead, he ate you."

Zerfall turned away. This was not Jateko, just the angry soul of some witless Swordsman trying to wreak vengeance on the man who killed him. "Tod," she said, nodding toward the nearby corpse. "Take me to that body."

Tod dragged her without complaint, stopping at the corpse, head hanging low over it as if examining the man. Zerfall doubted he was that interested. Clutching the reins in her teeth, she dragged herself to the priest. Whatever grace she may have once possessed was long gone and she mourned its loss. Looping the reins around the corpse's ankle, she prodded Tod's tatty leg. "Drag this to Jateko." She'd follow. She dare not test the reins with their combined weight.

With impossible weariness, Tod lifted his head to glance in Jateko's direction. Finally, huffing annoyance, he turned, dragging the corpse behind him. The reins snapped before he completed his turn and Zerfall stifled the urge to swear and curse the gods. Tod, unaware or uncaring, returned to stand over the motionless Basamortuan.

Crawling to the priest's side, she grabbed him by his shirt and tried to drag him. It was hopeless; the priest weighed several times more than her desiccated corpse. When she snarled in frustration one of her teeth shattered and she spat the fragments. Gripping the body again, she managed to drag it a hand's span before one of her fingers snapped with a dusty *crack*. This time, raging at the sky above, she did curse the gods. She didn't care that they weren't listening and, even if they were, wouldn't want her to succeed.

A dozen strides, an impossible distance for a dead girl to drag a fat priest.

She couldn't do it, she'd never—

Zerfall remembered Jateko lying in the sand after he killed Abiega, too weak to move. He wanted to eat the warrior's brain.

I can't drag this to you, she'd said, meaning the entire corpse.

His brain is really heavy? he asked, either joking or mad from dehydration.

She laughed and swore, remembering her thoughts at the time: *Why the hells am I trying to drag the entire damned corpse?* Jateko wasn't going to eat the arms and legs. He wouldn't need the stomach or most of the guts. The bones were useless weight. She glanced at the horse, spotting the depleted water skin hanging at his side.

"Tod," she said, "come here."

It would take time and she'd make many, many trips, but she'd do it.

First, she drained the priest of blood, capturing it in a water skin, and fed that to Jateko. Then she cut free the heart and liver and kidney and fed him that too, stroking his throat to trigger the swallowing reflex. When he finished those, she split the skull and fed Jateko the brain.

She repeated this with each and every corpse until Jateko had eaten all twelve. It took days. Maybe weeks. She didn't care.

Zerfall wouldn't let him die.

She needed him.

JATEKO AWOKE TO A cacophonous mob of voices, laughing, crying, arguing, and screaming.

"Quiet, please," he whispered. "I'm trying to sleep."

They ignored him, gibbering and ranting. He shifted, trying to get comfortable. Out there, out beyond his eyelids, the world was getting brighter. Not bright like fire, but—

Fire.

Jateko's eyes snapped open and he stared up into a sky dark with bruised clouds. The air felt heavy, damp against his skin. When he blinked, water trickled from his eyebrows and into his ears where it tickled.

The voices, as if sensing he was awake, grew in volume, scaling upward in pitch and frenzy. One screamed threats of violence and dire warnings of Morgen's vengeance. Who Morgen was, Jateko had no idea. Another wailed for mommy, sobbing like a terrified little boy.

Fire. He'd been on fire. His flesh had melted, sloughing away like a snake sheds its skin. He glanced at his arms. They were whole. No, they were better than whole. They were round, thick and bulging with muscle. He'd dreamed of arms like this. He remembered the stench of his burning hair and the agony of his skin bubbling and reached a cautious hand up to touch his scalp. He was bald except for the faintest trace of stubble.

The voices ranted, smashing themselves against his thoughts, demanding attention.

"Shut up."

Silence.

"You're awake."

He turned to see Zerfall sprawled in the grass beside him. She looked awful, worse than he remembered. One of the fingers on her remaining hand was broken and jutting at an odd angle. Clumps of hair had been torn free, the flesh on her scalp flaking to exposing the grey skull beneath. Her arms, always thin, showed bone where muscle and flesh had abraded away. Ribs showed through the tattered remnants of her shirt.

"Your foot," he said stupidly.

Zerfall glanced at the ragged stump at the end of her right leg. "It came off," she said, shrugging. "It's gone. Something carried it away one night."

"I had an idea for fixing it. Need some good leather and . . ." He trailed off. She needed more than minor repairs. She needed a new body. "There were two Hassebrand," he said, changing the subject. "I killed one but . . . What happened? Why am I not dead?"

"I fed you a dozen priests, hearts, livers, kidneys, and brains." She smiled a ghastly grimace of receding gums and rotting teeth showing through tattered cheeks. "The last few were pretty ripe. We've been here a while."

A dozen men and women, their thoughts and dreams, strengths and skills, now lived within him. He grinned, rolling his shoulders. "I feel good. Strong. I know things."

Zerfall pushed herself into a sitting position but sat canted at an odd angle; she was falling apart. "Tell me," she said.

"I know about the Geborene, and their god, Morgen. They made him, and yet they fear him. He seeks to make the world a better place, a *sane* place."

"Let me guess," she said. "He's deranged."

"I don't think there are sane gods," he answered. "The Geborene believe all the gods, no matter how old, are nothing more than Ascended mortals, powerful Geisteskranken who managed to convince enough people to believe in them before they reached their Pinnacle."

"They might believe that, but they don't *know*. Not for sure."

"True. But half of my thoughts are of those who believe this. It's difficult for me to believe otherwise."

"They're infecting you."

"Changing me," he corrected. "Infected has negative connotations. Were I perfect to begin with, it might be accurate." He laughed, enjoying the feel of his broad chest. "I'm growing. Getting smarter, more educated. Maybe wiser." He shrugged with a grin of straight teeth. "What is wisdom?" He held up his hands. His wrists were thick with muscle. "I feel amazing."

"You look good. I barely recognize the skinny boy within."

"I'm not him anymore."

"Don't abandon who you were," she said, her voice soft. "I like him."

Jateko took her hand, careful not to cause further damage. Frowning at the broken finger he bent it back into place. "I know who you are," he said, glancing up to meet her empty sockets. "Who you were."

She stared at him, unmoving.

"I don't know everything about you," he corrected, "just what the priests knew." He stood, rising gracefully to his feet, and glanced down at her. *She looks so small.*

"Okay," Zerfall said.

"One of the priests I ate knows quite a lot about you and the Täuschung. You're Zerfall Seele. You are the founder of the Täuschung, a religion preaching that when all humanity is united in the heaven of Swarm we'll be freed to be gods. The idea is that if everyone believes reality is some kind of paradise then it will change to become just that. If everyone believes we will become gods, we will." He held up a hand when she opened her mouth to speak. "But the Geborene have been watching the Täuschung, they have spies among your sane priests and the true religion that hides beneath. The priest says the true Täuschung are sect of psychotics who believe reality is a prison—his words, not mine—and that if humanity suffers enough, for some long forgotten and unknown crime, we'll be freed to become gods."

She watched him, silent.

"He says either you or your sister hallucinated a hell called Swarm so perfectly it came to be. He calls it a Minimalist Hell." Jateko frowned, listening.

"He's argued with his peers about this at length. He wants me to ask you a question."

Empty sockets looked through him.

"He wonders if you're a genius and knew that a hell of nothing would be the best torment, or if it was a stroke of luck, the result of a lack of imagination. Apparently," said Jateko, "most hells are rather richly imagined with all manner of demons and tortures. Yours has none of that. And is all the scarier for it."

"All people need to make hell is more people."

Jateko nodded his understanding; a week ago he wouldn't have been able to follow any of this. Now he saw things differently. Now he understood. "The priest calls it The Long Game. You see, adherents of other religions die, moving on to whatever Afterdeath they believe in. He says that souls spend time in whatever Afterdeath that person believed in, but eventually move on to something else. Most people believe they're wiped clean, their memories and souls purged and redeemed, and reborn. No one knows. The one thing everyone agrees on is that something comes after the Afterdeath. But those who go to Swarm *stay* there. Forever. Their souls never move on."

"I planned well," said Zerfall. "I knew exactly what I was doing."

"Think about it," said Jateko. "The Täuschung never lose a worshipper, it can only grow. The old priest posits that eventually there will be more souls in Swarm than without. At that point, the scale will tip."

Zerfall rotting brow crinkled, showing bone beneath.

"When the majority of people believe in Swarm, it will become reality. The only reality." He chuckled, nodding in admiration. "It's an amazing plan, really. The Long Game indeed. The Täuschung may well define our future."

"Unless I stop them."

"Unless *we* stop them," he corrected. "I understand now. I didn't before. I was only following you. This is awful and evil. It can't be allowed. We have to end it. Free the souls trapped there."

She nodded but looked away.

"If belief really can shape reality on that scale," he added, "we have to kill the Täuschung god. To do that we have to kill the religion. Completely. With no followers the god should die, starve." *Why isn't she happy? I can really help her now. I won't be a burden.*

"What if I changed my mind?" she asked. "What if I decided I wanted to return to Geld and reclaim my religion, take it back from my . . . sister?"

Why the pause? Jateko blinked at her, unable to answer.

You know what you'd do, said Abiega. *You'd follow her and help her. You'd do anything for her, whatever she needs.*

But that's not what she wants to hear, said Gogoko. *She wants him to say he will stop her.*

"It doesn't matter," said Jateko, as much to the voices within as to Zerfall. "I know you don't want that. I know you want to end the Täuschung."

Empty sockets examined him. "We need to keep moving," she said when he began fidgeting.

Glancing about, he spotted Tod loitering nearby looking depressed and bored. Lifting Zerfall, he carried her to the horse. What the hell was he going to do about her missing foot? He couldn't even repair the knee as the tents of the Geborene priests had all burned. She weighed nothing, a dry husk of humanity. Tears stung his eyes.

Lifting her onto Tod's back he swung up behind her and felt the beast's spine sag under his weight. "I have an idea."

"Yes?"

He was pleased to see an eyebrow lift in curiosity, a small hint of life. "That bank note you showed me, it names you as the account holder." He understood so much more about *hiria ero* society now.

She perked up, sitting straighter. "So?"

Jateko prodded Tod forward with a nudge of his knee, pointing the horse west toward Geld. Tod's hips ground and clicked with every step, his stride jolting and awkward.

Just make it to Geld, prayed Jateko. If Tod failed, he'd carry Zerfall. He didn't care how far it was or what stood in their way.

"We're going to empty their accounts," he said. "Somewhere, someone can bring you back to life. Someone must have such a delusion. We'll find them. Since the Täuschung murdered you," he shrugged, "they can fund our search."

She seemed to be holding her breath, though he knew that made no sense. "Likely a pointless quest," she said, sounding uncertain, scared.

"I don't care. This Geborene priest keeps babbling about a Responsive Reality. Well it can damned well bend to *my* will. I want you to live, and I don't care how many Geisteskranken I have to devour to make it happen."

"The Hassebrand," she said. "Can you start fires?"

Jateko polled the souls within. "She isn't here. The other Hassebrand must have carried her away."

"So we still don't know if eating them gives you their power."

"I believe it will," he said with iron finality.

"I awoke in Geld with an empty scabbard and have been thinking about Blutblüte, my missing sword, ever since." She laughed, a humourless sob of pain. "And now, even if I get it back, I can't use it." Her voice grew tight and she spoke through clenched teeth.

Jateko wanted to tell her she could still stand, that he'd repair her foot somehow, that even with only one hand she could be deadly, but it would have been a lie. Her body was fragile and falling apart fast.

"I dreamed of ending the Täuschung," she said. "I dreamed of undoing the evil I created."

"We will."

"I'm useless. I am a broken corpse. I can barely stand, much less fight."

"I can," said Jateko. *I'll kill all who get in your way.*

He held her from behind. She felt tiny and fragile, hollow like a bird.

"Geld is less than a day away," he whispered into her rotting ear. This city-state was, according to the priests now residing within him, the largest and wealthiest of all city-states. It was a centre of commerce, home to a dozen religions from the Wahnvor Stellung to the Geborene to the peaceful public face of the Täuschung—and the sick truth it hid—and every insane sect in between. They'd find their answers there. He'd bring Zerfall back to life. He'd smash her religion, kill the priests, and do whatever else she wanted done.

Nothing and no one—not Geisteskranken nor gods—could stop him.

THE SETTING SUN DISAPPEARED behind a wall of slate iron clouds reaching toward them like the grasping tendrils of some deep-sea monster. Fat bellied drops of rain fell and Zerfall seemed to cave in upon herself, shrinking against him. The remnants of her once thick black hair hung about fallen shoulders in depressed and sodden strands. She stunk of damp decay.

Tod shuffled ever onward, ignoring the rain. His coat, chafed to the bone and flaking away in frayed sheets, hung in tangled snakes, brushing his knees. The *grind pop click* of his rear hips grew in volume and Jateko felt like he was being kicked in the butt by an angry mule.

With a crack of thunder and a blinding slash of lightning the sky split like a gutted fish, dumping its icy load in a torrential downpour. Jateko stared into the sky, mouth open. He'd never seen so much water in all his life. Did this happen all the time?

Jateko stared over her shoulder, frowning at the strange, oddly geometric shape of the horizon. He blinked water from his eyes and hunched his shoulders against the frigid water trickling down his spine. "Geldangelegenheiten. I see the city."

If she heard, she showed no sign.

"Zerfall," he said, nudging her shoulder, "I see the city."

"I see them," she said. "I see her. She's me, but not me." The stench of rot rode on her breath. "They know I'm not dead." She wheezed something that might have been a laugh. "Not properly dead. Aas is coming to kill me. Again."

Jateko, holding Zerfall, urged the dead horse forward with a nudge of his knees.

Click pop grrrrrrind thump! It felt like riding a wagon mounted on square wheels.

"He won't hurt you again," he promised.

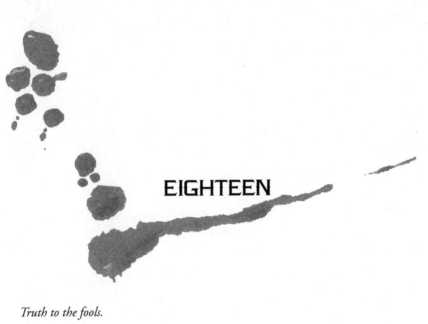

EIGHTEEN

Truth to the fools.
Lies to the wise.
Useful to the Gefahrgeist.

— "Religion", by Versklaver Denker, Gefahrgeist Philosopher

WHEN THE DOOR TO Hölle's apartments swung open, Aas found himself facing two women. He laughed and the shield of disgusting thoughts he built around himself fell away, forgotten. *{I'm such an idiot. Of course she's not dead.}*

Aas bowed low. "Hölle, we must talk." He scowled at Pharisäer. "Without her." *{She plots against you.}*

"I know," said Hölle. "I know what she is. I always have. I merely allowed her to think she had the upper hand." She looked exhausted, her skin grey and faded, cheeks gaunt. She hadn't bathed or cared for herself in weeks.

"Of course," said Aas. *{Who does she think she's fooling?}*

"Only herself," said Pharisäer, sounding unconcerned. "But you—" She grinned bright teeth. "You will die for what you did to me."

Aas saw Hölle's jaw clench in anger. *{They're going to kill me and I can't shut up. I have to get out of here before I think something truly damning.}* He glanced at Hölle's breasts, desperate to blanket his thoughts with puerile garbage. *{Gods, they're gorgeous. How soft they must be. I want to shove my face—}*

"No," said Hölle. "I need him."

Pharisäer laughed, a scornful and angry bark. "He can't kill me. What use is he to you?"

"You," said Hölle, "are not the only person I want dead."

Pharisäer's angry grin transformed, became sweet and innocent. "Come now, that hurts. Can't we all get along? You know I only want what's best for the Täuschung."

"She lies," said Aas. *{She cares nothing for your life's work.}*

"I know," said Hölle. "Pharisäer, leave us."

"It's not safe. You can't trust him."

{She can't trust me?} "I would never hurt you," he said to Hölle. *{Unless you wanted me to. Unless—}*

"I think he might be the only person I *can* trust," said Hölle. "Pharisäer, leave now."

"Or what?" Pharisäer demanded, hands on hips.

"Did it hurt when he killed you?" Hölle asked sweetly. "Yes, I see in your eyes it did. Leave, or I'll have him hurt you again."

{Please, please, please!}

"Fine," snapped Pharisäer.

"Aas," said Hölle. "You have displeased me. I will give you one chance to make this right." She let the threat hang.

Shoulders set, Pharisäer marched from the room. "You backed the wrong side," she hissed as she stalked past Aas, slamming the door behind her.

{She's right. Hölle is falling apart. I don't want to go to Swarm. No, I have my puppet, my escape—}

"Puppet?" asked Hölle.

"It's nothing." *{Hexenwerk will save me.}*

She glared at him. "You're dripping on my floor."

Aas glanced guiltily at his hand, realizing the makeshift bandage was soaked through with blood. "Cut myself." *{Don't ask. Don't ask about Hexenwerk.}*

Hölle shook her head in disgust. "I don't care about some sick puppet. I need you here and now."

{She needs me?} "I serve at your command."

"I need you," she yelled, advancing, fists clenched in rage, "because you failed me!"

{*Failed?*} Aas retreated before her anger. "No, I've done everything you asked." {*I even tried to kill Pharisäer.*}

Turning, Hölle snatched Zerfall's hand from where it lay on the desk, brandishing it like a weapon. Aas thought she would slap him with it. "She's alive. Zerfall is—" she stopped, blinking at the hand. "It's warm."

"That's impossible," said Aas. Terrified, he babbled. "She was already dying when I found her. I shot her in the gut. The arrow was barbed, dripping in Düster venom. I left her to suffer, as you commanded. I—"

"It's *my* fault?" Hölle demanded.

{*Yes. You should have just told me to kill her.*} "No, of course not. I just—"

"I didn't tell you to *leave* her to suffer, I told you to make *sure* she suffered. Fool! This isn't my fault."

{*Nothing ever is.*}

"What the hell does that mean?" Tossing the hand back on the desk where it landed palm up, she again advanced on Aas.

Shadows cavorted in response to her mood and once again Aas caught glimpses of an eternal nothing populated by millions of tortured souls. Humanity as its own hell.

"I'm agreeing," he said lamely. {*Will she believe—*}

"You think I'm an idiot?"

"No." {*But you flee responsibility like a child!*}

Her breath caught and for an instant he thought she would launch herself at him in a snarling attack. {*Do I kill her if she does?*}

Hölle's hands dropped to her side, and she regarded him with calm eyes a thousand times more frightening than her rage. "You failed me, but I will give you one chance to make this right. Find Zerfall. Kill her. Bring me her head."

{*She's alive? My love, she's really alive?*} "Of course."

"She's a Gefahrgeist. She's incapable of love. She used you."

{*She thinks I don't know that? Fool—*} Seeing Hölle's eyes flash with anger Aas clamped down on the thought. "I'll kill her." {*I did it once, I can do it again.*} He saw her look of disgust. "I'll bring you her head." *{Why can't she see beyond the surface? Why can't she see in me what Zerfall saw?)*

"Zerfall saw nothing I don't see," said Hölle. "Get out."

Aas fled, allowing terror to scramble his thoughts. Hölle already heard more than he liked. He hated that she knew of Hexenwerk. Not that she cared.

Did she understand that when he thought, *I did it once, I can do it again,* it wasn't a statement of fact? He was trying to convince himself.

If she knew, she'd have killed me already.

Aas strode the halls of the Täuschung church, leaving a trail of dripped blood. He had to get outside. He had to *twist,* to become the condor he was meant to be. The need drove him forward, relentless. The open sky was freedom, escape. He was choking in here, he couldn't breathe.

Zerfall is alive. Gods, she'd kill him for what he did to her. An eternity in Swarm would be better than suffering her vengeance. *I have to get out of here.* Where? He didn't know. *Anywhere but here.* All the petty shite going on between Hölle and Pharisäer ceased to matter. They were nothing. Zerfall. *She's alive. I tried to kill her, and I failed, and now she's coming back.* She was death. She'd kill them all, bring the world down around them. He needed to cash in his accounts and get the hells out of Geld before Zerfall found him. The Gezackt Mountains. Maybe he'd hide there. Maybe that was far enough.

Maybe it was time to see what was on the other side of the mountains.

He stepped into the same courtyard he stood in the last time Hölle sent him to kill Zerfall. The yard was empty. The Täuschung compound had been strangely devoid of its deranged priests for the last week. Aas fingered Hexenwerk, hidden deep in a pocket. The urge to *twist* grew, tugging at his thoughts, distracting.

He grinned, face tight. He'd been here in this mad city of greed and avarice for too long.

First, however, he needed to collect his bow and condor-fletched, Düster-poisoned arrows. And then there was the small library of rare books he treasured. He hated to leave those behind.

Aas scowled. When had he begun collecting possessions? Prior to coming to Geld and joining the Täuschung, he never stayed in one place long enough to accrue belongings. He felt dirty, soiled. Had Geld's obsession with money infected him?

I should leave the books and bow behind.

Just to prove he could? That seemed foolish. He'd keep the bow.

So, to his apartments first and then to the Verzweiflung bank.

HÖLLE WATCHED AAS LEAVE. *He'll find Zerfall. He'll kill her this time.* He had to.

She felt weak, drained. The world had lost all colour. She glanced at the mirror and for an instant thought she saw through herself. Closing her eyes, she turned away. *Minor hallucination, nothing more.* These things happened when you were a Halluzin.

Pharisäer returned, smirking. "You know you can't trust him," she said, as soon as she closed the door behind her.

Hölle felt hollowed. "What would you know of trust?"

Pharisäer shrugged, approaching, but stopping beyond arm's reach. "You underestimate him, as I did," she warned. "He's dangerous."

"Of course he's dangerous," snapped Hölle. "He's a killer. *My* killer."

"So you've got everything under control then? Hmm?" Pharisäer smiled honey laced with poison.

"I . . . yes."

"There's nothing you haven't missed?"

"Nothing. The One True God stands behind me. You could never achieve what I achieved."

"Don't you mean what *she* achieved?"

"*We* achieved."

"I don't know," Pharisäer said, shaking her head and looking doubtful. "I can't help but feel you've missed something."

"Your attempts at manipulation smack of desperation—"

"How about her," said Pharisäer, nodding toward Hölle's desk.

Turning, Hölle saw Zerfall's severed hand, palm up. The tattooed eye, open wide, stared at her.

Two women towered over Zerfall, staring down at her. Hölle, the Fragment she'd believed was her sister for so long, looked scared. The other woman looked exactly as Zerfall once had. They were in the chambers she and Hölle once shared.

My hand. She has my hand.

Hölle's eyes were wide with fear and fingers hovered at her mouth as if she cowered behind them. "Can she see us?" she said.

Damned Geisteskranken. Zerfall had never been able to control what she saw through the tattooed eye.

The Fragment Zerfall long thought of as her sister looked haggard, like she hadn't slept or eaten in weeks. Her clothes, filthy and stained, hung loose. *I'm coming for you,* she said. They didn't hear her. *Should have tattooed a mouth on there as well.*

The one who looked like Zerfall, thick dark hair falling about her shoulders, nodded. "I think so, Hölle." She winked at Zerfall. "Notice how the attention changes depending on who's talking."

Backing away, Hölle, still striking and beautiful, said, "Sister, why did you try and kill me? What did I do?"

The other looked disgusted. "You were never sisters. You're her Fragment. You've been working to replace her for hundreds of years, even if neither of you realized it. Well, she knows now."

"No. We were sisters. Once. I'm sure."

"Stop lying."

Hölle ignored the other, focussed on the tattooed eye. "She's returned. She's come to finish—" The woman grimaced, clutching her belly. "She's come to kill me."

"This seems like a win-win situation to me."

"Even if you survive my death, do you think she'll let you live?"

"The enemy of my enemy . . . What do you think, eh Zerfall? Shall I help you slay this pathetic manifestation?"

"You're mad!" screamed Hölle. "This is Zerfall. She's unstoppable!"

The lithe woman made a wet farting noise with soft, full lips. "You underestimate me at every turn. Get Blutblüte back from Aas. Give me the sword, and I'll kill her for you."

Tears streamed down Hölle's round cheeks as she backed away. She stared down at Zerfall, eyes pleading. "Why did you stab me? What did I do?"

Zerfall remembered lying on that stinking cot with her sister, feverish and dying. She'd been so scared, a terrified little girl. *No, you're not real.* Four hundred years was too long; her memories were so faded she could no longer discern truth from desire. She wanted company, she told herself, someone to hold her, someone to tell her it would all be fine. She wanted it so bad. And then Wahrergott, real or hallucinated she didn't know, wrote his words in her brain with fire. Sanity seared and melted and reality ran fluid, bending to her need.

I don't need you anymore. She remembered thinking that once before, many hundreds of years ago, when she first realized Hölle could run the Täuschung without her. She remembered that ancient jealousy. Her sister had always been better at—*No! I was—*

Strong arms held Zerfall cradled close and she found herself staring up at Jateko's square jaw. She couldn't equate what she saw to the weak-chinned, slope-shouldered boy she first met.

"You're awake," he said, glancing down at her with concern.

"The dead don't sleep."

"Whatever you were doing, you were gone."

"I was with Hölle. In Geld."

"We're in Geld," said Jateko, nodding at the surrounding buildings.

Zerfall struggled to sit forward. "I can barely move," she said.

Jateko flashed an apologetic grimace, but she saw sadness and self-recrimination in his eyes. "It rained. You're sodden."

A broken corpse, Zerfall barked a harsh laugh, a cough of rot and decay. "They were talking about me." She wanted to explain her sister who wasn't but couldn't. It was too painful. "Hölle, she fears me. She thinks I've come to kill her."

Jateko frowned, confused. "We have."

"Yes we have. Hölle has manifest a Fragment of her own." She glanced at Jateko. Had he caught it, her small slip?

Jateko shrugged, unconcerned.

Zerfall watched the city slide by, the jarring *grind pop click thump* of Tod's stride making it difficult to focus. Stone buildings towered overhead, signs advertising everything from clothes to food to rented companionship. Everything was for sale here.

Though the rain had ceased, few people were out on the streets and those who were huddled deep in luxurious coats.

"Is it cold?" she asked Jateko.

"I've been cold since we left the desert. Is the city always like this, so grey and depressing?"

"Yes." She watched a woman in a tall and awkward hat exit a colossal structure of stone polished to a glossy finish so bright she saw her reflection within. Pillars, soaring columns of marble, lined the palatial steps leading up to monstrous doors that looked to be made of hammered bronze.

Jateko, noting her attention, stared in open amazement. "Is that a church? What gods they must worship here."

"It's a bank," she said, gesturing at a sign and wondered if any of the people Jateko devoured could read. "This is the main office of the Verzweiflung Banking Conglomerate."

"A bank." Jateko shook his head in wonder. "I understand the word, but it makes no sense. This is still a church."

"The Verzweiflung worship money. People store their wealth here."

"It's full of goats and swords and food? That explains the size."

"Not that kind of wealth. Gold. Silver. Coins, and jewels."

He looked doubtful. "Your bank draft, we can exchange it for wealth here?"

"I believe so. Though I'm not sure if it will work. It's a little weathered." She laughed, a snort of wry amusement. "As am I."

As they reached the foot of the stairs Tod's rear hips gave out with a loud *crack* and pitched them backward off his bent spine. Jateko rolled, keeping Zerfall safe in the cradle of his arms, and stood in one smooth motion. Tod lowered himself until his ravaged skull rested on the cobbled road. The ragged edges of his opened belly splayed apart like an upside-down sack thrown to the ground. A shiver ran the length of his ruined body and he was still.

"Tod?" asked Zerfall.

"He's gone," said Jateko, pulling her into a hug.

I don't need him any more. The thought saddened her. *Was my need all that kept Tod moving?* She never gave the beast a choice, never spared his desires a thought. *That's who I am.* She hated herself. *I haven't changed.*

Nestled in Jateko's arms she wished she could close her eyes, shut out the world. She'd give anything to feel the heat from his body, to bask in the warmth of another living soul. Tod, her friend, was gone. She wanted to cry but had no eyes, no tears. No release for pain. Maybe she had changed a little; the old Zerfall could never feel such emotions for another. She clung to that thought.

"There's nothing here for us," she said. "This was a mistake. We—" The bank doors swung open, held by a fat man in small and unadorned hat who bowed low as a gaunt and hideous man exited.

Zerfall stared up the steps at the thin man. His face hung slack and sallow, his skin puckered with thick black hairs. A black long bow and a quiver of thick-shafted black arrows hung across slim shoulders hunched against the cold. Blutblüte hung at his hip. He shuffled down the steps in fits and starts like vulture hopping from branch to branch, bulbous eyes darting. One hand was wrapped in a bulbous and bloody bandage.

When she awoke in the desert, she remembered her life, and who she'd been. She remembered Aas but hadn't given the man much thought; there was no emotional connection to make him important, to make him worth remembering.

Seeing him now, here in Geld just a few block from the church brought back more memories. They returned in a torrential flood. She and Aas had been something like lovers, which is to say he loved her and she used him and hurt him whenever it entertained her. Her Gefahrgeist power kept him malleable, made him willing to do anything to please her, and she abused that.

I kept him around because I could hear his thoughts. He was the only person I trusted. And still she'd cut him, testing how far she could push him. She never found his limit.

He loved me. He loved her with unquestioning loyalty and she kept him distant. She felt nothing for him, had been incapable of such feeling.

Glancing again at Tod's gutted corpse she felt Jateko's arms around her, a distant pressure devoid of warmth, felt that dim spark buried deep in her, felt the shiver of fear at the thought of losing him. *I've changed.* But how much had she changed? Was Jateko here by choice, or did her need enslave him too?

"What is it?" Jateko asked when he noticed her focussed attention.

"That's him," she said, gesturing with her remaining hand. "Aas, the man who killed me. He took my hand."

Jateko froze, shoulders and arms tense, hard like rock. He watched the black-clad man descend the steps in their direction, not walking directly toward them, but likely passing not much beyond arm's reach.

"He looks thin and weak," whispered Jateko.

"He's dangerous." She remembered the barbed agony of the arrow Aas left buried in her gut.

"He has Blutblüte, my sword."

H*E CARRIES B*LUTBLÜTE*? J*ATEKO didn't know whether to be elated or terrified. What was it capable of? Zerfall never talked about it other than to say that Swarm, the hell of the Täuschung was somehow trapped within the blade. Could he possibly hope to defeat such a weapon?

"I need your sword," he said, drawing his own and sliding the Swordsman's second blade from where it hung at her side. He released Zerfall, stepped in front of her to shield her with his bulk. *No one will hurt her again.*

Aas stopped when he noticed Jateko's actions. He stood watching, left arm held cradled against his chest, the hand wrapped in tattered bandages seeping blood. He showed no hint of fear, just mild curiosity.

Jateko rolled his wide shoulders, loosening them. "You hurt my friend," he said.

"And?" asked Aas, relaxed and unconcerned.

"I'm hungry."

The gaunt assassin leaned forward and sniffed, testing the air with a hooked nose as if that might help him make sense of Jateko's words. "This is Geld. There are many restaurants nearby."

Jateko advanced, lifting the matched blades, testing their balance. He felt good, strong and fast. Invincible. Cold rage, tight wound fury, bathed his thoughts bloody crimson. Killing this wretched man wasn't enough; he must not be free to flee to Swarm or any other hell or Afterdeath. *He must be mine.*

Savage hunger threatened to wash away all thought. Grey clay brains. The oil slick sheen of liver. The soft squish of raw kidney. Jateko's mouth watered. He *needed* it.

"I am Jateko, the All Consuming. I'm going to eat your brain."

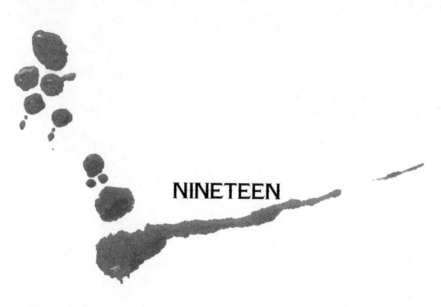

NINETEEN

Fear is the fulcrum.

—Versklaver Denker, Gefahrgeist Philosopher

THE TATTOOED EYE SLID closed and Pharisäer grinned madness at Hölle, eyes bright and victorious.

Fear flooded Hölle's veins like a rush of frigid water. Had that really been Zerfall watching through that eye, or was this just another manifestation of her Halluzin power? Neither option instilled her with hope. Either Zerfall had been watching for god knew how long, or Hölle was losing control of her delusions. Both meant the end.

Pharisäer turned on Hölle, leering clenched teeth shown in something between a snarl and a mad grin of ravenous hunger. "She's coming. She's coming to kill you for what you did to her."

"I didn't *do* anything!" She hated the whine in her voice.

"You've been running more and more of her religion for the last two hundred years. By the end, just before she stabbed you, she had almost nothing to do with the Täuschung."

"She didn't want—"

"Some part of you knew what you were. Some part of you knew what you needed to do. You've been slowly replacing her for centuries, taking all she built and making it yours. She stabbed you to protect herself, but I don't think she yet realized exactly what you were. I think she really did believe you were her sister." Pharisäer grinned prefect teeth. "At least until the end. Maybe she began to understand. Maybe she learned something, like you recently did."

"You don't know that," said Hölle, reaching toward the hand, wanting to turn it palm down, but hesitating.

"Go on," taunted Pharisäer. "Touch it. I dare you."

Hölle turned away. "No need," she said.

"Liar. It's over. Everything you worked for is dead." Pharisäer laughed, mocking. "Most of it never existed in the first place. Just like you."

"Swarm is real!" snapped Hölle. "Täuschung is real. Wahrergott is real. *I am—*"

"You're a fool. It may all be real, but it's not yours. You are nothing more than Zerfall's delusion given flesh. Powerless. Useless." Pharisäer loosed a slow, world-weary sigh. "It's no wonder she tried to kill you. You disgust her."

Hölle spun on her, advancing, fingers curled like claws. "No. *I* dreamt Swarm. Swarm is *mine.*"

Pharisäer, unafraid, held her ground. "You can't remember doing it, can you? And why is it in *Zerfall's* sword?"

Hölle stopped short.

"Look at you," said Pharisäer. "Desperate. Misery writ plain across your face." She leaned close as if to breath in Hölle's despair. "You're breaking. I can smell it. Doubt undoes you."

"I have no doubt," said Hölle and knew it for a lie. Doubt was all she had. The room darkened, clouded by the Halluzin manifestations of her fears. "It was a long time ago," she said, loathing how pathetically uncertain she sounded. "Four hundred years. You have no idea."

"Four hundred?" asked Pharisäer. "Are you sure? Can you truly remember four hundred years with Zerfall?"

She couldn't, not really. It was too much. The dim outline of a cot formed from coiling shadow, pressed against the sagging wall of a family home stricken with poverty and virulent plague. A single girl, emaciated and soaked in rank sweat, lay groaning, haunted by febrile dreams. A second girl faded in and out, uncertain. *I remember the cot. I was there.* But the memory was faded with time, translucent.

Pharisäer pressed close and Hölle retreated, hands up as if warding off an attack. "No one can remember four hundred years. It's too long."

"Really?" demanded Pharisäer, following. "How much *do* you remember? Two hundred years? A century?"

Hölle shook her head in denial and struggled to remember. *I remember . . .* But what was real, what was dream, and what was hallucinated madness?

"I said I was your guilt and your doubt," said Pharisäer. "I wasn't lying. I am. Do you know what guilt is?" She smiled, soft and caring and didn't wait for a response. "It's the acceptance of responsibility. Do you know what you doubt most?"

"I have no—"

"That you can do this alone. You can't."

Half a dozen adumbral bodies, the feverish girl's parents, lay sprawled where they had fallen, littering the hallucinated floor.

"I . . . I don't know," admitted Hölle in a small voice.

"Gods," snarled Pharisäer in disgust. "Did you manifest just weeks before she stabbed you? Is that why she tried to kill you? Was she staving off the manifestation of an unpleasant new delusion?" Pharisäer's eyes widened, her mouth hanging open as she nodded. "Yes, that's it. Maybe you signalled the end of everything *she* worked for."

No. I remember being a little girl. "I was there at the beginning." Hölle clung to that memory. *Wasn't I?*

The girls in the cot jerked and thrashed, their minds shredded by plague and the words of the One True God burned into their souls like lightning splitting a tree.

"Is that memory yours, or hers?" Pharisäer pursed her lips, doubtful. "I share some of your memories."

"You're lying."

The Fragment shrugged, uncaring. "I remember when she stabbed you, the incredible pain." Pharisäer shuddered, clutching her belly, and Hölle whimpered in response, tears leaking from her dark eyes.

"No," said Hölle. "I remember."

"No doubt she filled you with many of her own memories. It's only natural you confused them as your own." Pharisäer offered a comforting and understanding smile, tinged with regret. "It's not your fault; we're creatures born of insanity. It's no wonder we ourselves are deranged."

"Swarm. I hallucinated—"

"Come now," said Pharisäer. "Everyone thinks you're this powerful Halluzin, that you created an entire hell with a thought. But that's nonsense and we both know it. Beyond a few dancing shadows, what have you hallucinated lately? When was the last time you truly shaped reality? Eh? Was Swarm it, your only lasting hallucination?" Pharisäer lifted her hands as if offering apology. "You *know* that's not the way it works. People aren't delusional for one brief instant. It's a life-long curse. It defines them. Forever."

Hölle felt lost and bewildered, eyes darting like a cornered rat. "I'm Halluzin."

Pharisäer gestured at the flickering image of the bed-ridden girls. "Show me. Define reality. Make it real." She stared at the image, fading in and out of reality as if uncertain of its place. "No?" she demanded, not giving Hölle time to answer. "I thought not."

"It's not that easy. It doesn't—"

"Of *course* not," sneered Pharisäer. "And may I say how *convenient* it is, that you are unable to provide any kind of proof."

"It's not my fault!"

"Of course not," she repeated. "Since you've done nothing—achieved nothing—nothing is ever your fault."

"You're wrong!" screamed Hölle. "I run Täuschung! I matter!"

"What?" Pharisäer looked about in stunned disbelief as if searching for someone else to confirm she wasn't the crazy one here. "You? You sit in your room all day hiding from everything and every one. Hiding from responsibility. It's not my fault, *it's not my fault.* Coward."

The memory of pain stabbed into Hölle's belly, lit her guts on fire. The sword, Blutblüte. She'd been stabbed. She should have died. She remembered Aas' attempt to kill Pharisäer. *You didn't die because you're not real. No no no no.* "I was healing."

"I know, I know. It's not my fault," whined Pharisäer, mocking. "You were healed months ago. I've been running the Täuschung. I've been maintaining the church, looking after the day to day business. You've done *nothing*. You don't leave your bed except to whine and complain." Pharisäer made a show of examining her and tutting at what she found. "You know what I think?"

"I don't care what you think."

"You *used* to be strong. But now, you're a shadow of what you were."

Too close to her own thoughts, Hölle retreated.

Pharisäer followed. "I don't know what happened to Zerfall after she tried to kill you, but something has changed her. She no longer needs you. Whatever mental damage caused your existence has been healing." Pharisäer pursued Hölle around the bed, cornering her. "Think about it. Aas said she lost her Gefahrgeist power. I think perhaps she's becoming sane and her delusions are dying. You're fading."

Hölle shook her head in mute denial.

"Look at you," demanded Pharisäer standing before Hölle. "You stink. You're soft and you're weak." Pharisäer leered. "What will Zerfall think? You know how she views weakness."

Hölle took a deep breath, forced herself to stand tall, hands on hips. "I'm not weak."

Pharisäer slapped her hard across the face and Hölle stood shocked, blinking back tears. A thin line of blood trickled from the corner of an already swelling lip. Pharisäer raised an eyebrow, waiting, and then slapped her again when she opened her mouth to speak. The second slap crumpled Hölle to the floor.

The hallucinated girls and cot snapped out of existence.

"Weak," said Pharisäer, grimacing at her hand, now flushed red from the slaps. "Look, even your pitiful little hallucination is gone. You're worthless." She dropped to one knee, examining Hölle with pity. "It was so easy to trick you."

"You never—"

"I danced you like a gods-damned marionette. I manipulated you into sending Aas away with Blutblüte."

"What? Why?"

"Fool. Only Blutblüte can kill Zerfall."

Was that true, or was the Fragment lying? "Aas will kill her for me."

"He's gone."

"He betrayed me?"

"Betrayed?" Pharisäer laughed, an honest guffaw of startled pleasure. "I've been telling him how much you hate him for weeks. I told him all about how you planned to kill him."

"You?"

"Of course." Pharisäer rose and danced a mad jig, arms raised as if hung from strings above. "Dance puppet, dance!" She stopped, arms dropping, head hanging at an odd angle, like her strings had been cut. "Did you really think he'd kill Zerfall for *you*, a whiny bitch who hates him?"

"You turned him against me. It's not—"

"Your fault. I know. Nothing ever is." She cocked her head to one side as if considering. "You only have two delusions."

Hölle, face flushed and wet with tears, stared up at her in confusion. "Two?"

"First, you are deluded in thinking that you matter. At all. To anyone. But your second delusion, it's a beauty."

"It is?" The universe frayed apart like a cheap rug and hung tattered and abused. Who was she? Who had she been? If Zerfall was real and Hölle nothing but the dream of a feverish child, what of her life's work? Was it all just madness, did none of it matter?

"Yes. It's me!" Pharisäer offered a bright and cheerful smile. "I'm a product of your own self-loathing. You created me out of your pathetic need to flee responsibility." Again she danced about, flapping her arms and tottering her head back and forth in a deranged caper. Over and over she sang, "It's not my fault. It's not my fault," as she danced. Winded, she paused. "You created me to be your end. I am here as an act of self-sabotage, nothing more." Tears welling in her eyes, she dropped her shoulders as if in broken defeat. "You *want* to fail."

Hölle blubbered, drooled spit tainted red with blood and cried tears of heartbreak. "You said you'd take my doubt."

Pharisäer gazed at her, incredulous. "Sweetheart, I lied." She gestured at where Hölle cowered. "Look at you. You are nothing *but* doubt. Come on, admit it, you knew I lied. The entire time, you knew. You had to, you aren't stupid. And still you played along. You let me run your stupid church while you hid away in bed. You knew. This," Pharisäer opened her arms to encompass the room and scene, "is what you wanted."

"No. It's—"

"Not. Your. Fault. And once again I have done exactly what you wanted me to."

"What . . . what I want you to?"

"I've tricked you into sending Aas away, the one person who could protect you. And now I've stalled you for long enough Zerfall can finally kill you." Pharisäer glanced at the door. "She's almost here."

Hölle loosed a wail of terror, an incoherent scream of mind-shattering fear. "No!" She snatched a steak-knife off a food-encrusted plate that had held her dinner some days ago. Pharisäer, surprised, backed away.

"She can't kill me!" screamed Hölle.

"Kill you? You have met Zerfall, right?" she asked, sarcastically. "You know what she's like. Gods, I'm glad I'm not you." Pharisäer paced the room. "No, Zerfall won't kill you. At least not right away. I mean, you did send someone to kill her. And not anyone, you sent her own lover. How twisted was that? What the hells were you thinking? Damn, you don't even need me; you've been sabotaging yourself from the beginning."

"No. I—"

Pharisäer waved her to silence. "And then you ran the Täuschung—Zerfall's life's work—into the ground. You turned her priests against each other. You sold off all the property the church has bought over the centuries for a pittance of what they're worth. In the last few weeks you've ruined everything she worked so hard to achieve."

It all made sense. Her Geisteskranken battling in the streets in Täuschung robes. The church coming under investigation. "That was you. You did—"

"Right, *I* did that. It isn't your fault. I'm sure she'll believe you." Pharisäer nodded to herself, gnawing on her lower lip. "She'll take an eternity to kill you." She blinked, looking startled by an idea. "Literally! You're a Fragment like me. You won't die. She'll torture you forever."

Pharisäer was right. Zerfall would see it all as Hölle's responsibility. *She'll be so angry with me.* She shuddered in terror at the thought of her sister's anger. There was no hurt Zerfall wouldn't inflict.

Hölle clutched her knife to her heaving chest, clung to it like she'd drown without it. "I'll kill her," she sobbed. Her words lacked conviction.

"With that silly little knife?" Pharisäer cocked her head in thought. "Aas loves her, you know. I wonder if he went straight to her and gave her Blutblüte as an offering, some misguided attempt at buying forgiveness." She laughed, a tinkling of merry humour. "But we know Zerfall: That bitch is as cold and hard as iron, not an ounce of forgiveness."

Hölle sank to the floor and curled into a foetal ball, knife held tight, retching and twitching in bone-shaking sobs.

"Here she comes," purred Pharisäer. "She's in the hall."

She's coming. Fear shredded Hölle's thoughts. Nothing in all the world was more terrifying than an angry Zerfall. She'd torment Hölle for a thousand years. Swarm would be a release, an escape. "Help me," she pleaded. "I'll give you anything. Everything. Help me."

Pharisäer nodded. "I'll help you. I must. I am, after all, a manifestation of your desires. There's one escape."

Escape? Hadn't she just been thinking that? Hölle blinked up at Pharisäer, lips quivering, face streaked with tears, hopeful. "Where?"

"There, in your hands. Why do you think you grabbed it? You knew you'd never defeat Zerfall with a shite little knife; you knew you'd need it. It's your way out."

Hölle's eyes locked on the knife.

"Anything is better than being in Zerfall's hands," said Pharisäer

Swarm could be her escape. She'd survive the hell and someday be freed to rise as a god. The knife shook as Hölle turned it against her own throat. "I . . . I can't."

"You can," said Pharisäer, eyes damp as she knelt at Hölle's side. "I will help. But," she added, "not the throat. There's no need to suffer."

"Suffer," whispered Hölle. She remembered Selbs and how her Fragment, Beherrscher, died and faded shortly after Selbs's death. *Does Pharisäer not know?* Did she think she'd survive Hölle's death? There was some small comfort there, knowing she ended them both.

Together they held the knife, and Pharisäer turned it so the needle-sharp tip touched Hölle's chest over her heart.

"T HIS WILL BE PAINLESS," lied Pharisäer as she pressed her weight against the knife.

The moment the tip pricked the soft flesh of Hölle's breast her eyes opened in blossoming terror. *She understands now.* Pharisäer drank that moment. Hölle struggled, trying to push Pharisäer and the penetrating blade away. But Pharisäer was on top. Inexorably the knife slid, slow as a creeping glacier, into Hölle's chest. Pharisäer, realizing her advantage, didn't put her full weight behind the blade; no need to end this too swiftly. Straddling the woman whose delusions gave her birth, Pharisäer stared into beautiful dark eyes wide with terror and pressed the knife deeper.

"When I die," gasped Hölle through gritted teeth, "You'll die too!"

She still doesn't understand. But now wasn't the time for that truth. Not yet.

"It's okay," Pharisäer breathed into Hölle's ear, feigning exhaustion. "I'm tired. I'm ready for the end."

Had she not sufficiently broken Hölle first, she would disappear. Hölle's death would mean her end. But Hölle had cracked. She'd given up. Surrendered. This was Pharisäer's time.

It was all lies. Pharisäer had no idea if Zerfall was alive and no reason to think the psychotic bitch who gave birth to this pathetic delusion was becoming sane.

She said whatever she thought would most weaken and terrify Hölle, anything to undermine her belief in herself. All for this moment. All for this suicide. For in truth, there was only one woman in this room.

"I'm not real," she whispered to Hölle. "This is you killing yourself." She pushed the knife deeper. *But I will be real once you're dead.*

When Hölle sucked in breath, Pharisäer bent and kissed her hard, breathing in her last exhalation as the knife entered her heart. For a dozen heart beats after, Pharisäer stayed there, mouth pressed against Hölle's open lips.

When Pharisäer sat up, splashed in blood and drunk on victory, she surveyed her rooms. *It's mine. It's all mine. This stupid church and these stupid priests. They'll do anything for me.*

Assuming Aas found and killed Zerfall as he said he would—and she saw no reason to doubt the man—everything worked out perfectly. In truth, she was less than convinced Zerfall was alive at all. Far more likely she died out in the desert. Aas, for all his failings, was an excellent killer.

Pharisäer glanced at the tattooed hand. It remained unchanged, the eye closed. Its opening had probably been some minor hallucination of Hölle's.

Why isn't it rotting? The thought left a sour feeling in her gut.

"It's just me," she said to the empty room. "Me, Zerfall."

She frowned, confused.

"I am Zerfall."

It felt wrong. Empty.

"I am Zerfall Seele," she tried again. It wasn't true. "Shite," she swore. Zerfall was still alive.

Maybe Aas hadn't found her yet. *Yes*, she decided, *that has to be it*. Soon Aas would find and kill Zerfall. She licked her lips, examining the corpse at her feet. Soon.

A dark worm of doubt curled cold in Pharisäer's heart.

TWENTY

All civilization is built on fear.

—Versklaver Denker, Gefahrgeist Philosopher

EAT MY BRAIN? *WHAT a strange threat.* It must have cultural connotations of which Aas was unaware. It was difficult to even take seriously.

Aas' hand ached and throbbed. *Twisting* had mostly closed the wound, but the sodden bandage still leaked blood.

He examined the young man—Basamortuan, he guessed, judging from the dark mahogany of his skin and the tattered and burnt remnants of what looked like tent fabric. The youth, broad shouldered and slim hipped, was bald except for a hint of dark stubble. He brandished a matched pair of swords, looking all too comfortable with their weight. Did the desert tribals have roaming Swordsmen like the city-states? Aas didn't think so. It was odd to see one with a proper sword, never mind a matched pair of such quality. Usually they were armed with shoddy and rusting weapons or spears of bone and wood.

"Do I know you?" Aas asked.

The handsome warrior—and he could be nothing else for his balance was perfect, his poise ready to move in any direction—grinned straight white teeth. "No. But I will know you."

I will know you? What a strange thing to say.

I don't have time for this. Now he'd finally decided to leave Geld, the urge to spread his wings and fly drove him to distraction. "Begone," said Aas.

The man might be a warrior, but Aas was a killer, an assassin. He had more tricks—knives and poisons, garrottes and hooks—up his sleeves than this barbaric youth could imagine. The Basamortuan were fierce warriors, but they fought without finesse, relying on brawn and speed rather than skill.

"What happened to your hand?" the young man asked, noticing the blood leaking from Aas' makeshift bandage.

"I chopped off my finger."

The Basamortuan accepted this without question, nodding as if this were normal behaviour.

"Don't do this," a voice wheezed, and with a start Aas realized another figure stood partially concealed behind the Basamortuan warrior. "We should leave."

That voice. Weak and thin as it was, Aas recognized it. "Zerfall?" Excitement and fear warred for supremacy. Had she returned to reclaim her religion? Would she kill everyone who wronged her, or would she crush his will with her Gefahrgeist power and once again make him hers?

Aas leaned to look past the Basamortuan. She looked near dead last time he saw her, but she'd progressed far beyond that. She stood lilting to one side, one foot missing, the ankle ending in a ragged stump of splintered bone. The knee of that leg had been shattered and bound to a few sticks to keep it straight. Where her torso showed through the tattered remains of her shirt he saw what looked to have been patches of ratty horse flesh sewn to her. Aas understood immediately: She'd been repaired many times. Calling her a corpse would have been kind.

When she stood staring, dead face unreadable, he knew she was helpless. The old Zerfall would have crushed him already, wouldn't have given him a moment to think or act. *I could keep her.* He could study her. Cotardists were supposed to die when the rot reached their heart, weren't they? That's what he always heard. Oh, the mysteries to explore! Or she could be a trophy. A defenseless Zerfall; the thought intoxicated.

"We aren't leaving," the Basamortuan said over his shoulder, speaking to Zerfall.

Is she not here of her own free will? Had the Basamortuan somehow taken advantage of her in her weakened state? *I can save her!* Drawing a long black condor-fletched arrow from his quiver, Aas laughed aloud, spinning it in his fingers. He'd escape the Täuschung and their hell *and* get the woman of his dreams. Once he rescued Zerfall from this savage she'd see his worth. *She'll finally love me.* Gods he wanted that more than anything. Looking at her rotting corpse it was like nothing had changed, like she never left. Somehow he'd make her a new body. Could he make a good enough puppet, and if he did could he move her soul? Belief shapes reality. Somehow somewhere it would be possible. *She'll be mine. Forever.*

The Basamortuan stood waiting, swords at the ready.

Aas approached.

{That isn't right. That's the stance of a city-states Swordsman.}

J ATEKO GRINNED AT THE scrawny man. Aas was not at all what he expected; the man looked like a plucked chicken, all puckered skin and hanging wattles.

"That's right," he said. "I—you didn't speak."

Aas said nothing, sauntering forward, an arrow turning in a languid spin in the fingers of his unhurt hand. He didn't look at all like a man about to fight for his life.

"Wouldn't you rather use that sword?" Jateko asked, nodding at the plain blade hanging at the man's side.

"No thanks," answered Aas, the arrow continuing its lazy rotation. He made no attempt to retrieve the bow slug over his back.

He doesn't want to use Blutblüte? Why not?

He's an assassin, said Grausamer, *not a Swordsman.*

Oh, said Abiega, *decided to be useful, have you?*

Some goat-shagger ate my brain, snarled Grausamer. *Sorry if I needed some time to get used to the idea.*

I heard Aas' thoughts, said Jateko, but no one else seemed to care.

In a sword fight, said Grausamer, *I'd slaughter this man.*

"Good," said Jateko, receiving an odd look from Aas.

{Who is he talking too?}

This is not *a sword fight,* added Grausamer. *That arrow is poisoned.*

Jateko glanced at the arrow and, sure enough, the obsidian tip was coated in something dark.

The assassin noticed his attention. "Düster venom. Comes from a—"

"Snake. I'm familiar with them," said Jateko, circling to keep the assassin at distance. "Taste awful."

{So he is Basamortuan. That stance . . .}

Since no one else seemed to think hearing the assassin's thoughts was odd, Jateko decided to accept it and move on. "I ate a Swordsman," he said, explaining.

"Oh." The assassin changed stances, darting forward.

Jateko danced back, staying well clear of the poisoned arrow.

Why are you telling him this? asked Abiega

Maybe I can scare him, answered Jateko. *Frightened people make mistakes.*

He seems terrified, muttered Gogoko,

"Wendigast?" asked Aas, frowning. "No. You aren't manifesting as demonic."

Jateko feinted with one sword to draw out the assassin's defence and attacked with the second. He made the attack loose and sloppy, at half the speed he was capable of.

The assassin avoided it easily and shot him a look of disgust.

I thought you were trying to scare him, said Gogoko.

And I thought we decided that wouldn't work, answered Jateko.

"I don't understand your city-states classifications of Geisteskranken," Jateko said, again circling. "Aren't all Geisteskranken really Wahnist? Don't they all suffer false beliefs? You label things thinking it means you understand them."

Hey, said Abiega, *that's my line.*

The assassin halted. He bit his lip in thought and said, "There are differences. Nuances."

"I don't fit the Wendigast classification at all," pointed out Jateko, changing directions. "So am I Wahnist, or Halluzin? Are the strengths and skills I gain from eating my victims manifest hallucinations?"

The assassin's attention wandered as he frowned in thought. "Does everyone in your tribe—"

Jateko attacked, stabbing and slashing in a lightning dance of singing steel. Aas retreated, ducking most attacks and batting aside others with the flat of his empty hand. Jateko pressed forward, driving himself faster until his twin swords screamed a clear note of savagery and still Aas avoided his attacks. When he let up, the assassin was breathing heavily and nodding in appreciation.

"Which Swordsman did you eat?" Aas asked.

"Grausamer Schlächter," said Jateko. "He claims to have been quite good."

"He was," agreed Aas between breaths. "The best in Geld. Maybe the Greatest Swordsman in the World."

See, said Grausamer petulantly, *I told you I was great.*

Aas examined Jateko through slitted eyes as he once again circled away. "You aren't breathing hard."

Jateko shrugged non-committally. "I devour more than their skills."

{That should do it.} "I think I've stalled for long enough." said Aas, grinning and looking relaxed.

"I—what?" Jateko's knees wobbled under him.

AAS LIFTED THE ARROW and raised an eyebrow as a thin stream of red blood dripped from the obsidian tip. "I cut you."

"Really?" The young Basamortuan took a moment to search himself before finding the cut, a deep scratch, along one forearm. "That? It's nothing."

{Like all Swordsmen, he's none too bright.} "Remember the Düster venom?"

Jateko blinked and then laughed. "I was so excited about killing you, I forgot."

{It should be reaching his organs right about now.}

The desert warrior crumpled to the cobbled road, the beautifully matched swords skittering on stone. "Hardly seems fair," he growled through clenched teeth.

Aas approached, kicking away the young warrior's swords. *{Muscles should begin seizing.}* "Did you really kill and eat Grausamer?"

The Basamortuan's limbs shivered in tight paroxysms and he curled into a foetal ball, whimpering. "Yes."

"Good. I lost money when he killed Verlierer last year."

"He says sorry," hissed the warrior.

"That's unlikely. He was a prick." *{He should be paralysed already.}*

The young warrior's body stiffened, and Aas heard the creak of bone and tendon. "That . . ." The youth managed to gesture by moving his head the barest of a nod. ". . . Blutblüte?"

Aas nodded. Leaving it sheathed had been a wise choice; he never could have defeated Grausamer in a sword fight. "Yes. It was hers," he said, glancing at Zerfall. *{Once I've made you whole again I'll return it to you.}* He loved her so much it hurt. Having her this close clenched his guts like an iron fist. He couldn't breathe. Everything he always wanted stood but a few strides away. Finally, she needed *him*! Everything would be different now.

Zerfall watched him with empty sockets, her dead face unreadable.

"I'll take you away from here," Aas said. "I can make you whole again," he promised.

Her failure to react—either with appreciation or scorn, and he was more familiar receiving the latter from Zerfall—distracted him. *{I love you. I always have.}* It didn't matter that he'd had no choice. Things were different now, somehow he knew it.

Aas knelt by the Basamortuan's side, preparing to finish the youth with a thrust of the poisoned arrow. "He's carrion, he just doesn't know it yet." *{I know you need me. Need is love, I see that now. Before it was always just me needing you, but now . . .}*

"Aas," Zerfall croaked.

He looked up, met those dark sockets. "Just one moment—"

JATEKO TORE BLUTBLÜTE FROM its scabbard and rammed the sword up through the assassin's guts and into his chest, *twisting* and wrenching the blade to cause maximum damage. Aas gurgled and coughed a great gout of blood over the cobbled street. Jateko shoved him aside and pushed himself into a sitting position with much groaning and grunting.

{Not possible. Düster venom.}

"Mom used to make Düster soup. I had to collect the vicious bastards. I've been bitten hundreds of times. I may have developed a slight resistance."

{Not . . . possible.} The assassin's thoughts were fading.

"And I ate over a dozen people," said Jateko. "It would take twelve times the usual dosage to kill me. I felt pretty bad for a moment, but started healing immediately."

The assassin's eyes slid closed. *{Wendigast? It can't . . . work like that . . . never heard of . . .}* Even now, as he lay dying, the man struggled to understand.

"I believe it does. I *know* it does." Jateko appreciated the assassin's curiosity. He looked forward to possessing it. "But I don't think I'm Wendigast."

{Must get out.}

"I think I was so naïve I was capable of convincing myself of all manner of insanity. That's why I question your civilized classifications. You assume insanity has to fit nice neat labels, but surely that's crazy!"

{Get to . . .}

"Labelling something doesn't mean you understand it. In fact, I think it stops you from further questioning. Hello?"

The assassin lay motionless. No breath moved his chest, no pulse throbbed through the veins in his neck.

Jateko stood. "It's a good thing I heard what he was thinking. I wasn't sure what the symptoms of Düster poisoning were. Couldn't remember the order. I think if—what the hells?"

Aas' chest moved like something sought to claw its way free.

AAS LAY ON HIS back, watching the Basamortuan youth through fading eyes. The world grew dark, distant. The pain in his gut, the vicious rape of his internal organs, dragged him down, sank him in darkness. Drowned him in waves of agony. The cocky little bastard had murdered him.

How had he done it? How had the Düster venom not killed him?

The young warrior babbled, perhaps in response to Aas' own thoughts. He couldn't be sure. The man was too far away and getting farther with every failing beat of Aas' dying heart. And they were just words. Words didn't matter. Not now.

Swarm.

Oh gods no. All hells and shite. He believed in Swarm, absolutely.

If only Hexenwerk was the escape he needed it to be. How had that *salbei* been able to ignore the pull of his flesh body and move his soul into a lousy puppet? Was it the *salbei's* life of abstinence that made it possible, was it living an entire life in abject misery? What if Zerfall and Hölle were right and the key to everything was suffering. He'd laugh, if he could. At best he managed a bubbling cough of blood.

How many times had he been on the other side of this violent equation, standing over his victim, watching the eyes as the spark of spirit went to whatever Afterdeath awaited? How many souls had he sent to Swarm?

He'd know soon enough. They'd be there, waiting.

Aas remembered standing in the Basamortuan desert, watching Zerfall writhe around the poisoned arrow he left in her gut. Gods how he drank in that moment, gloried in her pain.

A wet sob—a bloody whine of fear—escaped his lips. He felt emptied, like a slashed wineskin, its contents splashed about the stones of the Verzweiflung courtyard. He remembered watching his father gut chickens in the cellar, their innards spattering about his feet. Is that what he looked like, a gutted chicken?

No, a condor.

Could he *twist*? Aas tried, struggled to find that place inside, that black core that hated who and what he was; that part of him wanting nothing more than to shed his humanity like a scorpion shedding its exoskeleton. He should have stayed in that cellar, died there. Eating the rotting corpse of his father, had been wrong. Evil. He deserved this.

That very same part which hated him, that which allowed him to *twist*, wanted him to die.

Escaping that pain would be a blessing.

Escaping.

Aas struggled to bring his scattered thoughts together, to focus. The *salbei* of the Ausgebrochene tribe, had he been escaping his body? Is that why he could leave it behind when Aas remained rooted in flesh? Had a lifetime of physical and mental abuse and suffering allowed the *salbei* to desire escape from his own flesh more than his soul wanted to remain there?

{Must get out.}

Aas reached for the Hexenwerk with his thoughts and found the puppet, an empty shell. His body, a failing meat prison soon to become carrion, did nothing to resist the flight of his soul.

There was no end, just more suffering. The Täuschung got that much right.

{Get to . . .}

Aas fled his dying body into Hexenwerk. He felt tiny, crushed. The puppet was too small, but it would do. He had to find another vessel. The drunken *salbei* told him it was possible to possess the body of another, though he refused to go into detail. Aas would have to make his way to the Ausgebrochene tribe in the Gezackt Mountains before Hexenwerk fell apart; a seemingly impossible voyage for a puppet of snot and hair and a single small finger. Somehow he'd force the truth from the *salbei*.

He struggled, trapped within the inner pocket of his robes. He should have thought this through, made the pocket easier to escape. He should have armed the puppet with a razor blade. Even a tiny weapon was better than none. He felt naked, unarmed and vulnerable.

There, the cobblestone of the road. He dragged himself from the pocket and pushed himself upright to stand on rubbery legs.

{I did it! I'm free! I—}

JATEKO RETREATED A STEP, eyes wide, as a hideous puppet of snot, hair, fingernail clippings, long black feathers, and what looked like a freshly severed finger, crawled from within Aas' robes. Small, ill-formed wings stretched wide.

{I did it! I'm free! I—}

In a fit of visceral disgust Jateko stomped on the puppet, crushing half of it to the road. It wailed a discord of shattered thought and agony and squirmed, shedding flakes of flesh and what might have been dried nuggets of shite. Jateko brought his foot down on the offending creature over and over until it stopped moving and he no longer heard its screams.

"What the hells was that?" he asked Zerfall.

AS STOOD NAKED, SURROUNDED by an uncountable swarm of people, each and every one of them also naked. Ceaseless screams shivered the air. The stench of breath and panic and blood and terror clogged his nostrils.

Men and women stood gathered, staring at him.

"I know you," said one, stepping forward.

Aas' chest tightened. *{No.}* "Nimmer. I—"

"You killed me." The man grinned bloody teeth. His eyes screamed where his voice remained eerily calm.

"And me," said another.

"And me."

"And . . ."

And on it went. They surrounded him.

"You sent us here," said Nimmer.

A nearby man dragged another to the ground, kicking and screaming, and began tearing at him with his teeth as if he meant to eat him alive. It went on, ignored, unworthy of comment. Elsewhere men and women rutted or were raped. Some stood dazed, eyes empty and mad, their minds long broken. Others clawed at their own flesh as if attempting suicide with nothing more than their own fingernails.

He had to get out, to escape this madness. *{If I can get above—}* But they heard his thoughts and were on him. Fists pummelling, nails raking at his flesh, they dragged him down, buried him under their weight. Nimmer straddled Aas, knees on shoulders, pinning him to the ground. For a brief instant he saw sky through a gap in the bodies. It was nothing. Not blue, just there. There was no sun, the entire sky gave off even, unchanging light.

"I only wanted to be left alone!" screamed Nimmer. Then he grabbed Aas' head—one hand each side of his skull—and slammed it to the ground. Bright slashes of color whited out Aas' vision, sent him away, and then someone kicked him in the balls, bringing him retching back into his body. Again Nimmer lifted his head and slammed it to the ground and Aas managed only a grunted, "Uhn."

Someone bit off one of his fingers and his hand was afire in agony.

"Uhn." Again his skull struck the ground, this time with a sodden *crunch*.

Snarling teeth locked around another finger, worried at it like a starved dog gnawing a tough bone. The knuckle broke. Skin stretched and tore. The finger came free.

Someone kicked him in the balls again. This time it didn't hurt so much.

"Uhn." His thoughts, soggy, broken, splintered apart each time his skull struck ground.

{They're . . . Uhn . . . killing . . . Uhn . . . me . . . Uhn . . .}

AAS BLINKED. HE STOOD, naked, watching as a crowd of raving men and women pulled a sallow and sagging corpse apart. He recognized that puckered skin, those thick, dark hairs.

{That's me.}

The mob looked up, grinning madness and blood lust. He recognized the man sitting astride the savaged corpse.

{Nimmer.}

Nimmer lifted the corpse's head and it came away from the ground with a wet sucking noise. The back of the skull was crushed flat. Streamers of blood and fragments of bone caught in strands of thin hair and torn flesh hung from the battered visage.

"No escape," said Nimmer.

{I have to get above—} They were on him again, dragging him down with their weight and numbers. Someone kicked in his ribs and he felt them splinter, sharp shards of bone tearing into his organs.

Thumbs found his eyes and pressed in with inexorable force. Vision sank into red, splashed bright as his eyes burst, and stuttered into darkness. Blows rained down upon him while someone bent one of his arms the wrong way until the elbow dislocated with a damp *pock*.

AS BLINKED. HE STOOD naked. The sky, empty as it was, beckoned. If he could just *twist*.

{I must—}

They dragged him down.

"THAT WAS WEIRD," SAID Jateko with a shiver. He nudged the crushed puppet with a toe to make sure it was dead and glanced at Zerfall. "You ever see anything like that before?"

She shook her head. "No."

"Thanks for distracting him."

"It was easy," she said, voice thin and sad, "He loves . . . loved me."

Did you just kill her lover? Abiega asked.

Jateko didn't know how to ask. *She seems sad, but not as upset as she'd be if I killed someone important to her.*

Have you listened to nothing she's said? Demanded Grausamer, the Swordsman. *She told you she's a Gefahrgeist. Such people are incapable of love.*

That's who she was, said Jateko. *She's changed.*

How would you know? Asked Abiega.

The thought bothered Jateko and he didn't want to examine it. *It doesn't matter.* She needed him.

"You arguing again in there?" Zerfall asked.

"Discussing." His stomach rumbled in hungry complaint and the corpse, hideous as it was, looked like the finest meal. All other thought fell away.

While not muscular, Aas' body possessed a wiry strength. The assassin had been fast too, quicker than Jateko, even though he'd eaten a dozen men. *I want that speed.* The crushed puppet drew his attention; had the man moved his soul there, used it as a vessel? It seemed that way. The body died and then he heard Aas' thought, "I did it, I'm free" and the puppet started moving. He glanced at Zerfall, again seeing her advanced state of decay. Her body was falling apart. Soon she'd be completely helpless. *I need what this assassin knows.*

Kneeling by the corpse, Jateko gripped the skull in both hands. *How strong am I?*

He split the skull open with ease, exposing the grey meat of brain matter within.

"Here?" asked Zerfall.

"Yes." He was so hungry. Tearing free the brain, he held it cupped in his palms. Much as he wanted the assassin's speed, he needed his knowledge most. *What will I learn from this man?* Jateko mused.

Assassins are scum, muttered Grausamer and Jateko ignored the Swordsman.

Ripping free a nugget, he popped it into his mouth and chewed quickly. Movement caught his eye, and he glanced at the crowd gathered on the steps of the Verzweiflung Bank. Most wore a variety of strange hats, varying from small and brightly coloured to towering constructions of deepest black that seemed to defy reality by staying on the heads of those who wore them.

The hats are called Geldwechsler, one of the devoured Geborene priests whispered into Jateko's thoughts. *The bigger and more uncomfortable the hat, the higher the rank.*

A small woman, face wrinkled like a sun-dried apple, massive black hat perched precariously, tottered down several steps to stand between Jateko and the church. *Bank*, he corrected. *These people worship wealth.* She stood like she personally would block him from the main doors.

"The Verzweiflung Banking Conglomerate stands above wars of religion," she called down to him.

He tore free another chunk of brain as he swallowed the first and popped that too into his mouth. "Oh. That's . . . uh . . . good to know," he answered, not knowing what else to say.

She scowled, managing to bite both upper and lower lips at the same time, making her face look even more like desiccated fruit. "You are aware you killed a priest of the Täuschung?"

Jateko nodded, chewing. "And now I'm eating him."

"Not here," she said with utter confidence. "Remove yourself from our steps."

Jateko was about to agree and drag away the body for later eating, when a thought stopped him. "This is Zerfall," he said, gesturing to where she stood. "Founder of the Täuschung." He stuffed more brain into his mouth, chewing fast.

The old woman's face puckered even further, looking like someone was trying to pull it inside out from behind.

Zerfall drew the crumpled and faded bank note from her pocket and held it aloft.

The banker's eyes narrowed as she squinted at the parchment. She made no attempt to approach. Next she turned her attention to Zerfall, examining what remained of the woman, before finally nodding. "Account Holder Zerfall Seele, so good to meet with you, deary." The woman stared off into space as if trying to remember something. "Your sister's Fragment attempted to access your shared accounts."

Deary? Jateko couldn't imagine anyone calling Zerfall deary, but this woman made it seem natural. Swallowing a lump of partially masticated brain, he forced more into his mouth.

"She's not my sister," said Zerfall.

The banker gave her an odd look and shrugged, accepting.

Zerfall gestured at Jateko with her stump. "Put all Täuschung funds in this man's name."

"And you are?" asked the old woman, turning slowly to keep the hat balanced.

"Jateko," he answered, his mouth full.

She stared at him for a long moment, and he wondered if she'd drifted off like his gran used to do before she died. Finally, she nodded. "Done. Jateko, honoured Account Holder, you may remain here to finish your . . ." she scowled disapprovingly. ". . . repast. Does this conclude our business?"

"Remove me from the accounts," wheezed Zerfall. "My delusions and I shall have no access from this point on."

The old banker looked disappointed but said, "Of course, deary."

"Is it a lot of wealth?" Jateko asked, shoving the last of the brain into his mouth and unsure what just happened.

"While the interest paid on such accounts is minimal, Account Holder Jateko, it *is* compound interest."

"And?"

"Interest has been paid for four hundred and thirteen years. In that time regular deposits have also been made. Also, many of the Täuschung holdings have been liquidated."

Liquidated? That sounded painful. Jateko avoided stepping on the stomped remains of the disgusting snot puppet. Still uncertain, he asked, "Am I wealthy?" He bent to retrieve Blutblüte, dragging it from the dead assassin's guts and then using it to hack open the man's rib cage to expose the heart.

"Quite," she answered with a polite little bow, though not enough to tip the hat from her head. If his actions disgusted her beyond their lack of class, she hid it masterfully. While her face still looked like a piece of rotting fruit, her entire demeanour changed. She even attempted a patient smile that came nowhere near reaching the wrinkled sacks around her eyes.

These civilized folks are damned strange. He'd never get used to this. Jateko pulled the assassin's heart free and tore off a mouthful with his teeth, chewing as he watched the banker. To free his hands he bit into the heart and held it with his teeth. Delicious hot blood ran down his throat and chin. Standing, he held Blutblüte to Zerfall in offering.

She held out the skeletal remains of her right hand, the fingers bone and parchment flesh, the broken finger once again jutting awkwardly. "You keep it."

Discarding Grausamer's beautiful matched swords, and ignoring the Swordsman's grumbled complaint, he strapped Blutblüte in place at his hip. The sword, plain and unadorned, felt right. It belonged there.

Jateko devoured more of the assassin's heart, his mind reeling. Both the Täuschung and the Geborene Damonen made use of the Verzweiflung.

The Wahnvor Stellung, a devoured priest informed him, *also bank with the Verzweiflung. They hold the wealth of virtually every religion and city-state.*

No matter what god each city-state claims to worship, thought Jateko, chewing the last of the heart, *this is the true religion of civilization.*

"Jateko," said Zerfall, distracting him. "You have a choice to make. You're free now."

"Free?" He turned to face her, the bankers, for the moment, forgotten.

"You have more wealth than you could ever spend."

He laughed, taking her right hand in his and bending the broken finger back into place. "I don't see what wealth has to do with freedom."

"You could unite the Basamortuan," she said. "Arm and feed your tribes, topple the city-states."

"You're testing me? You want to know if I'm serious about staying with you?" How could he turn his back on her now?

"You can have everything," she said.

"I have everything." He glanced to where the banker stood, respectfully silent. Strange how her behaviour changed once he had wealth. *These people make no sense.* How did the mere possession of gold make one worthy of respect? Particularly when he'd done nothing to earn that wealth. "Can you direct me to the Täuschung?" he asked. "We have unfinished business."

She gestured north west.

Stomach rumbling in a hunger that never quite abated, Jateko returned his attention to Zerfall. "Shall we pay them a visit?"

Empty sockets stared at him and he saw rotting teeth through her eroded cheeks. She shook her head, a weak side to side motion accompanied by the grind of bone and hardening cartilage. "I'm done. Go home."

Jateko bit down on the rush of emotion, forcing calm. "The assassin moved his soul into that puppet, and Hölle is a part of you, right? Your Fragment?"

"Different personality."

"We're going to find a way to move your soul into her body," blurted Jateko, the idea still forming.

"How?"

"I don't know. Harea guided me to you. The Etsaiaren Sea of Souls. It has to make sense. It has to mean something. There has to be a *reason.*"

"I don't think I am that reason," whispered Zerfall, air hissing from her lungs.

You are. You are all my reasons. "In all the endless Basamortuan desert you were where Gogoko and Dedikatu were going to kill me. I can't believe any of this is coincidence."

"Why?" That one word, dry and crumbling like the shed skin of a snake left long in the sun, broke his heart.

"Because I love you." For once, none of the voices in his head mocked him. "I can't let you go. I won't."

"You're a fool," she said, but there was no sting to her words.

"I know. Let's go visit your delusion," he whispered to Zerfall, pulling her into a gentle hug.

TWENTY-ONE

Every time you imagine a conversation with someone where you are trying to convince them of something, know that you are talking to yourself; it's you you're trying to convince.

—Traurige Tatsache, Philosopher

A N HOUR PASSED AND still Pharisäer couldn't convince herself she was Zerfall. *It's no good. Zerfall is alive.* It was the only answer. Until Zerfall lay dead Pharisäer would be doomed to this half-life of almost existence.

Glancing at the corpse sprawled on the floor, she said, "I am Hölle."

It was true, but a hollow victory. Becoming Hölle was pointless; the fool had nothing Pharisäer hadn't already taken.

I'm real. This too was true. She'd half expected that replacing Hölle would make her Zerfall's new Fragment. It hadn't.

Everyone feared and respected Zerfall. *I don't want to be Hölle. I want to be Zerfall.*

She'd have to continue pretending to be Zerfall until the bitch was dead. She'd been faking it for long enough the priests accepted her—even if she sometimes caught glints of doubt or distrust in their eyes. She'd play the role until she became it.

Pharisäer stalked over to Hölle and kicked her. It felt like kicking a side of gelid beef; the body barely moved, mocking her anger. In spite of what she told

Hölle, she had no idea where Zerfall was and whether Aas intended on killing her. Knowing the mad wretch, he would. *His predictability is probably his best feature.* But then he'd surprised her before. She definitely hadn't predicted his killing her in his own bed. It bothered her that she so completely misread the man. His worship of this body and her manipulation of his emotions should have been more than enough to guarantee his obedience.

Pharisäer shivered at the memory of Aas' knife sliding into her flesh, the look of abject sadness on his face as he killed her. He hadn't wanted to, and yet he had. She couldn't understand; what went on in that ugly skull?

What other mistakes have you made?

"None," she said, contemplating giving Hölle another kick. "He knew I considered killing him. It wasn't my f—"

She stopped and stood rooted, staring at the mocking corpse. She almost said it wasn't her fault.

That's Hölle. I never dodge responsibility for my actions.

She thought about how effortless it would be to truly become Hölle.

You're the delusion of a delusion. She's one step closer to real. You want that.

"No. I want *real*."

You tried. You can't convince yourself you're Zerfall.

"It's not my—*Shite!*" This time she did kick Hölle's corpse. Again it ignored her. She dropped to her knees to scream into Hölle's slack face. "You damned cunt! I killed you, and I'll kill her too!"

Zerfall would never crack like Hölle had. *She's a killer, bright steel and death, where Hölle was doubt and inaction.* Pharisäer had never met the woman, but there wasn't a Täuschung priest—even amongst the most insane—who wasn't terrified of her.

"I'll kill her!" she screamed at Hölle's unresponsive face.

A sharp knock rattled the door to Hölle's chambers. *My chambers.* Pharisäer corrected.

"What!"

The door swung open and Captain Gedankenlos stood at the threshold. He blinked when he saw her crouched over Hölle's corpse but kept his face carefully blank.

"Zerfall—" he began.

"Shite! Where?"

He blinked again, looking confused. "What?"

He thinks you're Zerfall, remember?

Right. He'd startled her. It wasn't—

It wasn't your fault?

Pharisäer ignored the thought. "Report," she commanded the baffled Captain.

Gedankenlos dipped a quick bow. "Aas is dead."

Pharisäer's breath caught. Was this good news, or bad? "How?"

"A Basamortuan killed him in Verzweiflung Square, on the bank's front steps. Teilweise Taub, one of our younger priests, saw it all. He rushed here to report."

Why had some savage from the desert killed Aas? And for that matter, *how*? "Aas awaits his rebirth as a god in Swarm," said Pharisäer, knowing it was expected.

Gedankenlos nodded but didn't seem to much care. "There's more."

"More?"

"Teilweise said the bank transferred all the Täuschung accounts to this Basamortuan."

"They—" Pharisäer, stunned, stared at the Captain. "Is he sure?" She'd sold off most of the Täuschung holdings at a vastly reduced rate, and now it was all gone? *Some damned sand flea has my money?* It wasn't her fault, she needed to damage Hölle and the church had been her greatest weakness. How could she possibly have known this would happen?

"Teilweise seemed sure, but was too far away to hear everything."

You've been the true head of the Täuschung for less than an hour and already the church is destitute.

"It's not my—" Pharisäer bit down on her tongue, cutting off the word. She spat blood at the floor. "How many Täuschung are in the temple?"

Gedankenlos' brow furrowed in thought. "You sent almost everyone away," he reminded her. "ängstlich and Dämonin Schwindel came back from Traurig last week. Starker Narr arrived from Selbsthass yesterday. He said he was unable to enter the city proper, was turned away at the gates. I believe Gefräßige Wut and Unbedacht are in the compound as well."

"Take them all. Find this Basamortuan. Bring him here. Alive."

He nodded another quick bow. "Of course." He turned to leave and stopped, hesitating.

"What?" she snapped.

"Teilweise mentioned something else."

"Really?" she asked, sweetly. "Would you like me to torture it from you?"

He flashed a quick glance at Hölle's corpse. "The Basamortuan was with someone."

I'm going to kill this idiot. "And?"

"Teilweise said he thought it was a rotting corpse."

"Those filthy tribals do all sorts of insane shite. Maybe he had some family vendetta with Aas and carried his father's corpse here so it might witness Aas' death."

Gedankenlos shuffled about on his feet, looking like he was trying to decide if he'd made a mistake bringing this up.

"Spit it out and then go get—"

"Teilweise said the corpse was alive."

Alive? Hadn't Aas said Zerfall was showing Cotardist tendencies? Could a soul remain in a body even in such an advanced state of rot? She'd never heard of anything like it; Cotardists died when the rot reached their heart.

We are talking about Zerfall here. Nothing can kill that psychotic bitch.

"Teilweise also said—"

"Shut up," commanded Pharisäer. "I need to think."

Gedankenlos stood motionless, face expressionless. She glanced at the hand lying atop Hölle's desk—*My desk*—and scowled when the Captain's gaze darted in that direction. "I think the Basamortuan will come to us. Be ready. I need him alive. We'll need him to transfer control of the accounts back to me." She slashed a sideways glance at Gedankenlos, but the Captain seemed oblivious. "To the church," she corrected.

"Of course." The Captain turned to go.

"What else did Teilweise say?"

Gedankenlos hesitated. "He said Aas had Blutblüte." He glanced to the empty scabbard hanging on Pharisäer's hip and she crushed the desire to curse and scream. "He said the Basamortuan took it."

Zerfall and some Basamortuan warrior were coming here? And the Basamortuan wielded Blutblüte? Pharisäer wanted to crawl into bed and cry.

She wanted to cower under the sheets, to hide away from this terrible and cruel world. What had she done to deserve this?

*That's what Hölle would do. It's not my—*She felt her lips peel back in a feral snarl and Gedankenlos blanched. "I am not Hölle," she said, and he glanced again at the corpse.

"Of course not," he agreed, retreating toward the door. "I never . . ."

Never what? Never thought I was real? She tried to crush the doubt down deep into her belly, but it festered there, threatening to rise like sour bile. She felt real, more real than she ever felt before. More real than when she stood in front of the congregation and they all saw her. Hölle was dead and she was Hölle. *Shouldn't there be more?* "You'll wait for the Basamortuan to come to us. Bring them to me. Alive."

"Them?"

"The Basamortuan and . . . the bones." She growled and gnawed hard on her lower lip until she tasted blood. "Alive but beaten. Helpless." She looked up at Gedankenlos and though he towered over her he retreated further into the hall. "Kill anyone and everyone who lays eyes on them or sees Blutblüte."

"Everyone?"

"Yes."

"Including myself?" Gedankenlos asked from the hall.

Pharisäer examined the Captain of her Guard. It was a laughable title at best. Zerfall clearly only kept him around for his physique. "Don't be an idiot." She'd kill him later.

"Sorry." Gedankenlos turned and fled.

How the hells had everything gone so wrong so fast? She should be feeling victorious, and yet more than anything she wanted to find somewhere to hide. Zerfall was coming for her, she knew it. Four hundred years the woman walked the earth, insane and yet apparently immune to the Pinnacle. This, more than anything, worried Pharisäer; how had Zerfall avoided the curse which haunted all Geisteskranken? One terrifying explanation loomed above all others: Wahrergott was real. Zerfall was backed by the One True God.

"It doesn't matter," Pharisäer told herself. "Teilweise said Zerfall was a corpse."

What about the Basamortuan warrior?

"A man, with the same weakness all men share."

Aas didn't find it terribly difficult to ignore your wiles and kill you.

"Ah, but he knows me. It should be no great task to lure this Basamortuan away from Zerfall." After all, what charms could a pile of bones have?

She's a powerful Gefahrgeist. It hardly matters what she looks like.

Pharisäer scowled at the thought. "I beat Hölle, I can beat Zerfall."

Hölle was no Zerfall.

As Jateko walked he dreamed of stretching his wings wide and flying high over the stink of this gold-worshipping city. The streets were eerily familiar and he easily found his way through their sprawling chaos. Spotting a massive glistening white pyramid—*The Geborene Damonen temple,* he thought—through a break in the buildings, he wanted to perch on its apex and shite.

That's weird.

Looking away, he caught sight of one of those ridiculous banker hats—*Geldwechsler,* he remembered—and felt a foreign stab of hatred and disgust. He glanced at Zerfall and his chest tightened with a savage crush of emotion. He already knew he loved her, but this was different. He wanted to cry to see her so broken. She'd been so viciously beautiful, so proud.

Zerfall walked at his side, a limping shuffle. She leaned on him for support, her missing foot making walking without help impossible. He stole a quick glance.

I never knew her like that. She was dead and rotting the day I met her.

He remembered what she looked like, before. She'd been gorgeous, perfection. Dark, penetrating eyes, bright with wit and intelligence. He remembered the curl and bounce of her hair as it fell around her shoulders like a waterfall or the curtains at one of those expensive theatres.

Theatre?

He remembered the way she smelled, sweet like fire-warmed honey, and the curve of her full lips as she cut him.

Cut me?

Gods, he wanted that so much. He wanted to hurl himself at her feet and beg forgiveness for leaving her in the desert, for turning his back on her when she needed him most. He deserved everything that happened to him and a thousand times worse.

This time of day, Verleiher Way will be quicker, he decided, following the narrow street.

Two blocks later he realized Verleiher Way was busier than expected. He pushed through the crowd. He towered over most of these people. Was he taller now? Even armed, with Zerfall—clearly a walking corpse—at his side, it was his dark skin and tattered *oihal*—now consisting mostly of torn and filthy *karpan* fabric—which caught people's attention. He heard 'desert savage' whispered over and over and many darted 'angry, sneering looks in his direction.

Why do they hate me?

The Basamortuan don't use money, Aas answered. *You have no real concept of wealth, or debt.*

We understand owing debts.

You owe debts of gratitude or honour. Money has nothing to do with either.

We don't have money, everything is trade. Barter, Jateko added, realizing he knew the word.

Exactly. It means the Verzweiflung have no hold over you.

That doesn't make sense. If these people don't want to be in debt, they should decide not to pay the bank back.

But then the Geld Guard come knocking and throw you in jail.

There were, Jateko noticed, an awful lot of guards patrolling the street. *All these guards work for the Verzweiflung?*

No, they're paid by the city-state.

Then why enforce the bank's rules?

Because Geld is indebted to the Verzweiflung.

"What's going on in there?" Zerfall asked, distracting Jateko from his internal discussion.

"The assassin is with me now," Jateko answered. "Aas and I were discussing economics."

"Oh." Did she sound less than pleased? "Learn anything interesting?"

"Aas is in love with you," he blurted.

She nodded, not looking at him.

"He says he's sorry he tried to kill you."

"Oh. I'm . . . I'm not the person he knew."

"I know." Jateko stopped at an intersection, glancing down two different streets.

There's a fantastic butchery down there called Medium Rare, Aas informed him. Jateko, having no interest in prepared charcuterie—*why do I even know that word?*—ignored him.

"Is this difficult for you?' Zerfall asked.

"Why would it be?"

Zerfall's eyebrows bespoke confusion. "I . . . I thought—"

"I was kidding. This is very strange. I have all these memories of you and I and the things we did together. Mostly things you did to me—painful things. But I wasn't there."

"I've changed." She hesitated. "I think I've changed."

"I like *this* you," said Jateko. "I don't think the old you and I would get along. At all."

She watched him and he saw her teeth clenched through a tear in her cheek.

"But part of me wants the old Zerfall back," he said. "Part of me loves and worships the old you. I miss her. I miss the way she cut me and taunted me and never let me touch her. And . . ."

"Yes?"

"The old you was beautiful."

"And the new me is a stinking, rotting corpse."

"Not too stinky."

"Thanks."

"Sorry. I already told you I loved you. Even before I ate Aas."

"You ate ass?"

"He still doesn't think it's funny."

AAS GUIDED JATEKO THROUGH the streets of Geld, pointing out dark alleys in which he'd murdered people and buildings he'd shite upon.

[Aas?] Jateko asked.

{Hmm?}

[What are we going to face at the Täuschung temple?]

{Hölle and Pharisäer. Pharisäer is a manifestation of Hölle's split personality. Hölle is the more dangerous of the two; she's a powerful Halluzin. Pharisäer pretends to be Zerfall, but has nothing on the real thing. Turn left here.}

Jateko followed the assassin's direction.

{What the hells is your delusion?} demanded Aas. *{You don't fit any of the classifications.}*

[As I said before, your civilized system of classifying insanity is flawed.]

{I missed that,} said Aas. *{I was dying at the time.}*

Jateko ignored this. *[Why would insanity would follow nice, neat rules?]*

{But it does,} said Aas. *{It's measurable. I studied this in detail. There are laws which govern the range of effect, the balance of power between Geisteskranken and the sane—}*

[You're missing something simple,] said Jateko. *[It isn't delusion that defines reality, it's belief. I was so incredibly gullible, ignorant and naïve, I was capable of convincing myself of almost anything.]*

{You're saying ignorance made you a powerful Geisteskranken?} Aas asked, incredulous.

[Yes.]

{So you're sane, but incredibly stupid.}

[I would have put it diff—]

{Maybe you're a very rare breed of Wahnist,} suggested Aas.

[That might fit,] admitted Jateko doubtfully. *[You're the first real Geisteskranken I've eaten. And I'm only guessing I can twist. I might be wrong.]*

"You're both missing something," said Zerfall.

"Yes?" asked Jateko. "What's that?"

"I can hear what you're thinking."

"Oh."

{Oh,} said Aas.

"Just in the last few minutes," she said. "It grew in volume. It sounded like we were approaching a crowd. It took me a moment to realize what it was I was hearing."

"But that means—"

"That means you suffer the delusions of those you eat," said Zerfall. "Eat a dozen Geisteskranken, and you'll face a dozen Pinnacles."

Can she hear me too? Abiega asked.

When Zerfall failed to react, Jateko answered, [*I don't think so, Abiega.*]

"Don't think what?" Zerfall asked.

"Abiega asked if you heard him too." He winked at her. "Typical Narcisstic, eh?"

Hey!

"I only hear you and Aas."

Jateko stopped walking, staring up at a group of squat buildings in a walled compound. The main gates, iron-wrapped timbers, the sharpened tips of which looked to have been dipped in molten metal, sat closed. To the right of the gates hung a hempen rope attached to a rusty bell hanging from the branch of a tree which looked to have died several hundred years ago.

"How do we get in?" he asked, nodding toward the closed gate.

{*I'd* twist *into a condor and fly in,*} said Aas. {*I suppose sane people ring the bell.*}

What are you *going to do?* asked Abiega pointedly.

The gate swung open, saving Jateko from having to answer. Within stood three men and two women. One of the men, a towering slab of muscle and sloping brow, looked like he'd been stuffed into his chain hauberk by force. Woven steel rings, stretched taught across a broad chest twice the girth of Jateko's, looked ready to burst. A morningstar of dull black iron, its bulbous head caked in flakes of dry blood and clumped hair, hung heavy in a scarred fist. The rest of the group twitched and picked at skinny arms and gave off an aura of ill health, mental and otherwise.

{*This is bad,*} said Aas. {*Really bad.*}

"Why?" asked Jateko.

{*They're expecting us.*}

"Sure, the big guy is, well, big, but the rest of them don't look like—"

A petite woman in stained homespun robes stepped in front of the huge warrior and he flinched away, retreating. She grinned sharp teeth, white and vicious, her gums black and oozing with open sores.

{*That's Gefräßige Wut,*} said Aas. {*Wendigast.*}

ZERFALL HEARD AAS BABBLING: *{Ängstlich, he's a Capgrast. Thinks his wife is a demon. Dämonin Schwindel, beautiful red-head in the green dress, that's his wife. Starker Narr, he's the huge Dysmorphic with the morningstar. Unbedacht, the twitchy one who looks like he's either about to cry or shit himself in fear, he's a Wütend, a berzerker.}* His thoughts, a rapid staccato, grew in volume and she barely kept up with the litany of names and mental illnesses. These were her people. She chose each of these mad souls, bent them to her purpose and bound them to her church. This was the core of the true Täuschung, not the sane fools preaching of heaven and salvation. This group murdered and sent countless souls to Swarm.

How had I thought this was right? How had this been a reasonable path? She hated what she'd built. It was sick. Swarm trapped souls. Forever. It robbed people of all chance at redemption. She didn't know what happened in the Afterdeath, but Swarm was wrong. It was a blight.

Zerfall wanted to crush them, to take up her sword and—*You're helpless.* Even if she had her sword she could barely stand without Jateko's help.

"Jateko," she said, looking up into his strong, square-jawed face. "Will you do something for me?"

"Anything."

She wanted to cry at the speed of his answer. Her soul, whatever that spark was deep inside her, shuddered and wailed in agony. Everyone answered that fast, with no time for thought, when she left them no choice. *Bring him away from here.* But she couldn't. She had to end the Täuschung. She needed him. God she hated that word. And she hated herself for what she said next. "The Täuschung, you have to stop them."

He nodded, returning his attention to the woman in filthy homespun. She approached in dainty steps, eyes alight with malice. "Once I've saved you," he said "we'll end the Täuschung and Swarm together."

Her dead tongue tasted of betrayal. "Promise you'll do this for me. No matter what happens."

Jateko's jaw clenched. *[What would be the point of going on without her?]*

"Promise," Zerfall begged.

"I promise I will end the Täuschung and Swarm," swore Jateko.

I'm sorry. I'm so sorry.

"Wait here," he said.

Drawing Blutblüte, Jateko stepped forward, putting himself between her and the gathered Täuschung.

Momentarily forgetting her missing foot Zerfall tried to follow and the shattered bones of her ankle slipped on slick cobblestones dropping her to the ground.

JATEKO EYED THE PETITE woman in homespun. She had the pale skin of those from the far north and carried no visible weapons. Aside from her sharpened teeth and unhealthy gums, she appeared utterly normal. "She doesn't look like much."

Gefräßige's grin transformed, slipping and twisting and disintegrating to become a deranged leer as she grabbed fistfuls of her hair with clawed fingers. With a wail of heart-rending sadness, horror, and defeat, she ripped downward, peeling skin and scalp from her skull to reveal the horrendous demon lurking beneath her flesh. Black eyes, too far apart and oozing purulence, sought Jateko. Those eyes both begged for and promised death. Quivering nostrils, ragged slashes dripping pus, tasted the air, searching. Someone—one of the Geborene priests within Jateko—squealed in terror. With a vicious wrench she peeled the rest of the human flesh from her body like a bloody wet sack. It hung from her fist, inside out and dripping bright crimson on the courtyard stones. She dropped it to the ground with a sodden *plop*.

"Ah," said Jateko.

Humanity shed like an unwanted dress, Gefräßige revealed a demonic body of cavernous ribs and gaunt starvation. An abattoir perfume, the stench of fresh rot, clogged Jateko's nostrils. Her skin, sagging and ripe with open sores, hung in translucent sheets.

Blutblüte. The sword felt different than the fine matched blades he took from the Swordsman. This wasn't just a sword. While he felt confident it would bring death, it was more than an implement of violence. It had a weight, a finality, that went beyond its mere physicality.

{How much does a soul weigh?} Aas asked.

Nothing and everything, Abiega answered instantly.

Jateko ignored them both.

Starker Narr, the massive Dysmorphic, hefted a morningstar that looked like it was designed to knock down buildings and followed the demonic Gefräßige. He angled out to her left, to flank Jateko.

Dämonin Schwindel, a green dress hugging her shapely form, glanced over her shoulder at her husband, Ängstlich, who hid at the rear of the gathering. She looked lost and forlorn, out of place with this group of mad priests, and Jateko realized a long chain joined an iron collar about her slim ankle. Ängstlich had the far end of the chain wrapped around his wrist.

Jateko heard her, voice pleading, say, "Please, not again. I'm not a demon." She reached a hand toward her husband.

Ängstlich screamed, cowering from the outstretched hand, his face a rictus of terror and loathing.

The rest was drowned out in her escalating scream as savage spasms tore her statuesque body. The green dress, one moment form fitting, stretched and tore as she grew in size. Within two heartbeats she stood seven feet tall. Her breasts, pendulous globes of veined flesh, grew far out of proportion to her size. Her hips and arse too were monstrous mockeries of the female form. The V of her womanhood swelled and darkened, became tangled, and oozed strange fluids. Something struggled in there like it sought escape. Her full lips promised everything—sex, warmth, and love—and her tongue writhed in an erotic dance of fellatic suggestion. Her face flickered between beautiful and evilly demonic, eyes leering and laughing, begging and pleading for release.

[Am I seeing the person under the skin?] Jateko wondered, standing his ground as she stalked forward to stand at Gefräßige's right side.

{The evil is Ängstlich's,} said Aas. *{He's a juvenile wretch, a gutless coward, terrified of her intimidating beauty and everything that makes her a woman.}*

[So if I kill her,] thought Jateko, *[I'm killing an innocent victim?]*

Seriously? snapped Grausamer. *You've killed and eaten how many souls and now you're going to start worrying about innocence?*

The last man, a short and scrawny retch with long greasy hair hanging over his eyes, wore a motley patchwork of ill-fitted armour. He dragged behind him a cudgel looking far too heavy for his slight form. He paced forward, staring at the ground, until he was several strides ahead of the others.

"Who?" Jateko asked aloud.

{Unbedacht,} said Aas. {Usually he's a moody cretin, but—}

He can barely lift that cudgel, pointed out Abiega.

{—he's Wütend,} finished Aas. {A psychotic berzerker.}

With a sigh of infinite weariness, Unbedacht raised his head to peer at Jateko through strands of tangled hair. With a grunt of effort, he hefted his cudgel, staggering under its weight. When Jateko raised Blutblüte in challenge, the man's eyes came alight.

"Yes," said Unbedacht. "Yes. Finally."

"What?"

Unbedacht dashed forward, screaming and spinning the cudgel as if it were nothing. Crouching, Jateko prepared to meet the mad charge, planning to side-step the heavy weapon and cut down the Wütend.

Instead, Unbedacht threw the cudgel at him, catching Jateko by surprise. The weapon's iron head smashed into his chest, shattering ribs and sending him reeling backward. Unbedacht loosed an inarticulate throat-tearing scream as he leapt upon the off-balance Jateko, staggering him back another step. The mad-man tore at the Basamortuan's throat with ragged fingernails and snapping teeth as if he planned to pull him apart by brute psychotic strength. For an instant Jateko wondered why they bothered sending the rest of the Geisteskranken when this insane wretch would kill him all on his own.

And then he remembered he was not one man. He was a dozen or more people. He was strong beyond any Wütend's delusion-derived strength.

Jateko peeled Unbedacht off him, held the raving, spitting mad man at arm's length. The Geisteskranken clawed at his arms, peeling flesh in long strips. The wounds healed in an instant, leaving white scars. Looking past the man he held, feet dangling and kicking, he met the eyes of the gathered Täuschung priests as he drove Blutblüte through Unbedacht's chest.

As the sword entered him, Unbedacht's eyes widened in glee and then terror. He sagged, limp and dead, and Jateko tossed the empty corpse aside. Was it his imagination, or did the sword seem heavier? A strange sigh passed through the gathered Täuschung Geisteskranken like a breeze through autumn leaves.

"Flee," said Jateko.

"Redemption," slurred Gefräßige through sharpened teeth.

Ängstlich sobbed in the background, cowering behind the others.

Tears leaked form Dämonin Schwindel's ever-shifting eyes. "Escape," she whispered, stepping toward Jateko.

"A challenge," said Starker Narr, eyes hungry with anticipation.

{I don't think that had quite the desired effect,} mused Aas. *{Expecting rationality from—}* His thoughts were interrupted as the Täuschung attacked Jateko in a chorus of insane screams.

ZERFALL WATCHED, HELPLESS, AS the demon which had been Ängstlich's wife hurled itself upon Jateko. The sword entered her gut, speared up into her torso, rending flesh and ripping an agonized cry somewhere between orgasmic release and incomprehensible terror from her lips. As she died she yanked on the chain attaching her to her husband, dragging the screaming Ängstlich closer to the fray. Her demonic body crashed into Jateko, toppling him over backward and pinning him under her dead weight. Impossibly, he lifted her bulk and seemed about to throw it aside, but Starker Narr brought his morningstar down on Jateko's exposed leg, shattering the knee and thigh bone. Jateko grunted in pain, trying to twist away from the grievous wound, and dropped Dämonin Schwindel. She landed pinning his right arm and Blutblüte to the ground.

Gefräßige leapt forward to land astride Jateko's chest and clawed at his face, tearing away a long flap of skin and scalp, exposing the bone beneath. With a wrench, Gefräßige tore it free. Unhinging her jaw like a snake, she popped it into her gaping mouth.

The ground shook as Starke smashed Jateko's other knee to jelly and, though Jateko made no noise, Zerfall heard the young Basamortuan mentally broadcast a scream of pain.

Gefräßige leaned in close to flay more flesh from Jateko's savaged skull with razor sharp teeth. An ear came free and she swallowed it whole.

Starke reached down to grab Dämonin Schwindel—who, once dead, returned to her human form—by the hair and drag her from Jateko, exposing the youth's torso so he could smash at it with his morningstar.

Both hands freed, Jateko grabbed Gefräßige by the throat, keeping his fingers clear of her frothing mouth and snapping teeth. And then another blow from Starke's swung morningstar splintered his hip, sending jagged shards of bone through torn flesh. This time Jateko did scream. Ripping Gefräßige's head from her demonic body, he hurled it away. Blood arced from the torn femoral arteries in graceful coils and hung in the air, reminding Zerfall of spirals in a sea-shell.

Jateko levered himself upright, reaching for Blutblüte, as Starke swung the monstrous morningstar at his head. Zerfall watched the exposed bone shatter and collapse beneath the gore-matted iron-studded globe. All broadcast thought from Jateko ceased in an instant and the youth collapsed backward, boneless and limp, to lay sprawled at Starke's feet. Blood leaked, slow and lazy, from the brutalized skull. His face looked misshapen and lopsided.

No! This was impossible. Jateko was the All Consuming. Zerfall reached for him, and collapsed back the ground.

The muscled Dysmorphic stood over Jateko, swinging the morningstar in slow circles, looking like he was trying to decide what to smash next. "That was odd. I heard his thoughts," he said. "It was like being near Aas." He ceased the morningstar's spin, apparently deciding his victim offered no threat. "You still in there?" he asked, nudging Jateko with a booted foot.

No thought leaked from the Basamortuan.

"The Captain said alive," whined ängstlich, who only now dared approach.

Starke glanced over his shoulder with a scowl. "Gutless. Your wife is dead." He bared brown teeth at the small man. "Isn't this what you always wanted?"

ängstlich eyed his wife's corpse. "Is she really gone?"

"That's Blutblüte," said Starke, nodding to where the sword lay at Jateko's side. "She's gone." He bent to retrieve the sword, hefting the weapon as if testing its weight.

Anger ripped through Zerfall, washing away all misery and self-pity. *Don't touch my sword!* She wanted to climb to her feet, take her sword from this muscled moron, and show them what death looked like. She dragged herself toward the Dysmorphic with a hiss of hatred.

"She's gone," laughed ängstlich, clapping and capering about in an ungainly dance. "I'm free of the evil bitch!"

"You're a cowardly idiot," grunted Starke. "She was a good woman. Your delusions did this to her."

"No, she was a demon."

"She'll be waiting in Swarm," pointed out the Dysmorphic with an evil leer.

"That's a long time from now" said ängstlich, halting his mad dance and looking annoyed at Starke for ruining his celebration.

"Ah, look," said Starke. "Here comes Captain Gedankenlos." When ängstlich turned to look, the Dysmorphic chopped him down with a casual swing of Blutblüte.

Zerfall watched as Captain Gedankenlos approached. Tall and handsome with broad shoulders and a strong, square chin, he looked every part the dashing hero.

He scowled at Starke. "I suppose you had a good reason for killing a fellow priest?"

Starke shrugged, looking unconcerned. "He missed his wife."

Zerfall froze when Gedankenlos glanced about, taking in the carnage with a nod of appreciation before returning his attention to Starke. "This Basamortuan killed Dämonin Schwindel, Gefräßige, and Unbedacht?"

Either they hadn't seen her, or they were doing a masterful job of pretending. Perhaps looking like a corpse had its advantages. Should she stay still, wait for one of them to get close enough? She loosened a knife in its scabbard.

If nothing else, maybe they'd turn Blutblüte on her and she'd die by her own sword; she had no doubt the weapon could end her hellish existence.

Starke shrugged again, grinning. "Killing the lad was nothing." He lifted the morningstar, giving it a flick so the iron ball, hanging from its chain, swung in a slow circle. "Smashed him to pieces."

Gedankenlos scowled at Jateko's crushed corpse. "I said *alive*."

"Sending five of us suggests you thought he was dangerous. I saw no point in taking chances."

"*She* wanted him alive."

Starke's massive shoulders hunched. "Shite."

"Right. Shite, indeed. You'll have to apologize."

"Of course."

"In person."

Starke sighed. "Fine," he said with resignation.

"Could *you* have killed Gefräßige?" asked the Captain, arching an eyebrow.

"Of course." He looked less certain than he sounded. "Particularly with this." Starke lifted Blutblüte. "The sand-sticker had Zerfall's sword. Any idea how he got it?"

Captain Gedankenlos held out his hand. "Ask Zerfall," he dared.

Starke frowned at the hand before surrendering the weapon. "You seem calm. I thought you might be angry at having lost so many powerful Geisteskranken."

"No," said Gedankenlos. "Just saves me some time."

"How so?" asked the Dysmorphic, sloped brow furrowing in confusion.

Gedankenlos glanced past him and nodded toward Zerfall. "Hey, is that rotting corpse watching us?"

Starke turned and stared at Zerfall. "Yes. Yes, it is."

Gedankenlos drove Blutblüte into Starke's back. The ancient blade passed through mail and leather and flesh and bone with ease. Starke died without a sound.

Gedankenlos wiped the blade clean on the dead Dysmorphic and examined the weapon with a critical eye. "So small. Such a little nothing, and yet so much."

Not sure whether he recognized her in her advanced state of decay, she levered herself up on her left arm leaving the right hand free to draw a blade should the chance arise. "Gedankenlos. It's me, Zerfall."

"No. Impossible." He looked doubtful, like he didn't believe his own words. Or didn't want to.

"You have always been loyal—"

"To strength." He made a show of examining her. "You don't look very strong."

Do you really want to know how much of the old you remains? Command him. Leave him no choice but to obey.

She said nothing.

Tucking the sword into his belt he stepped forward and kicked out her supporting arm. The bone broke with a *crack* and she collapsed to the ground.

"You're not Zerfall," he said, sounding relieved. "I don't know who or what you are, but you aren't her."

Gedankenlos stomped on the wrist of her right hand, pinning it to the ground. She prayed he hadn't broken the bone. He searched her with professional efficiency, rooting through pockets—hidden and otherwise—and discarding what few weapons she possessed. When he found her tattered copy of Halber Tod's poems he froze.

He opened the book at random, gaze flicking over the text before darting in her direction. "Where did you get this?" he demanded.

"It's mine," she croaked, voice a papery whisper.

Licking his lips, he leaned back to examine her face, frowning in distaste at the wreckage. "Truly?" he asked.

"Truly." She tested her wrist and found it still functional.

With a whispered "Shite" he tucked the book back into the pocket where he found it. "I'm going to take you to see . . . Zerfall," he said. "You and the Basamortuan. If you resist, or make this any more annoying than it already is, I'll break every bone in your body. Understand?"

Zerfall nodded. "One problem," she said, looking up at the man squatting over her.

After stooping to grab one of her ankles, he stood straight. "Hm?"

"I am Zerfall," she said, daring him to doubt.

Gedankenlos swallowed. "Then who was that," he said, "standing over Hölle's corpse?"

Hölle's corpse? Zerfall felt lost. Had she come all this way for nothing? Jateko had slain Aas and then been slain, skull shattered in an instant of violence. Shock left her numb, unable to know what she felt at the loss. She couldn't believe he was gone, that he died because he refused to abandon her. And now Hölle lay dead, murdered by a Fragment pretending to be Zerfall? What was left?

You came here to end the Täuschung. Nothing has changed.

Except everything had changed. She was broken, only capable of standing if someone propped her up. And Jateko. He hadn't been part of her plan, he had *been* the plan. She had thought to use him to kill Hölle and, if needed, hunt and kill her mad priests. With Jateko gone, she had nothing. If Hölle's Fragment was anything like the woman Zerfall had been, Zerfall had already failed.

She became aware of motion and realized she was being dragged along the uneven ground. Gedankenlos paused as he passed Jateko's corpse to bend and, with his free hand, grab the Basamortuan youth by an ankle to drag him alongside Zerfall. Some part of her raged at the impropriety of being hauled like a sack of trash. She ignored it. Anger was pointless.

The Täuschung compound was empty. There were dormitories enough for hundreds of priests, but they saw no one on their journey. Entering the largest of the buildings, a run-down church looking much older than its surroundings, she saw how decrepit the building was. Filth and long streamers of dust-clogged spider webs gathered in the corners. Anything not stone sagged and rotted. This wasn't the result of recent neglect; this was the product of hundreds of years of careless indifference.

And why not? she thought. No proselytizing happened within these walls. This part of the church was populated by the insane and damaged, those foul souls focussed on venting their self-loathing on the unsuspecting innocent.

This is your religion. No matter how much she wanted to tell herself this church's sorry state occurred after she left, she knew it wasn't true. For centuries she walked these halls, ignoring the growing filth.

She remembered the day she tried to kill her sister. *No, I never had a sister.* She remembered the soul-tearing pain of Hölle's betrayal. Her last memory of Hölle was of the woman pacing back and forth in their shared chambers, telling Zerfall of all the wonderful plans she had for the Täuschung, and how she was going to make the church the most successful religion in all the city-states in the next decade. Zerfall saw there was no room for her in those plans. Hölle no longer needed her.

Though the idea lurked for decades, growing stronger with the passing of each and every year, she knew at that moment what her sister really was: A Fragment. Everything made sense. Her memories of lying in that cot alone, feverish and mad. The way her sister slowly replaced her, slowly pushed her out of her own life. She knew why she felt like she'd been unravelling for years.

And she knew what happened when a Fragment no longer needed the original.

Halber Tod made so much sense. Everything she ever worked for was rot. If her Fragment could fool her for centuries and then take it all away, nothing mattered. Not the Täuschung, and not Wahrergott.

Somehow, waking in the desert and finding Jateko returned her purpose. The thought of killing the Fragment who stole her life and ending the evil religion they created gave her the will to go on.

Is it really nothing more than vengeance which has kept me moving all this time? She hated the idea. That was something the old Zerfall would have been quite comfortable with.

I deserve everything I have suffered and a thousand times worse.

Jateko's corpse, limp and flopping, head bouncing off every uneven stone, rolled against her as Gedankenlos turned another corner.

I'm sorry. She wanted to pull herself apart, be nothing. She couldn't take the sight, the reminder of what she did to the boy. *I should have left you in the desert. Once I realized how useful you'd be . . . once I understood how you felt about me . . . I couldn't let go. I was selfish.*

Her own skull struck a rock jutting from the floor with a hollow *pock*. She felt nothing.

[I don't . . .]

What? Where had that thought come from? Zerfall turned her head to examine Jateko. Did the damage to his skull look a little less severe? Was he healing even from these grievous wounds? She wasn't sure; the Basamortuan looked very dead, his limbs shattered, his skull crumpled.

Gedankenlos stopped and stood listening, still gripping Zerfall and Jateko by the ankles. "Did you hear something?" he asked.

"Just my head bouncing off these stones," said Zerfall.

He glanced at her over his shoulder before shrugging and continuing on his way.

Zerfall reached out with her stump to nudge Jateko's corpse. He didn't react, showed no signs of life. *If he were alive, I'd hear his thoughts.* She wanted to try whispering to him but didn't dare lest she alert the Captain.

Gedankenlos approached a door, larger and more ornate than the rest, heavy oak finished in intricately worked iron that had long ago rusted red. He stood for a moment gripping the two corpses, scowling at the door as if trying to make up his mind about something. Finally, he leaned forward and knocked by banging his forehead against the door.

Zerfall heard a muffled "Enter" from within and watched as Gedankenlos shoved at the door with his forehead. When it failed to open, he growled in frustration and dropped Jateko's ankle to free a hand with which to open the door. After swinging the door open, he bent to retrieve the ankle and dragged the two of them into the room. He halted once he cleared the doorway as if awaiting permission to enter further.

Within, a woman waited.

Zerfall examined her. Thick dark hair fell about slim shoulders in waves. Her dark eyes were bright with intelligence and curiosity. The woman's body, slim and yet curvy, reminded Zerfall of her own when she first woke in that puke-filled alley.

This what I looked like when alive.

Not quite. Something was missing. There was a softness to this woman Zerfall never possessed.

"Is he leaking blood all over my floor?" the woman asked.

"A little," admitted Gedankenlos. "He's not bleeding too much now that he's—" He swallowed.

"That he's what?"

"Well, dead."

"Did you bring me two gods-damned corpses?" the woman demanded petulantly.

PHARISÄER SCOWLED AT CAPTAIN Gedankenlos, waiting. "Well?"

"Yes," he answered, standing at the entrance to her chambers like an idiot. "But—"

"Did I not say I wanted the Basamortuan alive?"

"Starke killed him. Crushed his head with that ridiculous morningstar."

"He'll rot in Swarm for this," she swore.

"Already done," said Gedankenlos.

"Is that . . ." she gestured at the sword stuck awkwardly in his belt. "Is that her . . . my . . . Blutblüte?"

Gedankenlos nodded. "The Basamortuan had it."

When he started forward, she waved him to a stop. *Idiot.* "Don't track blood in here. Leave the savage by the door. The other one. Is it alive?"

"Kind of," he answered, looking like he wanted to say more.

"Is it broken? Helpless?"

He nodded without answering.

"Bring it here."

Releasing the Basamortuan's ankle, Gedankenlos dragged the desiccated corpse into Pharisäer's chambers. Tattered shreds of flesh fell off it and stuck to the carpet and it left behind a clump of dark hair attached to a patch of scalp. *What a mess.* She decided it didn't matter. Once she was real she'd move out of this dilapidated dump.

Snapping her fingers, Pharisäer held out her hand. "Give me the sword."

Still dragging the other corpse, Gedankenlos drew Blutblüte from his belt as he approached, spun the weapon and handed it to her hilt first. Releasing the corpse, he retreated without turning his back on her.

What's he so afraid of? Does he think I'll kill him?

Which of course was what she planned on doing, just not yet. If this husk at her feet was all that remained of Zerfall, soon Pharisäer would be the real Zerfall. And Gedankenlos was the last living soul who might know the truth.

"I'm not going to kill you," she told the Captain. "You are far too useful." *And dangerous. I'll wait until your guard is down.*

Gedankenlos blinked, looking surprised like the thought hadn't occurred to him, and backed farther away.

He wasn't that good an actor. Something else must have rattled him.

The corpse at Pharisäer's feet levered itself upright on an arm ending in a ragged stump and Pharisäer's gaze darted to the hand on the desk. *It's her. It must be her.*

The corpse drew a slow and strangely intentional breath. "I am Zerfall," it said. "Give me my sword."

Pharisäer retreated before the vehemence, the barely controlled rage. Empty sockets, pits of soulless black, saw her. Saw through her. *She knows me.* Fear shivered through Pharisäer. Hölle had been nothing. Zerfall was everything. This was the founder of the Täuschung. This was the woman whose madness birthed a hell and gave life to a god. *And I brought her here.* What the hells had she been thinking?

She glanced at Gedankenlos and he swallowed and backed toward the door sputtering, "Maybe I should . . ."

This garbage is nothing to me! I *will be Zerfall.* "Captain," she said, feigning casual ease. "I have changed my mind." She pointed at the corpse struggling to push itself into a sitting position. "Break it apart. Render it utterly helpless."

Gedankenlos stopped, stood rooted, attention darting between Pharisäer and the living corpse at her feet.

"I am Zerfall," said the corpse, louder this time.

Gedankenlos licked his lips. "I think I shall return later," he said, bowing in their direction. "Whoever remains I shall serve."

"Look at her," snapped Pharisäer. "She can't even sit up. Do as I command!"

Zerfall pushed herself to her feet, stood lilting at an awkward angle. She ignored Gedankenlos, attention locked on Pharisäer. She held out her right hand. "Give. Me. My. Sword."

Over Zerfall's shoulder Pharisäer saw the Captain hesitate and take a tentative step in her direction, reaching for his own blade.

Zerfall turned to glare at him. "I am Zerfall. I am four hundred years old. The One True God watches over me. This . . ." She nodded at Pharisäer. "This *shadow* is nothing."

Pharisäer watched, helpless, as Gedankenlos fled, leaving them alone in the room. *I'm no shadow. I will be the real Zerfall.*

Her words felt hollow. She could never be this woman.

Z ERFALL WATCHED GEDANKENLOS FLEE the room. *That's what the loyalty of a coward is worth.*

She wanted to lie down and await the end. She wanted to scream and rage. She wanted her sword.

Zerfall turned to face Pharisäer. "Just us, *Fragment.*" Again she held out her open hand. "Give me the sword, and I'll let you leave." For an instant she thought the woman would hand it over and then those dark eyes hardened.

Pharisäer backed away, lifting the sword into something close to a guard position. "You can barely stand. I'm going to hack you apart." She grinned bright teeth, waving the sword in front of her.

"You're afraid," said Zerfall, limping one small step toward Pharisäer, dragging her shattered ankle across the rough stone of the floor. "You're afraid I'm going to take it all away."

Pharisäer threatened with the sword but retreated, eyes darting. "I'm not afraid—"

"You're looking for a way out." Zerfall shuffled to position herself between Pharisäer and the door. "But you're not leaving with my sword." She had no plan. Everything she thought she knew had fallen apart. But she couldn't let Blutblüte go, couldn't allow Swarm to escape. As long as she held the sword she could fool herself there was some chance at ending Swarm and bringing down this sick religion she created.

Pharisäer leapt forward, stabbing.

Zerfall batted the sword away, smacking the flat of the blade with the palm of her hand.

"You telegraphed your attack," she said, shuffling after the once again retreating woman. "Your shoulders tensed. I saw it in your eyes." Zerfall grinned. "What do you see in my eyes?"

Again Pharisäer stabbed clumsily, telegraphing the attack, and again Zerfall knocked it aside.

"You really must do better—"

Pharisäer screamed and hacked at Zerfall, flailing with the sword. The first swing crashed into her chest, shattering ribs and spinning her off balance. The second fractured her hip and dropped her to the ground. Still screaming, Pharisäer hacked at Zerfall, bashing as much as cutting. Bones broke and thin flesh tore. Zerfall fought to fend away the attacks, but Pharisäer, while not as strong as Zerfall had once been, was far stronger than the desiccated corpse she now was. A wild swing shattered the bones in Zerfall's right arm and she sagged to the floor.

Pharisäer backed away, gasping, sucking in deep breaths.

"I'm done," Zerfall whispered to the floor, lungs empty of air. "Enough. Jateko's dead. I can't do this any more." But it was a lie. Now that she lay here, broken and helpless, facing the end, she didn't want to die. Not yet. Not like this. *Not at the hands of this* Fragment.

"What are you mumbling about?" Pharisäer demanded between breaths.

Zerfall used her stump arm to roll herself onto her back. "That's my sword," she said. Her right wrist had broken and a sharp shard of bone poked through the flesh. A weapon, all she had. *All I need.* Maybe, if she lured the Fragment close enough, this might not be the end.

"Mine now," said the woman, grinning. There was something wrong with that vicious smile; doubt ate at its corners.

"You're nothing." said Zerfall, hoping to provoke Pharisäer. "Fragment," she sneered. *If I can kill her, I can call that Captain back into the room. He'll do as I command.* She didn't know what she'd command him to do, but anything was better than dying like this. "Coward."

"Coward?" Pharisäer paced around to Zerfall's legs and stomped on the remaining foot, shattering the small bones. "Coward?" She lifted her foot and brought it down on Zerfall's shin and it snapped with an arid *crack.* "Why should I fear you?" She stomped on Zerfall's other shin, breaking it too. "What will you do to me?" It took several attempts, but finally she managed to crush Zerfall's right knee to dust and splintered fragments of bone.

Zerfall watched, preparing to lunge forward should Pharisäer move within reach. *A little closer.* "Hölle was nothing, a figment of my imagination. You are even less, the dream of a dream."

The woman lifted her foot preparing to crush Zerfall's other knee, and then stopped. She was panting, breathing hard from the effort. "I am nothing? Look at you! A broken corpse. Helpless. Powerless." She stomped on Zerfall's chest, snapping several ribs. Leaning down she pushed Blutblüte's point against Zerfall's throat parting dry flesh in a bloodless wound. "It's you who are nothing. In a moment I will be everything."

Zerfall stabbed her in the side, driving the sharp shard of bone into the soft flesh beneath her ribs. Pharisäer screamed and threw herself backward, scrabbling and kicking to put distance between herself and Zerfall. A flailing foot struck Zerfall's arm, shattering the elbow joint.

Pharisäer rolled to her feet with a groan of agony, clutching her side, blood leaking between her fingers. She laughed through gritted teeth, a choked sob of pain and dark humour. "You tricky bitch."

The wound wasn't nearly deep enough to kill. What little hope Zerfall had died and she flopped back to the ground. She lay, head turned to one side and watched the blood pooling around Jateko's battered corpse.

Pharisäer laughed and shook her head in amazement. "You killed yourself, you know. You and Hölle. You stabbed her, and she sent Aas to kill you. Your religion will die with you. I don't care about the Täuschung or your helpless One True Git." She shook her head, lips puckered in disgust. "What a pointless faith."

Zerfall wanted to feel something at that but couldn't. It wasn't her religion either. Täuschung was the old Zerfall's dream. If Pharisäer destroyed the religion to spite Zerfall could she count that as a victory? That had been her goal after all. Except if the Fragment was anything like the woman Zerfall had been she wouldn't end the Täuschung. Religion was too useful.

"You're done," said Pharisäer. "I'm going to send you to Swarm. Your church is in disarray. Without leadership it will fade to nothing. I've destroyed everything you ever worked for. You have nothing left."

Zerfall watched as the woman limped circles around her, careful to stay out of reach, Blutblüte hanging forgotten in her fist. "Who are you trying to convince?" And then she laughed, her first real amusement in what seemed like forever. "You're trying to manipulate me, to break me down. You seek to crush my spirit. Is that what you did to Hölle?" She waved the woman to silence. "It doesn't matter. I don't care."

Pharisäer seemed to remember Blutblüte and hefted the weapon with a triumphant gleam in her eye. "I don't need to destroy what you are, you've already done that." Pointing the sword at Zerfall's chest, she approached. "All I need to do is end you."

Zerfall wanted to lie back and await the end. She wanted to surrender all she was. She couldn't. She swore to end Swarm and she would fight to do that until the very end. She struggled to get the desiccated remains of an arm under her and braced herself, ready to again lunge at Pharisäer. It was hopeless, but she had to try. *Give the old Zerfall credit for one thing, there was no quit in her.* Maybe, if she tripped the woman up, toppled her to the ground, she could choke her or smash her unconscious. She laughed at the thought of Pharisäer waking in an alley, her skull smashed, with no recollection of who she was or how she got there.

Pharisäer screamed "Why are you laughing!"

"I'm not Hölle. You can't break me."

Pharisäer drove Blutblüte toward her heart.

TWENTY-TWO

A wise man would rather suffer defeat today than win years from now.

—Basamortuan Proverb

DARKNESS.

Stuttering light.

Darkness.

Vision flickered in and out of focus, a bloody smear of light and a stone floor canting at an odd angle. Some woman, beautiful and lithe, something like the way Zerfall used to look when Jateko first met her, paced around a crumpled pile of garbage. She held a sword in her hand and snarled at the heap on the floor.

Darkness.

What happened?

Some Dysmorphic caved your skull in.

Oh. Right. He had a dim memory of facing several Geisteskranken but couldn't remember how it ended.

Not well, someone told him.

He groaned in pain as he tried to stretch out a leg.

Quiet, someone else said. *If Pharisäer hears you, we're dead.*

Pharisäer?

Hölle's Fragment.

For a moment the word was meaningless city-states babble. *Right, a manifestation of her split personality.*

I can't believe you survived that. This time Jateko recognized the voice as Aas'.

I have the health and strength of over a dozen people, Jateko explained. *I heal quickly.* His entire body screamed in agony at the damage it suffered. *I think I need more souls.*

You better heal faster, said Aas. *Pharisäer's getting angry.*

Jateko cracked open an eye and tried to blink away the haze of blood washing his vision in a sanguine stain. The pile of refuse at Pharisäer's feet was Zerfall, he realized. He watched, helpless, as Pharisäer stepped forward and brought her foot down on Zerfall's foot. He heard bones snap and break.

Leave her alone! He tried to push himself upright, but his arm had been shattered and his hand slid on the blood-slicked stone beneath him.

Not yet, said Aas. *Don't give yourself away until you're ready to fight.*

I have to save her. I have to try.

If you move before you're ready, you'll die with her.

Jateko tried to lift his head to better see, but his body ignored his commands. *I'd rather die trying than do nothing.*

Aas is right, said Abiega. *Don't spoil your chance at saving her with some foolish display of ill-thought heroism.*

Cursing, Jateko realized they were right. He couldn't sit much less stand and fight. He could do nothing to help her now. He heard Zerfall taunt Pharisäer and watched as Pharisäer stomped more of her bones to dust.

I'm going to kill Pharisäer. I'm going to send her to Swarm. I'm going to—
Wait.

He watched, helpless, as Zerfall stabbed Pharisäer and the Fragment retreated, wounded, but very much alive. And angry. Pharisäer grinned deranged rage, left a trail of blood as she circled Zerfall, Blutblüte swinging in slow threat.

No no no no.

Slowly straightening his leg Jateko felt the bones of his knee click into place as he healed. Tentatively he bent the leg. The pain was incredible, but the leg moved. *Hold on Zerfall, stall a little longer.* Did Zerfall know he was alive? He glanced in her direction, saw Pharisäer lift the sword menacingly.

Jateko ground his teeth in helpless rage. *Aas, if she kills Zerfall, I'm going to kill you.*

Too late.

Straightening his other leg, Jateko felt bones pop into place and couldn't believe the two women didn't turn in his direction at the sound. *Hey, she can't hear our thoughts. Am I cured?*

No, answered Aas. *We're too far away.*

Jateko rolled onto his stomach, getting both hands beneath him. The pain was excruciating. Muscles and tendons in his arms and legs writhed around healing bones and he felt stronger with each breath.

When you try and kill her, said Aas, *she'll hear us coming. Focus your thoughts on your base desires. Focus on how beautiful she is, on how much you want her. She'll make promises. You'll want to believe them, but don't. Instead, think about how much you* want *to believe.*

That sounds impossible.

It's your only hope

"All I need to do is end you," snarled Pharisäer, menacing Zerfall with the sword.

As Jateko pushed himself into a kneeling position he heard Zerfall's mocking laughter. *Zerfall's not stalling, she's antagonizing her.*

With a grunt of effort, he rose to his feet and stood, knees wobbling, as Pharisäer screamed, "Why are you laughing!" and lunged toward Zerfall with Blutblüte.

Zerfall tried to parry the attack with her own thin arm. Even dead she moved fast, catching the flat of the blade in exactly the right place. Brittle bone betrayed her and her arm snapped.

Pharisäer drove Blutblüte into her chest.

Zerfall, dead since the day Jateko met her, sagged lifeless to the floor, a dry sack of shattered bones.

PHARISÄER STOOD OVER THE limp corpse, eyes and mouth wide in disbelief. She drew Blutblüte from Zerfall's chest and stared, blinking, at the blade.

No blood stained its surface. *Of course not*, she thought numbly. *She's been dead for ages.*

She nudged the body with a foot; it was surprisingly light.

"I did it," she whispered. "I killed Zerfall."

Tentatively, almost reverently, she pushed the sword again into Zerfall's torso and withdrew it. Was she faking? Was this a trick? Pharisäer snarled and stomped on the near-fleshless skull, shattering the jaw and cracking the occipital bone. She tittered, madness scraping at the sharp edges of her laughter, and again brought her foot down. Bones snapped like twigs.

"I did it. I am Zerfall." It felt wrong. It wasn't true.

It is true! I made my new reality. I won!

But it wasn't.

How was this possible? It made no sense! She killed Hölle, Zerfall's Fragment and became Hölle. Now she'd ended Zerfall. Had she missed something? Had Zerfall's imaginary god somehow intervened?

"I am Zerfall. Head of the Täuschung. Founder of this shite religion."

No, you aren't.

She wanted to dance on this corpse, defile it. She wanted to peel what skin it had and make for herself a scarf or . . . something! Did it matter that she wasn't Zerfall? "One True God be damned, I'm going to rape this place for everything."

Zerfall may have given most of the Täuschung wealth to that damned desert savage, but there was a lot she could pawn off and sell. Hells, even this compound—run down and decrepit as it was—had to be worth *something*. Maybe she'd even convince the Verzweiflung bankers that the accounts were rightfully hers. Anything was possible. She was real.

"I am Zerfall!" she screamed.

[I am going to kill her.]

"What?" Pharisäer turned to see the Basamortuan shuffling unsteadily toward her. "You're . . . you're alive?" Or was he dead, like Zerfall had been. It didn't matter; she had Blutblüte.

As he passed the desk he glanced at the hand still resting there, unchanged. *[I lost her.]*

{You're not focussing,} said a familiar voice.

Pharisäer glanced about her chambers. "Aas? Is that you? You can serve me. Kill this fool and I'll—"

{Remember what I told you,} said Aas, ignoring her promises.

The Basamortuan limped closer, standing taller, baring bloody teeth in a savage snarl. His head looked bent, crushed on one side.

[She killed Zerfall. I'm going to kill her,] the first voice said again.

He must be dead. She raised Blutblüte, threatening. Where were Aas' thoughts coming from? Why could she hear the Basamortuan's thoughts?

"I *am* Zerfall," she said with all the feigned certainty she could muster.

The Basamortuan stopped, blinked stupidly at her. "You are?"

The beautiful sound of doubt. Doubt and need. With a groan he straightened his back and she was surprised at how strong and tall the lad was. She would use him. *If he was Zerfall's, he will be mine.*

"Of course," she lied. "The moment I killed *that*," she gestured at the haggard corpse with Blutblüte, "I became Zerfall." She took her time examining him, knowing her eyes were dark and smoky, full of promise. "Aas, tell him I speak truth."

[Is this true? Is she Zerfall now?]

Was that desperate hope she heard?

{Yes,} said Aas. *{She was Pharisäer, but if she's killed both Zerfall and Hölle, she is real now. She is Zerfall.}*

The Basamortuan shuffled forward, putting himself between her and the door. "She's not lying?" he asked aloud.

{No.}

The Basamortuan limped closer, and she saw hunger in his eyes. He wanted this. Had always wanted this. *Just a man,* she thought. The boy probably spent every night dreaming of a whole and living Zerfall, warm, and soft to the touch. She took a deep breath, wincing at the pain in her side, swelling her chest, and let a slim finger trace the curve of her hip.

[Gods, look at her. She's perfect. So beautiful. I need her. If she's the real Zerfall . . .] Longing tainted the boy's confused thoughts. *[Then maybe I haven't lost her.]*

Pharisäer licked her full lips and let her gaze crawl across the youth's strong body like a caress. Soon, he'd beg to serve. "I'm better," she promised, moving toward the bed. He followed like a dog. *I have him.* "Aas knows this. I'll give you what she," she nodded at the corpse, "never could."

The Basamortuan stopped, turned sad eyes on the skeletal remains at her feet, his thoughts a chaotic maelstrom of lust, and need, and loss. He took another tentative step toward her.

Was he limping less than he had been?

"She's nothing now," purred Pharisäer. She touched one of her breasts, cupping it. "This is what you want. Warm flesh. Not that *rot*. This is what you love."

[What I love.] The Basamortuan reached a hand toward her and stepped closer.

Pharisäer let a warm whimper dancing the thin line between fear and excitement escape her lips. *That's right, this is what you want.*

[It wasn't the body I loved.]

"Come now," said Pharisäer. "You can't tell me you don't want this."

[Gods I do.] He moved another step toward her. *[A little closer. Then she dies.]*

PHARISÄER SQUEAKED IN SURPRISE and danced lithely beyond Jateko's reach. "You're a fool. You're both fools. I would have been everything for you but you'll throw it all away for a damned rotting corpse." She raised Blutblüte. "Come then. You love her so much; I'll send you to meet her."

[Damn.] Had he been able to keep himself distracted a moment longer, she'd have been cornered between the wall and the bed. Jateko slowed his advance. *[I knew I couldn't kill her without thinking about it.]*

He moved to keep himself between her and the door. He was healing quickly, but if she got past him he'd never catch her. With the desk on one side of the room and the bed on the other, he could cut off her escape, but she had plenty of room to wield a sword.

{It takes a lot of practice to control such thoughts,} said Aas. *{The trick is having something else to think about, something that really worries you.}*

[Well this worries me,] answered Jateko. *[She has Blutblüte, and we don't even have a sharpened stick.]*

"That's right," hissed Pharisäer, stabbing with Blutblüte to keep him back. "Now you'll die."

{I know a secret,} said Aas in a bouncy sing-song.

Jateko darted forward and Pharisäer sliced the air before his eyes, forcing him to retreat.

"And what is that?" she asked. "Is it something pathetic? Something sad? Will you tell this fool he *wants* to die, that if I kill him he'll get to spend eternity with his love, and that in Swarm she'll be whole and beautiful?"

[Is that true?]

{Yes, but—}

"Don't you want to see her again? I can make that happen. Just stand still."

[What the hells am I fighting for? She's gone. I want to see her.]

{There's more at stake here—}

Pharisäer lunged at Jateko and he hurled himself away, narrowly avoiding being impaled as she thrust the sword at his belly.

"Aas is a fool," said Pharisäer, following. "A dreamer. He's wandered the world, reading and studying, and understands *nothing*." She laughed again, forcing Jateko back, thrusting Blutblüte at his face.

[What was the secret?] Jateko asked Aas.

{She has no idea how to use a sword.}

Jateko stepped toward Pharisäer and this time when she stabbed at him he ducked under the clumsy thrust and grabbed her slim wrist. It was easy. She was small and lithe, but she had none of Zerfall's strength, none of her skill. He twisted until he heard the bones pop. When Blutblüte dropped he caught it with his free hand and drove it into her soft belly.

For a dozen dying heartbeats Jateko stood motionless. Pharisäer—everything he ever wanted Zerfall to be—hung limp, dangling from his fist, Blutblüte jutting from her gut. She blinked once and all reason faded from her eyes.

He lowered her to the floor, sliding the sword free of her flesh. Tears ran, falling like pattering rain on Pharisäer's beautiful face. "I needed her."

She wasn't the Zerfall you loved.

"That's not what I mean," sobbed Jateko. "I needed her body. I was going to find a way to move Zerfall's soul into this body, and we killed it."

It would never have worked. Zerfall's soul is in Swarm. It's beyond our reach. She's gone. Forever.

"Are you sure?" Jateko blinked, confused.

Blutblüte's proximity guarantees she is in Swarm.

"Blutblüte?"

Zerfall told me the sword's secret once, years ago: Blutblüte is Swarm, explained Aas. *The hell is within the blade. That's how they started this religion, how they sent the first souls. It was only much later, once they convinced enough fools to believe, that they were able to send souls to Swarm without Blutblüte's direct use. As the number of souls in Swarm grew—as the number of souls trapped within the blade increased—proximity to the blade guaranteed the destination of those who died.*

Jateko listened, too numb with loss to interrupt.

The sword is an epicentre of faith, continued Aas. *Millions of souls believe in Swarm and they're all right there in your hand. There are perhaps one hundred thousand people living in the city of Geld and maybe another fifty thousand in outlying dependencies. The population in that sword dwarfs the entire population of the Geldangelegenheiten city-state. At this point, I wouldn't be surprised if everyone who dies in or near Geld goes to Swarm.*

"She's in the sword," said Jateko, lifting it to stare at its brutal simplicity. Hope surged through him, kicked his heart like an angry goat kicking an annoying child. "We break the sword. Her soul will be—"

It's unbreakable, said Aas.

Jateko searched Zerfall's chambers for something to lean the sword against. He'd stomp on it near the hilt, typically where swords were weakest. "I can break it. I have the strength of a dozen men."

Millions believe they will be trapped in there until they're freed as gods. Can you break that?

Jateko found a stack of musty books looking like they hadn't been touched in centuries and leaned Blutblüte against them. Leaping into the air, he brought his feet down on the blade side of the guard. The sword ignored him, didn't so much as bend. He might as well have been stomping on a mountain. With a scream of rage he jumped on the sword again and again.

Jateko, it won't work, Aas said.

"I have to be stronger. I'll eat more people until—"

It won't work. You will never be strong enough to break the belief of millions. In fact—and I found this quite clever—Zerfall once told me that the first few hundred souls she sent to Swarm were her own priests. They were the vanguard, there to preach to the souls that followed. They were there to convince all who entered Swarm that they would remain trapped until humanity Ascended.

Jateko collected Blutblüte from the ground and glared at the cursed sword. "I used to dream of coming to the city-states and finding a magical sword." He laughed, a mirthless bark of anger.

There is no such thing as magic swords, said Aas.

"Then what the hells is this?" demanded Jateko, shaking Blutblüte.

It's the embodiment of the manifestation of the delusion of a powerful Geisteskranken. One, I believe, backed by the will of a god.

"A god? You don't believe that One True God garbage, do you?" asked Jateko, incredulous.

I didn't. And then I doubted. Now . . . Jateko sensed the assassin's difficulty in expressing his thoughts. *I once read about a rather systematic means of asking questions and finding answers. Or possible answers. Look at the evidence.*

"What the hells are you talking about?"

The Pinnacle. It's more than an idea or a theory; it's a law. Geisteskranken grow in power as their minds fall apart. They are at their most powerful at that moment when they lose control of their delusions. That law is why the city-states aren't dominated by Geisteskranken.

Jateko glanced about the room, wanting to destroy something and yet wanting to understand the assassin's strange words. "I thought they were."

Well, kind of. But the Gefahrgeist running every government or church are minor in comparison to one nearing the Pinnacle. You've never met a truly powerful Gefahrgeist. You've never been in the presence of a Slaver.

"I don't see—"

How did Zerfall and Hölle last four hundred years without reaching the Pinnacle?

Jateko snarled in frustration and swung Blutblüte against the wall with all his strength. Mortar and flakes of shattered stone exploded into the air. The sword's edge wasn't even nicked.

There's one obvious answer, and we'd be fools to ignore it.

Again Jateko attacked the wall, screaming and hacking with mad abandon.

Aas prattled on in the background: *She had help. It is the simplest explanation.*

Jateko stopped and stood scowling at the sword clutched in his trembling fist. "Help."

Yes. The One True God.

Begrudgingly, Jateko's mind began to focus on Aas' words. "A god who wanted all humanity to suffer?"

Yes. And if she was backed by a god, what else is true? What if this reality is a prison? What if Swarm is the way out?

Jateko contemplated Aas' words. Could Swarm and the Täuschung really be the work of some distant god? The idea was madness and yet made as much sense as anything he learned since leaving the desert. Could Blutblüte be humanity's salvation?

The Täuschung worshipped the One True God, a distant and uncommunicative deity. Their religion seemed insane to Jateko.

"I promised Zerfall I'd end the Täuschung and Swarm. I'm going to crush this religion, end their hell. I *will* save Zerfall. Gods be damned."

TWENTY-THREE

The burial shroud has pockets for a reason.

—Basamortuan Proverb

OW? ASKED AAS. *SHE'S gone.*

Jateko felt a surge of hope. "You came back when I ate you."

You ate my brain, my heart and whatever else you managed to stuff into that insatiable face-hole. Look at her.

Jateko stared at Zerfall's desiccated corpse.

That's right, said Aas. *No heart. No liver. No internal organs. What will you eat, her bones? That won't work and you know it.*

"I'm going to get Zerfall back. I promised her I'd end Swarm. I'm going to do that too."

Impossible.

"Where belief defines reality, *nothing* is impossible."

What's your brilliant plan.

"You died in close proximity to Blutblüte."

You ran me through with it.

"You went to Swarm, after I stomped your disgusting puppet?"

Yes.

"When you were there, could you see and interact with the other souls?" Jateko asked Aas.

He felt the assassin shudder at the memory. *Yes. It was another reality. Like this, but very different. Empty, and yet crowded.*

"Everyone there has a body?" asked Jateko, struggling to picture what Aas described.

Yes. Millions of people crammed onto an endless plain of nothing.

"Good." Jateko took a long slow breath and marshalled his thoughts, trying to fit the chaotic mix of disparate ideas into a unified plan. "I define a very small local reality around me because I am over a dozen people and the number of people who believe something matters. Correct?"

Correct, answered Aas. *Weight of numbers also affects the range; one person believing something has a smaller sphere of influence than a thousand believing the same thing.*

"So Swarm defines a larger and yet still localized reality around Blutblüte because there are millions of souls trapped in one place."

Yes, answered Aas, sounding like a patient teacher. *Correct.*

"I'm going to Swarm," said Jateko, with more confidence than he felt. Had he thought everything through? It seemed damned unlikely.

What will that achieve? demanded Abiega, butting in.

"Once there, I am going to kill and devour every single person."

Impossible, said Aas. *There are millions—* He stuttered unintelligible thought for a moment before saying, *You'll never succeed.*

"Once I've killed and eaten everyone," explained Jateko, "I'll define that reality."

There are huge and rather obvious flaws in your plan, said Aas.

"What did I miss?" asked Jateko, eyeing the fresh corpse at his feet. His stomach rumbled in ravenous complaint. He was so hungry it was becoming difficult to think.

The Täuschung are still sending souls to Swarm, said Aas. *And if I'm correct in my theory that Blutblüte's proximity is sending souls to Swarm as well, the hell is growing faster than you could kill and eat people.*

Aas was right. It was impossible. He'd never keep up with Swarm's rate of growth.

Aas is wrong, said Abiega. *The assassin's arguments work for you as much as against you.*

"Explain," demanded Jateko.

Proximity matters, said Abiega. *We take the sword far out into the Basamortuan and bury it where it will be close to no one.*

I suppose that solves part of the problem, Aas grudgingly admitted. *But there's still the Täuschung.*

And then we hunt down and kill every single living member of the Täuschung, said Abiega.

You'd have to eat them too, said Aas as the idea sparked his imagination and he explored its merits. *Otherwise they'll go to Swarm and you'd have to kill and eat them later.*

Right, agreed Abiega. *Once the Täuschung are dead and devoured and Blutblüte is too far away to send people to Swarm, the hell will stop growing. Then, and only then, can you go.*

"How many Täuschung priests are there?" Jateko asked Aas.

Only a few hundred Geisteskranken in the inner core—

"That's not too bad—"

And a *few thousand relatively sane priests leading the public face*, the assassin answered. He hesitated and then said, *Damn.*

"What?"

She'd know.

"She? Pharisäer?"

No. That one over there, Hölle.

Jateko glanced at the other corpse. He'd ignored it as unimportant. Now that he looked closer, he realized the woman bore a familial resemblance to Zerfall. "If I eat her . . ."

You'll know where most of the priests are located. You'll know any secrets she knew.

"I'm eating her," said Jateko, stalking to the body. Leaning down he touched the flawless skin of her face. She was warm. *Good. Fresher is better.* His stomach burbled in happy anticipation.

More problems, said Aas.

"Really? Killing and devouring thousands of Täuschung priests—after hiding a magical sword in the middle of the desert—wasn't problem enough?"

How strong and smart will you be after killing and eating thousands? And remember, hundreds of them are Geisteskranken. How sane will you be?

Jateko, who had just survived having his skull crushed by a morningstar, stood lost in thought. Aas' was a dangerous and frightening question. Though the assassin was, as far as Jateko knew, the only Geisteskranken he'd eaten, already he felt like he strode a slippery slope. He broadcast his every thought, unable to control what those around him heard. Over a dozen voices babbled within him, sometimes vying for attention, sometimes holding conversations amongst themselves. Some worm of self-loathing gnawed at his guts, begged to shake off his humanity and become a glorious condor. Memories that weren't his bubbled to the surface at odd times; had he really eaten his father? He had no hope for sanity. What would he be after devouring hundreds of Geisteskranken priests bent on worshipping a god of suffering? Their thoughts would taint his, *become* his.

None of it changed anything.

He made Zerfall a promise. He'd end this mad religion and end Swarm. He'd set her free.

There's more, said Aas. *How will you get to Swarm?*

"I'll kill myself."

You survived having your head smashed in, pointed out Aas. *How will you kill yourself when you have the health and healing ability of thousands?*

"I'll find a way." He thought for a moment. "Blutblüte."

Okay, said Aas. *Let's say you kill all the Täuschung priests and end the religion. Let's say you manage to kill yourself and get to Swarm. Let's say you manage to kill and devour the millions of people there—a task that will take centuries. Let's say you do all of this. You will have devoured millions of souls. You'll be a god. Now what?*

"I leave Swarm," stated Jateko as if it were the simplest thing in all the world.

How? demanded Aas.

"I will define its reality. I will free myself. And then, with millions of souls residing within me and Swarm being empty, I will shatter Blutblüte."

You're insane, repeated Aas.

"That's why it will work."

Jateko saw Zerfall's hand, palm up, on a desk. The tattooed eye was closed. He retrieved it. Though grey, it showed no sign of rot. He remembered Zerfall saying she'd seen Hölle through that eye, overheard conversations with Zerfall.

"I'll bring the hand. If the eye opens I can tell her what I'm doing, give her hope."

Hunger dragged him back to Hölle's corpse, he could wait no longer. Kneeling, he looked one last time at that flawless skin. So beautiful on the outside, but what had been within was something dark and ugly. Self-loathing killed this woman and now he would devour all she was. Would it end him too?

Opening her shirt, Jateko placed a hand between her breasts, feeling the soft perfection of her flesh. He had to eat. The hunger left him no choice. Next he'd devour Pharisäer and then the corpses of the Täuschung priests he'd slain. He'd take on their delusions, yet more insanity. Would he someday be a god?

He remembered Halber Tod's poem.

"What kind of god does this?"

He split her ribs with his bare hands, exposing the feast within.

TWENTY-FOUR

I don't understand why we need so many hells and Afterdeaths when it's all right here.

— Einsam Geschichtenerzähler

ZERFALL STOOD NAKED, PRESSED on all side by a seething crush of sweating, breathing, screaming humanity, all as naked as she. Hands and mouths sought her, groping, pinching and biting. She barely noticed them. Millions of voices lifted in cresting waves of torment, driven to insanity by the eternal emptiness of this hell. She ignored the symphony of torment.

She thought back to the book of poems Aas gave her. She remembered becoming increasingly aware of the decaying state of her church. The rot she ignored for hundreds of years seemed to infuse her skin, taint her thoughts. She remembered the poem. *What kind of god—*

Memories returned in a crushing tidal wave, memories she found so painful, so steeped in self-loathing, her mind had hidden them from her.

She remembered everything.

She remembered being a little girl, lying feverish in a sweat sodden cot, surrounded by the rotting corpses of her parents and siblings. With dawning horror, she remembered her sister, Hölle, lying beside her.

She remembered how Hölle grew, slowly, over decades, stepping out from under the shadow of her sister. At first Zerfall was proud of her sister's accomplishments. But the self-centred Gefahrgeist in her grew to see Hölle as a threat.

Zerfall, never one for planning, needed Hölle more than Hölle needed her. Over the course of years Zerfall's jealousy at Hölle's many successes ate at her.

The Täuschung had been hers, but now Hölle didn't need her at all, hadn't needed her in decades. Zerfall's sister made all of the church's decisions. She felt as if she was being pushed into the background and no Gefahrgeist could stand that. One hundred years after waking on that cot she looked back at that blurred past, each passing decade making that day less real. Had a god really talked to them?

That blurring gave her an idea. Hölle thought Zerfall couldn't plan, but she'd prove her wrong. Zerfall remembered making the decision to retake her church, to put her sister back in her place. As a powerful Gefahrgeist she knew that to convince others she must first convince herself. She spent decades telling herself she never had a sister, pretending Hölle was nothing but a Fragment, knowing that after centuries she would forget the decision. Once the idea took root, she played with it every day, tasting it, pretending it was real. She spent weeks and then months pretending Hölle was a Fragment

And then years.

Another century passed and that decision blurred. One hundred years after that she forgot it completely. Another century later and she forgot the entire plan. Hölle was right, Zerfall wasn't good at long term plans. But the damage had been done, and the idea lurked deep within.

Zerfall remembered that last day, the way her sister paced the room with such utter confidence, explaining her plans for the church and how, in the next decade, she'd make the Täuschung the most successful religion in all the city-states. She remembered how her every suggestion was waved away, how her sister always had a reason why things should be done her way.

That day in the cot, blurred by centuries, came back to her. She remembered being alone, that her sister had died. She knew then, beyond any doubt, that Hölle was a Fragment.

And Zerfall was a powerful Geisteskranken. Her fear and madness defined reality.

Hölle was real. She wasn't a Fragment, not in the beginning. I stole her life, I made my sister a manifestation. She loathed herself, hated what her selfish need did to her sister. To Jateko.

Zerfall would have laughed at the sick futility of it all, but her mind shuddered and quaked under the strain of understanding and the absolute wretched grief that gripped her heart in its crushing fist.

"What have I done?"

The crush of humanity about her heaved and writhed. Hands clutched and fingers probed and she ignored it all. She sent them here. Humanity with no distraction but more humanity. She'd done this.

"I didn't understand," she said into the stretched and silent scream of the man before her, his face so close to hers she felt his lashes when he blinked. He made small heaving noises, fighting to draw breath in the press of the crowd. No hint of comprehension showed in his wide eyes. Madness. She turned her head, trying to look elsewhere. Madness. Madness in every face. Insanity choked every breath and sound. Some of these souls had been here four hundred years.

Swarm surged and heaved and Zerfall saw her sister pushing through the mob, coming ever closer.

She's dead. We're both dead.

She remembered everything.

She remembered the god speaking to them—remembered for the first time in four centuries—the message, writ into their brains like a herder's brand driven against a cow's flesh.

This responsive reality should be your heaven and yet you make it a hell. I enforce the laws of this reality. What humanity believes defines what is. You can save them. You can make this the utopia it should be. For I too am bound by rules. I serve you, humanity. You shape your own reality. You <desire>, and I am your <manifestations>. You should be as gods, free to shape and play. You must unite humanity. Convince the world that if they believe this is their paradise, it will be so. End this eternal suffering. This is not your prison. You made this hell. You can unmake it.

She remembered waking beside her sister. Each retained only fragments of the message. As they lay huddled on their cot, surrounded by death, breathing the stench of their dead family, recovering from the plague that decimated their village, they pieced it together.

That scene no doubt tainted their translation.

This responsive reality is a hell. I am The One True God and Enforcer of the laws. To save humanity you must unite all in suffering. Penance for your crimes. Convince the world. This is your prison. Make your hell. Beyond this, is paradise. You will be free, as gods.

They made their hell—this childish and poorly imagined reality of suffering—hallucinated it as they huddled together on that rank and rotting cot, terrified and alone.

Four hundred years they spread their doctrine of suffering and now countless millions were trapped here in Swarm, robbed of whatever Afterdeath should have been theirs. Täuschung was a plague, had been built that way on purpose.

Zerfall watched Hölle push through the crowd, fighting to get closer to her twin sister.

Will she hug me or try and kill me?

Zerfall had never been capable of forgiveness, but that wasn't Hölle's way.

When she reaches me, I'll tell her everything. I'll tell her how sorry I am. She wanted to laugh at the thought. The old Zerfall would never apologize, was incapable of even considering it.

She blinked, lost and confused. Hölle was gone. Not lost in the crowd, she winked out of existence

The press of humanity heaved and turned like fish in the ocean, like a flock of birds dancing to some unheard tune. Zerfall moved and turned with it, trapped.

"Where . . ." This time Zerfall did laugh. "Jateko." He must have eaten the woman's corpse, devouring her soul.

Lost and alone, trapped in a hell of her own devising. She rode the swarm, unresisting.

Swarm had no time; the rising and setting of a sun would have been a distraction from the suffering. Nothing broke the eternal monotony.

Days passed. Weeks.

Years.

Sometimes the eye tattooed on her left hand opened and she saw Jateko. He talked to her, telling her of his plans to rescue her. Telling her not to lose hope. He changed, was different each time. The souls he ate took their toll and she saw it in his eyes. Madness. He got stronger, smarter. He developed new Geisteskranken powers.

It was killing him. Or at least killing the youth she loved.

She'd plead with Jateko, begging him to leave her, to save himself.

He couldn't hear her.

Sometimes Zerfall died, raped and murdered, or beaten to death by someone who recognized her. Sometimes people killed her for no reason other than a moment's diversion.

Each time she awoke, once again riding the sea of Swarm.

She never got hungry and she never needed sleep.

Swarm went on forever.

TWENTY-FIVE

Condone the torture of the powerless.
What kind of god does this?
Preaching pain and emptiness.
What kind of god does this?
    —excerpt from the poem, "The Täuschung", by Halber Tod, Cotardist Poet

NORTH, IN THE FARTHEST-MOST reaches of the boreal forests separating the Verschlinger tribes from the civilized city-states, Jateko crouched over the gutted remains of his last victim, licking his fingers clean. One more small voice joined the cacophony bubbling about his thoughts. There were so many now—thousands—that conversations with individual souls rarely took place. Still, Abiega, Gogoko, and Aas sometimes managed to make themselves heard. He wasn't sure why. Was it because they were among the first, or was it more a matter of their strong personalities? Or maybe he turned to them because they were familiar.

A colossal bear, winter coat moulting and hanging grey and tattered in knotted curtains, shambled from the forest. Rearing onto its hind legs, it watched Jateko, nostrils flaring. The beast towered over eleven-feet-tall and must have weighed over two thousand pounds.

"What's left is yours," Jateko called to the bear as he sauntered away; such a creature was no danger to him. "I've taken what I need."

He walked through the trees, enjoying the crunch of snow and the dry snap of pine needles beneath his feet. He breathed deep the sharp and commingled scents of hot blood and white spruce.

"That's the last of the Täuschung, is it not?" he asked aloud.

It is, answered Hölle, knowing the question was addressed to her.

Thousands of strange desires niggled at his thoughts. Many of those he devoured were Geisteskranken; the mad and delusional of the world. He had their strengths and their weaknesses.

Jateko knew thousands of delusions. All within a thousand strides heard his thoughts. He sparked raging infernos with a thought, *twisted* into a myriad of animals and monsters, swelled impossible muscles, or caused his flesh to rot and peel.

Much as Zerfall's flesh rotted and peeled, pointed out Aas.

"Ah, the assassin of my conscience speaks," said Jateko.

You're trying not to think of her.

Jateko ignored Aas' words. "It's time to return to the desert. I must retrieve Blutblüte." Jateko buried the sword in the desert thousands of miles east of where even the hardiest Basamortuan tribes dared venture.

He twisted, his body crumbling apart and reforming as a monstrous condor with a thirty-foot wingspan. He pushed himself into the air, the powerful beat of his wings toppling trees beneath him as he rose.

He flew east and south. Not a god, but not a man either. Eight hours later he watched the last of the Kälte Mountains pass beneath him. Aas babbled on about how he grew up south of here, living in his father's basement, terrified of the world. Jateko, long accustomed to hearing voices in his head, ignored him. To the east stretched the endless wastes of the Basamortuan Desert. And beyond that . . .

"Someday I want to cross the Basamortuan," said Jateko. "I want to see what is west of the Gezackt Mountains, north of the Verschlinger tribes, and south of the Salzwasser Ocean."

There is no someday, said Aas. *You made Zerfall a promise.*

Jateko flew on, beyond the lands of the desert tribes and into the unknown heart of the Basamortuan. Far below the dunes faded to a soft pink and then darkened to the deep sanguine of rotting blood. Nothing lived out here, no life moved beneath him. His belly grumbled in complaint. *Soon*, he told it. *Soon you'll have your fill.* Swarm's millions. Would that satisfy his insatiable hunger?

No. There could be no end to this. The more he ate the more he needed to eat. When he was a boy, mocked for his weak chin, concave chest, and scrawny build, he ate once every other day. Sometimes, when food was scarce, he ate every third or fourth day. Now, a muscled hulk of a man, he ate several times a day, given the chance. And he ate nothing but human brains, hearts, livers, and kidneys. He remembered how difficult—impossible, even—it had been to devour the brain and organs of a grown man in one sitting. It was all too easy now.

Jateko landed in an endless rolling wasteland of red sand. No rock or plant or dune differentiated this spot from any other and yet he knew Blutblüte was buried here. His memory was flawless. The desert wind brought him the scent of blood and souls far to the east.

"I knew the desert wasn't the end. I knew something was out here."

I wonder what they're like, mused Aas. *I wonder what they believe? Is their reality like the city-states or have they shaped it differently?*

"We should go look. It wouldn't take long."

No, said Aas. *You just want to eat them.*

Jateko couldn't argue that. Hunger built in his belly, clawing for attention.

Stooping, he dug his hand into the sand, wrapping strong, thick fingers around the sword's pommel, and drew it forth. He examined the blade. Years in the sand hadn't changed it. It was plain and simple.

So small. Such a little nothing, and yet so much, muttered Gedankenlos from somewhere within.

How will you kill yourself? Aas asked. *You've been stabbed and beheaded, burnt and trampled. What can kill you now?*

"Belief," answered Jateko.

But the problem wasn't killing himself, the problem was *wanting* to kill himself. He'd devoured Slavers, Gefahrgeist teetering at the Pinnacle, and ignored their desperate need for worship. They were nothing. He was legion, defined reality as only a population of thousands could. He'd been burned by Hassebrand, walked through sheets of fire, unscathed. He'd shrugged off the savage attacks of deranged Wütend, ignored the reality twisting beliefs of Micropics and Macropics, devoured the swollen and festering flesh of the Befallen. They were all within him now, part of who and what he was. He suffered their delusions.

You aren't Wahnist, Aas said, catching Jateko's attention. *I was wrong about that. You're a Narcisstic; it is your original, and I'd guess only, innate and personal delusion. And, as you devour souls and grow in strength, your Narcisstic tendencies grow in power as well. Think about it. In spite of an absolute lack of evidence, you left the desert convinced you were bound for greatness. It was nothing but a grandiose fantasy.*

Jateko stood for a long time, staring at the sword clutched in his fist. The sun dropped toward the horizon and the temperature plummeted until he saw his breath as plumes of swirling mist. Cold was nothing to him and he ignored it.

Is all this delusion? Was every choice he made the result of an inflated sense of self-worth?

The thought he might not be important tightened his chest. *I matter. I am the All Consuming!*

The voices in his head fell quiet.

"Zerfall," he said. "Even if I don't matter, she does."

Does she? Aas asked. *Why? Is it her, or your need for her that matters?*

"What's the difference?" demanded Jateko.

And therein, I suspect, lies our answer.

"I'm about to kill myself," said Jateko. "I am about to send myself to hell. All for her. That's not love?"

If that's really why you're doing it. You don't feel a touch of excitement at the thought of millions of trapped souls, waiting to be devoured?

Jateko licked his lips. Gods he was hungry.

Exactly, said Aas. *You think you're going to be a god. You think you're* destined *to be a god.*

"Think of all the good I could do," protested Jateko. "You yourself said that every religion and city-state was run by Gefahrgeist. I could replace a hundred petty tyrants, unite all humanity under one benevolent god. I could bring peace to all—"

And there we have it, said Aas. *Just like the gods-damned Geborene.* He laughed, mockingly. *Maybe a little Narcisstic?*

Again the assassin was right. Jateko wanted to tell Aas to shut up but he had no control over the voices in his head.

You made Zerfall a promise, Aas reminded him.

"I remember," growled Jateko.

But do you understand why?

"Because she thought Swarm was evil."

She thought Swarm was evil because it trapped souls there, robbed them of their Afterdeath.

"I remember."

Robbed them of all chance of redemption.

"I remember!"

You're doing the same thing.

Jateko opened his mouth to argue and then stopped. Once again, the assassin was right. Every soul he devoured was trapped within him for all time. Or at least until he died.

"I don't want to die," Jateko admitted. "Life is special. It's amazing. Death . . ." he shuddered.

The only way to save her, is to devour her too. Even if you escape Swarm, she'll be stuck in here with the rest of us.

"Stuck?"

You think we want to be here? We're the mad little voices in your head. And most of the time you ignore us. We're helpless. Hopeless. Prisoners. And soon there will be millions in here.

With only a few thousand devoured souls he was already near godlike. With millions . . .

How ravenous will you be then? asked Aas. *Will you be able to resist the hunger?*

It was already too much. Yesterday he ate pounds of human meat and now he felt like his gut was devouring itself. He'd have to eat soon.

You know how to free the souls within you.

He'd have to die.

Jateko remembered Zerfall reading Halber Tod's poems to him as they rode: "What kind of god does this?"

"What kind of Afterdeath awaits someone who has done the things I have done?"

Aas ignored his question. *If you love Zerfall, prove it.*

"You've been building to that the entire time," muttered Jateko, knowing it was true.

Consume the world. Or keep your promise to the woman you claim to love and give it all up. For her.

"Aas, you're right." Jateko turned Blutblüte and pressed its sharp point into his chest, sliding it between his ribs. "I promised Zerfall I would end Swarm." He felt the blade prick his heart and paused, hesitating.

Do you know what Zerfall liked most about you? Aas asked. *Think back, remember how ignorant and helpless you were. She could have abandoned you at any time and chose not to. What do you think she saw in you?*

Jateko couldn't answer. What had she seen in the scrawny youth he'd been?

You were honest, said Aas. *You never lied. Not to her, not to anyone. Not once.*

Jateko drove Blutblüte into his heart—

—and stood naked, surrounded by an impossible crush of seething humanity. Millions of throats screamed deafening torment.

He added his own voice to the clamour, screaming "Zerfall!"

Someone grabbed at Jateko, clawing with sharp fingernails and raking long gashes along an arm. He turned to see a woman, fingers stuffed into her mouth, greedily sucking them clean of blood. She laughed and giggled and screeched incoherent noise. It wasn't Zerfall. Jateko punched her, shattering her skull and killing her instantly.

"One down. Fifteen million more to . . ."

He watched, jostled by the heaving crowd, as the woman's body faded and, nearby, an identical one appeared. A score of heartbeats later her eyes snapped open and she clawed her way back to her feet, screaming the entire time. Once upright, she hurled herself at him again, fingers raking and clawing. He killed her again, this time tearing her head from her body.

An old man groped at Jateko's genitals and the Basamortuan killed him without a thought. Turning back to the woman, he saw her—once again whole—climb to her feet and search the crowd for him.

{I forgot to mention that, didn't I,} said Aas. *{You can't keep just killing her. Death is no escape from Swarm. You have to eat her before she returns. I'd suggest the brain first.}*

This time, when she attacked, he grabbed hold of her by the arm and snapped her neck. Pulling her skull apart he tore free wet worms of brain and stuffed them into his mouth. Next he tore open her ribcage and tore free her heart, slamming that too into his still chewing mouth. Kidney and liver followed. He stood over her corpse keeping the crowd at bay through sheer inhuman strength, waiting.

A small, mad voice joined the other in his head and he felt fractionally stronger.

[*I can do this. I can kill and eat them all.*] Jateko grinned bloody teeth at the crowd around him and, having heard his thoughts, they howled, throwing themselves upon him. Jateko killed. He killed and ate. Sometimes those he killed fell beyond his reach and again rose to hurl themselves at him in mad abandon. Did they understand he offered an escape? He had no chance to explain.

Jateko killed. He grew stronger.

He killed. He ate.

No sanity could survive this hell. He made a terrible mistake in coming here. He should have found some other way of saving Zerfall, of keeping his promise.

Time meant nothing and yet he remained painfully aware of every passing second.

Jateko killed. Reality was blood and brains. Stringy strands of heart muscle caught in his teeth, threatened to choke him. And still he killed.

Sheer numbers dragged him down and they piled upon him, massed human flesh, slick with sweat and blood. They crushed him beneath their weight, punching and biting and clawing. Calling the Hassebrands he devoured to the fore, he loosed their self-loathing and burnt those crushing him to ash. They'd rise again, but he needed space.

He stood.

They came, crashing upon him like a tidal wave of psychotic flesh. Death meant nothing to them; they knew they'd rise again.

He killed, stuffing bits of humanity into his mouth whenever circumstances allowed.

[*Zerfall, where are you?*]

Jateko killed and he ate.

Stronger.

Crazier.

Hungrier with each life devoured.

His sanity stretched thin, like sinew pulled so tight as to become translucent.

{What will be left of you once you have slain and devoured the last soul? Will you retain enough self to do as you promised? Will you kill yourself?}

[I don't know,] answered Jateko honestly. He swallowed another bloody mouthful, not even knowing what it was. *[Gods, I am so hungry.]*

Jateko pulled limbs off people and used them to club others to the ground. Sometimes he gnawed on arms and legs, knowing it was pointless, but desperate to fill the insatiable pit within.

[Aas, you made a terrible mistake.]

{Me?}

[You tried to trick me. You thought getting me to come here would save the city-states, save the world. You were wrong. Before, I had some chance of controlling the hunger. Not now. I will kill and eat every one of these people. I won't be able to stop. Already can't. I'll kill them, and then I'll go back. I'll be too hungry to choose otherwise.]

{What about Zerfall?}

Jateko sobbed mad laughter. *[For all I know, I've already killed and eaten her. I see nothing but blood.]*

Jateko killed and ate, his mind detached from his actions. The screaming within his head had long since become as loud as the screaming without. There was not a single sane soul in all Swarm. He ate them all. Took on what they were.

[Aas, I've been thinking.]

{Yes?}

[There are roughly fifteen million souls here.]

{That's Hölle's best guess.}

[Assume I kill and devour one every twenty seconds.]

{It will be slower at first,} said Aas. *{But the rate should increase when the population is reduced.}*

[It will take me roughly five million minutes to depopulate this hell.]

{You sound oddly calm.}

[That's eighty-three thousand, three hundred and thirty three hours.}

{*Three thousand, four hundred and seventy two days,*} said Aas.

[*A little over nine and a half years,*] said Jateko. [*The city-states have perhaps a decade before I return.*]

Jateko tore life apart and devoured it.

Stronger.

Crazier.

Doomed.

TWENTY-SIX

The sane never truly live.
The crazy never truly die.

—Versklaver Denker, Gefahrgeist Philosopher.

I N A LAND WITH no sun, no day or night, time became a myth. With nothing but pain and suffering to hold against the passing seconds as measurement, each heart beat was an eternity.

Zerfall floated among the souls she'd sent to her hell. Sometimes she was ignored and took the opportunity to dredge her thoughts over and over trying to remember Wahrergott's message. Sometimes someone recognized her and the mob would turn on her, beating and biting, clawing, and choking, until she died. If she had the misfortune of arising near enough to her tormentors to be seen, she'd die again. Sometime she died dozens, even scores of times before she returned beyond the easy reach of those who sought her death.

Each time she died Wahrergott's words became less real. Had she imagined everything? Was the One True god nothing more than the fevered nightmare of a young girl dying of some plague?

Jateko hadn't contacted her through the tattooed eye in her hand in what seemed like years. Maybe longer. Was he dead? Had someone finally dragged him down? Had the gods of the city-states turned against him?

Or had he changed his mind? Had he seen the madness of his path and walked away?

She hoped so.

She decided to discover what lay at the edge of Swarm. She pushed through the mob for an eternity, trying to stay to a true course. She died more than fifty times and killed twice that before she gave up. She never found an end. Maybe Swarm went on forever or curved somehow back in on itself. Maybe she'd been too deep in the sea of souls and given up before she escaped. She thought back to her time in the desert, *Santu Itsasoa*, the living corpses lashed to cacti, and wished she was still there.

If Swarm was endless, shouldn't there be space without people? Did these souls crowd together in some need for company only to torture each other, or was there no escape?

Someone behind her screamed and wrapped stick-thin arms around her neck. She died, choking and kicking, fighting to the last. She never saw who killed her.

She missed her parents, her little brother. *I miss my sister.*

Someone pulled out a fistful of her hair before they were moved beyond reach by the teaming swarm. Humanity compressed and expanded in response to something she couldn't see, waves passing through a medium of souls.

If only Hölle hadn't sent Aas to kill me. She could have died in the desert, rotted to nothing. None of this would have happened.

Swarm crushed her, and she couldn't breathe. Screams shattered the air, all the world tasted of panic and the stench of loosed bowels. The mob retreated from something, pushing and punching in a desperate attempt to flee. There was nowhere to go.

Who here hasn't died a thousand times? What could move undead and undying souls to fear?

Blood rained down upon her but when she looked up the sky was as clear as always.

A severed arm windmilled past, spiralling blood in lacy expanding wheels. A man barely visible through the crowd clawed at his own arms, raking flesh and washing himself in gore. He screamed, eyes clenched and heat pulsed off him in waves. Zerfall's hair curled and shrank, blasted to dust as her scalp boiled.

Hassebrand. A powerful one if he could define reality even in this crush of humanity. Not that there were any sane here to contradict his insanity.

He cleared an area around them, turning countless souls to ash.

They're not dead. Not really. No one escaped Swarm.

A man, bound in bulging muscles, impossibly handsome, strode into the cleared area. He was as naked as every soul in Swarm but clothed from head to toe in a thick sheen of blood.

Jateko. He'd aged, looked to be in his late thirties now. *How long have I been here?* Madness haunted his eyes. Reality twisted around him, writhed and suffered. The mud at his feet boiled and he was unhurt.

The Hassebrand lashed him with fire and Jateko crossed the distance in two long strides, tore the man's heart from his chest and devoured it in a single bite. Zerfall watched as her friend split the still living man's head and scooped out the brain, shovelling it into his mouth. Jateko tore the rib cage open, casting aside the sundered cage of bones and ripping free the kidneys and liver. These too he ate. It all looked so very practised. When he finished he looked up, scanning the crowd fighting to retreat from him. Swarm had compressed and there was nowhere for them to go. His eyes passed over Zerfall before returning to her. He licked his lips, ravenous hunger writ across chiselled features, and stalked toward her.

He's going to eat me. She should have felt something more. Fear. Something.

"Jateko."

He stopped, blinking down at her. He'd grown taller.

"Jateko," she said again. "You came." Guilt crushed her and she crumbled to the ground. Her need had done this to him. Her selfish desire had driven this innocent boy mad.

All of this is my fault.

He too dropped to his knees, tears spilling free. "Of course I came. I love you."

"You shouldn't have. I should have let you go home—"

"I never would have left you. You needed me. No one ever needed me before."

She loathed herself. The person she'd been, the person she'd become.

"I ended the Täuschung," he said, reaching toward her. "For you. I killed them all. I ate them all. No new souls have come to Swarm in years."

She listened in mute horror as he explained his plan, as he revealed the terrible mistake he made.

"I can't stop," he said. "I am the All Consuming. I will devour every soul in the city-states. I will eat the world clean until only I remain." He hung his head in shame.

Zerfall crawled to him, held him in her arms. "This is my fault. I thought I was doing the right thing. I always did. Even at the very beginning. Evil is doing the right thing no matter what the cost." She laughed without humour, tears spilling free. "Evil is thinking you know what the right thing even is."

Jateko wrapped his arms around her, held her close, face buried in her hair. They clung to each other, naked, caked in gore. The gathered souls of Swarm gave them space, fear keeping them back.

"If you don't somehow kill yourself once you've finished here," she whispered into his ear. "You'll be just as evil as Swarm. You can't trap these souls within you forever. You need to let them free."

He leaned back, regarding her with bright intelligence. "Would that be the *right* thing to do?"

She examined him through her tears. He was beautiful, perfect in every way. "You know the answer to that," she said.

"I'm sorry," he said.

"It's—"

JATEKO KILLED HER, CRUSHED her in his arms. She'd been beautiful, everything he ever imagined. He waited for so long for this moment and now he had her he couldn't stop. The hunger left no room for thought. He split her apart and devoured all she was, sobbing as he chewed. Numb terror emptied him. He killed his love. She needed him and he failed her.

Her voice joined the cacophony within. There were too many now, millions of voices clamouring for attention.

Hunger drove Jateko to his feet.

He stalked Swarm, killing and devouring, only nominally aware that the voices within him one by one fell silent.

He hunted, a thoughtless predator, until he stood alone, a Swarm of one. Millions of souls existed within him and yet no one spoke. An empty hell of nothing and silence.

A dim memory fought for attention. *You define this reality now.*

That meant something, was important. He came here for a reason.

To eat.

No, there'd been more. There'd been love.

What was love in comparison to hunger?

How much does a soul weigh?

He felt heavy with souls. Each was its own burden.

He was a god.

What kind of god does this?

Zerfall. He killed her. He ate her.

Jateko had a distant memory of thinking this would somehow make them closer. He remembered thinking they'd be one. It wasn't like that at all. She was inside him but he couldn't hear her. Such utter stillness; the silence of the empty grave.

You made a promise. End Swarm.

Promises mattered. He remembered that.

Jateko laughed, a choking sob. "I should stay here forever. If I end Swarm I'll return to the city-states."

You have to kill yourself once you return. You promised.

He had no choice. He couldn't stay here in this empty hell. He was hungry.

Jateko defined his reality.

He ended Swarm with a thought and stood in the depths of the Basamortuan desert, surrounded for thousands of miles in every direction by sands stained red. Standing exactly as he had decades ago when he first killed himself. Blutblüte still pierced his heart. Jateko drew the sword free and the wound healed. He examined the blade. It was nothing, just a sword.

Souls. He smelled souls. Thousands and thousands of souls. And the reek of madness.

Turning, he found himself facing a disordered mob of people and for a moment thought he was back in Swarm. Insanity pulsed through the crowd in waves; not a single sane person stood before him. They were all Geisteskranken, but not all were mortals. Also gathered here were the gods, numen, and Ascended of Geld and the Basamortuan.

Harea, God of the Desert, Lord of the Sands, stood shoulder to shoulder with Schuld, a minor Geld god who oversaw the punishment of defaulting debtors. Heriotza, Goddess Death, Harea's estranged wife, stood among a gaggle of preening Swordsmen. Every breed of Geisteskranken was represented here a thousand times over. There were even dozens of Kleptics trying to sneak up behind Jateko. He ignored them.

The air shimmered and twisted over the mob, ravaged by competing delusions. Reality was stretched thin here and he felt like the very fabric of existence might tear.

A young girl no more than sixteen stepped from the crowd. She carried a bloody shard of broken mirror in slashed fingers and her arms and legs were covered in long self-inflicted welts. She held up the mirror and he saw the same young girl reflected there even though the mirror faced him.

"I have seen the futures," said the Reflection.

Futures, plural. Interesting. "Tell me," said Jateko. He had no fear. Not all the madness in the world could stop him.

"In one future you surrender to us. You allow us to end you. Humanity lives on."

"And in the other?"

"You are the end of all life on this world. You are the last evil of mankind."

"I am the All Consuming," agreed Jateko, hunger bubbling up from his gut.

"You don't have to—"

Jateko killed her, pulled her head from her shoulders with a single hand, crushed her skull in his fist, and sucked the brains out.

"There is no future," he told them, tossing the corpse aside.

Thousands of deranged voices rose in deafening challenge and they were upon him. This wasn't like facing the tortured souls of Swarm. These were Geisteskranken, they embraced their madness, honed it. They were the most dangerously broken souls Geld and the Basamortuan had to offer.

A mob of Swordsmen surrounded him, cutting and stabbing, and Blutblüte shattered blocking the first attack. Jateko knocked swords aside with his bare hands, smashing those who came within reach. Half a dozen long blades found his flesh, opening him wide. A woman eviscerated him, spilling his guts into the sand before he sent her shattered corpse spinning away with a backhand blow.

Micropics tried to diminish him and Getrennt sought to distance him from reality. Such utter madness unleashed in such a small area sundered reality and the world frayed apart. Nothing was real. Everything was real. Hallucinated monsters came screaming from the darkest depths of the blackest souls to hurl themselves at Jateko. Therianthropes, wolves and dragons and bears and tigers, swarmed him, biting and clawing. Ascended heroes, trapped by the stories built around their lives, immortalized by the need of the sane masses for hope, threw themselves at him. Howling Hassebrands lit the world alight with their misery, fused sand to glass, and did as much damage to their fellow Geisteskranken as they did to Jateko. Bodies burned. The world burned.

The mad are not well suited to teamwork.

Had that been Zerfall's' voice?

Harea, God of the Sands, backed by the belief and worship of thousands of Basamortuan tribes, towered above Jateko. The god bent his will against him, tried to erase him from reality, tried to undo the knot of his story, remake reality as if Jateko had never been.

But a few thousand deranged souls incapable of working in concert were nothing; Jateko was millions. Jateko was reality.

I am legion.

Jateko, having devoured scores of Unwirklichkeit, turned his attention on the desert god. *[You're nothing more than the manifestation of the beliefs and fears of ignorant savages.]* Reality thinned around the god, holes tearing in the fabric of what was, exposing the decaying chaos beneath. *[I don't believe in you.]* Harea became indistinct, as if viewed through a heavy fog. And with a thought, the winds of faith blew that fog apart. The desert god was no more.

Jateko stalked through the nightmare of riven reality, killing with his bare hands, sometimes stuffing bits of humanity into his mouth. His bowels trailed along behind him, dragging corpses who had become entangled there, and he ignored the wound.

Jateko, stop. I need you. You have to listen.

He knew that voice.

Jateko stopped, stood motionless. He ignored those who sought his death. "I can't stop," he said. "I don't want to stop. I am the All Consuming, foretold by a thousand generations of sorgin."

WHILE JATEKO DEVOURED THE last souls of Swarm, Zerfall found she could communicate with the others trapped within him. She sought out Aas and Hölle, her sister. She apologized to both, begged forgiveness for her crimes. They immediately forgave her and she came to a realization. She hadn't changed. They forgave her because she needed their forgiveness and they had no choice.

She understood: Jateko wasn't Swarm, he was worse. Much worse. There was no physicality, just the crush of souls demanding attention, begging to be heard. Jateko was their only window to reality, and he ignored them. Here she was helpless, had no influence on the world. Even the brutal interactions of Swarm were better than this fleshless existence. He'd kill and eat, and she'd be trapped here, helpless, forever.

She knew what she had to do.

While not a Slaver, she was nonetheless an incredibly powerful Gefahrgeist. As Jateko devoured Swarm, Zerfall spread like a plague, bending the millions of trapped souls to her will. They had nowhere to go, no escape, and she crushed them, silenced them with her need to be heard. There might be millions of souls in here, but she was Zerfall. Her need had birthed a god. Her delusions spawned a hell. She was by far the most broken soul within the Basamortuan.

And she would rule here. She had to. She needed to. It was the right thing to do. It was her only way out.

She knew what she had to do and hated herself for it. Her selfish need had brought him to this, and now it would end him. *He deserves better*. But she couldn't give it to him.

By the time Jateko faced the gathered madness of Geld and the Basamortuan tribes, Zerfall ruled the souls within him. All bowed to her need. She commanded their every thought, their every belief. She was the god within the god.

Jateko, stop. I need you. You have to listen.

His love and her need stopped him and he stood listening.

You promised me, she said. *You promised you'd kill yourself. We fought to end Swarm, to free those souls. What you are doing is wrong.*

She knew he had never really understood who she was, what she was. For all his faults, he never would have followed her if he'd known her evil.

All these souls he devoured infected him, but they remained separate too, retained the shape of the people they'd been. Zerfall was whole. And while he devoured hundreds of Gefahrgeist and could make use of their power, he never had. Not once. That kind of foul manipulation wasn't Jateko, never would be. He might kill and eat people because his hunger left him no choice, but he'd never willingly steal their freedom. Trapped within him, it seemed a contradiction, but Zerfall understood and appreciated the difference. What he could never do she did with ease. Ever since that day she awoke on that cot she'd bent people to her needs. Her sister. The people of Geld. The priests of the Täuschung. Jateko.

Much as she hated herself for it, it was easy.

And now she had a driving need. She needed to free these souls. She needed to undo the damage she had wrought. But those were the surface needs, the lies she told herself. Zerfall knew this truth, but hid from it. To fool the masses one must first fool oneself, and she'd been doing it for centuries.

What she truly needed was to escape the horrors of her crimes. She needed to end herself.

Jateko thought he defined reality. He was wrong, as deluded and confused as ever.

He didn't define reality, she did.

She hated herself for what she would do, for what she had done. But as with all Gefahrgeist, she too was a slave to her needs. And now, with the combined belief of the millions of souls trapped within Jateko, she turned her need against him.

The man I loved would never do this, she said. *Everything we suffered through was all to free the souls in Swarm. You've replaced one prison with another. All the evils of my long life pale before the crime you now commit.*

She felt him hesitate, his need to please her stalling him where his own will could not.

I can't—

You made me a promise, she interrupted, knowing how important honesty was to the Basamortuan. *You promised you'd free the souls, and the only way to do that is to end yourself.*

The deranged of Geld hurled themselves upon Jateko and he ignored them. His wounds healed and their madness was nothing. *I hunger.* Yet he stood motionless, held by her voice.

You can't let all this be for nothing, she said.

Some city-states god Zerfall didn't recognize smashed at Jateko with stone fists, and Jateko channelled the hundreds of Hassebrand within him and seared the area around him clear of life. The god was gone, hot ash in the desert wind.

This isn't who you are, she said. *The man I loved was good, wanted to help people. It was his greatest trait and what I loved most about you. I miss that man. I need you to be that man again. I'm trapped in here with the others. Don't do this to me. Free me. Free everyone.* She loathed herself.

Jateko listened, bound by the chains of her desires. Everything he'd done since she found him had been to please her. She understood all to well: Jateko's need was to be needed. Had he made a single free choice since that day he found her in the sands? Zerfall didn't think so. Even when she told him to leave her, to return to the tribes, she hadn't wanted him to and he stayed.

She'd lied to herself, told herself she was someone different, that she'd changed. She knew who she was. She was who she had always been.

Freeing these souls was the right thing to do, but that wasn't why she did it.

Zerfall bent the united will of the millions of souls in Jateko against him.

I need you to die. I need you to kill yourself. For me.

She left him no choice.

"For you," he said. "Anything."

PERSONALITIES

CITY STATES

Aas Geier: Priests of the Täuschung. Therianthrope - condor.

Ängstlich: Täuschung priest. Capgrast. Husband of Dämonin Schwindel.

Beherrscher: The manifestation of Selbs Bitterkeit's self-hatred.

Dämonin Schwindel: Täuschung priest. Wife of ängstlich

Einsam Geschichtenerzähler: Geisteskranken poet and story-teller to whom an impossible number of works is attributed.

Forscherin: A natural scientist living in Auseinander. She studied the mechanisms of the world and the laws governing reality.

Gedankenlos: Täuschung priest. Captain of the inner guard.

Gefräßige Wut: Täuschung priest. Wendigast

Giernach Reichtum: Highly ranked member of the Verzweiflung Banking Conglomerate, worshipper of the One True God.

Grausamer Schlächter: Self-proclaimed greatest swordsman in all Geldangelegenheiten.

Halber Tod: Cotardist Poet.

Hexenwerk: Aas's doll. Made of his hair, snot, and feathers.

Hölle: One of two founders of the Täuschung.

Morgan: Ascended god of the Geborene Damonen.

Nimmer: Täuschung priest. Getrennt.

Pharisäer: A fragment of Hölle's crumbling personality. A manifestation of her pain caused by her attempts to distance herself from what she plans.

Selbs Bitterkeit: Doppelgangist. Täuschung priestess.

Starker Narr: Täuschung priest. Dysmorphic.

Tod: Zerfall's dead horse.

Unbedacht: Täuschung priest. Wütend.

Unterwürfig: High priest of the public face of the Täuschung.

Vergangener Traum: Once the best Swordsman in Grenzstadt, slain by Grausamer Schlächter.

Versklaver Denker: Gefahrgeist Philosopher.

Wahrergott: The One True God, enforcer of the rules of reality. Worshipped by the Täuschung.

Wahrheit Ertrinkt: Philosopher.

Zahlen: Accountant for the Täuschung.

Zerfall: Founder of the Täuschung. Powerful Gefahrgeist.

Zweifelsschicksal: Mehrere Philosopher who eventually lost control of his multiple personalities and fragmented. Legend has it that he is still alive and travelling as a large crowd of people in search of the original.

BASAMORTUAN DESERT

Abiega: First warrior of the Etsaiaren tribe.

Axolagabe: Warrior of the Etsaiaren tribe.

Etsita: Mother of Jateko.

Gazte: Young warrior in the Etsaiaren tribe.

Gogoko: First warrior of the Hasiera tribe.

Harea: God of the desert, worshipped by most tribes of the Basamortuan Desert.

Heriotza: Goddess Death.

Jakintsua: *Sorgin* of the Hasiera tribe.

Jateko: Outcast from the Hasiera tribe.

Urutiko: Previous *sorgin* (wise woman) of the Hasiera tribe—before Jakintsua.

GEISTESKRANKEN
[THE DELUSIONAL]

Attonitatic: Hears two voices—one (on the left) says to do good things, the other (on the right) says to do evil.

Befallen: (Ekbom's Syndrome): Believe they are infested with parasites, bugs, or insects crawling on or under the skin.

Capgrast (Caprgras Syndrome): Believe a relative or spouse has been replaced by an impostor (often demonic in nature).

Comorbidic (Comorbidity): A person with multiple delusions that have reached the manifestation stage. Konig is a Comorbidic as he is a Gefahrgeist, Doppelgangist, *and* a developing Mirrorist. Comorbidity often marks the final days of a Geisteskranken as it signifies an increasingly decaying mental state.

Cotardist (Cotard's Syndrome): Believe they are dead. Often combined with the belief they are rotting or missing internal organs.

Doppelgangist (Syndrome of Subjective Doubles): Believe a double of themselves is carrying out independent actions.

Dysmorphic (Dysmorphic Syndrome): These folks are overly worried about a perceived defect in their physical features. They want to look different so badly their appearance actually changes. Due to their obsession, they are unable to see the changes and still think themselves defective. Many believe they are so unspeakably hideous they are unable to interact with others. This will eventually spiral out of control. Most Dysmorphics eventually withdraw from society and end in suicide. Many become abnormally thin, muscled, large-breasted, or exaggerated specimens of physical perfection . . . in one area.

Fregolist (Fregoli Delusion): Believe various people are actually the same person in disguise.

Gefahrgeist (Sociopath): Sociopaths lack empathy (the ability to feel for the pain and suffering of others) and morality. They are driven by their need to achieve and rule in social circles.

Geisteskranken (Delusionist): Reality is responsive to the beliefs of humanity. Under normal circumstances it requires large numbers of people—all believing the same thing—to affect change. The more people who believe something, the more real their belief becomes. Geisteskranken are capable of believing something so utterly and completely—are insane enough—to affect noticeable changes in reality all by themselves. Most are only mildly neurotic and can cause minor or subtle changes. The truly powerful are also that much more deranged.

Getrennt: (Depersonalization Disorder): Disconnected from one's body, detached from own thoughts and feelings. Disconnected from reality. These folks often feel as if they live in a dream state (some will deny reflection in a mirror is theirs, and can be confused with Mirrorists. Some have out-of-body experiences. Depression, low self-esteem, panic attacks, self-harm, and extreme phobias often result. Some feel as though time is 'passing' them by and they are not in the notion of the present. Getrennt are also often comorbidic and suffer from Unwirklichkeit (Derealization).

Halluzin (Hallucinations): These folks are capable of manifesting hallucinations in one or more senses. Minor Halluzin might just cause people to smell whatever the Geisteskranken is thinking about. Powerful Halluzin can hallcinate in all five senses and twist local reality.

Hassebrand (Pyromaniac): Set fires as an outlet for their repressed rage and loneliness.

Intermetic (Syndrome of Intermetamorphosis): Believe people swap identities with each other while maintaining the same appearance.

Inverse Square Law: (Inverse Square): The further one gets from a Geisteskranken, the weaker the effect of their delusions. Stand next to a Gefahrgeist, and you'll soon be desperate to be their best friend. View that same Gefahrgeist from a safe distance, and you'll see them for the manipulative arse they are. As a Geisteskranken's mental state decays—and their delusions gain in strength—the range of that power increases, but the inverse square law still applies. There are rare exceptions, where the Geisteskranken's delusions pertain specifically to distant objects.

Kleptic (Kleptomaniac): Are compelled to steal things (usually of little or no value). They are often not even aware they've committed the theft.

Körperidentität: Body Integrity Disorder: The belief life would be so much better as an amputee. The feeling is accompanied by the actual urge to amputate one or more healthy limbs to actually follow through on those feelings.

Krankheit: (Somatoform Disorder): Believe they are always sick and or injured to the point that they are. Extreme cases believe they have lost bodily functions—they might become blind, deaf, numb, or paralysed due to their delusions. These folks are often comorbidic and Dysmorphic as well, believing a limb is particularly weak and withering.

Macropic: (Macropsia): Objects are perceived to be larger than they are . . . and so they become larger. This could apply to a person, limb, or object of any type. A spider can be seen to be the size of a house. Run! These folks are responsible for many of the world's monsters. This is sometimes combined with Micropesia.

Mass Delusion: Some Geisteskranken are capable of convincing the sane masses of all manner of craziness. Typically the stolid beliefs of the sane masses counteract the delusions of the insane. There are however exceptions to that rule. If a Geisteskranken gains followers at a slow enough rate, they can effectively create a new normal. The beliefs of the Geisteskranken become the beliefs of the masses. This is particularly common with the smarter Slaver-type Gefahrgeist. Erbrechen Gedanke (Beyond Redemption) is a perfect example. In these cases, the belief of the masses actually supports the Geisteskranken increasing their ability to twist reality and the range of that ability.

Mehrere (Schizophrenic): Are so sure they are more than one person . . . they actually are! The various people they become can have wildly varying physical and mental traits. The truly deranged can be an entire crowd of people; either one at a time, or all at once.

Micropic: (Micropsia): Objects are perceived to be smaller than they are . . . and so they become smaller. This could apply to a person, limb, or object of any type. These folks can shrink you down to the size of an ant or turn your home into a doll-house. This is sometimes combined with Micropesia.

Mirrorist (Eisoptrophobia): Some believe the reflection in a mirror is someone other than themselves. Some Mirrorists believe their reflections know things, can see the future, or travel freely between different mirrors (useful for long distance communication). Others believe mirrors are portals to other worlds or dimensions. Some Mirrorists fear their reflections are trying to escape where others fear their reflections are trying to drag them into the mirror.

Narcisstic: (Narcissism): A personality disorder where the patient has an exaggerated sense of self-importance and individuality. The excessively crave attention and admiration and tend to be preoccupied by grandiose fantasies about themselves. They find interpersonal relationships difficult and tend to exploit others and lack empathy.

Phobic: Anyone suffering a strong phobia.

Somatoparaphrenic (Somatoparaphrenia): Believe one or more limbs (sometimes an entire half of their body) belongs to someone else. Often this means they have no control over that limb. In extreme cases the limb develops a 'mind of its own' with its own agenda.

Synesthesia: (Synesthesia): is a disorder resulting in the sufferer experiencing an alternate sense as a result of the first sense. Ex: experiencing the sense of sight as the sense of taste.

The Pinnacle: The ultimate leveller of the playing field. Embracing one's delusions comes with a price. Sure, holding one's emotional scars tight and constantly picking at one's mental wounds might cause a Geisteskranken to grow in power, but embracing insanity is not healthy. As a Geisteskranken loses their grip on reality they become stronger, more able to utterly believe all manner of insane shite. As their sanity crumbles apart the range and strength of their delusions increases. Eventually, however, those delusions come to completely define that Geisteskranken's reality. They take over. That moment, that teetering instant when delusion crushes sanity, is The Pinnacle and, for a brief instant, the Geisteskranken might become so powerful as to challenge the gods. Unfortunately, (at least for them) they are no longer sane enough to do anything with that power. What happens after depends on the delusions in question. A Mirrorist might be dragged into the mirror by his reflections. The Doppelgangist might be replaced by a Doppel. The Hassebrand might incinerate themselves in an orgy of flame.

Therianthrope (Therianthropy): Believe they are possessed by (or sometimes were born with) animal spirits. Many believe they can transform partially (or completely) into their animal form.

Trichotillic: (Trichotillomania): a disorder resulting the urge to pull out hair (facial or otherwise). The ritual activity brings comfort to the afflicted.

Unwirklichkeit: (Derealization): The external world seems unreal, lacking spontaneity, depth, or emotional impact. This is most commonly a comorbidic disorder and occurs as a symptom of other disorders. This can manifest as something separating the Geisteskranken from the rest of reality. A wall of glass, thick fog, or gauzy veil are common manifestations of that separation. Sometimes the sufferer believes reality is actually just a particularly intricate play they are watching.

Wahnist: (Schizophrenia): A Form of Schizophrenia (false beliefs): Includes: believing people can hear your thoughts, that you are famous, or (falsely) believing the Geborene are out to get you.

Wendigast: (Wendigo Psychosis): An insatiable craving for human flesh. Typically the person will become a demonic monster, but still recognizable from human origins. This is more common in the tribes to the far north where every winter starvation becomes an issue. In appearance they combine the emaciation of severe starvation—along with open sores—with demonic strength. They also stink of death and decay. Some turn into massive giants, growing in strength and size as they eat. These guys have nothing to do with Chuck Wendig. I have no idea if he eats human flesh.

Wütend: (Amok, or Militant Explosive Disorder): Periods of brooding followed by a berserker killing frenzy (usually armed with a sword or knife) against people or objects. Most Wütend are killed during their frenzy or commit suicide after, but the few who survive typically have no memory of the event.

GLOSSARY

Abgeleitete Leute: Semi-mythological city populated solely by copies of a single Mehrere. This Mehrere is said to believe that he is many *different* people and that no two of his copies look or act the same.

Albtraum: The nightmares of man given flesh. These creatures take shapes relevant to those they haunt. They feed off the delusional and mostly attack Geisteskranken.

Aufenthalt: Independent city-state.

Auseinander: A kingdom defeated by the Sieger Clans. A Sieger Geisteskranken lost control during the Battle of Sinnlos after raising an army of the dead. The Kingdom is now populated by the raised undead and ruled by what was the strongest of the Geisteskranken's inner demons.

Basamortuan Desert: East of the city-states.

Befallen: (Ekbom's Syndrome): Believe they are infested with parasites, bugs, or insects crawling on or under the skin.

Bide Sinple (In the ancient and long dead language of the Basamortuan tribes): A Basamortuan philosophy routed in the idea that the simplest path is usually the correct one. This isn't just a case of choosing the path of least resistance, but also of achieving one's goals with the least fuss and effort.

Bizkarrezurra erantsita (In the ancient and long dead language of the Basamortuan tribes): The ultimate trophy is to collect an opponent's head with the spine still attached. The complete version of the ritual involves forcing the victim's soul from the belly—where it resides—into the skull by filling the belly with sand. For best results, this must be done while the victim is still alive.

Blutblüte: Zerfall's rather plain looking sword. She believes it is unbreakable and that Wahrergott gave it to her. It never dulls, never needs sharpening.

Borrokalaria: Harea's *Hall of Blooded Warriors* in the Afterdeath.

Buruzagi (In the ancient and long dead language of the Basamortuan tribes): Basamortuan for Chief of the tribe.

Düster Snake: Deadly poisonous snake found in the Basamortuan desert.

Etsaiaren: Tribe of the Basamortuan desert, sworn enemies of the Hasiera tribe.

Flussrand River: The physical boundary defining the border between the Kingdom of Gottlos and the Theocratic Kingdom of Selbsthass.

Folgen Sienie: Small city on the eastern border of Reichweite.

Geborene Damonen: Believe that the universe was not created by the gods, that somehow it came before them, and that humanity created the gods with their desperate need to believe in something.

Ausgebrochene : Tribals living on the edge of the Gezackt Mountains, north of Auseinander. The tribal wisemen—*Salbei*—practice the art of moving their souls and possessing inanimate objects.

Geldangelegenheiten: Extremely prosperous city-state, commonly referred to as Geld by its inhabitants. Centre of the Verzweiflung Banking Conglomerate. Centre of the Täuschung.

Geld Guard: City guard of Geldangelegenheiten.

Geldwechsler: Hats worn by members of the Verzweiflung Banking Conglomerate. Colour and size denotes rank. The darker and more somber, the larger and more uncomfortable, the higher the rank of the wearer.

Gottlos: Grubby little Kingdom run by King Dieb Schmutzig who had been the previous king's greatest general. Dieb is a fairly powerful Gefahrgeist.

Selbsthass City: Capital of Selbsthass. Home to Konig Furimmer, High Priest of the Geborene Damonen.

Grenzstadt: Walled city on the eastern edge of Geldangelegenheiten. Stands between the city-state and the tribes of the Basamortuan desert.

Grunlugen: Independent city-state ruled by a family of petty Gefahrgeist.

Harea: God of the desert, worshipped by most tribes of the Basamortuan Desert.

Hasiera: Jateko's tribe.

Heriotza: Basamortuan goddess of death.

Hildako (In the ancient and long dead language of the Basamortuan tribes): The wandering spirits of those who have died and have neither been accepted by Harea or Ascended into some local watering-hole godling.

Hilen deabru (In the ancient and long dead language of the Basamortuan tribes): The undying, whose souls have been rejected by Harea, god of the Basamortuan Desert. Linked with Cotardists.

Hil Ostean: The Basamortuan Afterdeath. Ruled by Heriotza, goddess of death.

Hiria ero (In the ancient and long dead language of the Basamortuan tribes): Dismissive/insulting term for the people of the city-states.

Kälte Mountains: Mountain range to the north of Geldangelegenheiten.

Karpan: Tent, large enough for an entire extended family. Plural is karpa.

Krieger: The warrior sect of the Geborene Damonen.

Leichtes Haus: Tavern in Selbsthass City

Menschheit Letzte Imperium: The last of humanity's great empires to fall. This entire continent had once been united under a single despotic ruler, perhaps the greatest Gefahrgeist ever to live.

Mitteldirne: Capital of Gottlos.

Müll Loch: Birthplace of Stehlen.

Neidrig: City just beyond the north-western border of Selbsthass.

Oihal: Long flowing robes worn by most tribes.

Pozoia: Cured nuggets of cactus guts. Highly hallucinogenic.

Rand: City belonging to the Auseinander Kingdom

Reichweite: Small kingdom west of Selbsthass, beyond the free cities (including Neidrig).

Ruchlos Arms: Inn located in Neidrig

Salbei: Witch doctors of the Ausgebrochene tribes. They practice the art of moving their spirits into inanimate objects and possessing them.

Santu Itsasoa (In the ancient and long dead language of the Basamortuan tribes): The Sea of Souls. Where souls rejected by Harea are taken to wait out eternity.

Schatten Morder: Cotardist assassins of the Geborene Damonen.

Schlammstamm: Nomadic grassland tribes whose society is based around who owns the most horses. At the centre of each tribe is a deranged shaman who thinks he can control the weather and talk to tribal ancestors.

Schlangenbeschwörer: Therianthrope snake charmers of the SumpfStamm swamp tribes found at the mouth of the Wüten River.

Schwarze Beerdigung: Tavern in Neidrig

Selbsthass City: Capital of Selbsthass.

Selbsthass: Theocratic kingdom. Ruled by a reflection of Konig Furimmer, High Priest of the Geborene Damonen. Originally an independent kingdom with its own royal family, Selbsthass long ago fell under the sway of the Geborene. The strength of the religion's faith conquered the Kingdom in a bloodless coup and the royal family stepped down.

Sinnlos: Small city located on the border of Auseinander and the lands held by the Sieger Clans. Famous only due to the fact that the final battle between the Sieger and the Auseinander occurred here.

Sorgin (In the ancient and long dead language of the Basamortuan tribes): Shaman, witch doctor, healer, wise-one

SumpfStamm: Snake-worshipping tribes found in the swamps at the mouth of the Wüten River.

Swarm: The hallucinated hell of the Täuschung.

Täuschung: A dark cult worshipping deception and illusion. The ranking priests are powerful Geisteskranken, most being Halluzin.

Traurig: City in the Kingdom of Geldangelegenheiten. Birth place of Wichtig.

Unbedeutend: Backwater kingdom that's been at war with itself for three generations.

Unbrauchbar: Small city just within the borders of the Kingdom of Gottlos.

Verrottung Loch: The worst tavern in all of Neidrig.

Verschlinger: A tribe of savages in the far north who believe they gain strength and wisdom by devouring their foes. The Verschlinger do not believe in an Afterdeath.

Verteidigung: Garrisoned city to the north of Selbsthass City.

Verzweiflung Banking Conglomerate: Organized banks/money lenders based in the kingdom of Geldangelegenheiten.

Wahnvor Stellung: The largest and most powerful religion. They believe the gods are crazy. Crazy enough, in fact, that through sheer divine belief, they created the universe and everything within it. Only truly insane creatures could believe strongly enough to create something this complex. They worship the old gods that pre-date recorded history.

ACKNOWLEDGEMENTS

As always, first I must thank my wife and daughter. You keep me grounded, you keep me sane. You are the lights of my life and the centers of my universe. All I am orbits around you two. Hmm. Kinda want to write some science fiction now.

My agent, Cameron McClure, deserves a special thanks for this one. Long before you, the reader, gets to see any of this, before the publisher sees the first manuscript, Cameron reads my books. She critiques them. She is honest, and sometimes blunt to the point where I flop about the floor hemorrhaging blood. Ok. Slight exaggeration. When Cameron read *Swarm and Steel* she sent back several pages (soooo many pages) of notes and suggestions. There was one suggestion in there—a question, really—that triggered a landslide. The book changed. The characters changed. The ending changed. I suddenly saw everything in a different light (there was a lot more red). The rewrite was massive and the end product is something I could not have achieved without her input. This book is so much better than the one I first wrote. Thank you!

There are so many amazing fantasy-related communities online and I'd love to a part of all of them, but if I did that I wouldn't have time left for writing. There are three where I spend most of my time. If you're unaware of them, look 'em up and you'll find me there. The **Grimdark Fiction Readers and Writers** Facebook group is friendly and supportive and awesome. Marc Aplin's **Fantasy-Faction** is a champion of all things fantasy. Whenever I'm trying to decide what to read next, FF is my first stop. And finally, the **r/Fantasy** subreddit. A great community and an excellent place to find fantasy-related topics and discussions.

The lads at the **Grim Tidings Podcast** deserve a special mention. Phil and Rob have chatted with everyone who is anyone, from Anthony Ryan to Joe Abercrombie to Brian Staveley, and they're hilarious. Easily my favorite podcast. I'm writing this in American. Can you tell it isn't my first language?

There are a number of SFF reviewers/bloggers who have championed my books. In particular, James of **MightyThorJRS**, Petros of **Booknest.eu**, and Rita of **Leona's Blog of Shadows**. Thank you!

Oh shit. I haven't mentioned my parents yet. Hi Mom, I love you! And I promise to call soon! As I've said before, my parents are the reason I'm here, literally and literarily. Their love of books shaped my youth. My father and I still chat regularly about the art of writing and he still manages to teach me things. When I wanted a different perspective on Halber Tod, the Cotardist poet, I asked him to write a couple of poems for me. After grumbling that I was only asking because he was closer to death than I, he did. "Cotardist Lament" and "Untitled" are both his. Thank you! Dad, stop fucking about and let's get *Price of a Pint* published. It's a good book.

And finally, I must thank you, the readers who have demanded more Manifest Delusions. Keep demanding, it's a world I love to play in! In particular I want to thank all the folks who took the time to contact me directly to share your reactions to my books.

You keep reading, and I'll keep writing.

ABOUT THE AUTHOR

Michael R. Fletcher lives with his wife and daughter in the endless suburban sprawl north of Toronto, Canada. He dreams of trees and open fields and long grass. When he grows up he either wants to be a ninja, or a racecar driver. He can't decide.